GIGI BLUME

SODASAC PRESS
PUBLISHING HOUSE

SODASAC
PRESS

FIRST EDITION

Library of Congress Cataloging-in-Publication Data has been applied for.

ISBN: 979-8-9924331-1-1

Cover design and illustrations by Gigi Blume - Once Upon a Cover

Editor: Kristyn Fortner - Delightfully Booked

For Silvia
La Suiza Sonrisa
My sister from another mister
Myni schwester
Mi hermana
My dearest friend
You inspired this book and loads of laughter during LA traffic (LA traffic SUCKS) and now that day is a core memory I will cherish forever.

Dating Goals

Courage is just panic that kept skating.

CHAPTER ONE

GRIFFIN

Nothing says fun quite like worrying if we'll be out of a job tomorrow, but Coach Knight seems determined to ignore it, just like he ignores the sweat dripping down our backs and the way some of the guys have that freaked-out look in their eyes. I'm determined not to let the possibility of an NHL lockout distract me, though. I focus on blocking puck after puck, soaking in the smell of the ice and the sound of it scratching beneath my skates. Coach Knight is on some sort of cruel marathon kick, dragging out the session until we're ready to drop.

My teammates are firing shots with extra oomph today, probably channeling their frustration about the looming lockout deadline. I drop into the butterfly position, my pads hitting the ice with a satisfying thunk as Owen's slap shot whistles past my blocker.

The puck pings off the post. A close call that has me grinning behind my mask.

"Getting slow there, Crash!" Owen taps his stick on the ice, but I can see the tension in his shoulders. Everyone's wound tight today.

"Coming in hot!" Sawyer barrels down center ice and winds up for a slap shot that could probably punch through concrete. I barely snag it with my glove—the force sending vibrations up my arm.

"Easy on the merchandise!" I flash him a thumbs-up with my blocker hand. "I need these hands to eat my feelings when we're all unemployed tomorrow."

The reminder of the Collective Bargaining Agreement deadline hangs over the practice rink like a storm cloud. My teammates' shots are getting harder, faster, angrier.

Owen lines up for another shot, his face set in stone. "Focus up. If this is our last practice for a while, let's make it count."

My pads are too heavy. My eyes sting with sweat. I've got to show Coach I can outlast everybody. Just in case I don't see the guys again until Christmas. Just in case the CBA talks fail and some of my friends head off to Europe.

Hendrix swoops in next, bearing down on me. He fires five quick shots in succession...left pad save, blocker, catch glove, stick save, and...the last one squeaks through my five-hole.

"Finally!" Hendrix raises his arms in triumph. "Thought you were turning into a brick wall there, Griffin."

Another missile from Owen's stick comes screaming at my face. I snag it with my glove, but just barely.

"Easy there, Jablonski," I say. "Take it out on the net, not me."

I have the feeling that if I move out of the way and put up a picture of the Titans' owner, Malcolm Chase, the guys would go to town on it.

I try to stay focused on the pucks flying at me, but my mind keeps drifting to the ticking clock.

Midnight.

That's when everything changes if the league and players can't agree. The franchise owners are still playing hardball over everything. Salary cap, revenue sharing, free agency age. The whole thing's a mess.

"McGregor! Eyes up!" Coach Knight's voice cuts through my thoughts. He's running drills like it's any other day, face set in his signature scowl. "I don't care what's happening off the ice. Right now, you're here."

Another shot from Owen catches the corner of my net. Crap.

"Again!" Coach barks. "Until we get it right."

The whole thing makes my stomach churn. If they don't reach a deal by midnight, we're locked out. No more practices, no access to team facilities, no games. And a whole lot of angry fans.

I shake the sweat from my eyes beneath my mask as the guys line up for another round of rapid-fire shots. One after the other, they come at me. I miss half of them.

"Focus, Griffin!" Coach's whistle pierces the air. "One more time. Sawyer, Owen, give me that power play setup we worked on."

I stretch my legs between shots, trying to stay loose. My agent has been negotiating with a team in the Swiss National League for a few weeks now. EHC Visp Föhn. The name rolls around in my head during quiet moments. At least I have a backup plan if this all goes sideways. Their offer sits in my email inbox, but I haven't opened it yet. I don't want to jinx the CBA. I guess I'm just too superstitious.

After what feels like hours of drilling, Knight finally calls it. Just in time. The players are so ready for practice to be over, I think we might actually drop if we have to skate another minute.

"Hit the showers! And whatever happens tonight, I expect every one of you to stay ready," Coach says.

Sawyer and Hendrix clatter toward the lockers, where the rest of the team seems to think the showers will be much less torturous.

My legs burn as I skate off the ice.

I manage to unlatch my chest piece and clatter down the hall with it before collapsing on the bench. My gear's soaked through. My entire upper body aches. My lower body too. Heck, I think my hair aches. Coach really put us through the wringer today.

The locker room carries a heavy silence. Everyone's lost in thought, probably thinking about what comes next.

"So," Kevin Tate breaks the silence first, unlacing his skates. "Anyone else got plans if this goes south?"

"DEL reached out," Owen says, his voice tight. "Emily's not thrilled about Germany. Think I'll wait it out, see what happens."

"You speak German, right?" I say, jutting my chin at Hendrix.

"Yeah. Not great, but yeah."

Sawyer tosses a towel over his shoulder. "Maggie's already told me she'd follow me anywhere, but I don't know. With everything going on with my dad right now..." He runs a hand through his sweat-soaked hair, not finishing his thought. But we all know. Most of us anyway. If Sawyer can survive the revelation that he's the son of an Irish mob kingpin, we can get through a lockout. But it's still going to hurt.

"My agent's got feelers out in Sweden," Kevin says, unlacing his skates. "But Leigh's pregnant, and the kids are in school. I can't just up and leave them."

"She's pregnant again?" Sawyer bellows, slapping Kevin on the back. "Way to go, my man."

"You animal!" Owen gives him a high-five. "What's your secret?"

"What can I say?" Kevin flexes dramatically. "The Tate genes are just too powerful to contain."

The locker room erupts in groans and wadded-up tape balls flying at his head.

Owen's already typing on his phone. "Hold up, gotta tell Emily. She's gonna flip."

"Oh no, don't give her any ideas," Sawyer mock-whispers. "Maggie will hear about it and next thing you know, the whole WAG squad will be planning some kind of pregnancy pact."

Kevin beams. "Leigh's already in the group chat. Trust me, they know."

"The real question is," I say as I lean forward, wiggling my eyebrows, "did you score with a slap shot or power play?"

The guys howl with laughter as Kevin turns bright red. "I'm not discussing my...shooting methods with you clowns."

"The man, the myth, the baby-making legend," Hendrix declares in his best announcer voice.

Owen starts a slow clap that quickly turns into the whole locker room chanting "Stud! Stud! Stud!"

Kevin just grins wider, if that's even possible. "When you've got it, you've got it."

When the jeering dies down, Kevin asks me, "So what about you, single guy. Any plans for the lockout?"

"I've got a team in Switzerland sending me emails." I wipe my face with a towel, trying not to think about how empty this locker room might be tomorrow.

"Are you going to go for it?" Sawyer asks.

I shrug. "It's not like I have anybody to stay here for."

"So sad for you, bro," Hendrix grumbles, stuffing equipment in his bag. "Colette and I are already doing medium-long distance. Long-long distance would suck."

"Could be worse." I start unbuckling my pads. "You could end up like Beckett over there, who's dating his PlayStation."

"Hey!" One of our latest rookies, Dominic Beckett, chucks a rolled-up sock at my head. "At least my PlayStation doesn't complain when I hang with the guys."

"Dude, you have no clue about women, do you?" Sawyer teases.

"He's never been kissed," says Jonny Tolliver, making obnoxious kissing sounds. Jonny is new this season too. Practically fresh out of high school.

It feels like yesterday and yet a hundred years ago when I was a dork-faced rookie like them.

True to character, Beckett gives Tolliver the bird and says, "At least I don't spend my Saturday nights knitting sweaters for my cat while watching *The Great British Bake Off*!"

"Hey!" Jonny's face turns tomato red. "It was ONE sweater, and my mom's cat gets cold!"

The guys burst out laughing. Who knew Tolliver was a secret knitter?

"All right, shut up, all of you." Hendrix's voice cuts through the laughter. He's standing by his locker, still half in his gear, looking more serious than I've ever seen him. "I've got something to say."

We all quiet down, though Sawyer's still chuckling under his breath.

"I'm gonna propose to Colette."

The room goes dead quiet for about two seconds before exploding.

Owen whistles through his teeth, and Sawyer lets out a whoop that probably echoes all the way to the practice rink.

"That's why I can't go to Europe," Hendrix continues, trying to maintain his serious face but failing as a grin breaks through. "Can't exactly pop the question over FaceTime."

"Better not," Kevin laughs. "Leigh would kill you if you did that to Colette."

"So would Emily," Owen adds.

"Our little class clown, all grown up!" Sawyer pretends to dab away tears with his jersey.

I lean forward on my bench. "Does she suspect anything?"

"Nah." Hendrix smirks. "She still thinks I'm the same idiot who put a whoopee cushion on her chair at the teacher's meeting last month."

"You ARE the same idiot who put a whoopee cushion on her chair last month," Owen supplies.

"Seriously," Kevin says. "I don't know how she puts up with you."

"Do you need our help, man?" I say. "I mean with the proposal."

Hendrix twists his face, as if thinking takes too much effort. "Ummm…I'll let you know."

"Well, let's all hope there's no lockout," says Kevin grimly. "For all our sakes."

I feel a twinge of guilt. While they're all wrestling with family decisions, my biggest concern is whether Swiss food will agree with me. "Maybe they'll reach a deal at the last minute?"

"Yeah, and maybe Malcolm Chase will start paying the female staff fairly," Owen snorts. "Not holding my breath."

"Did you guys see his latest press statement?" Hendrix says, yanking off his shoulder pads. "Trying to spin this whole CBA thing like he's protecting the stockholders." He makes air quotes with his fingers.

Owen snorts. "Right, because he's such a humanitarian."

"Guy's worth what, half a billion?" Kevin shakes his head. "And he's crying poor about player salaries?"

"Anyone else buy in when they offered?" Hendrix asks. "I've got the automatic deduction from my paycheck. Don't even notice it's gone."

I nod, remembering the investment package Malcolm's office circulated a few months back. The promise of being a stockholder of the team we play for had seemed too good to pass up.

"Guilty." Owen nods. "Emily wasn't sure about it at first, but the projected returns looked promising."

"I did," I admit, raising my hand. "Seemed like a solid investment at the time."

"Same," Kevin says. "Leigh thought it would be good for our retirement portfolio."

"Not me." Sawyer holds up his hands. "No offense, but after everything with my dad...I'm staying away from anything that smells like creative financing. I prefer my money where I can see it."

"Fair enough," Hendrix says. "But Chase makes it sound like we're all going to be billionaires." He snorts. "Well, millionaire-aires."

"Honestly, Hendrix," Owen says, pulling a face. "How on earth did you get that English teacher to fall for you?"

"It wasn't for his grammar," I say.

Hendrix just grins. "You know what I mean. Anyway, maybe someday we'll actually have a say in how this team is run."

"Malcolm's full of it," Sawyer says. "Using the stockholders as shields when we all know he's just being greedy. Like, dude. You're not fooling anyone."

The whole thing leaves a bad taste in my mouth, but the investment numbers don't lie. The returns have been solid month after month. Still, something about Malcolm's latest spin raises my hackles.

"We should have a lockout party!" Beckett's eyes light up like he just invented sliced bread. "My place, pizza, beer. We can watch the negotiations play out and drink every time someone says 'good faith bargaining.'"

"Pass," Kevin says, zipping up his bag. "Leigh's got weird pregnancy cravings. Last night she wanted pickles dipped in Nutella at three AM."

Owen shakes his head. "Emily's got early training tomorrow."

"Count me out too," Sawyer says. "Maggie's cooking tonight, and I value my life. Plus, Otto gets anxious when I'm out late."

"Your parrot gets anxiety?" Beckett's eyebrows shoot up.

"Don't judge my bird, rookie."

"What about you, Griffin?" Beckett turns to me. "You're not married."

I zip my bag, already dreaming of my bed. "Thanks, but I'd rather get some sleep. No point staying up worrying about something we can't control. Getting worked up won't change anything that happens at midnight."

"Come on!" Beckett whines. "Where's your team spirit?"

"Worrying won't add a single hour to your life," I say, channeling my inner fortune cookie. "Actually, pretty sure it does the opposite."

The guys groan in unison, but I talk over them. "My grandmother used to say worrying is like a rocking chair. Gives you something to do but doesn't get you anywhere."

"Who let Yoda in here?" Sawyer launches his sweaty jersey at my head.

I dodge, but Owen's sock catches me right in the face. "Hey!"

"Nice try, Buddha!" Hendrix pelts me with his compression shorts.

"Gross, man!" I swat them away. "I'm just saying!"

A barrage of sweaty gear flies at me from all directions. "Real mature, guys." A jockstrap nearly hits my mouth. "Okay, that's just nasty. Who threw that?"

"The wisdom of Griffin McGregor, everyone," Beckett announces in a mock-announcer voice. "Next up: how to die alone while spouting inspirational quotes!"

"Oh wise one." Sawyer bows dramatically, hands pressed together like he's praying. "Please bestow upon us more of your infinite wisdom!"

I roll my eyes. "You guys are ridiculous."

"I bet he has a Pinterest board full of inspirational quotes," Hendrix says. "Live, Laugh, Love...Hockey."

"Dance like nobody's watching!" Kevin adds with a twirl.

"That's it. I'm never trying to be helpful again."

"No, no, please!" Beckett clasps his hands together. "Tell us more about how goals are like butterflies. Beautiful but fleeting."

"I hate all of you."

"That's not very Zen of you, Master Griffin," Owen says in a mock-serious tone. "Remember, hatred leads to the dark side."

"That's *Star Wars!*" I protest.

"Should we get you one of those little desktop calendars?" Sawyer wipes tears from his eyes. "Daily Griffin-spirations?"

"With pictures of fluffy kittens hanging from tree branches?" Hendrix adds. "Hang in there...probably."

"I bet he has one of those meditation apps," Tolliver says.

"The ones that play rainforest sounds while someone whispers about finding your inner peace."

I give him a hard stare. "For your information, I prefer ocean sounds."

The guys lose it completely. Owen actually doubles over, clutching his stomach.

"I'm leaving now," I announce, shouldering my bag.

"Wait, wait," Sawyer cries, barely able to speak without laughing. I need you to explain how life is like a box of chocolates."

"You never know what you're gonna get!" the rest of the guys all chorus after me as I head for the door.

"Keep calm and Griffin on!" Beckett calls out.

Owen adds, "When you get home, don't forget to meditate and align your chakras."

"I'm about to align *your* chakras," I snap.

This sets them off again, and I leave to a chorus of "Namaste!" and "May the Force be with you!" following me out the door.

Confidence is just pretending until
everyone else believes it.

CHAPTER TWO

C runching along the path, the fall colors alight, my lungs fill with the clean mountain air.

And my bladder fills with dread.

The morning sun peeks through the evergreens as I power up the loop trail. This is my sanctuary. No beer taps to fix, no invoices to process. Just me and The Cure's "Just Like Heaven" pumping through my vintage Walkman headphones.

The trail curves around a rocky outcrop, and I pick up my

pace, belting along with the song at the top of my lungs. A red squirrel darts across the path, giving me the side-eye. *"Ja, ja,* I see you too, *kleiner freund."*

I've named him Herbert. He's usually here at this time—probably judging my singing.

The trail opens to a clearing where the village of Grächen spreads out below, morning mist still clinging to the rooftops. S'Holzfass (the bar I inherited from my father last year) is just a tiny dot from up here.

Strange how something so small can feel like such a weight sometimes. Of course, it's not without its charm, with its creaky floorboards and regulars who think they're comedians.

I stretch my arms overhead, feeling my muscles warm despite the cool air. The trail winds ahead through golden larches, their needles creating a soft carpet underfoot.

I could stay in this zone forever. Except for the urgent need to pee.

At first, I tell myself I can make it all the way home. If I up my pace a bit, I'll be at my own place. Only a few more kilometers to S'Holzfass. My 80s playlist will get my blood pumping enough to get me there without incident, and then it's another day of pouring pints and dodging bad pickup lines.

My father used to say these morning hikes kept him sane during tourist season. Now I understand why. Running a pub isn't just serving drinks. It's playing therapist, bouncer, and sometimes babysitter to grown men who can't handle their alcohol.

On my mental list: everything. But the top few are keeping the lights on, reordering house beer, and making sure the accounts don't bounce.

Herbert scampers back across my path with a pine cone in his mouth. "Show-off," I mutter, adjusting my headphones.

The mountainside is painted in shades of amber and gold.

Autumn is my favorite time of year, when the air gets that special crispness that makes everything feel more alive.

My playlist shifts into Blondie's "One Way Or Another," and I find myself with the urge to belt it out, badly and gleefully, right into the vast fall wilderness. A vast fall wilderness that now has the distinct and unsettling sensation of being one big public restroom with not an actual public restroom in sight.

"*Scheisse*," I mutter, doing a little dance on the spot.

The situation progresses from you-might-want-to-think-about-a-bathroom to I MUST PEE NOW!

Either I find a bathroom fast, or I'll need new jeans before I open the bar.

I can't believe I'm doing this, I think as I change course, speed-walking to Walter Egger's cabin.

Walter has known my family forever, and his cabin is just around the bend, thank goodness. It's been vacant for ages while Walter's off pretending he's Indiana Jones.

He left for South America several months ago, planning a trip around the world. But he met a lady in Buenos Aires and kind of just stayed in Argentina indefinitely.

He told me I could use his spare key if I needed it. I've only gone in a few times to dust and air it out, but right now, that key is my salvation.

I round the bend where Walter's cabin sits nestled among the pines, my bladder screaming in protest.

"Do not think about waterfalls," I mutter while fishing behind the loose stone near the foundation. "I'm gonna get ya, get ya, get ya…" I belt out as I snatch the key, doing what can only be described as an urgent potty dance. My bladder has exactly zero patience right now.

The lock clicks open, and I burst inside with a happy sigh because I can see the bathroom door just off the entryway and I know I'm not a minute too soon.

I sing-sing-sing along to Blondie as I make my break, flinging the bathroom door open, flipping up the toilet seat, and yanking my jeans down.

Sweet relief floods through me as I finally get to pee, my heart rate slowing from red alert to *Aaaaah*. Victory is mine.

I take a moment to be grateful for indoor plumbing. And to regain my dignity. Mostly the plumbing.

Sighing, I grin at Walter's tacky fish-themed shower curtain and the ancient orange shag rug that belongs in a 70s time capsule. The man loves his fish...and orange paired with the color avocado green.

I sing with even more gusto. With the echo-y acoustics of a cabin bathroom and a carefree willingness to overlook the fact that I'm tone deaf. Singing in bathrooms is my jam. It doesn't matter if my neighbors for five miles in any direction think I'm crazy.

After washing my hands, I throw open the bathroom door, belting out, "I'm gonna trick ya, I'm gonna—*HEILIGE SCHEISSE*!"

I freeze. There's a man. A very tall, very muscular man, leaning against the wall with his arms crossed.

He's wearing sweatpants, a worn T-shirt, and a bemused expression. The T-shirt says TITANS HOCKEY, and the man wearing it is built exactly like you might expect a hockey team to be built.

The fabric stretches across his shoulders, which have the nerve to bulge enticingly. Then, my gaze makes its way up to his face and...Boom! Dimples. He has the boyish good looks of someone with everything in the world going for him, and he's using them against me right now.

His wavy brown hair catches the morning light streaming through the window, and...Wait. Why is this ridiculously handsome intruder in Walter's cabin?

"Interesting choice for a morning serenade," he says, grinning.

Heart hammering against my ribs, my brain kicks into survival mode. I look around wildly, hoping for an improvised weapon and find Walter's decorative fish mounted on the wall.

Maybe I have a prayer if I swing hard. Maybe. I've fought off handsy drunks with less.

"I have a fish, and I am not afraid to use it!" I warn in my native Swiss German.

Did this guy follow me from the village? Has he been stalking me on my morning runs?

His eyebrows shoot up, his dimples getting even dimplier. Then he puts his hands in the air like the most adorable surrender of all time. "Whoa there, Debbie Harry. I come in peace."

His accent is American, maybe. Whatever it is, it means I should switch to English, and if I switch to English, he can't even suspect how panicked I am.

"How long have you been following me?" I grip the fish tighter. "And don't move! I will whack you with this trout faster than you can say '*schweizer käse*!'"

His eyebrows shoot up, and he actually has the audacity to chuckle. "I wasn't following you."

"Then why," I demand in a much slower voice, "are you in this cabin?"

"I think the bigger question is why are *you*?" he says. The easy laugh in his voice tells me he's maybe not afraid at all, but the charm in it tells me I should still be worried. Just about different things. My sanity, for instance.

"I'll be asking the questions here, mister. What are you doing here?"

My mind goes straight to worst-case scenario and hopes the man I found in an otherwise vacant cabin doesn't want to murder me. His master plan might be to bludgeon me, while smiling and having dimples.

But I can bludgeon right back. I could take him. Throw him off balance long enough to escape. Time to summon my inner ninja.

"I live here," he says.

"Liar! Walter Egger lives here!" I edge toward the door, keeping the fish between us, Blondie still playing through my headphones, which now dangle uselessly around my neck.

"Walter's in Argentina. Though I've got to say, this is the first time someone's threatened me with a singing fish."

The fish suddenly bursts into "Don't Worry, Be Happy" in a tinny electronic voice, making me jump and nearly drop it. The plastic fish head bobs side to side in time with the music, its mouth opening and closing mechanically while the fin flaps in my hands.

His shoulders shake with silent laughter. "Do you want to club me over the head with that before or after I tell you who I am?"

Heat floods my cheeks. Of all the weapons I could have grabbed.

"*Du meine güte*," I mutter, heat creeping up my neck as the fish continues its performance. I jab frantically at its side, trying to find the Off switch, but somehow only manage to make it start over. "Stop singing, *dummes ding*!"

"Here, let me help." He reaches for the fish, but I snap it back.

"Stay where you are! Just because you know Walter is in Argentina doesn't mean—" The fish launches into an encore.

"*Ach, halt die klappe.* Shut up!" I scream.

His dimples deepen as he watches me wrestle with the mechanical trout.

"I'm renting the cabin. I can show you the lease agreement if you'd like, though you might have to put down the fish."

The fish mercifully stops mid-verse, leaving us in awkward silence except for Falco's "Der Kommissar," which is now crackling through my ancient headphones.

I'm still not entirely convinced this man is not a burglar, but something about his open face and the way his eyes crinkle at the corners makes me lower my makeshift weapon. Just slightly.

"You're...renting Walter's cabin?"

"For the next few months, yeah." He gestures to a suitcase by the door I hadn't noticed before. "Just moved in yesterday, actually. I really appreciate the welcome committee, by the way."

I narrow my eyes, keeping the fish at the ready. "How do you know Walter?"

"Through a rental agency in Visp." He leans against the wall, completely unfazed by my interrogation. "Though I did meet him on a call before he approved the lease."

"You spoke to Walter?"

"Would you like to call him? I have his WhatsApp number."

"Ha! Walter doesn't use WhatsApp. He says social media is for—"

"People who have nothing better to do than stare at their phones all day." He mimics Walter's gruff voice perfectly.

The fish slips a little in my grip. "Okay, what is Walter doing in Argentina?"

"Living his best life in Buenos Aires with a tango instructor named Rosa."

"Ha! Wrong! Her name is Rosita." I thrust the fish forward. "What's Walter's favorite cheese?"

He laughs. "I have no idea."

"Your name?"

"Griffin." He extends his hand to shake mine, then thinks better of it.

"American?"

"Canadian."

"Favorite color?"

"Blue. No. Red!"

I make a buzzer noise. "Wrong."

"Wrong?" He squints at me with a puzzled expression.

"What," I say as I adjust my grip on the fish, "is your quest?"

A grin spreads across his face as he takes a daring step toward me, getting closer than he probably should. He holds the other end of the fish. "To seek the Holy Grail."

My breath catches as his fingers brush against mine. The warmth of his hand lingers on my skin, sending tingles up my arm. I tilt my head back to meet his eyes, and oh, what eyes they are. Deep brown with flecks of gold, crinkled at the corners from his smile.

His height towers over me, and despite my usual dislike of feeling small, there's something about his presence that makes me feel...things.

"May I?" His voice is low, intimate, and does strange things to my insides. My fingers release the fish of their own accord, betraying my brain's protests about stranger danger. The way he's looking at me makes my face flush hot.

"I...um..." Since when do I stutter? I never stutter. I'm the one who tells drunk men where to stick it when they get handsy at the bar. But something about the way his fingers are still touching mine around this stupid singing fish has short-circuited my brain.

"I was just making sure you weren't, you know, a burglar or something."

"I'm not a burglar." His eyes twinkle. "Are you?"

"Me?" I scoff. "No."

His dimples wink as he sets the fish on a nearby shelf. "Says the woman who broke into my cabin to use the bathroom."

"I did not break in! I used the spare key that Walter—" I stop, realizing this isn't helping my case and I blurt, "A girl's got to pee."

He steps closer, catching me off guard as he finds my Walkman and clicks the Off button, right in the middle of Falco singing, "*Dreh dich nicht um.*"

He flashes those dimples, almost disarming me. His arm brushes mine, this solid and steady maple wood beam of an arm, and the touch ricochets.

"So I've noticed. What's your name, girl-who's-got-to-pee?"

His voice is a low rumble that is not helping my resolve one bit. I've never felt this immediate attraction to anyone before, and it's...unsettling.

I take a step back, needing space to clear my head. "Anika."

"Nice to meet you...Anika." The way he says my name, slow and rich like dark chocolate. And I'm Swiss. I love chocolate. His voice wraps around each syllable as if savoring it.

I take a second to look at my surroundings. And, okay so maybe he's been here a while, because my oh-my-güte-must-pee situation was such that I didn't even notice anything when I made a beeline to the bathroom. I didn't notice the unfamiliar jacket hanging by the door, the big boots by the couch. And when I popped out of the bathroom, singing, "I'll get ya, get ya, get ya, get ya..." Surprise! I didn't have to get him. He was right there, and, clearly, very amused.

I edge toward the door, my face burning hot. "Right. Well. Sorry about the...fish. And the breaking and entering. And the singing. Actually, let's pretend none of this happened."

His eyes follow my retreat, sparkling with amusement. "What, and miss out on this delightful first impression?"

I fumble behind me for the doorknob, missing it twice

before my fingers finally close around it. "I should go. Places to be, you know."

"So..." He crosses those muscular arms with casual grace, and wow, those biceps. "Should I expect more surprise visits? I could keep the bathroom stocked with extra singing fish."

I fling the door open, nearly tripping over my own feet. "Definitely not. Never again." I gesture vaguely at the bathroom, then at myself, then at him, which only makes things worse. "This was a one-time emergency situation."

"Shame." That one word, delivered with a hint of a smirk, makes my stomach do a backflip.

"I have to go!" My voice comes out froggy. "Many important things to do. Very busy. Goodbye!"

I sprint out the door, my face flaming, and dash into the trees, desperate to get away from the dimples, the laughter, and from...whatever that was.

Behind me, I hear his warm laugh floating on the morning breeze, and I pick up my pace. This is what I get for drinking that extra cup of tea this morning. Next time, I'll just hold it.

Trust is the most dangerous currency.

CHAPTER THREE

Griffin

The crowd erupts as I block a shot from HC Davos's center, Stefan Weber. These Swiss players are fast. Especially Weber, who's been dancing around our defense all night.

"Nice save, McGregor!" Peter Koch, our center, taps my pads with his stick as he skates past.

I've been with EHC Visp Föhn for three weeks now, and the team's already starting to feel like family. Peter is teaching me Swiss German curse words I probably shouldn't repeat.

Christoph "Speedy" Rüeger lives up to his nickname as our right wing. And then there's Tyler Matthews, another NHL lockout refugee. He's from the Minnesota Bandits, playing defense for Visp and helping me adjust to European ice.

The arena here isn't as big as the Blizzard Dome, but these Swiss fans make up for it in pure passion. They're waving flags and singing songs I still can't understand.

"Watch the trailer!" I shout as I spot Davos's sniper, Jonas Müller, sneaking in behind our defense.

Tyler picks up on my warning and cuts off Müller's angle. Seconds later, Peter scores on the other end. The horn blasts, and our fans start chanting "Föhn! Föhn! Föhn!"

"That's how we do it in Visp!" Peter circles back, spraying ice as he stops. "Griffin, you're bringing us luck, my friend."

I flash him a thumbs-up, then reset for the face-off. The game here is different. Wider ice, more passing, less hitting. But hockey is hockey, and right now, with the NHL locked out, there's nowhere else I'd rather be. Well, maybe one place, if I'm being honest. My mind drifts to a certain bathroom intruder with fierce eyes and a deadly trout...

The whistle snaps me back to reality as Davos's center wins the draw clean.

I track the puck as it ping-pongs between players, my muscles coiled and ready.

A shot rings off my mask, and I instinctively snag the rebound before it drops. The crowd roars, and I can't help scanning the sea of faces. Is she out there? The pretty strawberry blonde with perfectly pink cheeks?

I shake my head, refocusing as Weber dekes past our defense.

"McGregor!" Tyler shouts from my left. "Two-on-one!"

I drop into my butterfly stance, tracking the puck as Weber dekes left, then right.

Not this time, buddy.

The puck's a blur, but I track it off his stick, kicking out my right pad. The save isn't pretty, but it gets the job done. The crowd roars their approval.

"Your mother was a hamster!" Peter shouts at Weber as he skates by.

I've learned that's one of his tamer insults.

The game flows back and forth, and between saves, my mind keeps drifting to the girl with the terrible singing voice. *Who breaks into a cabin belting at the top of their lungs?*

The memory makes me smile behind my mask.

Another shot, another save. The crowd starts chanting something that sounds like a mix between a drinking song and a war cry. I still can't understand half of what anyone says here, but hockey? Hockey I understand perfectly. The sound of blades cutting ice, the hollow thwack of stick on puck, the surge of adrenaline as I track the play. It all speaks the same language.

The final horn blares, and we've done it. Squeaked out a 3-2 win against Davos. My heart's still racing from that last sequence, where I had to make three saves in quick succession.

As we line up for the post-game handshakes, I spot a familiar face that makes me do a double take. "Holy smokes, Dex Campbell?"

We played juniors together back in Calgary. I didn't see him on the ice tonight, but goaltenders rarely share a game 50/50.

"Griffin McGregor, you beauty!" He grins through his beard as we fist bump. "Sick saves tonight, man."

We can't chat more, as the line keeps moving, but Dex taps his wrist as if to say, 'let's catch up later.'

After showering and changing, I find him waiting outside our locker room. "There's a great coffee place around the corner," he says. "Unless you've got team obligations?"

"Nah, I'm free. Lead the way."

The café is cozy, with wood-paneled walls and the rich smell of fresh-roasted beans. Dex orders something complicated in perfect Swiss German while I stumble through pointing at the menu.

"So how long have you been over here?" I ask once we're settled with our drinks.

"Three seasons now. Swiss league's been good to me." He stirs his coffee. "Better than riding buses in the AHL, that's for sure. But what about you? Starting tendy for the Titans. That's huge."

"When we're not locked out."

"Could be worse places to land than Switzerland." Dex grins. "The mountains, the chocolate, the beautiful women..."

I almost choke on my coffee, as if Dex knew I'd been thinking about my bathroom intruder all night.

Dex raises an eyebrow at my reaction, but I quickly change the subject. "Wow, it's good to see you, man. Juniors seems forever ago."

Dex leans back in his chair. "Yeah. Remember that time the bus broke down outside Red Deer?"

I snort. "Coach made us do jumping jacks to stay warm and what's-his-name complained the whole time."

"Bryce Sheriton."

I snap my fingers, memories flooding back. "Yes! Oh my gosh, Bryce Sheriton. Except we used to call him—"

"Bryce Krispies!" we both exclaim in unison, laughing at the memory.

"What a weenie," I say. "He was the laziest player I've ever seen."

"Man, junior hockey was something else. Remember when someone filled your blocker with shaving cream?" Dex smirks proudly while pointing at himself.

"That was you?" My jaw drops. "I blamed Aiden Harrison for months!"

Dex's eyes shine with mischief. "The look on your face when you went to make that first save."

"I had foam shooting up my sleeve! The refs had to stop the game."

"Hey, it made you more flexible. You were doing splits trying to shake that stuff out."

I shake my head, still amazed after all these years. "Speaking of games, I didn't see you out there tonight until the handshake line. Everything okay?"

"Yeah, just my rest game, but I was suited up just in case. We've got a good rotation going. Coach likes to keep us both fresh. Tonight was Eric's night. He's a solid keeper. This way we're both sharp when it counts." Dex takes a sip of his coffee. "You know how it is. Play too many games and suddenly your reflexes are shot come playoff time."

"Tell me about it. Back in Toronto, Coach Knight practically has to drag me off the ice sometimes. But he's right. By game sixty, those cross-ice one-timers start looking a lot faster."

"At least we're not stuck in some AHL barn playing three-on-threes anymore." Dex raises his cup in a mock toast. "To Switzerland."

"To Switzerland," I echo.

"So, how long are you planning to stick around here?" I ask. "Think you might head back to Calgary anytime soon?"

Dex's face lights up in a way I've never seen before. "Actually, I'm pretty settled in Davos. Met someone special." He pulls out his phone, showing me a photo of him with a stunning blonde. "This is Marta. She's a physiotherapist for the team."

"Wow, doctor girlfriend. Fancy."

"Yeah, she's incredible. Speaks five languages, loves hiking, and somehow puts up with my terrible attempts at Swiss German. We travel all over Europe during the offseason."

"Living the dream, huh?"

"Can't complain." Dex tucks his phone away, but his smile remains. "Living here, playing hockey, being with her...it just feels right, you know? Can't imagine going back to Canada anymore."

I nod, but something in my chest tightens. "Really? You'd stay here permanently for a girl?"

"When you know, you know." He shrugs. "What about you? Any Swiss misses catching your eye?"

My mind flashes to strawberry blonde hair and a brandished trout, but I shake it off.

"I mean, there are beautiful women here, but..." I trail off. "I can't imagine staying in another country for someone unless we're married. Even if..." I catch myself before finishing that thought.

"Even if what?" Dex's eyebrows shoot up with interest.

"Even if...there might be someone worth getting to know better."

"Oh? Do tell."

"It's nothing. Just this crazy encounter at my rental." I wave it off, but I can't help smiling. "She tried to attack me with a fish."

"A fish?" Dex bursts out laughing. "Only you, McGregor. Only you."

"It wasn't a real fish," I amend.

"Does she live here? In Visp?"

"Actually, I'm not living in Visp. The team set me up with this sweet apartment downtown, but..." I lean back in my chair. "I found this perfect little cabin in Grächen. It's like stepping into a postcard."

"Grächen?" Dex furrows his brow. "That's a bit of a drive, isn't it?"

"Only thirty minutes to the arena. The commute's worth it." I pull out my phone to show him some photos. "Look at this view from my deck. Reminds me of growing up near Banff. Dad used to take us hiking there every summer."

"Man, you and your mountain obsession." Dex shakes his head, but he's smiling. "Most guys would take the fancy apartment in the city."

"Yeah, well, I'm not most guys." I swipe through more photos. "The cabin belongs to this guy Walter, who's traveling. It's got this old stone fireplace, these massive windows overlooking the forest. Total silence. Just me and the mountains. Here's the hiking trail that heads into the village."

"And that's where you met the fish lady?" Dex smirks.

I feel my cheeks heat up. "She was just using my bathroom."

"Hold up." Dex wipes tears from his eyes. "She...used your bathroom? A random woman walked into your cabin...to pee?"

"Well, technically it wasn't random. She knows the cabin owner." I wince. "Apparently she has permission to use the spare key for emergencies?"

"And her emergency was...?"

"Nature called during her morning hike, I guess? Look, she was listening to music and probably didn't notice my stuff everywhere. Then she came bursting out of the bathroom singing Blondie at the top of her lungs."

"Blondie?" Dex interrupts, shoulders shaking with laughter.

"One Way or Another." I can't help grinning. "Not her best performance."

"So she's singing Blondie, sees you, and grabs...a fish?"

"It was this musical trout thing. Like a wall decoration." I mime wielding it like a weapon. "She started yelling at me in two languages."

Dex is practically doubled over now. "Please tell me you got her number."

"No, she kind of...ran away." I scratch the back of my neck. "But I'm pretty sure she lives in town somewhere. Grächen's small, so..."

"So you're gonna casually lurk around street corners in case she happens to walk by?"

"What? No! I just might keep an eye out. You know, in case she needs to use my bathroom again."

A crooked smile is often more honest than a straight one.

CHAPTER FOUR

Anika

This is the stupidest idea I've ever had. I clutch the plate of homemade Chräbeli, which is balancing on the pack of Goldeimer toilet paper. It's a practical peace offering, I think. After I made a fool of myself last week.

The cookies are still warm from the oven, and the sweet anise scent wafts up, reminding me why I'm here. To apologize. That's all. Nothing more.

The door knocker echoes through the cabin, but no answer comes. My knuckles rap against the wood.

Still nothing.

My shoulders slump with relief and maybe a little disappointment.

Just as I'm about to leave the gifts by the door, a rhythmic thunking sound draws my attention around the corner of the cabin. I follow it, my boots crunching through fallen leaves, until...

Oh. Mein. Guete!

Griffin stands in a clearing, wielding an axe. Sunlight streams through the autumn leaves, catching the beads of sweat on his bare shoulders and back. His muscles ripple and flex as he brings the axe down, splitting a log effortlessly.

I freeze mid-step, cookies and toilet paper almost forgotten in my suddenly slack grip. I've seen shirtless men at the lake in summer, but none like...this.

My mouth goes dry as I watch him work, time seeming to slow down. Each powerful swing showcases the play of muscles across his back, his biceps flexing as he positions another log.

What am I even doing here? The cookies were just an excuse, if I'm being honest. A pitiful attempt to make up for breaking into his bathroom and threatening him with a fish. But now I can't tear my eyes away from the way his wavy hair curls damply at his neck, or how his jeans hang low on his hips as he bends to gather more wood.

He pauses to wipe his brow with the back of his hand, and I duck behind a tree like some creepy forest stalker. What am I doing? Ogling him like he's the star of a lumberjack calendar?

But I can't stop watching. The way his shoulders bunch and release. The pure strength in his movements that somehow still holds a dancer's grace.

"Enjoying the show?"

I jump, nearly dropping the cookies. Griffin turns around, propping the axe casually on one shoulder. His smile shows off those dimples that should be illegal.

Heat floods my face as I realize I've been caught staring. "I... brought cookies."

I straighten, shaking off the embarrassment. I'm just going to set the offering on the ground and back away like I'm at the mouth of a volcano leaving a sacrifice to the angry volcano gods.

"You came all this way to bring me cookies?" His voice holds warm amusement that makes my insides flutter. He sets down the axe and steps closer, still gloriously shirtless.

I nod mutely, wondering if it's possible to spontaneously combust from proximity to male perfection. He's just a man, I remind myself. Just. A. Man.

"These are Chräbeli," I blurt, still holding the plate and toilet paper like a complete idiot. "And...toilet paper. For breaking in. To use your toilet."

I freeze as the implications hit me. "Oh no. Not that the cookies will make you need to...I mean, they're perfectly safe. The toilet paper is separate. Not related. Just practical." I clamp my mouth shut. Why can't I stop babbling?

Griffin's eyes dance with amusement as he crosses his arms, making his muscles do...interesting things. "So, to summarize, your apology gifts are questionably edible cookies and emergency toilet paper?"

Heat crawls up my neck.

"I should've just brought a fruit basket," I mumble.

He reaches for a cookie, his fingers brushing mine. My skin tingles at the contact. With exaggerated caution, he takes a dramatic bite, his eyes never leaving mine. "Guess we'll see if I have to make a run for it."

I'm about to make a run for it. Down to the village and away from this man.

The way he's looking at me makes my stomach do backflips. I watch his face, holding my breath. The Chräbeli are my Oma's recipe. Crisp, sweet anise cookies shaped like tree branches. I've made them a hundred times, but suddenly they seem inadequate. Also, the toilet paper isn't helping.

"Delicious," he says around a mouthful of cookie.

I lift my chin, thrusting the plate and toilet paper at him. "Now we're even."

"Even?" Griffin's dimples deepen as he rakes his eyes down my body and back up. "For what, exactly?"

"Never mind. And you can stop looking at me like that, mister."

"Like what?"

I force the items into his hands. "Just take these. I need to go."

"If you need to go that badly, I have a fish-themed bathroom you can use."

"I need to go to WORK."

"Oh? Where do you work? I could walk you down."

"No thanks."

I spin on my heel, ready to bolt, but his voice stops me. "You know what Wayne Gretzky says?"

"Who?" I turn back despite myself. I know perfectly well who Wayne Gretzky is.

"The Great One. Hockey legend." He sets the gifts on a nearby stump. "He says you miss one hundred percent of the shots you don't take."

"Is that supposed to mean something to me?"

"It means maybe you breaking into my bathroom was the universe's way of making sure we met. And here you are again. It's fate."

I snort. "I don't believe in those sorts of woo-woo things."

"Another hockey quote then. 'It's not whether you get knocked down, it's whether you get back up.'"

I blink at this strange man and his oddly optimistic way of seeing things. Most people would be annoyed about finding someone using their bathroom without permission. But he seems...amused? Even pleased? He's treating it like some cosmic matchmaking service.

"Are you always this..." I wave my hand, searching for the right word. "Friendly to people who break into your house?"

His grin widens. "Only the cute ones who serenade me with Blondie songs."

"No! Don't remind me of that!"

"One wayyyyy da da da da," he sings, badly off-key, butchering the words. "I'm gonna gonna gonna gonna."

"Stop." I press my lips together to hide a smile. "That's terrible."

"I never claimed to be a singer."

"Shouldn't you put a shirt on? It's October." My voice comes out higher than intended.

Griffin stretches lazily. "Am I making you uncomfortable?"

"*Nein.* I mean no. I just...wouldn't want you to catch cold."

Real smooth, Anika.

He reaches for his T-shirt draped over a nearby log, but instead of putting it on, he dangles it from one finger. "You sure? Because I'm actually quite warm from all the wood chopping."

My eyes betray me, tracking a bead of sweat as it trails down his chest. I snap my gaze back to his face, finding him watching me with that infuriating dimpled smile.

"Fine. Freeze to death. See if I care." I cross my arms.

"Well, if you insist..." He unfolds the shirt with deliberate slowness, making a show of sliding one arm through, then the other. The fabric clings to his damp skin as he works it down his chest, somehow managing to make getting dressed look like a scene from *Magic Mike*.

"Better?" He smooths the shirt over his stomach, his movements deliberate.

I tilt my head, studying him more carefully. Years of bartending have given me a sixth sense about people—the way they carry themselves, the stories behind their eyes. But this guy? He's throwing me off balance.

"What are you even doing here?" I wave my hand at the cabin. "A Canadian, renting in Grächen of all places?"

He runs a hand through his damp hair, tossing me a flirty look. "Playing hockey for Visp, actually. There's this whole lockout situation back home."

"Hockey?" I roll my eyes dismissively, even though my heart skips. "That's the one with the little white ball?"

His jaw drops. "You're kidding."

"Oh wait, no. That's golf." I tap my chin, playing dumb. "It is the one with the sticks, *ja*? Like golf, but chasing the ball around the ice."

"It's nothing like golf," Griffin corrects, looking personally wounded. "And it's not a ball. It's a puck. Hockey is an art form. The speed, the skill, the strategy..."

I bite back a smile, remembering how I'd won a lot of money last season betting on my favorite teams. But he doesn't need to know that.

"Sounds boring." I examine my nails.

"Boring?" The poor man seems to be gasping for air, the way he's sputtering. Yeesh, you'd think I'd just insulted his mother.

"I prefer real sports," I say. "Like skiing."

"Real sports?" He clutches his chest. "Maybe you should come see a game, let me change your mind."

"Shouldn't you be splitting more wood or something?"

"Come on, I'll get you tickets." He steps closer, and I catch a whiff of pine and fresh sweat. "Front row, right behind the goal. Best seats in the house."

"So I can watch sweaty men slam each other into walls? No thanks."

"Hey, some of those sweaty men are quite charming." He winks. "One in particular."

"Let me guess. You?"

"I've been told I clean up nice."

"Are you trying to get me to come to your game, or ask me out?"

"Can't it be both?" He grins. "Come watch me play. If you still think it's boring, I'll buy you dinner to make up for wasting your time."

Such a smooth talker.

"And if I like it?"

"Then I'll definitely buy you dinner." His eyes sparkle with mischief. "But you'll have to admit you were wrong about hockey."

"Not happening."

"Oh I think it's happening. We have a home game this Friday. I'll leave your ticket at will-call."

"I work Friday." Thank goodness for that convenient truth.

"Saturday then."

"I work every night."

"How is it you work every night? I think I need to have a word with your boss."

I stare him down, hands on my hips. "I am the boss."

"Well then it's settled."

I turn to leave, fighting a smile. "Some of us have to work for a living instead of playing games on ice."

"So you're coming Friday?"

"Definitely not."

"I'll take that as a maybe."

I don't look back as I head toward the trail. "Just eat your cookies, Wayne Gretzky."

Danger has a way of showing up in formal wear.

CHAPTER FIVE

S taring at the wooden beams crossing my cabin's ceiling, I replay that backhand shot from tonight over and over in my mind. The puck sailed right past my blocker side, a shot I should've had. The red light behind the net still burns in my memory like a taunting reminder. Sleep? Not happening.

"Get it together," I mutter into my pillow, punching it into a more comfortable shape. But comfort isn't coming tonight.

Three-four. That's how it ended. If I'd just caught that backhand in the third period, we might've pushed it to overtime. The whole sequence unfolds behind my closed eyes. I should've shifted left.

The sheets tangle around my legs as I toss and turn. My teammates played their hearts out tonight, and I let them down. That final score might as well be tattooed on my eyelids.

I grab my phone, pulling up the game highlights. Maybe if I watch it enough times, I'll figure out exactly where I went wrong. The video plays in the dark room, casting blue light across my face as I scrutinize every movement.

There it is. Minute fifty-eight. I was positioned too far right, anticipating a different play. Rookie mistake.

The worst part? I saw it coming. That slight shoulder drop, the way he shifted his weight. All the telltale signs were there. Yet somehow my brain decided to take a coffee break at that exact moment.

The clock on my phone reads 12:15 AM. I need to get my mind off the game so I'll be rested for tomorrow. I flip my pillow to the cool side for the hundredth time, but all I can think about is how I let my team down.

Too restless to sleep, I get out of bed, my feet hitting the cold wooden floor. The kitchen's just a few steps away in this cozy cabin, but right now it feels like a mile. My throat's dry as sandpaper.

The tap water here tastes different than back home. Cleaner, fresher, straight from the mountain springs. I down one glass, then another. What I really want is a beer, but that's not gonna help my head or my game tomorrow.

My stomach growls, reminding me I barely touched dinner after the game. There has to be something open in the village, right?

I pull on my thermal shirt and jeans, adding my heaviest sweater, and grab my coat from the hook. The temperature's been dropping fast this past week. Soon this whole valley will be buried in snow. The thought makes me smile despite my mood.

My boots are still muddy from earlier, but they'll do. Keys, wallet, phone. Check. I lock up and start down the path toward town, hands stuffed in my pockets. The night air hits my face like a slap of cold water as I step outside. Stars blanket the sky above the village, way more than you'd ever see in Toronto. The village below looks like a Christmas card, all twinkling lights against the dark mountain backdrop. There's gotta be something open down there. A coffee shop, a late-night café...anything to get me out of my own head. And if not, at least the walk might tire me out enough to finally sleep.

Halfway down the hill, I realize I should've taken the car. The temperature must've dropped another ten degrees since sunset. My toes are already going numb inside my boots. Real genius plan here. Who needs a nice warm vehicle when you can stumble around in the pitch black like an idiot?

The moon's only a thin sliver tonight, and my phone's flashlight only illuminates a small circle at my feet. This seemed like a brilliant idea ten minutes ago. The smart thing would be to head home. But the thought of lying in bed, staring at the ceiling for another three hours...

A branch snaps somewhere in the darkness. I freeze mid-step, heart pounding.

"Just a rabbit probably," I grumble, pulling my coat tighter. "I couldn't just raid the kitchen like a normal person."

The cold air bites at my exposed face, and I wish I'd grabbed my scarf. Or better yet, stayed in my warm bed with my regrets.

The village lights twinkle below, looking deceptively close. But I know better now. It's still a good twenty-minute walk down this winding trail.

Another noise in the woods makes me pick up my pace. Could it be a bear?

I'm not sticking around to find out.

My breath comes out in quick white puffs as I half jog down the trail. The village lights seem farther away now than when I started. How is that even possible?

My nose is going numb, and I can feel the cold seeping through my jeans.

Finally, the trail gives way to paved streets. The town square opens up ahead, dominated by the old church whose spire pierces the star-filled sky. Its clock face glows faintly. 1:07 AM.

I pause in the middle of the square, hands deep in my pockets, breath clouding in front of my face. The mountains loom black against the starry sky, their peaks lost in darkness. During the day, this square bustles with locals and the occasional tourist.

I make my way through the sleeping village. Stone and timber buildings line the narrow streets, their wooden shutters closed tight against the night.

Most windows are dark, but warm light spills from between wooden shutters here and there. Someone's probably up late watching TV or reading.

Everything's so quiet I can hear water trickling somewhere in the darkness, probably from one of those fountains where you can drink fresh water coming directly from the mountains.

I follow the narrow alley past a closed bakery that still smells like fresh bread. My stomach growls again, reminding me why I'm out here freezing my butt off in the middle of the night.

Around the corner, a faint glow catches my eye. There's a wooden sign hanging from wrought iron brackets that reads "S'Holzfass" in old Germanic script. It's creaking slightly in the night breeze. The windows are dimly lit, and I can hear muffled voices inside.

I push open the door, hit by a wave of warmth and the smell of beer. 99 Luftballons plays on the overhead speakers.

Inside, the pub is all exposed stone walls, dark wooden beams, and brass fixtures. There's a handful of locals clustered around a worn table. They all turn to stare as I enter, conversations pausing mid-sentence.

I shake off the cold and claim an empty barstool, unbuttoning my coat. No bartender in sight. The men's conversation drops to whispers, and I feel their eyes on my back. Someone mutters something in Swiss German, followed by rough laughter. I keep my eyes forward, waiting for whoever's running this place to appear. The locals keep chattering and laughing behind me, occasionally calling out something in English that I pretend I don't hear.

I drum my fingers on the weathered wooden bar top as the stereo switches to "Take on Me" when one of the men calls out in accented English.

"Hey, American!"

I look over my shoulder to face their table. They're red-faced and grinning, clearly several beers in.

"Canadian, actually."

"Ah, Canadian!" One of them raises his beer. "Come, drink with us!"

I hesitate, glancing between their table and the empty bar.

The smart play would be waiting for the bartender, but these guys aren't letting up. They're waving me over like we're old friends. Something about those smiles and snickers give me pause.

"We need one more player, Canadian guy."

I slide off the barstool, sizing up the group as I approach

their table. The oldest one, sporting a mustache, pulls out an empty chair.

"Sit, sit! We are playing Jass. Do you know it?" He shuffles a deck of cards.

"Can't say I do." I lower myself into the chair.

"It is a Swiss game," another one pipes up. "Very simple. We will teach you."

They introduce themselves in rapid-fire. Colin, Evan, Lars—their names blurring together as they deal the cards. The rules seem straightforward enough, but there's something off about how eager they are to teach me.

"First round is just for fun, yes?" says Colin, the mustached one.

The others nod eagerly. Too eagerly.

One of them, (Evan, I think) wearing a red flannel shirt, slides a beer in front of me. I haven't even ordered one yet.

"Lars always wins," he says. "Maybe you can bring him bad luck, eh?" He elbows his friend, both snickering.

I pick up my cards, trying to make sense of the unfamiliar suits. They're not like regular playing cards. There are bells and shields and acorns instead of hearts and spades.

"How about a small bet to make the game more interesting?" Colin suggests, pulling out his wallet. "Twenty francs each? For beginner's luck?"

The others quickly agree, tossing bills into the center. Three pairs of eyes fix on me expectantly.

I've played enough poker to recognize when I'm being set up. These guys aren't as drunk as they're pretending to be, and that practiced shuffle wasn't just showing off. They think they've found an easy mark. The clueless foreigner they can fleece for some cash.

"Sure," I say, pulling out my wallet. "Twenty sounds good."

Colin's eyes light up as he deals the cards. They exchange

looks that clearly say they think this is going to be like taking candy from a baby. They're probably right.

Colin fires off instructions while Lars and Evan nod along, adding bits and pieces that only muddle things further.

My head is already spinning. "Wait, so the acorns are..."

"Yes, yes, highest suit," Lars cuts in, already playing his first card. "You will catch up quite quickly."

"This is Under, very important card." Colin points to what looks like a medieval knight. "And here, these are your trumps."

I stare at my hand, trying to make sense of the symbols. Before I can ask another question, Evan slaps down a card.

"Your turn," Colin prompts, nodding at my cards.

"But I don't know what—"

"You will catch on, you will catch on!" Evan waves his hand dismissively. "Play anything."

I randomly select a card with what looks like a bell on it. The others groan dramatically.

"No, no, you must follow suit!" Colin taps my discarded card. "Unless you have no bells, then you can trump."

"Right..." I have no idea what that means.

Lars leans forward, studying my face. "Hey, I know you. You're that new goalie, yes? For Visp?"

"Yeah, that's right." Finally, something familiar to talk about. "You follow hockey?"

"Of course! I am a big hockey fan!"

"Cool."

Meanwhile, they're all throwing cards down in some pattern I can't follow. I stare at my hand, completely lost.

"I saw the game with Davos." Lars leans forward. "That save in the third period was good."

"Thanks, man." I feel myself relaxing a bit. Hockey fans are hockey fans, no matter the country. "That was a tough game."

"Play your card," Colin interrupts, tapping the table impatiently.

I glance down, having completely lost track of what's happening.

"So, this card beats that one?" I ask before laying down a card. The others exchange knowing smirks.

I second guess my choice, picking up another card at random, earning groans from around the table.

"Ah, you had the shield!" Lars shakes his head.

"Right, sorry, I—"

"Ha!" Evan slaps down a Jack with a flourish. "Trump suit! Pay up, hockey man!"

The guys burst into cheers as Evan sweeps my twenty francs from the pile. I watch my money disappear, feeling like I just got played in more ways than one.

"Maybe we should go over those rules again?"

"Next hand will be better!" Colin declares, already dealing new cards. "Now you understand the game, yes?"

I really don't, but their eager faces make it hard to back out now.

A sharp voice cuts through the pub, making the men at the table freeze. The Swiss German words snap like a whip, and even though I don't understand them, the tone is crystal clear.

"Ich han euch scho hundert mal gseit, ihr söllet nid mit touriste charte spiele!"

The guys groan collectively.

I know that voice.

I turn around and there she is. Anika comes around from behind the bar, hands on her hips, glaring at my new "friends." Her hair is pulled back into a high ponytail, wisps framing her face. She's wearing a vintage Depeche Mode T-shirt that looks like it's been well-loved.

My new card buddies shrink under her fierce gaze as she

continues her tirade. Colin's mustache twitches nervously while Lars suddenly finds his empty beer glass fascinating.

"These gentlemen," she switches to English, turning to me. "They know very well that Jass takes years to master. And they are playing with a special Swiss deck." She extends her hand toward Evan. "Give his money back."

"But, Anika!" Evan starts to protest.

"Now." Her eyes narrow. "Or maybe we can discuss your tab?"

Evan's face turns as red as his flannel shirt. And just like that, my twenty francs slide back across the table.

"Sorry," Lars mumbles, studying the floor.

I pick up the money, fighting back a grin as I watch these grown men squirm under Anika's disapproving stare.

There's something about the way she carries herself, like she could take on a bear and the bear would apologize. I'm finding it absolutely fascinating.

She signals me to follow her to the bar, and like a puppy, I trail after her. I claim the same barstool as she sets a shot glass in front of me.

"These guys," she tells me. "They pull this trick on tourists all the time. I tell them to stop, but they're stubborn."

She gets a bottle of whiskey and opens the lid.

"Oh no, thanks," I say, waving it off. "I don't want a shot."

She squints one eye at me and pours anyway. "This is for me."

"Oh."

"Anyway, why come to a bar if not to drink?"

I'm about to explain about not being able to sleep after losing the game, but something stops me. Maybe it's the way she's looking at me with those sharp eyes, like she can see right through me. Instead, I lean forward on my elbows and grin.

"We have to stop meeting like this. What were you doing when I first got here? In the bathroom again?"

Anika rolls her eyes, but I catch the hint of a smile. "I was in the office, doing paperwork. It's usually dead this time of night."

She takes her shot of whiskey in one smooth motion, then wipes the bar with a cloth that appears from nowhere.

"So this is why you couldn't make it to the game?"

The reason she shot down my invitation to come watch me play. Probably for the best. We got our butts handed to us tonight.

"Someone has to keep these troublemakers in line." She jerks her head toward the Jass players, who are now quietly nursing their beers.

"Wait a minute." I straighten up as I remember something from our conversation at the cabin. "You said you were the boss. Are you the manager, or do you own it?"

"It was my father's. Now it's mine."

The way she says it, quick and matter-of-fact, tells me not to push that topic. "Tainted Love" comes on, and Anika hums along as she wipes down glasses, completely in her element.

I nod along. "So what's with the retro playlist? Not that I'm complaining."

Anika shrugs, stacking clean glasses. "I like what I like."

A crash from the Jass table makes us both turn. Colin's knocked over his empty glass, and they're all laughing way too loud.

Lars waves an empty beer mug in the air. "Anika! One more round!"

She shakes her head. "*Nei.* You've had enough."

"Come on!" Lars staggers to his feet. "Just one more!"

"We're closed," Anika says firmly, crossing her arms.

"But it's early!" Evan protests, his words running together.

Anika's eyes narrow dangerously. She points to the door. "Go!"

The men exchange glances, then slowly gather their jackets, grumbling under their breath.

"We'll just go to Alpenglow, then!" Lars announces, trying to sound dignified as he wobbles toward the door. "They have better music."

Anika's laugh rings through the bar, a rich sound that makes me want to hear it again.

"Oh please! They won't even let you through the door at Alpenglow."

Colin's mustache droops. "That's not true."

She wipes down the bar, completely unfazed. "You'll be back tomorrow anyway."

"Maybe we won't," Evan mutters, but there's no conviction in it.

"*Tschüss!*" Anika calls after them as they file out into the cold. The door closes behind them with a soft thud, leaving the bar suddenly quiet except for Soft Cell still playing overhead.

I chuckle as I watch those guys shuffle out, but now that they're gone, maybe I can finally talk to her properly. I've been thinking about her ever since she dropped off those cookies. No. Ever since she broke in to use the bathroom, to be honest.

"You too." Anika points to the door. "Out."

"Wait, what?"

"Bar is closed." She switches off the stereo mid-song, plunging us into silence.

"But I just got warm!" I protest. "I froze my butt off walking down here."

She raises an eyebrow, unimpressed. "You walked all the way from the chalet? Through the forest trail? In the dark?"

"Hey, I was hungry."

"We don't serve food here."

"Wait." I glance toward the door where the card players disappeared. "Those guys aren't driving, are they?"

"Grächen is partly car-free," she says, starting to stack chairs now. "Those guys all live in the village. Five-minute walk, maybe ten if they stop to sing."

I scoff. "It's a thirty-minute walk for me. Uphill."

"Then you better start heading back." She gets a broom from behind the bar and starts to sweep broken glass from under the table where the men were just sitting.

"Can I at least call an Uber first?"

That gets a real laugh out of her. Not the polite kind, but a full belly laugh. A snort even comes out.

"What's so funny?"

"There is no Uber in Grächen." She wipes tears from her eyes with the back of her hand. "We have one taxi, and Kurt is sleeping by now."

I blink at her, not quite believing this is happening. "You're seriously kicking me out?"

"I have things to do." She props the broom against a wall "Glasses to wash, floors to mop..."

"I could help." The offer slips out before I can stop it.

She moves behind the bar, pulling out cleaning supplies, and gives me a look that could melt ice. "And why would you do that?"

"Because I'm a nice guy?" I flash my most winning smile, the one that usually gets me out of trouble with Coach.

"Nice guys who help clean bars usually want something." She adds soap to running water to wash the rest of the beer glasses. "What do you want?"

"A ride home would be nice."

"Ah." She nods sagely. "There it is."

"Come on, it's freezing out there!" I gesture toward the

window, where frost is already forming on the glass. "I'll probably get eaten by a bear."

"There are no bears in Grächen." She doesn't even look up from her cleaning. "Maybe some foxes."

"Foxes can be vicious!"

"They are more afraid of you than you are of them," she says, hands full of suds. "Unless you're carrying chicken in your pockets?"

"If I had chicken, I wouldn't be hungry."

"Then you don't have anything to worry about." She shuts off the water. So please go. I have work to do."

"What about wolves?"

"No wolves either. Just hockey players who don't know when to go home."

"Are you sure you don't want my help?" I offer, already reaching for a rag.

"No." She snatches it away before I can grab it. "Out."

"But—"

"Now." She plants her hands on her hips.

I raise my hands in surrender, sliding off the barstool. "All right, all right. But if I don't make it back to the cabin, it's on your conscience."

"I'll light a candle for you," she says dryly.

I toss the twenty francs on the bar for a tip, even though I didn't drink anything. "You're really not going to give me a ride?"

"*Guete Nacht*, Griffin." She makes a shooing motion with her hands. "Watch out for the foxes."

Luck looks suspiciously like preparation.

CHAPTER SIX

Anika

Dodging pink and yellow balloons that brush against my face, I squeeze between chattering couples at my friend Ivy's baby shower. Their apartment in Bern feels cramped with all these people, most of whom seem to be sporting matching rings and baby bumps.

Ivy's British husband James hovers nearby, refilling everyone's champagne glasses (except Ivy's, of course) as everyone makes an effort to speak English for his benefit.

"Have you picked names yet?" Maja asks, adjusting the pink "It's a Girl!" banner hanging crookedly on the wall.

"We're thinking Sophia." Ivy beams, rubbing her belly. "Or maybe Lucy."

I'm the only one here without a ring on my finger. Even wild-child Heidi got married last spring in a barefoot ceremony on some beach in Thailand.

"The nursery is almost ready," Ivy says, rubbing her swollen belly. "We went with a woodland theme."

Maja chimes in from across the room. "Oh, you must see what we did with Luna's room! The unicorn wallpaper is so cute."

Lisa and Sarah compare notes on their recent promotions at their banking firms. Beside them, Eva cradles her six-month-old while discussing sleep training methods with Alessia, who's due any day now.

I sit down on the sofa and take a sip of my champagne, trying to focus on the bubbles dancing on my tongue instead of the growing hollow feeling in my chest. These women used to share my adventures. Backpacking, spontaneous road trips, late nights singing and dancing.

The conversation swirls around me like I'm watching a movie. Career women discussing their latest promotions and upcoming business trips. Mothers swapping stories about first steps and preschool applications. And me, somehow belonging to neither world, stuck in a limbo I never noticed creeping up on me.

When did I become the outsider in my own friend group?

"How's the pub doing?" Lisa asks between bites of carrot cake. "I keep telling Gustav we should drive down there for a weekend."

"Great!" I force a smile, the lie tasting bitter. "Really great. Busy season's coming up with winter tourism."

Eva nods, bouncing her baby on her knee. "That's wonderful. Though I can't believe you've never remodeled."

"The tourists love it," I say, which isn't exactly untrue. The few tourists who wander in seem charmed by the vintage vibe. But charm doesn't pay the bills.

Truth is, most of them head to that new place, Alpenglow, with its Instagram-worthy craft cocktails and LED light displays. Meanwhile, I'm lucky to fill half my tables on weekends. Last month, I had to dip into my savings just to keep the lights on.

Ivy claps her hands. "Your father would be so proud."

My chest tightens at the mention of Papa. He poured his heart into S'Holzfass for thirty years. He knew every regular by name, remembered their drink orders, their stories. The pub was more than just a business to him. It was home.

But maybe that's the problem. I'm trying to preserve something that doesn't fit in this world anymore. Like my vintage records and ancient cash register, I'm stuck in a time that's passed.

Ivy waddles over with a plate of mini quiches. "Remember when we used to spend every weekend at S'Holzfass? Dancing on the bar?"

"Now we're lucky if we can stay awake past nine," Maja laughs.

The feeling of being adrift hasn't subsided even as conversations shift toward everyone's new lives.

"How's Zürich treating you?" Lisa asks Maja, who launches into a detailed account of her family's move from Basel.

"The commute is worth it for the schools," she explains. "And Daniel's firm has been so accommodating with my flexible schedule."

"Same with Geneva," Sarah adds. "The banking sector there offers much better maternity benefits than I had in Lausanne."

I nod and smile at appropriate intervals, amazed at how scattered we've become across Switzerland, yet they've all maintained this shared rhythm of life...marriages, mortgages, babies. Everyone seems to have built these sophisticated lives in bigger cities, while I've stayed rooted in our little alpine village, running Papa's pub.

Ivy and James start opening presents, exclaiming over tiny clothes, toys, and practical items like a breast pump that makes James blush furiously. Ivy unwraps another pastel-colored onesie to exclamations of delight.

I'd spent hours picking out a handcrafted wooden music box from an artisan in my village. Ivy seems genuinely touched when she opens it.

"Oh, Anika, it's beautiful!" She runs her fingers over the carved forest animals. "This is so special."

"I'm glad you like it," I say, relieved in some way. I wanted to give the baby something unique that will last for years. Maybe even pass it down as an heirloom.

The games start next. I try to look engaged during "Guess the Baby Food" and "Measure Mama's Belly," but my smile feels increasingly stiff. I manage to win the "Baby Word Scramble" and receive a scented candle as my prize.

By four o'clock, people begin checking watches and mentioning drive times.

"We should hit the road before it gets dark," Maja announces, gathering her designer handbag. "It's a long drive back to Geneva."

"We should go too," Heidi says, kissing Ivy's cheek. "This one gets cranky in the car." She nods toward her husband, who playfully rolls his eyes.

One by one, they gather diaper bags and purses, exchanging promises to meet up again soon, though we all know it might be months before schedules align. I remain behind, stacking plates and gathering champagne flutes as the apartment empties.

"You don't have to clean up, Anika," Ivy protests, but looks relieved when I insist.

With just the three of us left, the apartment feels spacious again. James collects torn wrapping paper while I gather stray napkins and deflate balloons, grateful for something to do with my hands.

We work quietly for a few minutes, the soft clink of dishes and rustle of garbage bags the only sounds until the apartment looks presentable again.

"That wasn't so bad, was it?" Ivy asks, sinking onto the sofa with a sigh of relief, hands resting on her belly.

"It was lovely," I say, sitting across from her on a soft armchair. "Everyone seems to be doing so well."

James emerges from the kitchen with three mugs of tea. "They all talk so bloody fast. I caught maybe half of what everyone was saying."

"You're getting better," I assure him, accepting the steaming mug. "At least you've mastered '*Grüezi*' without sounding like a complete tourist."

Speaking of tourists, a flash of that Canadian hockey player's face comes into my mind's eye. I immediately push that way down.

We settle into a comfortable silence, the kind only possible with old friends. Ivy kicks off her shoes and props her swollen feet on the coffee table.

Then Ivy and James exchange one of those married-couple glances, the kind that contains an entire conversation.

"So, Anika," Ivy begins, with an attempted casualness that immediately puts me on alert. "We've been meaning to ask you something."

James sits beside Ivy, their shoulders touching. "My

colleague Thomas is moving to Switzerland next month," he says. "British bloke, about our age, very nice."

"Very handsome," Ivy adds with a significant look.

"Oh no." I set my mug down carefully. "I know where this is going."

"He's brilliant," Ivy adds eagerly. "He's a landscape architect, loves hiking and skiing. Totally your type."

"And he doesn't know a soul here except me," James adds. "It would be a friendly gesture, really."

"We were thinking dinner here, very casual," Ivy says. "No pressure, just...meeting someone new."

I stare at my oldest friend, trying to process how we arrived at this moment. Her feeling she needs to rescue me from my singlehood.

Oh the shame!

"I'm not looking for anyone right now," I say finally, the words coming out more defensive than intended. "The pub keeps me busy enough."

I shift uncomfortably in my chair as Ivy and James exchange another one of those married-people looks. I hate those looks.

"It's just dinner," Ivy presses, leaning forward. "If you don't like him, no harm done."

"He really is a nice guy," James adds. "Loves the outdoors, very down-to-earth. Nothing like those finance bros Maja's always trying to set you up with."

I take another sip of tea to buy myself time. How do I explain this without sounding like a complete failure at life? I'm twenty-five years old, and I've never been on a proper date. Not one.

"I'm just...not good at that sort of thing," I finally mutter, staring into my mug.

"What sort of thing?" Ivy asks, genuinely confused.

"Dating." The word feels foreign in my mouth. "I wouldn't know what to do or say. It would be a disaster."

There's a beat of silence, and I can feel their surprise without looking up.

"Wait," Ivy says slowly. "When was your last date? I don't think you've mentioned anyone since...Actually, have you dated anyone since my wedding?"

Heat creeps up my neck. "Not exactly."

"Not exactly as in...?" James prompts.

"As in never," I blurt out. "I've never been on a date. I've never had a boyfriend. I just...never got around to it."

Ivy's eyebrows shoot up. "Never? But what about that ski instructor? The one from St. Moritz?"

"We had drinks with a group after lessons. It wasn't a date."

"And the bartender from Zürich? The one with the tattoos?"

"We exchanged numbers, but I never called him." I twist my fingers in my lap. "The pub needed new plumbing that month, and by the time things settled down, it felt too late."

Ivy and James exchange glances again.

"It's not that weird," I say defensively. "Some people focus on other things."

Ivy sets her tea down. "Oh, Anika."

"Don't 'oh Anika' me," I say, suddenly irritated. "Not everyone's life follows the same timeline. I run a business. I own property. I'm doing fine."

"Of course you are," James says quickly. "But don't you get...lonely?"

The question hits harder than I expect. Do I? Most nights, I'm too exhausted to think about it. I fall into bed after closing, sometimes still smelling of beer, and sleep until it's time to do inventory or place orders. The days blur together in a rhythm of work that leaves little room for reflection.

"I have the pub," I say. "I have customers I see every day.

Old Herr Ziegler, who comes in for his afternoon beer. The hiking guides who stop in after tours. The seasonal workers who become regulars for a few months before moving on."

Like certain hockey players...

But even as I say it, I realize these aren't real relationships. They're transactions wrapped in pleasantries. No one asks how I'm really doing beyond the polite "*Wie geht's*?"

"The worst that happens is you get a night off," James says reasonably. "You work too much."

"It's not just that I'm busy with the pub. I'd be terrible at a setup. Seriously! You know how I am."

"What do you mean?" Ivy asks, rubbing her belly absently.

"I'm..." I search for the right words. "Intimidating, apparently. That's what Lisa told me after your wedding, when I asked why none of the groomsmen talked to me. Too direct. Too opinionated. Too...much."

James chuckles. "You did tell my cousin his speech went on too long."

"It did! Twenty minutes about your rugby days? Come on." I roll my eyes. "See? This is what I mean. Guys want someone sweet and agreeable. I'm the woman who tells them their fly is down or their opinions are wrong."

"The right person would appreciate your honesty," Ivy insists.

"Right. Because men love when women correct them about whiskey brands or call them out when they exaggerate their skiing abilities." I set my cup down with a decisive clink. "Every guy I've ever said three words to gets this terrified look when I even so much as look their way. You've heard of resting grump face? I have resting I-will-drop-kick-you face."

Ivy bursts out laughing. "Maybe what you need is a dating coach."

"A *what*?" I blink at her.

"You know, like in that movie. James, what was it called? The one with the woman who kept having awful dates?"

James groans good-naturedly. "That terrible romantic comedy you made me sit through last Christmas? *Dating Doctor* or something equally ridiculous?"

"Yes!" Ivy snaps her fingers. "She hired this coach to teach her how to be more dateable. It was hilarious."

I stare at them both. "You're joking, right?"

"Of course I'm joking," Ivy says, still chuckling. "Though honestly, you don't need a coach. You just need practice."

"Right," I mutter.

Ivy reaches across and squeezes my hand. "One dinner. Just the four of us. If it's terrible, I promise to never try setting you up again."

"And I'll let you leave early if you give me our secret signal," James adds, demonstrating by tugging his earlobe.

I laugh despite myself. "You two are impossible."

"Is that a yes?" Ivy asks hopefully.

I take a deep breath. Maybe it's the champagne from earlier, or the peculiar vulnerability of having just confessed my complete lack of romantic experience, but suddenly the idea doesn't seem quite as terrifying.

"One dinner," I agree reluctantly. "But if I tug my ear, you better come up with an emergency."

Ivy claps her hands together. "Deal!"

"I'm already regretting this," I groan. "Can I change my mind? I'm changing my mind."

Ivy shakes her finger at me. "No takesies-backsies. You promised."

"You somehow tricked me into this," I protest. "I was emotionally vulnerable after watching you unwrap seventeen onesies with ducks on them."

James chuckles, gathering our empty mugs. "If it helps,

Thomas isn't even moving here until next month. And he'll need time to settle in, find his flat, that sort of thing."

"How long?" I ask, suddenly feeling like a death row inmate who's just been granted a temporary stay of execution.

"Probably about six weeks before we'd do the dinner," James says, heading toward the kitchen. "So you have plenty of time to prepare."

"Or panic," I mutter.

"Or prepare," Ivy corrects, her voice firm. "And don't you dare use that time to come up with excuses. I know all your tricks."

I sigh dramatically. "Six weeks of anticipatory dread. Wonderful."

"Six weeks to practice not scowling at men who try to talk to you," Ivy counters with a smirk.

"I don't scowl," I protest. "Okay, maybe a little."

James returns from the kitchen. "Look at it this way. If it's horrible, you'll have a funny story to tell the regulars at S'Holzfass."

"Great," I say sarcastically. "Old Herr Ziegler will love hearing about my dating disasters while he nurses his afternoon lager."

Ivy shifts on the sofa, adjusting her position to accommodate her belly. "Just promise you'll actually show up. No last-minute pub emergencies."

"When have I ever..." I begin, then stop myself when I see her knowing look. "Fine. As long as the pub isn't literally on fire, I'll be there."

"That's all we ask," James says with a satisfied nod.

Even the coldest ice remembers warmth.

CHAPTER SEVEN

Griffin

The adrenaline from tonight's win against HC Basel has mostly faded, replaced by a weird cocktail of confusion and annoyance.

I'm cruising down the road back to Grächen, one hand on the wheel, the other massaging my shoulder that's still throbbing a bit from where that maniac grabbed me. I'd have thought it would be great to come across a Titans fan here in Switzerland. But that guy? Somebody should have denied him a passport.

"You'll pay for this!" The man's words echo in my head. His face had been red with rage, spittle flying as he screamed about his life savings and the Titans stock. None of it made sense. Sure, stocks have ups and downs, but his reaction seemed extreme.

I flex my jaw, still feeling the sting where his fist grazed me before Peter and Tyler yanked him back. Christoph had positioned himself between us, speaking like a horse whisperer to calm the situation.

"Should've gone with the side exit," I mutter to myself, taking the turn toward home maybe slightly faster than necessary. The secret, non-crazy person exit.

"Your owner's a crook!" The man's words echo in my head. "I can't get my money out! What are you people doing with our investments?"

"Hey, man, I just play hockey," I'd told him, hands raised. "I don't know anything about the stock stuff."

But his eyes had been wild. Desperate. "You're lying! Three months I've been trying to get my investment back! They keep saying the Titans stock is frozen!"

My phone buzzes on the passenger seat. Probably Tyler checking if I'm okay. He'd offered to go get a drink with me, but I'd waved him off. I just need some quiet to process what happened.

The thing is, that fan's accusations nag at me. I invested in Titans stock too, straight from my paycheck like Hendrix suggested. Malcolm Chase had made it sound like such a sure thing, a way to be part of the team's success. But that guy tonight...there was real fear beneath his anger.

The headlights catch the reflective markers along the curves. Usually, this drive helps clear my head after a game, but tonight, my mind keeps replaying how my teammates had to drag that guy off me.

"Where's my money, McGregor?" He'd grabbed my coat, knuckles white. "Chase promised..."

The win against HC Basel should have me floating on cloud nine. That glove save in the third period was highlight-reel material. Instead, my gut churns with unease.

A car coming the other way flashes their high beams, snapping me back to the present. I ease off the gas, realizing I've been speeding. The last thing I need is to wrap my rental around a guardrail because some unhinged fan got in my head.

Still, something feels off about the whole thing. Malcolm Chase's name keeps popping up lately, and not in a good way. First the CBA negotiations, now this? The fan's accusations swim through my thoughts: "They're stealing from us...your team owner...It's all a lie."

I'm about two minutes from home when I make a snap decision. I can't face an empty cabin with nothing but that crazed fan's words bouncing around in my head. Without really thinking it through, I signal and veer away from the turn that would take me up to my place.

"Screw it," I mutter, heading toward the village center instead. Maybe some human interaction will drown out the noise in my skull.

I find a spot to park at the edge of Grächen's pedestrian zone, turning off the engine and sitting in silence for a moment. My shoulder throbs dully as I reach for my phone. Sure enough, there's a text from Tyler making sure I got home okay. It's nice of him to check up on me. Us expats need to look out for each other. I send a quick reply that I'm good, then shut off my phone.

The streets of Grächen are quiet this time of night, but I can see the warm glow from the pub windows up ahead. A few locals nod at me as I walk past. I've been here long enough that I'm no longer a complete novelty, though I still catch the occasional double-take.

When I push open the heavy wooden door of the pub, the scent of beer and wood polish greets me. The place isn't packed, but there's a comfortable buzz of conversation. My eyes immediately land on Lars, Colin, and Evan huddled around their usual table, cards in hand. They're deep in another round of Jass, focused expressions on their faces.

The guys haven't noticed me yet, so I stand there for a moment, watching their intense concentration. Lars has his "poker face" on, which isn't much of a face at all, just a stoic expression. Colin keeps bouncing his leg under the table while Evan absently rubs his beard. He's probably got a good hand.

"Room for one more?" I ask, pulling out the empty chair.

Their heads snap up in unison, expressions shifting from surprise to welcome.

Lars arches an eyebrow. "You sure about that, Canadian? Last time didn't go so well."

"I'm a slow learner, not a quitter," I shoot back with more confidence than I feel. Truth is, this Swiss card game still confuses the hell out of me, but tonight I need the distraction. "I've been practicing."

They all laugh at the obvious lie.

"Yeah, with who?" Lars snorts. "The mountain goats?"

I sit down, trying not to make it obvious I'm looking around for Anika.

"Maybe I've been watching YouTube tutorials," I say, which only makes them laugh harder.

Evan starts dealing the cards. "All right, Griffin, if you're serious about learning, we'll go slow."

The cards hit the table with a soft snap as he deals. I pick up my hand, studying the unfamiliar suits of bells, shields, acorns, and roses. Just as I'm trying to remember if the Under trumps the Ober, Anika appears beside our table.

"Oh no." She crosses her arms, fixing me with a stern stare. "Don't come crying to me when they clean you out. I won't bail you out this time."

"I appreciate the vote of confidence," I say dryly.

Lars chuckles. "She's right. We're not taking it easy on you, hockey star or not."

"Wouldn't expect you to." I organize my cards, still not entirely sure what makes a good hand. "And to prove it, the next round is on me."

Colin raises an eyebrow. "Feeling generous after winning against Basel, or softening us up before we take your money?"

"A little of both," I admit, earning chuckles from around the table.

I reach for my wallet, pulling out my credit card to give to Anika. She looks at the card like it's made of Anthrax. "Cash only."

I pull out my wallet and hand Anika a hundred franc note. Her eyes narrow.

"What? Too much?" I flash her my most winning smile.

"I don't have change for this." She taps the bill against her palm.

"Keep the change then."

"I don't want your pity money." She slaps the bill back on the table.

I fish out a few smaller notes. "Better?"

She snatches them with an eye roll that somehow makes me grin wider.

Colin drums his fingers on the table. "Twenty francs to play, hotshot."

Right. I'd forgotten about the buy-in. I place another twenty on the table, trying to remember the rules Lars explained last time. Something about trump suits and not being allowed to play lower trumps unless...My head hurts already.

I arrange my cards carefully, pretending I know what I'm doing. The game moves faster than I can follow, cards flying onto the table in some pattern that makes sense to everyone but me. I'm pretty sure I've broken at least three rules.

Anika returns with our beers, and I catch myself watching her walk away instead of paying attention to my cards. Lars clears his throat meaningfully.

"Your play," he says, and I realize everyone's waiting on me.

I stare at my hand. Bells? Roses? What beats what again?

"Today, McGregor." Evan taps his cards impatiently.

I slap down what I think is a high card. The king of roses.

Colin snorts. "Trumps are acorns this round."

"Right. I knew that." I didn't know that. I'm almost positive they're making stuff up at this point.

My head spins a little. This is perfect. Exactly the distraction I needed. I catch Anika watching from behind the bar, watching me crash and burn. I'm okay with that. When our eyes meet, she quickly looks away, but I swear I see the ghost of a smile.

Colin grins, gathering the cards for a new deal.

"Okay we'll try again, *ja*?" Colin begins to explain, lining up his own cards. "Swiss Jass. Four suits, nine cards each. The Jack is the highest card. We call it the Bauer. Then the nine, the Nell, then King, Ober, ten, and so on."

Seriously, they might as well be speaking Martian.

As I study my cards, the guys fall into their usual banter. It's comfortable. Normal.

"So I announce my trump suit?" I clarify, trying to keep up.

"Exactly." Lars nods. "Choose wisely. We're playing for pride here."

I look at my jumble of unfamiliar cards and take a shot in the dark, throwing down a random card.

The guys exchange looks.

"What? What did I do?"

"You just played your trump," Colin says slowly.

"Is that...bad?"

"You just won the hand," Evan says, shaking his head. "With possibly the worst strategy I've ever seen."

I stare at the pile of cards. "Really?"

"Pure luck," Colin mutters, pushing some coins my way.

"Oh!" I allow myself to gloat a little, giving a side glance toward Anika. "Cool."

The game goes on for the next hour to a soundtrack of 80s eurorock, but my dumb luck wore out after that first win. Oh well. I knew it couldn't last. Now I'm down about sixty francs, but I don't care, because I'm too busy watching Anika work.

I'm only half focused on my cards. My eyes keep drifting to her, mesmerized by how she moves behind the bar, singing along to The Clash and Erasure.

When she catches me looking, she gives me this half-glare that should probably terrify me but instead makes my pulse skip. The beer is hitting just right, making everything feel warm and pleasant. I signal for another round.

"Your funeral tomorrow," Lars says, but doesn't stop me from ordering.

"Worth it," I mumble, watching Anika as she pulls the tap handles. My head's already fuzzy from the first two, but whatever. I'm not playing tomorrow, and these guys are actually pretty fun when they're taking my money.

The door bangs open, letting in a blast of cold air along with two guys who look like they stepped out of a 90s grunge band. The taller one's got a leather jacket with too many zippers, while his buddy's sporting a patchy beard. They swagger up to the bar, reeking of cigarettes.

"Hey! Two beers!" The tall one slaps his hand on the bar.

Anika doesn't even look up from wiping glasses. "We're closing soon. One round only."

"Come on, sweetie, don't be like that." The shorter one leans on the bar, grinning.

The way they're leering at her makes my jaw clench. I start to rise, but Lars catches my eye and gives a tiny head shake.

She sets down her cloth, fixing them with a look that would freeze hell. "One round. And don't call me sweetie."

The guys grab their beers and drop into chairs at the next table, shooting smug looks our way. The tall one props his feet up on an empty chair. My attention keeps drifting to their table, muscles tensing every time they snicker or whisper to each other.

"Your turn again," Evan says pointedly.

Right. Cards.

But I can't stop watching the two newcomers out of the corner of my eye. They're laughing too loudly and staring at Anika with predatory grins every time she walks by. One of them makes a comment that causes the other to laugh and elbow him, both turning to watch her as she moves behind the bar.

Lars looks between me and the two guys, then shakes his head slightly. "Ignore them. They're just drunk idiots."

"Yeah, they'll finish their beers and leave," Colin adds, sounding unconcerned. "Focus on the game."

"I am," I lie, stealing another glance at the two men. The taller one is now openly staring at Anika, making a comment to his friend that produces more laughter.

Evan leans in, voice low. "She can handle herself. Trust me."

I reluctantly turn back to the game, trying to concentrate on the cards in my hand. But every laugh from the next table sets my teeth on edge. Maybe I should just call it a night. My head's already swimming from the beer.

Anika begins making her way around, collecting empty glasses. She passes their table, and my blood freezes as the tall one suddenly lunges forward, grabbing her arm.

"Let go," Anika says sharply, trying to pull away.

The guy just laughs, his grip tightening. "Come on, just one drink with us."

Anika yanks her arm free. "Keep your hands to yourself."

My back stiffens as the shorter one grabs Anika around the waist and pulls her onto his lap.

"Don't be like that," he says.

She struggles, clearly furious, but he's got his arms around her waist.

"Hey!" I'm on my feet before I even realize what I'm doing. My chair flies backward. "She asked you not to touch her."

The guys look at me, then exchange amused glances. The taller one says something that makes his buddy laugh.

"The lady asked not to be touched," I growl, crossing the space between our tables in two strides. My voice comes out low and dangerous.

The guy holding Anika smirks at me. "Mind your business, American."

"Canadian," I correct automatically. "And I'm making it my business."

"Griffin," Lars warns from behind me.

I ignore him. "Let her go. Now."

Lars, Colin, and Evan are on their feet now too, moving around the table but not jumping into the fray.

The tall one stands up, sizing me up. He's a few inches shorter than me but built like a tank. His breath reeks of cigarettes and beer. "Or what?"

The next moment happens in a blur. He throws a punch that catches my eyebrow, sending me staggering backward until my back hits the wall. Pain explodes above my eye, warm blood immediately trickling down.

"Griffin!" I hear Anika shout.

I push off the wall, ready to charge back, but the guy holding Anika suddenly yelps in pain as Anika's heel crashes down on his foot.

She twists in his grip, her elbow connecting with his solar plexus. In one fluid motion, she's out of his lap, spinning to deliver a palm strike to his nose that makes a sickening crunch. He howls, hands flying to his face.

The taller one roars and barrels toward her. Anika doesn't even flinch. She drops low, her leg sweeping out in a perfect arc, catching him behind the knees. He crashes to the floor like a felled tree.

The shorter one, blood streaming from his nose, makes another grab for her. As he lunges for her, she pivots, using his momentum against him. One moment he's charging, the next he's flying through the air, crashing onto an empty table.

My jaw drops.

The taller guy staggers to his feet, face contorted with rage. He pulls a small knife from his jacket, and my heart stops.

"Anika!" I yell, pushing off the wall.

Anika is already moving, her stance low and balanced. She blocks his arm with her forearm, delivers a palm strike to his chest, an elbow to his temple, and suddenly his face is to the floor, arm bent at an angle.

"I said, keep your hands to yourself," she says calmly, releasing him with a little shove that makes his head thunk against the floorboards.

The entire bar has gone silent. I'm standing there with my mouth hanging open, my own injury forgotten, and completely sober. The entire exchange takes maybe fifteen seconds. Both men are groaning on the floor while Anika stands over them, barely breathing hard, smoothing her hair back into place.

"Get out," she says coldly. "Now."

They stumble to their feet, shooting venomous glares at her (and me) before limping toward the door.

"You crazy witch," the shorter one mumbles through his hands, his nose is still gushing blood.

But Anika just stares them down until they disappear into the night.

The bar is silent for a beat, then, like a dam breaking, the Jass players erupt into cheers and applause.

Lars is whistling through his fingers, and Colin is doubled over laughing.

"Did you see their faces?" Evan howls, slapping his knee. "Priceless!"

I'm still frozen in place, blood dripping down the side of my face, completely shell-shocked by what I just witnessed.

Anika brushes her hands together like she's just taken out the trash, then turns her attention to me. "Sit," she commands, pointing to a chair. "Don't move."

I obey without question, sinking into the nearest seat.

"You're bleeding on my floor," she says matter-of-factly, then disappears behind the bar.

"What...What just happened?" I finally manage to ask no one in particular.

Lars claps me on the shoulder. "Meet Anika Gisler, three-time regional champion in Wing Chun kung fu."

"You're joking."

"Nope." Colin grins. "Those idiots picked the wrong bartender to mess with."

Evan is collecting our cards and stacking them neatly. "And you, my friend, are an idiot for thinking she needed your help."

"I..." My cheek feels hot, and it's not just from the punch. "I didn't know."

"Obviously," Lars says, gathering his winnings from the table. "But it was still nice of you to try."

Anika returns with a first aid kit, setting it on the table with a deliberate thunk. She opens the kit and pulls out an antiseptic wipe. Without warning, she leans in and dabs at the cut above my eye. I hiss at the sting.

"Such a baby," she mutters, but there's no real bite to it.

The Jass players are collecting their things, still chuckling among themselves.

"We'll leave you to your nursing duties," Colin says with an exaggerated wink that earns him a glare from Anika.

"Thanks for the cash, McGregor," Lars adds, patting his pocket where my money now resides.

They head for the door, leaving a stack of bills on the table as a tip that's suspiciously close to what they won from me tonight.

"*Tschüss!*" they call in unison, and then they're gone, their off-key singing fading as they head down the street.

I'm alone with Anika, who's still gently cleaning the cut on my eyebrow, her face inches from mine. Up close, I can see flecks of gold in her blue eyes that I never noticed before.

"That was..." I shake my head, searching for words. "Amazing. Terrifying. Incredibly hot."

The corner of Anika's mouth quirks up. "Are you drunk?"

"No," I say, then reconsider. "Maybe a little. But I'd think that was hot sober too."

She applies a butterfly bandage to my cut, her fingers surprisingly gentle for someone who just took down two men twice her size.

She steps back, examining her work. "This will bruise, but you'll live."

"Thanks," I say, reaching up to touch the bandage. Our eyes meet, and there's a charged moment of silence.

"That was stupid, you know," she finally says. "Getting involved."

"Maybe." I shrug. "But I'd do it again."

Anika studies me, her expression unreadable. Then she starts packing up the first aid kit. "You hockey players." She huffs. "Always looking for a fight."

"I still have all my original teeth," I say with a big grin.

She doesn't seem impressed.

The bar suddenly feels too warm as Anika finishes packing up the first aid kit. I resist the urge to touch the butterfly bandage she's placed on my forehead.

"Did you walk all the way from your cabin again?" she asks, studying me for a moment, seemingly weighing her options. "I can give you a ride home. Just this once," she adds quickly. "Since you're injured and..." She gestures at the glasses. "Probably shouldn't drive anyway."

"Thanks, but my car's parked at the edge of the pedestrian zone." I nod toward the door. "I'm fine to drive, I swear. That little..." I gesture vaguely at my face. "...situation sobered me right up."

She doesn't look entirely convinced but nods slowly. "I'll walk you to your car after I close up."

I'm about to tell her that's not necessary, that I can manage just fine, but the words die in my throat. Five more minutes with Anika? Yeah, I'm not turning that down.

"Thanks," I say instead. "I'd appreciate that."

Anika moves around the bar, doing a quick job of closing down. I can tell she's leaving some tasks for morning, probably because I'm just sitting here watching her like an idiot. I should offer to help, but the last time I tried, I was unceremoniously kicked out.

"Ready?" she asks finally, pulling on a light jacket and grabbing her keys.

I nod, following her to the door. She locks up, giving the handle a quick tug to make sure it's secure, then starts walking. I fall into step beside her.

The night air is crisp and clean, the kind that fills your lungs and makes you feel more alive. Stars blanket the sky above us, impossibly bright away from city lights. So different from Toronto. I'm hyperaware of Anika's presence beside me. The faint scent of her shampoo, the rhythm of her breathing.

"So, Wing Chun, huh?" I break the comfortable silence.

She glances at me, a small smile playing at her lips. "Since I was ten."

"That explains a lot." I can't stop grinning. "Seriously, that was the most impressive thing I've ever seen. The way you handled those guys."

She shrugs, but I can tell she's pleased. "They were drunk and sloppy. Not exactly challenging opponents."

"Still. You could probably take down half my team without breaking a sweat."

She laughs at that. A real laugh, not the restrained chuckle I've heard before. The sound does something to my chest, like a face-off win in overtime.

"Maybe not half," she says, raking her eyes down to my feet, then back up. "You hockey players are built solid."

Is she checking me out? The thought sends a buzz through me that has nothing to do with alcohol.

We walk in silence for a few more steps. Our hands brush accidentally, and I swear I feel a current run up my arm. I steal a glance at her profile—the slight scoop of her nose, the way her lips curve upward, even when she's not specifically smiling.

The pedestrian zone ends, and we turn onto the street where I parked.

"This is me," I say as we approach my rental. I don't want this walk to end. There's something between us. I'm not imagining it. A tension, an awareness that's been building since the first day I walked into her pub. Maybe even before that, like the universe was just waiting for us to notice each other.

I fish the keys from my pocket, then hesitate. "Thanks for patching me up. And for the escort."

"You're welcome." She stands there, making no move to leave, her eyes reflecting the moonlight. "Does it hurt?"

"My pride or my face?"

Her mouth quirks up. "Both."

"Face is fine. Pride..." I mime an explosion with my hands. "Completely shattered."

She laughs then, and something in my chest expands. I realize I want to make her laugh again, as soon as possible.

We're standing face-to-face now, close enough that I can see those blue and gold flecks in her eyes even in the dim light. My pulse is racing like I'm in the final minutes of a tied game.

I should say something clever or charming, but my mind's gone completely blank. All I can think about is how much I want to kiss her.

She seems to read my thoughts. Her eyes drop to my lips for just a second, then back up to meet my gaze.

I can't look away from her face, memorizing every detail—the way her dark lashes cast shadows on her cheeks, the subtle curve at the corner of her pretty mouth.

She wets her lips, a quick, nervous flick of her tongue that makes my breath catch. My heart hammers against my ribs. Is she leaning closer? Her body shifts almost imperceptibly toward mine, and I swear the space between us has shrunk without either of us taking a step. Her eyes drop to my mouth again, lingering there, then meeting mine with an intensity that makes my breath catch.

My entire body hums with anticipation. I've been in high-pressure games, penalty shootouts with championships on the line, but nothing compares to the electricity coursing through me right now.

Anika's breathing changes, becoming quicker, shallower. Her head tilts up toward mine, almost imperceptibly, but I notice because I'm noticing everything about her. The slight flutter of her eyelids, the way her fingers fidget with the edge of her jacket, how she doesn't step back even though I'm definitely in her personal space now.

I lean in, slowly, deliberately giving her every opportunity to pull away if I'm reading this all wrong. But she doesn't move. There's a vulnerability in her expression that makes my chest ache.

My thoughts are a chaotic jumble. Part of me can't believe this is happening, while another part feels like we've been moving toward this moment since she first walked into my cabin.

Time stretches like honey between us, but in reality, only five seconds have passed. Probably less. I'm acutely aware of everything—the distant sound of music from somewhere up the street, the whisper of wind in the trees, the way Anika's breath hitches slightly as I move closer.

Our lips are a whisper apart. I can feel the ghost of her breath against my skin.

And then, suddenly, her eyes go wide with panic and her hands are against my chest, pushing me away with surprising force. And in the next second, pain explodes across my cheek as her fist connects with the side of my face.

"What the—" I stagger backward, hand flying to my jaw.

"*Scheisse!*" Anika claps her hands over her mouth, eyes huge with horror.

I blink rapidly, working my jaw to make sure it's still attached. "Wow you really clocked me." I manage to croak out.

"I'm so sorry!" She reaches toward me, then pulls back like she's afraid to touch me again. "I don't know why I did that. It was instinct, I—"

"It's fine," I mutter. I fumble for my car keys, needing to escape this mortifying situation as quickly as possible.

She's stammering now, her composure completely shattered. "It wasn't you, it was me. I might still be in fight mode."

"Seriously, don't worry about it. I misread the situation. Totally my fault."

My face throbs where her fist connected—the same side that lunatic Titans fan got me, because of course it is, but my pride hurts way more than my jaw at this point. I finally get the door open and practically fall into the driver's seat.

"Thanks for the, uh, first aid earlier. And the self-defense demonstration. Twice in one night. Lucky me."

I close the door and turn on the engine. Through the window, I see her still standing there, looking stricken.

"You should ice that cut when you get home," she says, almost pressed against the window. "Twenty minutes on, twenty off."

"I know the drill," I reply.

"Of course you do, Hockey player."

"Goodnight, Anika."

So much for chemistry. So much for reading the signs. Whatever I thought was happening between us, I was clearly wrong.

Finally, she takes a small step back. "Goodnight, Griffin. Try not to get punched again."

I smile as well as I can after getting punched thrice in one night. "No promises."

Espionage is lying with better stationery.

CHAPTER EIGHT

The village market is tiny but packed today. Elderly Frau Weber inspects tomatoes with her magnifying glass while Frau Mueller gossips about someone's wayward grandson.

This market is my happy place. A charming labyrinth of locally sourced everything, with strings of fairy lights crisscrossing the timber beam ceiling year-round. There's Herr

Baumgartner's artisanal cheese stall with the samples I absolutely do not take more than my fair share of (okay, maybe I do), Frau Abold's spice corner that makes my nose tingle in the best way possible, and the produce section, which is where I'm currently deliberating between two identical-looking bunches of kale.

"They're exactly the same, dear," I mutter to myself, turning both bunches over. "Just pick one and move on with your life, Anika."

My basket is already groaning with bread, strawberry jam, and a wedge of brie that cost more than I can afford. I need to focus on practical items like vegetables an actual adult would buy. Not the chocolate-covered pretzels I've been eyeing since I walked in.

And then I see him.

Griffin is standing across the produce section, looking unfairly gorgeous in a navy beanie, his brown hair peeking out from underneath.

Our eyes lock over a display of organic bell peppers, and I briefly consider diving behind the potato bin. But it's too late. We've done that awkward recognition thing where we both wave at precisely the same moment. His confident, and mine more like I'm having a small seizure.

Oh no, he's coming over. He's actually walking toward me.

"*Entschuldigung*," I mutter to Frau Weber as I bump into her cart. She clicks her tongue, adjusting her thick wool scarf while giving me the side-eye.

Griffin arrives at my side, looking like he's stepped out of a winter fashion catalog while I'm wearing my laundry day leggings and a sweater with a suspicious stain that might be last night's chocolate binge.

"Hi," we both say simultaneously.

"Sorry—" we both start again.

"You—" we try once more.

Frau Weber and Frau Mueller pause their produce inspection to watch us with undisguised interest.

Griffin glances at our elderly audience and leans closer to me. "Maybe we should talk somewhere else? Unless you're really committed to this kale decision."

I look down, realizing I'm still death-gripping both bunches. "Oh! No. I mean, yes. Let's go somewhere...not here."

We both hurriedly buy our groceries—Griffin somehow making the purchase of milk and eggs look like a GQ photoshoot—and exit the market together.

"The fountain?" he suggests, nodding toward the town square.

I nod, suddenly aware that I've forgotten how to form actual words. The fountain isn't running now that it's November, and there's a light dusting of snow on the ground, but we sit on the edge anyway, our grocery bags between us like some kind of barricade.

"You go first," Griffin says after a painful silence.

"No, you," I counter, because apparently, I've regressed to playground communication skills.

"I insist," he says with a small smile that does funny things to my insides.

I take a deep breath. "Fine. I'm sorry I punched you in the jaw. It was a reflex. Not that I go around punching people regularly. It's not like some weird hobby of mine or anything."

Griffin touches his jaw, grinning. "I deserved it. I wasn't thinking straight. It's all but forgotten."

"Oh." I feel a strange disappointment settle in my stomach. Forgotten? Just like that? Of course it meant nothing to him. He probably goes around almost-kissing girls in every country he visits. I guess when you're a famous hockey player, you have girls throwing themselves at you all the time. "Right. Good. Glad we cleared that up."

"Your right hook is impressive though," he adds. "You should have been a hockey player."

"Well, the Alpine Wrestling Club had to be good for something," I joke, then immediately regret it, because I've never been in any wrestling club. Why am I like this?

Griffin shifts, adjusting his beanie. "Look, it was a weird night for me. Earlier at the game, some fan went totally berserk and sucker punched me outside the arena."

"Oh my, I'm so sorry."

He waves it off. "No, no. That's not why I brought it up. I just...I was looking for somewhere quiet to unwind after all that. I wasn't exactly in my right mind."

Here it comes. The awkward letdown.

Of course. He wasn't trying to kiss me at all. He was just emotional and probably drunk, despite what he said about being sober. I clutch my grocery bag tighter, the brie probably turning to mush under my death grip.

"And then everything happened so fast with those guys at the bar, and you were amazing with your kung fu moves, and I was already kind of..." He trails off, gesturing vaguely. "And then, when you walked me to my car, I wasn't...I mean...Not that I...unless you...But if not, that's totally..."

I want to crawl into the frozen fountain and die. He's trying so hard to let me down gently without actually saying he doesn't want to kiss me. Just like every other man who's ever met me.

He stutters, shaking his head. "Anyway, I didn't mean to put you in an uncomfortable position." He squints at me like he wants me to finish his sentence for him.

"Right," I say, my voice unnaturally high. "That's...that makes sense."

"It does?"

"Absolutely," I agree too quickly.

Maybe he wasn't about to kiss me at all. Maybe he was actually just checking my face for lint.

"You probably just want to be f...f-f-f...

"Friends?" I say slowly.

"Yeah. Okay. Sure. I completely respect that."

Is that what he thinks I want? That I didn't want him to kiss me last night? The irony that I've replayed our almost-kiss approximately 473 times in my head isn't lost on me.

A comfortable silence falls between us, which I promptly destroy by blurting, "Well, good thing really, since I am practically spoken for."

Griffin's eyebrows shoot up. "Practically spoken for?"

"Mmhhmm, my friend Ivy is setting me up with someone." I nod firmly, even though this arrangement consists of exactly zero concrete plans so far.

"And this makes you 'spoken for'?" His eyes dance with amusement.

"It could!" I announce, lifting my chin. "Once I meet him. And if we like each other. And if he's not scared of me."

"Scared of you? Never." Griffin grins.

And we're back to easy conversationalist Griffin. Just like that.

"His name is Thomas. Ivy says he's very nice and has all his hair, which apparently is a dating prerequisite I wasn't aware of until now." I'm talking too fast, but I can't seem to stop. "He's an architect. Or maybe a gardener? Something with landscaping and possibly a pocket protector."

Griffin's mouth twitches. "Well, he's a lucky guy."

I snort. "I'm not so sure about that."

"Any man who gets to take you out is a lucky guy," he says simply, and I feel my cheeks heat despite the cold.

I almost don't say it, but something about this easy rapport with Griffin—sitting here on this snowy fountain edge with our groceries between us—makes me feel brave.

"I can't guarantee I won't drop-kick Thomas when we meet," I blurt out.

Griffin laughs, his eyes crinkling at the corners like I've just delivered genuinely funny stand-up comedy and not a confession of my social ineptitude.

"I'm serious," I continue, fidgeting with my grocery bag. "I will somehow find a way to completely destroy any chance of a normal human interaction. It's my superpower."

Griffin's still smiling, but his expression has softened to something more curious than amused.

I suddenly remember Ivy last week, laughing about getting me a dating coach. She'd meant it as a joke. But sitting here with Griffin, an actual professional athlete, who probably has women lining up around the block, I realize it might not be such a terrible idea.

"This might sound completely insane," I start, my heart hammering against my ribs. "But you seem to know what you're doing when it comes to...people." I gesture vaguely at his entire perfect self.

"People?" he repeats, raising an eyebrow.

"Women," I clarify with a wince. "Dating. Social interactions that don't end in disaster or property damage."

His expression is unreadable, which I find deeply unfair. My face broadcasts every emotion like a jumbo screen at a hockey game.

"What exactly are you asking me, Anika?" His voice has that hint of amusement that makes me want to simultaneously continue talking and hide forever.

"Would you...maybe...consider being something like... my dating coach?" I squeeze my eyes shut as I say it, like I'm ripping off a Band-Aid. "Just some basic pointers so I don't terrify Thomas into moving to another country."

When I dare to look, Griffin is fighting a smile. "Your dating coach?"

"Never mind." I backpedal immediately. "It was a stupid idea. Completely ridiculous. Please forget I said anything."

"I'm just curious what makes you think I'd be qualified for such a position," he interrupts, leaning forward slightly.

I feel my cheeks flush hot despite the winter chill. "Well, you're...you know." I gesture at him again, more frantically this time. "And I've never had a boyfriend, so..."

That gets his attention. His eyebrows shoot up, and I immediately regret opening my mouth.

But instead of the shocked horror, or worse, pity, that I expected, he just smiles and says, "Good for you."

I blink at him. "Good...for me?"

"Yeah. Why rush into commitment? Better to date casually and figure out what you want."

Oh dear. He thinks I mean I've never had a *serious* boyfriend. Like I've been casually dating all this time, just playing the field, having a grand old time.

"No, Griffin," I say carefully. "I've never been on a date. Period. Not one."

His expression shifts from casual confidence to something I can't quite place. Surprise, certainly, but something else too.

"I don't know how to do any of it without scaring men off," I continue, dropping my gaze to my grocery bag. "Hence the need for a dating coach."

Griffin's lips curve into a slow smile. "Let me get this straight. You want me...to teach you how to date other men?"

When he puts it that way, it sounds completely ridiculous. Which it is.

"Yes?" I say, making it a question. "Unless you think it's a terrible idea, which it probably is, in which case, forget I said anything, and we can pretend this conversation never happened."

Griffin scratches his head, dislodging his beanie slightly. "I'm not sure this is the best idea."

"What's in it for you, right?" I rush in. "I totally get that. How about a fair exchange? I'll teach you Swiss German."

Griffin curls up his lip, considering. "You'd really teach me?"

"Absolutely. I'm a killer language teacher. Just ask my cousin's kids who now know all the swear words their parents didn't want them to learn."

That makes him laugh, and the sound does something warm to my insides.

"All right," he says finally, extending his hand. "Deal. I'll be your dating coach, and you'll teach me Swiss German. I'm going to be here for at least a few months with the team, and I'd like to understand what people are saying around me. Plus, learning the local language is respectful when you're in a foreign country."

I shake his hand, trying to ignore the little zing that shoots up my arm at the contact. "Really? You'll do it?"

"On one condition," he adds, his eyes glinting mischievously.

"Name it."

"We'll need to spend a lot of time together to make any progress." His smile turns a bit wicked. "Think you can handle that?"

I swallow hard, wondering if I've just made the best or worst decision of my life.

"I think I can manage," I say, trying to sound casual despite the butterflies having a rave in my stomach. "For educational purposes, of course."

"Of course," Griffin agrees, but his smile suggests he knows exactly what he's doing to me. "For education."

Sure. Easy peasy. I can totally spend lots of time with Griffin just as friends. Even if he does look unfairly perfect in a beanie.

Dating is just improv comedy with more awkward pauses.

CHAPTER NINE

GRIFFIN

There are roughly two thousand eight hundred and thirty-eight bones in the human body. Okay, I lied. It's just two hundred and six. But the way my head is spinning, rattling around with every shot, it feels like so much more.

It's when the puck hits my helmet with a clanging thud that I realize Sawyer's really glad to see me. Or maybe he's trying to take my head off. Either way, that's a real nice howdy-do from the guy who's normally on my side of the ice.

We're at an away game tonight, squaring off against Zürich and it's a madhouse on the rink. Fans pack the arena like sardines, buzzing with hockey madness, and I'm seeing a whole lot of blue jerseys charging my way. Sawyer came over from Toronto to play for Zürich during the lockout, and this is the first time I've been on the receiving end of his missile-grade slap shots. If I didn't like him so much, I'd hate him.

He gives me a wink. This is all very fun for him, isn't it?

"Thought we were friends, O'Malley!" I yell across the ice, rubbing my helmet for dramatic effect. He just laughs, that devil-may-care grin plastered across his face as he circles back, taking a lazy loop around the center ice.

To be honest, it's pretty amusing, if not a little unsettling.

The rink buzzes, and Zürich 's fans stomp their feet, chanting Sawyer's name like a bunch of Swiss hooligans. EHC Visp has its diehards who travel for games, but they're hopelessly outnumbered here. I feel like the last man standing in a sea of navy and gold. And maybe that's the appeal for Sawyer. This isn't Toronto. It's a whole new world of ice, and I have to admit he's making it his own. He sweeps through the defense, the puck glued to his stick like it's got a crush on him. I brace myself for the onslaught, focusing on his movements. He shoots. I stretch to block it with my glove.

"Legend!" Sawyer shouts. He's enjoying this a little too much.

"Stop hitting on me!" I yell back, flicking the puck toward the boards. "Or at least buy me dinner first."

We have possession of the puck now. The Visp crowd roars as we race it up ice. Christoph charges through the opposition, with Peter on his flank. Tyler crashes into the mix, setting the tone. But Zürich 's relentless. Their defenders converge, pinning us back. The tension is a living thing, hovering over the ice like a bad smell.

Peter makes a hard pass to Christoph, who rockets it straight at Zürich 's goalie. The rebound is brutal, and a Zürich player with red hair and a scrappy attitude jumps in. They've got my number and aren't afraid to dial it.

"We'll take it from here, McGregor!" Christoph calls, his accent thick with Swiss determination.

I chuckle. "Sure, just let me know when it's safe to open my eyes!"

The crowd's a monster, swallowing every play, and before I know it, a streak of blue has broken through our line. My stomach drops. It's Sawyer. The man with a shot straight from hell.

He fires. I brace. The puck screams toward me. It slams into my pads with a resounding thump, and my heart is in my throat. This guy really doesn't know the meaning of the word 'friendly'.

Zürich 's got some real firepower. A guy with a shaggy mustache takes a crack at me. The puck skitters past my foot. A close call. I dive, arms outstretched, catching it with my glove. Saved!

This game is personal, and Sawyer's out to prove he's the new Swiss hotshot.

"You always this quiet?" Sawyer hollers from his spot on the ice, baiting me with his famous smile.

"Just thinking about how that blue jersey matches your pretty eyes," I fire back, flicking the puck over to Tyler. It sails across the rink like a gift, and Sawyer's all over it.

But then a Zürich defenseman mishandles the puck near center ice. Christoph swoops in, passes to Tyler. Tyler fakes a shot and gives it to Peter, who's found some magic, putting it past the Zürich goalie. Goal! The Visp fans lose their minds, and for a brief, glorious moment, I think we're in this.

The next few minutes are chaos. Bodies fly, blades slice, and

I'm bombarded by blue jerseys and even bluer language amidst the friendly red of Visp's jerseys. My brain's whirling. Zürich ties it with seconds to spare, sending us to sudden death overtime.

It's three on three, and Sawyer's still in play. An assist here, a play there. Before I can blink, Zürich steals it with a deflected goal off Sawyer's assist.

The buzzer sounds, and it's bedlam. Fans cheering, players congratulating each other. First game against Sawyer, and now I know what he's made of. It's strange being on this side of his madness. He flashes those pearly whites at me and salutes mockingly. If this were a Titans game, we'd be celebrating this win together. Now, I'll never hear the end of it.

"Good job!" Sawyer says as I slump over to center ice for the post-game rituals. He beams and slaps me on the back, nearly sending me sprawling.

"Yeah, yeah." I feign a grimace, pulling him into a quick headlock before pushing him off. He looks like a rock star, waving at his wife Maggie in the stands, pumping fists with every member of the Zürich team.

Maggie is jumping up and down like a maniac, bellowing and contorting her face like she's at a WWE match instead of a hockey game. It's good to see her in the crowd.

After the game, we hit a café, the three of us cozied around a little table with tiny mugs. Maggie is chatting like she hasn't seen anyone in years.

"You played great, Griffin!" she says, slugging my arm condescendingly. "That helmet trick was my favorite."

I roll my eyes. "I aim to dazzle."

Sawyer smirks, nudging Maggie. "I think we scrambled him good."

Maggie leans in, all animated and full of stories. "Isn't it amazing here? I talked Sawyer into signing with Zürich the minute I heard we could live in Switzerland. Best decision ever."

"We are loving it," Sawyer says, wrapping an arm around her. "Even brought Otto with us."

I chuckle. "Crazy parrot. Please tell me he's speaking German curse words now."

Maggie gives a satisfied little nod. "He speaks more German than Sawyer."

"Whatever." Sawyer shrugs, playing it off. "I'm loving Switzerland. Maybe I'll just stay."

"Please," Maggie sighs dramatically, draping herself over his shoulder. "Say yes. I need at least two months to buy all the cheese. And chocolate! Oh. My Gosh. The chocolate."

"The stuff back home doesn't even compare," Sawyer says.

"Um, hello!" I counter. "Remember the fudge in Brookking Sound? And the hot chocolate at Tuckers? Life changing."

"You and your sweet tooth," says Sawyer, kicking me under the table.

"So, you got to admit," Maggie says, jabbing at me with her hot pink fingernail. "You love Zürich ."

"Beats getting pucks to the head." I shrug. "But it's a little loud, you know? And I'm used to small village charm these days."

"Oh, you mean your little alpine fairy tale?" Maggie teases.

"Grächen." I let my voice go all dreamy. "Fresh mountain air. Stone cabins. Tiny goats."

She tilts her head, studying me. "And beautiful women?"

I nearly choke on my coffee. "Where?"

"Everywhere you look!" Sawyer says, raising his mug in a toast.

Maggie gives him a hard stare, and Sawyer timidly sets his mug back down. "Everywhere I look because I'm only looking at MY WIFE! Ha ha!"

Maggie rolls her eyes dramatically, then leans on her elbows to ask me, "Do the locals know you're a hockey player or think you're just an enormous tourist?"

"Har har. I've actually made a few friends at the local bar, so there."

Maggie leans closer, perching her chin on her palms. "Oh, do tell."

"Just some guys that play Jass. It's a card game. They take all my money, and I get to learn some Swiss German. Which is apparently just German, but a lot more confusing."

"So they're giving you lessons or what?"

"Well, I mean, not exactly. The bartender said she'd teach me."

The minute it slips out, Maggie pounces. "She? Griffin McGregor, ooh la la!"

I groan, knowing where this is headed. "It's not like that," I insist. "She's got a guy she wants to date, and I'm going to help her in exchange for language lessons."

They both share a look that screams disbelief, then burst into laughter.

"What kind of language exactly?" Maggie blurts out. "Body language?"

"And you're going to teach her...tonsil hockey?" Sawyer gaffaws.

"Are you two in middle school?" I put my hands up, knowing I'm outnumbered. "Look, she wants to learn how to impress this guy. I'm her dating coach. That's it."

If I didn't love these guys, I'd be terrified. It's like a two-against-one cage match with an enthusiastic wife and her tenacious husband.

"The best-laid plans, Griff," Sawyer says, shaking his head. "That's all I gotta say. Best-laid plans."

I give him a sarcastic smile. "I can be an adult about this. Try not to faint."

Sawyer leans back in his chair and crosses his arms over his chest. He ticks his chin at me. "What's her name then?"

The corner of my mouth twitches as I say, "Anika."

It couldn't be helped.

Maggie gasps and slams her hand on the table. "You're crazy about her!" She practically sings the accusation.

"No."

"Oh yes you are!" She claps her hands and squeals. "You're grinning ear to ear!"

"I think you're exaggerating, Maggie."

"Ha ha!" She dances in her seat, twisting back and forth, pumping her arms, and tapping her feet on the floor.

I'd say she needs to get out more, but I fear the opposite is true when it comes to Maggie. Maybe she just misses the girl talk she'd normally get with Emily and the other Titans WAGS.

"Have you heard news about the lockout?" I say, totally trying to turn the conversation around. "Any developments?"

"Nice segue, man," Sawyer says. "Just seamless."

I grin. "As Heraclitus once said, 'The only constant in life is change.'"

Maggie snorts.

Sawyer face palms. "Okay, okay. I'll let you change the subject. The franchise owners aren't budging. Malcom, especially."

"I thought he'd cave by now," Maggie says, brow furrowed.

"So did I." I glance at my coffee, its warmth already cooling. "Worried about that investment of mine."

Sawyer shoots me a knowing look. "Glad I stayed out of it."

I squirm a little under Sawyer's "*I-told-you-so*" gaze.

"Listen, I might be worried, but I'm not panicking," I say, leaning back in my chair. "Not like that lunatic the other night."

Maggie's face twists into a worried frown. "What lunatic?"

I wave my hand dismissively. "Oh, it's nothing."

"Nothing?" Sawyer sits up straight, suddenly all business. "What happened?"

Great. Now Sawyer's hackles are raised. Ever since he had a run-in with the mob, he's Mister Cautious. I suppose I don't blame him.

"Just some overexcited fan," I say. "This guy comes up to me, totally unhinged, screaming about his Titans stock tanking."

Sawyer's eyebrows shoot up. "Titans stock. A Swiss guy?"

"No, Canadian. Had on a Titans jersey at the Visp game. He was ready to throw down right there in the parking lot."

Maggie leans forward. "Did he hurt you?"

"Nah."

"Wait," Sawyer interjects, his face serious now. "Some Titans fan came all the way from Toronto and attacked you because of the Titans stock?"

"Guy was probably just a conspiracy nut who lost some money on the market," I say. "Security handled it."

"Did you follow up? Check your accounts?" Sawyer asks.

"Yeah, first thing next morning. Everything looked fine. Better than fine, actually. Upward trajectory all the way." I take a sip of my coffee. It's ice cold now. "The guy was clearly off his rocker."

Sawyer exchanges a look with Maggie that I can't quite read.

"That's...odd." Sawyer drums his fingers on the table. "Want me to get Siobhan to take a peek? She could probably hack the Pentagon in her sleep. Checking your stocks would take her two seconds."

I consider it. Sawyer's sister is a computer genius. Whether all her hacking is legal or not is questionable.

"Maybe keep that as plan B? I mean, the numbers look good."

"*Too* good?" Sawyer's voice has that edge I recognize from when he's about to lay a monster hit on the ice.

"Maybe." I shrug, trying to shake off the nagging feeling in my gut.

"At least you didn't invest your whole signing bonus," Sawyer says, giving me a pointed look.

"Unlike some people we know," Maggie adds quietly.

I think about Hendrix, who's got more skin in this game than any of us. "Yeah. Starting to think you were smart to stay out of it, man."

"I'm sorry, what did you say?" Sawyer cups his hand around his ear and leans over the table. "I couldn't quite hear."

I sigh. "I said you were smart to stay out of it. Yeesh. Doesn't your wife stroke your ego enough?"

Maggie chokes on her coffee, coughing uncontrollably.

Sawyer pats her on the back. "There, there."

I roll my eyes at these two. "Seriously? Are we twelve?"

"You love us," Maggie says, flashing that megawatt smile of hers.

Sawyer grins, completely unrepentant. "Hey, you started it with the ego-stroking comment."

"You two need a hobby," I say, checking my watch. It's getting late, and the café staff has started giving us those polite "we'd like to close" looks.

"We do have a hobby," Maggie says, giggling. "It's called—"

"Wow would you look at the time!" I stand up and stretch, not in the least interested in hearing the rest of...whatever she was going to say. "We should probably call it a night. Don't you have practice at the crack of dawn or something?"

"Five AM," Sawyer confirms with a grimace. "Coach doesn't believe in sleep."

"Hey," I say as we head toward the door. "You guys should come down to Grächen for a visit sometime. Assuming your grueling hockey schedule will allow it, superstar."

Maggie perks up. "Really? Can we?"

"Sure. The train ride isn't bad, and now that the snow's here, the skiing is amazing. Plus, I've got this little cabin that—"

"We're coming to meet your girlfriend," Maggie cuts in, her eyes sparkling with mischief.

"Anika is not my girlfriend," I insist for what feels like the hundredth time. "How many times do I have to say it?"

"Oh, I'm sorry," Maggie says, not sounding sorry at all. "I meant your *future* girlfriend."

"My language teacher," I correct her.

"Your language of *love* teacher," she counters.

"The woman who's helping me learn Swiss German," I try again.

"The woman who's helping you learn the language of *looooove*," Maggie sings, drawing out the word.

Sawyer laughs. "Give it up, man. You're not winning this one."

"You two deserve each other, you know that?"

"We know," they say in unison, and something tugs in my chest that feels suspiciously like...longing for what Sawyer and Maggie have.

My heart skips a beat in anticipation for tomorrow's first official dating coach session with Anika. I'm already planning what we'll cover. Confidence building, conversation starters, maybe a little role-playing to help her practice. Not *that* kind of role-playing, obviously. Just...friendly practice.

Oh, who am I kidding?

Outside the café, we say our goodbyes with promises to meet up soon. As Sawyer and Maggie head off toward their

Swiss home-away-from-home, I pull out my phone to check the time and see a text from Anika that came in while we were talking.

Anika: *Can we reschedule tomorrow's lesson? Something came up.*

I feel a ridiculous stab of disappointment. Without overthinking it, I type back:

Me: *Nice try. I'm not letting you off that easily. Be ready at noon. We've got work to do.*

I stare at my phone for a moment, then add:

Me: *Trust me. This will be fun.*

I pocket my phone with a secret smile, thinking about what Sawyer said about best-laid plans. I definitely have plans. Oh boy, do I ever.

Practice dates have a way of becoming real ones.

CHAPTER TEN

If I wait any longer for this guy to text, my phone might just self-destruct. He said to be ready at noon. It's noon now, but without directions where to meet for our so-called date.

My clock taunts me. Maybe Griffin has come to his senses, decided I'm beyond repair, and bolted in the other direction. I'm teetering between swapping these absurd earrings for a pair of worn slippers and collapsing in a heap of defeat on my couch, until a knock at the door shatters my brooding. It's the kind that sends your heart racing if you're a homebody like me.

I stare at the door like it might spontaneously combust. If I wait long enough, maybe whoever it is will just go away.

Another knock comes, louder and more persistent this time. I sigh, telling myself I shouldn't just sit here to see what happens. Nope. I'm just gonna take an innocent stroll over to the door and...*hello*, Griffin. The smile on his face could melt glaciers, and the flowers he's holding aren't bad either.

"Hey there," he says, looking way too relaxed and completely at home in my doorway. "Brought you these."

He holds up the bouquet like it's some grand trophy and not just more evidence that I was wrong about him bailing. It smells of fresh-cut azaleas and a little bit of the universe playing a cosmic joke on me.

"Flowers? How...traditional." I cross my arms and try not to breathe them in. "How did you find out where I live?"

He cocks his head to the side, indicating someone (or three someones) across the street. Of course. Lars, Evan, and Colin. Shameless traitors, waving like it's some kind of hometown parade and Griffin's the main float.

"Lars told you?" I can barely hide my irritation. I just know it was Lars.

"And Evan. And Colin." Griffin's grin practically spreads to his ears. "They said it would impress you. They also said they've got bets you wouldn't answer the door."

"I wish I hadn't."

His face falls. "You were going to leave me standing outside your door? With flowers?"

My cheeks go nuclear.

"I...uh, well, I just thought you might be better off...uh..." I fumble for anything that doesn't make me sound like I was bailing but finally shrug. "Okay, fine. I got cold feet."

Griffin raises an eyebrow, clearly amused at my little meltdown.

"But the flowers are lovely. Thank you," I say, reluctantly accepting the bouquet. They're obnoxiously beautiful. "Anyway, they're just part of the coaching, right?"

"If you say so. And you're welcome. I was going to pick you up at the pub, but then I ran into those guys."

He points his thumb over his shoulder where Lars, Evan, and Colin are suspiciously exchanging money.

"Should have known," I mutter. I wonder how many francs Lars got from Griffin for the intel.

"*Wer ist an der Tür?*" my mother's voice calls from the living room, asking who's at the door.

Griffin's brows shoot up, and a flicker of genuine surprise crosses his face.

"It's my mom," I explain, reluctantly glancing back inside.

Griffin looks utterly bewildered. "If I'd known you lived with your mother, I would have brought two bouquets."

Over my shoulder, in a hasty mix of practicality and protest, I call out in Swiss German, "*Nur ein Freund, Mama!*"

Griffin wags his brows. "Just a friend, eh?"

I study him, only slightly impressed. "You understood what I said. Not bad."

"Lucky guess," he says, leaning against the doorframe like he's the most comfortable man in the world. I'm caught off guard by his easy demeanor. "Anyway, I'll just have to come back tomorrow with more flowers."

I invite him in, partly to regain some footing, partly to stop the neighbors from enjoying the spectacle.

"Come in while I find a vase."

He follows me into the living room, where my mother is practicing tai chi, dressed in layers of flowing, bohemian sweaters, her silver-streaked hair in a loose braid. Beads around her neck jingle as she turns. And with Griffin here, I'm more aware of the smell of patchouli clouding the whole house.

"Griffin is here to learn Swiss German," I say quickly before she can ask questions. The less she knows about this dating coach arrangement, the better.

But Griffin has already charmed her. She flies to him immediately, all warmth and sparkles, clasping his hands in hers. "Would you like to sit, Griffin? Can I make you some coffee?"

"Oh, no. We're not staying." I hold up the bouquet as if it's a timer, as if the flowers will die if they're not in water within the next ten seconds. But he's already sitting across from her, soaking up every embarrassing thing she has to say. How nice it was of him to bring me flowers. How my favorite color is yellow. How when I was six, I went through a phase where I would only wear yellow.

Griffin is taking it all in, totally making himself comfortable, like he'll settle in and never leave. I blame the patchouli.

"So, what brings you to our little village?"

"I'm a hockey player. I'm with Visp right now, but usually, I'm with Toronto."

Her reaction is completely over-the-top, but that's my mother for you. "I traveled to Canada years ago in my backpacking days."

Here we go. Mom could go on about backpacking for at least an hour if I let her. So I hastily toss the flowers onto the kitchen counter and call back, "I'm just going to get these into some water, and then we can go."

Their voices float back to me as I fill up a vase. Mom is drilling Griffin about his travels and telling him about that one time she camped on a mountain in Peru.

I finish arranging the flowers, and before Mama can get Griffin set up with some pillows and a blanket, I seize his hand, pulling him off the couch. "Okay! We're going! *Uf Widerluege, Mutti*!"

She beams up at Griffin. Most likely imagining what a nice son-in-law he'd be, probably since he's the only man to ever visit me in the history of forever. "Very nice to meet you. Come back soon!"

"You can count on it, Frau Gisler."

Griffin laughs as I drag him outside. "Are you always this demanding?"

"I had to save you from her. She'd never let you leave otherwise."

He ducks under a cascade of brightly colored wind socks that flap above the front door. "I don't know what you're talking about. Your mom's great."

He takes my arm and guides me around the icy sidewalk. The whole dating practice thing is throwing me off. It's like Christmas and Easter at the same time. I don't know what I should prepare for.

We head toward the town square. Griffin sets a brisk pace, the crisp mountain air barely registering to him, but my breath hangs in little clouds between us. He watches me from the corner of his eye. "So, can you guess where we're going?"

"I'm not a mind reader," I reply.

He laughs. "Good thing I'm coaching you, then."

"You love bossing people around, don't you?" I tease.

He flashes me a grin. "What do you think about hiking?"

I stop dead in my tracks. "Without snowshoes?"

"We'll take the gondola up to Hannigalp. There's a trail called the Questioning Round Tour."

"I'm quite familiar with all the trails. I've lived here my whole life."

"But you haven't seen them...with me."

"You do realize it's winter, right?"

"Best time to go! It's like having the whole mountain to ourselves."

"It's the worst time to go. Nobody else does because the trails are closed."

Where's your sense of adventure?" he retorts. "It'll be awesome."

I groan, but there's no shaking him. I have to laugh. "You're crazy, you know that?"

"Aw, thanks. That's the nicest thing you've ever said to me."

I punch him playfully on the arm and pretend my fist doesn't sting. "Not a compliment, big guy."

We board the gondola, just the two of us, and somehow, this little box car feels smaller than usual. Outside, white mountain peaks tower dramatically against a cobalt sky. I try to focus on the view, pretending that having a drop-dead gorgeous Canadian willing to spend time with me is totally normal. The ascent is slow, and with each passing meter, my resolve thaws a little more.

When we hop out, we find ourselves on a plateau over-looking the vast valley.

"Let's get this crazy thing over with," I say.

The path winds through snow-blanketed trees as snow crunches beneath our boots. There's a signpost marking the trail with a big question mark painted on it.

We stop to read the inscription by author Rolf Dobelli. It's in both English and German, which is helpful so Griffin can practice.

It says:

Would you mind if the contents of your brain could be read like a hard drive after your death?

. . .

Griffin pulls a face. "Whoa. That one's creepy."

"That question is as ridiculous as this entire date," I say.

"I'd say the date is definitely my favorite of the two," he counters softly.

He waits, like he actually wants an answer to the trailhead question.

"Not sure the world needs a complete map of my inner mind," I admit. "They'd fall asleep from boredom."

Griffin's eyes soften as he says, "I beg to differ."

GAH! What is happening? I run ahead to the next marker and read what it says.

What if you lost all your possessions? Could you be happy?

He catches up. "I've moved enough times for hockey that it's like I'm a pro minimalist."

I grin, knowing this is way easier than if this were an actual date. Not that this is actually a date. That's why it's fun. I won't get embarrassed if Griffin doesn't seem interested.

We tramp on, snow crunching beneath our feet, the sun sparkling off white-dusted trees.

Griffin removes his gloves, enjoying himself far too much for someone supposedly helping me learn to date. It feels comfortable, companionable, a hundred times better than I imagined it would be. I'm more relaxed than ever. More relaxed than I've ever been, with anyone. It's a nice feeling.

We reach another marker.

"Would you like your work to make you rich?" I recite, scanning the sign.

"Pass," Griffin says, probably because he's already rolling in all that hockey money. "What about you?"

"I'd settle for keeping my bar." I answer the question almost without thinking. There's a note of vulnerability in it, one I hadn't meant to reveal. I feel a twinge of awkwardness and try to play it off.

"So," I say, as lightly as I can. "Learning anything?"

"Lots." He sounds genuine. "Learning I like hanging out with you."

I smack his chest with the back of my hand. It's a strong, sturdy chest. "I meant German. From the signs."

He wraps his enormous hand around my wrist, pulling me closer to him. "I'm going to need a lot more lessons than this, *mein lehrerin*."

The way he says it. All gravelly and breathy. He might as well have said "my love" instead of just "my teacher."

"Your accent needs work," I tease, feeling far too aroused this near to him.

"Does it, now?"

I lift my chin and take a step back. I'm not good at this flirting stuff. I suppose that's why he's coaching me after all. He's not actually into me, even though the way he's looking at me sure feels like he is.

"Oh, it's pretty bad," I say, trying to cool down the heady mood. To clarify, I'm the only one that's hot and bothered. He's the picture of easy confidence.

We cover the rest of the route at a steady pace, moving like we don't have to make up answers or decisions or minds. The air is razor-cold, but the way he nudges me along, making sure I stay warm, I don't feel the full brunt of it.

Eventually, we stop at a small restaurant with a terrace overlooking a snowy panorama. The majestic white mountains loom before us, as impossible as the man sitting across from me with those dimples on full display.

"Don't think I didn't notice what you did," Griffin

comments as we sip our drinks. "When you conveniently didn't tell your mom the real reason for our outing."

I stifle a laugh, studying his face as if searching for imperfections. "Like I'd admit I need dating lessons. And by the way, you're not getting extra points for flowers."

He shrugs, teasing. "Didn't expect any. Probably need more than flowers to win you over."

I feel my cheeks burn again, but I cling to the fragile strength in my hands around the glass. He's talking about Thomas winning me over. Not him. Definitely not him.

"I wouldn't turn down chocolate," I say flippantly.

The wind howls outside, rattling the windows as if it's trying to shake loose my guarded heart.

"Anika," he ventures after a long pause. He looks at me seriously, his smile taking on an unexpected warmth. "Want to practice something?"

I keep my tone casual, not ready for what I think he's going to say. "Aren't we...doing that already?"

"How about this?" He reaches across the table, takes my hand. Gently, like it's the easiest thing. My fingers are warm in his.

I'm on the verge of reminding him this is supposed to be for practice, not fun, but there's something about his touch. Something that undoes me. My hand stays in his. Griffin plays with my fingers. Soft, careful circles with his thumb. A surprising ache settles in my chest, moving slowly to where our hands meet.

His eyes stay on mine, and for a brief second I'm unguarded. I have to fight the urge to tell him I would have been perfectly happy being single until he ambled into my bar. But that's not the kind of truth anyone wants read like a hard drive of my thoughts. At least, not until I know whether he really likes being here with me or if this is just pretend.

"*Ich halte gern deine hand*," he says.

Ooohhh-kay then. Starting out with feelings and body parts, are we? Even if all he said was that he likes holding my hand. This is all just part of the dating lesson, right?

I fumble. Pull back too fast, but not as quick as the flash of disappointment I catch in his eyes. Is he disappointed I took my hand away or that I failed the dating experiment? The second. Definitely the second.

"That's enough practice for today," I say, even though there is so much more I wish to express.

Griffin laughs gently. "Okay. What's next?"

I take a sip of my drink, needing a moment to compose myself so I can go back to acting like a normal human.

"Your German lesson," I say, trying for casual indifference. "We can start with numbers."

I figure that would be much safer than starting with something like feelings or body parts.

There's beauty in being
misunderstood.

CHAPTER ELEVEN

Anika skips toward the Visp arena entrance, bundled in a big puffy coat. I'm holding her ticket in my increasingly sweaty hand, but it's not the upcoming match making my heart pound. It's the giddy anticipation of Anika seeing me play tonight. She smiles when she notices me, and I'm officially done for.

"You made it," I call out, trying to sound casual and not like I've been checking my watch every thirty seconds.

"Did you think I wouldn't?" She scrunches her nose in a way that somehow manages to be both challenging and adorable. It makes my heart do that weird flutter thing it's been doing lately whenever she's around.

I hand her the ticket, "Your pass to this evening's entertainment."

She takes it with a suspicious squint.

"Consider this part of your dating education," I continue. "Dating 101, if you will. Sports Edition."

"How romantic." She rolls her eyes, but I catch the hint of a smile.

"Dating isn't just fancy restaurants and moonlit walks. Sometimes it's screaming your head off while men with knives strapped to their feet chase a rubber disk."

She examines the tickets like I've handed her instructions to defuse a bomb. "And how exactly am I supposed to pretend it's a date if I'll be sitting in the stands by myself while you're playing?"

"Trust me, watching me defend that goal will get you so hot and bothered, you'll feel like you're on a date." I wink at her, earning an eye roll.

"Your ego is showing, McGregor."

"Plus, after the game, you'll get to meet the team. Perfect practice for talking to new guys without immediately putting them in a headlock."

She scoffs. "You're going to throw me in with the wolves? Not even going to ease me into it?"

"Don't worry." I flash her my best reassuring smile. "Something tells me you'll end up leading the pack. Or at least walk away with a nice fur coat."

"That's not funny." But her lips twitch with the hint of a smile. "And for the record, I only put people in headlocks when they deserve it."

"Noted. Now let's go find your seat before you miss my stunning performance. And try not to swoon too hard when I make my first save."

She lets out a slow breath, acting as if she's contemplating whether or not to cancel me entirely. "I suppose I could give it a try. For educational purposes, you know."

We make our way through the turnstiles, the familiar sounds and smells of a hockey arena washing over me. The sharp scent of ice, the low rumble of the crowd, the occasional shout from vendors. It's my second home.

I lead her to her seat, front row with a perfect view of the net so I can keep an eye on her during the game. If this is her first hockey game, I want her to have the best seat in the house.

"Want me to take your coat?" I offer before she sits down.

"Sure." Anika shrugs out of her coat, and I nearly drop it when I see what she's wearing underneath.

She's in a Visp jersey. Not a new one, either. This thing has seen some serious action. Faded in all the right places, with a slight tear at the shoulder seam that's been carefully stitched. The name on the back belongs to Hämmerli, a player who retired at least five years ago. This isn't some souvenir shop purchase. This is a jersey with history.

"That jersey's seen a lot of action," I say, pointing to the faded player name across the back. "Must be a collector's item. Was it your dad's?"

She shrugs like it's no big deal. "No, it's mine."

I blink, processing this information against my memory of our first meeting when she acted like hockey was some obscure winter ritual performed by bearded men from the north.

"You're a Visp fan?" I ask, trying not to sound as bewildered as I feel.

"I've been to a few games," she says, which is clearly the

understatement of the year given the well-loved state of that jersey.

My brain starts reassembling everything I thought I knew about Anika. The mental image of her cheering in the stands, wearing this exact jersey, possibly screaming profanities at referees, is doing things to me. Confusing, wonderful things. I've never been more attracted to a woman wearing another man's jersey.

And suddenly, all I can think about is how she would look in Titans red and black. With "McGregor" emblazoned across her shoulders.

God help me.

"You told me you didn't know anything about hockey," I say, unable to keep the accusation from my voice.

Her lips curve into a mischievous smile. "I never said that. You assumed."

Who is this woman?

The announcer's voice booms through the arena, and I know I'm cutting it close before I need to get into my gear. But for the first time in my life, I'm at a hockey game and not thinking about hockey at all.

"I've got to go," I say as the crowd roars in anticipation. She smiles prettily at me and waves me off. I think she'll be more than okay. I might not be though.

The first period starts with a thunder of applause as we take the ice. Lugano in their black and yellow, us in our trademark red and white like the Swiss flag. The familiar scrape of blades on fresh ice centers me as I take my position in goal.

But not completely. My eyes keep drifting to the stands where Anika sits, front row, in plain sight of my net, that worn Hämmerli jersey practically glowing under the arena lights.

The referee drops the puck, and we're off. Peter wins the face-off, sending it back to Christoph, who immediately pushes it up the boards. I roll my shoulders, getting comfortable in the crease, but my focus is split. Half on the game, half on Anika.

Lugano's first line presses hard, their center dangling through our defense and firing a wrist shot from the high slot. I track it all the way, catching it cleanly in my glove. A routine save, but I can't help glancing over at Anika.

She's already on her feet, pumping her fist in the air, shouting something I can't hear over the crowd.

Five minutes in, Tyler strips the puck from Lugano's defenseman, creating a two-on-one with Peter. They execute a perfect give-and-go, and Peter buries it top shelf. The horn blares, the crowd erupts, and my teammates pile onto Peter along the boards.

I scan the stands for Anika. She's jumping up and down, high-fiving strangers around her. "Richi" by Stubete Gäng blasts through the loudspeakers, just like it does every time we score a goal. Anika knows all the words, singing along with the new friends she just made and...Wait, is that a sign? She's unfurled a handmade banner reading *"Hopp Schwiiz!!"* in bold letters, which is apparently a national war chant here in Switzerland. She holds it high above her head with two hands, singing and swaying with abandon.

I'm still processing this when Lugano counters with a quick rush. Their sniper gets alone in front, dekes once, twice. I stay with him, stretching my pad to make the save. The puck deflects wide, and our fans roar in approval.

My eyes dart back to Anika, who's now leaning over the glass, shouting what appears to be very specific tactical advice to Kovy, our defensemen. She's gesturing wildly, looking like she's been coaching from these stands for years.

I laugh behind my mask. The woman who pretended she didn't know the difference between hockey and golf is screaming like a season ticket holder.

Late in the first, Lugano's power play puts me to work. Three quick shots in succession. Blocker save, kick save, and then a sprawling desperation move to keep a rebound from crossing the line. The whistle blows, stopping play.

I lift my mask to take a quick drink, and that's when I see Anika mimicking my save sequence to the guy next to her, analyzing my technique with surprising accuracy. She catches me watching and gives me a thumbs-up that sends a ridiculous jolt through my chest.

The second period starts with more intensity. Christoph shows off his stickhandling, weaving through Lugano's defense before getting hooked. Penalty shot.

The crowd holds its breath as he approaches slowly, then accelerates, fakes backhand, and tucks it forehand past their goalie. 2-0 Visp.

I pound my stick on the ice in celebration, but I'm already looking for Anika. She's hugging complete strangers, jumping and screaming like we just won the championship. There's pure joy on her face, and it's doing dangerous things to my heart rate.

Midway through the second, Lugano catches us in a line change. Their captain breaks in alone. I come out to challenge, take away the angle, and stone him with my shoulder. The rebound pops high in the air, and I bat it away with my blocker as I fall backward.

When I get up, Anika is standing with both hands pressed against the glass, focused entirely on me.

She mouths something that looks suspiciously like "Don't screw this up, McGregor."

There's fire in her eyes. It's slightly frightening.

The third period turns into a goaltending duel. Their netminder finds his groove, and I'm called on to preserve our lead. Tyler delivers a bone-crushing hit that sends the crowd into a frenzy, and Anika is right there with them, pounding the glass.

With five minutes left, Lugano pulls their goalie. Six attackers bearing down, cycling the puck around our zone. Peter blocks a shot with his body, grimacing through the pain. Christoph clears once, but they regroup.

A point shot through traffic. I lose sight of it momentarily but drop to my butterfly anyway, feeling it hit my pad and skitter wide. The crowd exhales collectively.

I glance at Anika. She's chewing her thumbnail, completely invested, her eyes tracking every player's movement. When I make the save, she clutches her heart dramatically, then gives me a look that's half relief, half...something else. Something that makes me want to stop every puck in the universe if it'll make her look at me that way again.

Final seconds tick down. Lugano's last desperate attempt is broken up by Tyler, who feeds Peter for the empty netter. 3-0 final. The buzzer sounds, and we've got the win.

I'm riding the high of the win as I make my way through the arena tunnels, freshly showered, my hair damp against my Titans hoodie. My body aches in that satisfying post-victory way, but my mind is fixated on one thing only.

Anika.

Anika and her mysteriously well-worn Visp jersey. Anika and her "*Hopp Schwiiz!!*" banner. Anika, who sings along to Richi.

I spot her waiting near the player exit, chatting animatedly with a couple of other fans. She's thrown her puffy coat back on over her jersey, but the collar still peeks out. When she sees me, she breaks into a dazzling smile that hits me square in the chest.

Breaking free of the group of Visp fans to greet me, she lets her gaze unabashedly rake over me. "Hey there, hockey star."

"Hey there, hockey fan," I counter, unable to keep the amusement from my voice.

She shrugs innocently, but she doesn't fool me for a second. But before I can call her out, I hear the voices of my teammates behind me.

"Griff! You coming to celebrate?" Tyler calls out, followed closely by Christoph, Peter, and Kovy, our star defenseman from Russia.

"Yeah, in a bit," I answer, then gesture toward Anika. "Guys, this is Anika. Anika, these are some of the guys. Tyler, Kovy, Christoph, and Peter."

"*Jungs!*" Anika calls out, launching into rapid-fire Swiss German that has Christoph and Peter laughing and responding just as quickly. Her hands gesture wildly as she recreates what must be key plays from the game.

Tyler shoots me a confused look, and I shrug. I'm just as lost. But watching Anika's eyes light up as she talks hockey makes my chest feel tight in the best way.

"*Was für ein hammer Spiel!*" Her eyes are bright with excitement, hands flying as she acts out what I think is a goal from the second period.

I stand there, understanding maybe one word in ten, feeling both impressed and slightly out of the loop.

I think she just said it was a great game. Christoph is nodding enthusiastically. She even surprises Kovy by responding to him in what sounds like passable Russian, which earns her a booming laugh and a clap on the shoulder that makes me instinctively step closer to her.

The guys are being friendly but not overly so, and I find myself cataloging each interaction with unusual scrutiny.

Watching her, I feel something shift inside me. It's that feeling when a perfect pass lands right on your tape, or when you make a glove save that even you didn't think was possible. That click of everything falling exactly into place.

Tyler grins and gives me a look and whispers, "Where did you find her?"

"Oh!" She suddenly catches herself and switches to English. "Sorry, Griffin. Tyler. I was just saying that diagonal pass across the neutral zone in the second period was chef's kiss. I haven't seen anything like it since Aebischer retired."

"You know your hockey," Peter says, impressed. "And what do you think of our netminder, Crash McGregor?"

Peter slaps me on the back, making me stumble a little closer to Anika.

Anika throws a disinterested side-eye my way. "Eh. Not bad for a backup goalie!"

"And that banner!" Peter suddenly exclaims, setting off a round of laughter among the Swiss players. "*Hopp Schwiiz*! For a league game?" He mimics her enthusiastic sign-waving, and several of the Swiss players burst into laughter.

Anika's cheeks flush pink, but she's laughing too.

"You were the loudest person in section three," Christoph says, grinning as he pops open a sports drink. "Very passionate."

"What's so funny about her sign?" I ask, feeling like I'm missing the joke.

Peter claps me on the shoulder. "Griffin, my friend, '*Hopp Schwiiz*' is what we chant when Switzerland plays against other countries. Like in international tournaments or the World Cup. Not for club games, where Swiss play against Swiss."

"It means 'Go Switzerland' not 'Go Visp,'" Tyler adds. "It would be like bringing an American flag to a game between the Rangers and Bruins."

"Actually, that would be a very American thing to do," Peter says.

Tyler nods thoughtfully. "You have a point there."

"So she wasn't cheering for the team?" I look at Anika, who's trying and failing to look innocent. "She was just cheering for you Swiss guys, and ONLY for you Swiss guys?"

"In my defense," she says, raising her hands. "I didn't make a sign that said 'Everyone But Griffin.'"

"But you thought it," I tease.

Tyler laughs. "Man, Griffin, she had you at hello, didn't she?"

The guys laugh at my expense, but I don't mind. Seeing Anika so comfortable with my teammates, joking and smiling, does something to me.

I find myself studying the guys' reactions to her, an unfamiliar tension creeping into my shoulders. But Peter and Christoph treat her like a knowledgeable fan, nothing more.

The relief I feel is...unexpected. And telling.

I feel my cheeks warm as Anika bumps her shoulder against mine. The guys exchange knowing glances that I choose to ignore.

"Anyway," I say, clearing my throat, "I should probably walk Anika to her car."

As we turn to leave, I puff out my chest a little with the satisfaction that none of guys seemed to give Anika the extra attention they usually reserve for attractive women who come to the games.

It's only when we're walking toward the parking garage and I realize my hand has somehow found the small of her back that it hits me. I'm feeling jealous. Possessive, even. I barely know this woman, and yet the thought of any of my teammates catching her eye makes something primitive stir in my chest.

"Your friends are nice," she says, glancing up at me with that smile that makes my stomach flip.

"And you are an absolute fraud."

She stops in her tacks. "Fraud? *Moi?*"

"You played me! That day you came to my cabin with cookies and toilet paper. You acted like hockey was the most boring thing in the world."

"Did I say boring? I don't recall saying boring."

"You absolutely did. And then I said…" I pause, suddenly remembering my exact words that day. "I said if you found hockey boring, I'd buy you dinner to make up for wasting your time. And if you liked it, I'd definitely buy you dinner."

She tilts her head with faux confusion. "I remember no such conversation."

I should be annoyed at being played, but all I feel is fascination. And something else, something deeper that I'm not ready to name yet. But watching her celebrate our win, seeing how she lives and breathes this game like I do…I'm falling for her. Hard and fast, like a winger losing an edge at full speed.

And unlike on the ice, I have no protective gear for this kind of fall.

"Oh really? '*Hockey seems boring,*'" I mimic her words from weeks ago. "And then there was that whole thing where you mixed up hockey and golf."

Her lips twitch. "I have no idea what you're talking about."

"Anika." I give her a look. "Clearly, you're some kind of super fan. You were screaming at the ref about a missed interference call in the second period.

She adjusts her coat, a mischievous glint in her eyes. "Was I?"

"You sang team chants. You knew all the words to our goal song." I'm laughing now, completely charmed by this ridiculous woman.

She laughs, and it's my new favorite sound. "Guilty."

"How did I not see through you?" I marvel.

"Maybe you were too busy looking at my legs."

"That..." I feel heat climbing up my neck. "That's actually fair."

We stand there for a moment, smiling at each other like idiots, and I feel something settling in my chest. Something warm and solid and terrifying.

"So," I say, rocking back on my heels. "About that dinner I apparently owe you either way..."

Her smile falters slightly, a hint of vulnerability breaking through. "I believe I was tricked into that offer under false pretenses."

"Dinner, Anika." I step closer. Close enough to catch the scent of her shampoo mingling with the arena smells still clinging to her coat. "Let me take you to dinner."

"Are you asking me on a date, McGregor?"

"Yes." No hesitation.

She looks at me with those beautiful pale blue eyes, and I find myself stepping closer still. Aching to touch her. Counting the faint freckles playing against her nose.

"For practice, you mean," she says.

Ouch. My confidence just took a serious hit.

"Right. For practice. We can go to my place," I suggest, trying to keep my voice casual, even though I'm feeling zero chill right now. "I make a pretty decent pasta. We could do candles, wine..." I trail off with a hopeful smile.

Anika gives me a flat stare. "Nice try, Casanova."

I laugh, holding up my hands in surrender. "Can't blame a guy for trying."

After a moment, she looks thoughtful. "You know, I've been thinking about all our...sessions so far."

"Yeah?" I shift my weight, suddenly anxious about where this is going.

"All these practice dates have been so casual. Hiking, pizza, movies. It's been fun, but..." She tugs at her jersey. "I've basically been in my comfort zone the entire time. Jeans, sweaters, boots."

I tilt my head, studying her. "Is that a bad thing?"

"No," she says quickly. "But..."

"But what?"

Anika hesitates, then meets my eyes. "I'd really like to dress up. Go somewhere nice."

Something warm blooms in my chest. "Yeah?"

"It doesn't have to be expensive or particularly fancy," she adds hastily.

The image of Anika in a sexy dress flashes through my mind, and my mouth goes a little dry. "Money's not an issue, Anika."

She shakes her head firmly. "That's not what I mean. It's just...if Thomas wants to take me somewhere I need to dress nice, I need to know how to handle myself. What if I use the wrong fork or something?" Her voice gets smaller. "What if I completely mess up the date?"

My chest tightens at the mention of Thomas, but I push past it.

"I will definitely plan something like that for you," I say, my voice softer than I intended. I reach out and tuck a strand of hair behind her ear, my fingers lingering against her cheek. "Something where you can get dressed up and feel comfortable with the whole experience."

Anything she wants, I'll do it. Anywhere she wants to go.

Looking at her now, with snowflakes catching in her hair

and her eyes bright from the game, I realize I'd probably take her to the moon if she asked right now.

I put my arms around her. She does not put her arms around me, but she doesn't punch me either, and I decide not to be so needy.

Longing is just hope wearing black eyeliner.

CHAPTER TWELVE

GRIFFIN

The fact that I've been in the team gym for over four hours, doing every single workout possible, proves that, apparently, I have decided that physical pain is preferable to thinking about...her.

Pretending with every grueling rep that Anika isn't making plans with Thomas right now.

I heave the barbell up for what has to be my fiftieth rep,

muscles quivering until I'm pretty sure my arms are about to fall off.

"Just ten more," I mutter to myself, ignoring the burning sensation in my biceps that suggests I should've stopped twenty reps ago.

The thing about crushing on a woman while simultaneously helping her win over some other guy? It's a special kind of self-inflicted torture that no amount of endorphins can fix. Yet here I am, bench pressing my feelings away like the world's most pathetic loser who's been friend-zoned.

With every painful set, all I can think is that she's only using me to prepare for this Thomas guy. Meanwhile, she has me falling for her so hard that the physical strain of heavy lifting is actually a relief.

A few teammates grunt their encouragement and throw me what looks like concern from the corners of their eyes, so I step it up even more.

Thomas, you lucky jerk, are going to reap all the benefits of my handiwork, and it's driving me mental.

I collapse back onto the bench after my final rep, staring at the ceiling. Every flirting lesson I gave her, every conversation tip I suggested, every single thing I taught Anika about the art of dating. It's all just Thomas prep work.

Thomas. Even his name sounds smug. I bet he does CrossFit and drinks protein shakes made from endangered plants.

Thomas, with his stupid perfect hair and his stupid perfect job. Thomas, who gets to be on the receiving end of Anika's actual interest, while I'm relegated to the role of dating coach.

Now all I can think about is his hands all over her.

I grab my towel and wipe the sweat from my face, wondering if I could somehow use it to also wipe away my feelings. No such luck.

On to the treadmill. Maybe if I run fast enough, I can

outpace my own thoughts. I crank the speed to just shy of *death wish* and start pounding away.

"She's using you as a practice boyfriend," I pant between strides. "Get. It. Through. Your. Thick. Skull."

Each footfall hammers the point home. Anika sees me as safe. Convenient. The human equivalent of those plastic food displays in restaurant windows. All the appearance of the real thing with none of the substance.

And the worst part? I volunteered for this position. Practically begged for it.

The treadmill beeps angrily as my pace falters, and I realize I've been so lost in my Anika-centered spiral that I've drifted dangerously close to the back of the belt. I correct my position and push harder, sweat dripping onto the console.

I'm about to die for a woman who isn't even mine.

After three hours of sweating more from my own frustrations than from the weights and cardio, I finally give it a rest and collapse into a heap.

A shadow falls over me, blocking out the blinding gym light.

"Hallo, McGregor."

I look up to see Dieter, our facilities manager, hovering near the weight rack with the expression of someone who's just found a dead fish in their mailbox.

"Yeah?" I gasp, still trying to recover my breath and dignity simultaneously. Neither is going well.

"There are two men here to see you."

I blink sweat out of my eyes. "Did I order something?"

"Don't think so. They look..." He pauses, searching for the right word. "Official."

"Official?"

"In suits."

Great. Men in suits never bring good news. They either want money or your signature on something legally binding.

"Tell them I'll be right there," I say, grabbing my towel and dabbing at the small lake of sweat I've created. "Just need a minute to...you know...splash some water on my face, throw on a clean shirt.

Dieter nods and disappears, leaving me to contemplate which transgression of mine has finally caught up with me. That time I accidentally took two mints from the restaurant bowl? The parking ticket I contested because the sign was in German and I swear "*Parkverbot*" could mean "party spot" to any reasonable English speaker?

Walking into the lobby, I spot them immediately. Two men in dark suits standing with perfect posture, scanning the room like they're cataloging escape routes. They don't look like fans, sponsors, or anyone who'd normally visit a hockey rink.

"Griffin McGregor?" the taller one asks, with the kind of severity that makes my last name sound like a war crime.

"That's me," I confirm, offering my hand and my most charming I-haven't-done-anything-wrong smile. "What can I do for you gentlemen?"

"Agent Bruderlin, Federal Intelligence Service," the tall one says, flashing a badge that indeed looks very federal and very serious. "And this is Agent Showalter."

The shorter man nods curtly without offering his hand.

Very encouraging.

My mind launches into a greatest hits compilation of "Things Griffin Might Have Done Wrong"

1: My visa. It's definitely my visa. Which is a ridiculous thought, because the team managers handled all that paperwork.

2: That time I accidentally wandered into a restricted area at the airport because I was looking for my lost luggage.

3: The Instagram photo where I'm posing with what I

thought was a historic monument but might have been a military installation.

"Is there somewhere we could speak privately?" Bruderlin asks, his eyes sweeping the lobby as if the potted palms might be concealing hidden cameras.

"Uh, sure," I manage, brain still cycling through worst-case scenarios. "There's a meeting room just down the hall."

I lead them to our team's strategy room, which is thankfully empty. The walls are plastered with training schedules and nutritional charts, and I suddenly feel like I'm in one of those movie scenes where the protagonist is about to learn he's been unwittingly involved in an international espionage plot.

"Please, sit down," I offer, gesturing to the chairs around the conference table. I take a seat across from them, trying not to look as nervous as I feel. "So...Federal Intelligence Service, huh? Is that like Immigration and Customs Enforcement? Because I'm pretty sure my work visa's current."

"Mr. McGregor, this isn't about your visa," Agent Bruderlin says with the kind of patience usually reserved for children or confused tourists.

"Oh. That's...good?" My relief is short-lived as my brain scrambles to figure out what other trouble I could be in.

"The Federal Intelligence Service is more akin to Britain's MI6 or America's CIA," Agent Showalter explains, his voice clipped and precise.

"So you're like...spies?" The word tumbles out with embarrassing enthusiasm.

Well, this took a turn. I'm suddenly eight years old again, sitting cross-legged in front of our TV. I've watched every James Bond film at least three times. Okay, who am I kidding, more like ten times each. I still have annual 007 marathons, complete with themed snacks and terrible attempts at a Sean Connery accent.

Both men stare at me blankly.

"Sorry," I mutter. "Please continue."

Bruderlin opens a thin folder and slides a photograph across the table. "Are you familiar with this man?"

I look down at a high-resolution surveillance photo of Malcolm Chase exiting what looks like a luxury hotel.

"Malcolm Chase," I say, my stomach dropping. "Yeah, I know him. He's the owner of the Titans."

"Mr. McGregor, we have reason to believe that Mr. Chase is conducting some highly questionable business activities here in Switzerland," Bruderlin says.

"What kind of activities?" I ask, suddenly on high alert.

"Mr. Chase recently made a significant deposit into a Swiss bank account," Showalter explains. "He seems to be operating under the outdated belief that Swiss banking secrecy laws will protect him."

"They won't?" I ask. I'll never watch wire transfers in spy movies the same again.

"Not like they used to," Bruderlin says. "Swiss banking secrecy has largely been dismantled in recent years. However, since Mr. Chase has maintained his accounts for many years, it creates certain...challenges for us."

I shift uncomfortably in my seat. "What does this have to do with me?"

"We're aware of the so-called Titans stock that Mr. Chase convinced you and your teammates to invest in," Showalter says.

My heart sinks, and my thoughts rush to that aggressive fan that attacked me a few weeks ago. And about the substantial chunk of my money currently sitting in Malcolm's "guaranteed growth" investment fund.

Bruderlin's expression tightens. "We have strong reason to believe it's part of an elaborate Ponzi scheme. Our financial forensics team has traced funds moving through offshore shell companies that appear designed to obscure their origins and destinations."

"Are you telling me our investments are gone?" I ask, my voice sounding hollow even to my own ears.

"That's what we're trying to determine," Bruderlin says.

I stare at the documents, but the numbers and diagrams swim before my eyes. This can't be happening. "No." I shake my head. "No, that can't be right..."

My voice trails off as I remember the team dinner where Malcolm had jovially convinced half the roster to invest. How excited we all were about getting in on the ground floor of something big. How I'd sunk most of my savings into those shares, dreaming of the security it would provide when my playing days were over.

"How much?" I ask, my voice shaky.

"Pardon?"

"How much has he stolen?"

Bruderlin's face remains impassive. "We believe the total amount approaches eight hundred and fifty million euros, though the exact figure is still being calculated."

Eight hundred and fifty million. That's a whole lotta hockey sticks.

"I...Thank you for telling me this," I say, trying to sound calm while my entire financial future collapses around me. "Please keep me updated on the investigation."

Bruderlin and Showalter exchange a look that makes my stomach clench.

"Actually, Mr. McGregor," Bruderlin says carefully. "We were hoping for more than just your acknowledgment. We need your assistance."

I blink. "*My* assistance? I'm just a hockey player," I protest.

"I don't know anything about offshore accounts or shell companies."

They're either giving me too much credit or not enough, depending on how you look at it.

"That's precisely why you're valuable to us," Showalter says, leaning forward.

"What could I possibly do that the Federal Intelligence Service can't?"

"We believe you may be the best way to infiltrate his inner circle," Bruderlin says. "Chase trusts you. You have access he doesn't give to just anyone."

"What...what exactly would you need from me?" I ask, trying to keep my voice steady.

"Information, primarily," Bruderlin says. "Your relationship with Chase, details about his interactions with the team, any patterns you might have noticed in his behavior or business practices."

"And your discretion," Showalter adds firmly. "This investigation is ongoing, and we'd prefer Mr. Chase remain unaware of our interest in his activities."

"Malcolm Chase is hosting a black-tie event in Zermatt this weekend," Agent Showalter explains. "It's an exclusive gathering for his select investors and business associates."

"And since you've invested in his stock," Bruderlin continues, "your presence at this event would not raise any suspicions."

"Wait." I hold up my hand. "Are you asking me to spy on Malcolm Chase? At a fancy party in Zermatt?"

"You're the closest significant stockholder in proximity to Zermatt," Showalter says, as if that's a perfectly reasonable explanation. "You're a practical choice to infiltrate the party and gather intelligence."

I stare at them, waiting for the punchline. When none comes, I let out a short, nervous laugh.

"Is this a joke? Am I being pranked right now?" I look around for hidden cameras. "Did Sven put you up to this? Because this has his sense of humor written all over it."

"This is not a joke, Mr. McGregor," Bruderlin says with the patience of someone working for the Department of Motor Vehicles.

"So you're seriously asking me to be...what? Your secret agent?" I can't help the excitement creeping into my voice. "Like James Bond? Because I have to tell you, I look damn good in a tux."

Showalter's expression remains impassive. "We're asking you to attend an event you'd reasonably be invited to anyway and keep your eyes and ears open."

I laugh nervously. "Wait, you're serious? You want me to spy on Malcolm Chase? At a fancy party?"

"We wouldn't characterize it as *spying*," Bruderlin says, looking mildly offended. "Think of it as...assisting an investigation."

"By spying," I counter.

Showalter sighs. "By observing and reporting back. Nothing more."

"Why don't you just send in your actual spies?" I ask. "You know, people who are trained for this kind of thing?"

"There will be FIS presence at the event," Bruderlin assures me. "But you won't know who they are."

"We believe Malcolm Chase won't think twice about seeing you there," Showalter adds. "He might even be open to discussing additional business opportunities with you, which could provide valuable intelligence."

"So I'd be like a hockey player by day, secret agent by night?"

I immediately picture myself in a tuxedo, ordering martinis shaken not stirred. McGregor. *Griffin* McGregor. License to spy. I'm not entirely sure if I'm joking anymore.

Bruderlin sighs. "Mr. McGregor, this is a serious matter. Hundreds of millions of euros are at stake, including your own investment."

I sit back in my chair, trying to wrap my head around this surreal conversation. Here I thought the biggest crisis in my life was watching Anika fall for someone else, and now I'm being recruited for an undercover operation by the Swiss intelligence service.

"What exactly would I have to do?" I ask, curiosity getting the better of me.

"Attend the event. Mingle. Listen. Observe who Malcolm speaks with, what they discuss. Note anyone who seems particularly close to him or who might be handling financial matters," Bruderlin explains.

A slight thrill runs through me. "Do I get spy glasses with a tiny camera and a watch with a laser beam?"

Bruderlin's expression suggests he's reconsidering his life choices. "No, Mr. McGregor. This isn't a film."

"Right, of course not," I say, trying to sound serious despite the adrenaline now coursing through my veins. "But you do understand that I'm a hockey player, not a spy? My idea of stealth is trying to sneak an extra dessert past our nutritionist."

"We're aware of your occupation," Showalter says dryly. "That's precisely why you're perfect for this. No one would suspect you."

I consider the proposition. On one hand, it's absolutely insane. On the other hand...Well, it's still insane, but it's also kind of exciting. Plus, if Malcolm really has stolen millions from my teammates, I want to help take him down.

"What about the team?" I ask. "We have games this weekend."

"We've already spoken with your coach," Bruderlin says. "As far as anyone knows, you've been selected for a special NHL European ambassador event in Zermatt. Your absence has been cleared."

Of course they've thought of everything. These guys are professionals.

"So," I say. "If I agree to this—and I'm not saying I am yet—what happens after the party? Do I just go back to normal life? Pretend none of this happened?"

"If all goes according to plan, yes." Bruderlin nods. "Though we may need your testimony later if the case goes to court."

As the agents begin to outline the details, I can't help but wonder what Anika would think of all this. At the very least, it would make for a better story than "I spent three hours at the gym trying not to think about you."

Plus, I'd get to wear a tuxedo and infiltrate a fancy party in Zermatt. It's the closest I'll ever come to living out my James Bond fantasies.

I'm suddenly struck by a thought that should've occurred to me immediately.

"Wait. Is this dangerous? I mean, if Malcolm is running some massive financial scam and I start poking around..."

Bruderlin holds up a reassuring hand. "Mr. McGregor, your safety is our priority. We'll have several agents at the event, keeping eyes on you at all times."

"That's...comforting, I guess?"

"From a discreet distance, of course," Showalter adds. "They'll monitor the situation without compromising your cover."

"So basically, I'll have my own security detail, but they'll be invisible?" I ask, still trying to wrap my head around all this.

"Precisely," Bruderlin confirms. "They'll be circulating throughout the party as guests, staff, security personnel. All positioned to intervene if necessary."

"You won't even know who they are," Showalter adds. "But they'll be ready to act if necessary."

I nod slowly, processing this information. Then another thought hits me, and I can't help the small smile that forms on my lips. I promised Anika I'd take her somewhere fancy, where she could dress up.

"Before I agree to any of this, what about a date?" I ask. "Would I be allowed to bring someone with me?"

Both agents look momentarily thrown by the question.

"A date?" Showalter repeats, as if I've just suggested bringing a pet rhinoceros.

"Yeah, you know. Wouldn't it look suspicious if I showed up alone to something like this?"

The agents exchange glances. Bruderlin's brow furrows. "We hadn't accounted for that variable."

"Most of these guys bring dates to these things, right?" I press. "It would seem weird if I didn't have someone on my arm."

Showalter looks skeptical. "The fewer people involved, the better."

"But consider this," I say, channeling every negotiation tactic I've ever used with coaches. "Having a date gives me a natural reason to move around the room, introduces me to different social groups, and provides cover for conversations."

The agents share another one of those silent communication glances.

"Who did you have in mind?" Bruderlin asks cautiously.

"Just..." I clear my throat. "Just a friend. She's been wanting to dress up and go somewhere swanky. This would be perfect."

"Is this 'friend' someone we should be concerned about?" Showalter asks, his eyes narrowing slightly.

"No, no. She's just...someone I know." Someone I'm hopelessly falling for while helping her pursue another man. But I keep that part to myself.

The agents step aside for a moment, conferring in hushed German that I can't quite catch.

After what feels like an eternity, they return to the table.

"We will permit you to bring a date," Bruderlin says, his tone making it clear this is a concession. "But we will run a thorough background check. If anything raises red flags, you go alone."

"Understood."

"This person must be completely trustworthy and discreet. They cannot know the true nature of your attendance."

"Absolutely." I nod vigorously. "She's the soul of discretion."

Showalter interjects, his tone stern, "As far as she's concerned, this is simply a high-end party you've been invited to as a team investor."

"You got it," I agree quickly, trying not to look too eager. "She won't suspect a thing. She'll just think it's a fancy date."

A date with Anika. An actual, proper date! Even if she doesn't know that's what it is. Even if she's still hung up on Thomas. Even if I'm technically working as an undercover agent for the Swiss intelligence service.

Yeesh, my life has taken a strange turn.

"So we have an agreement?" Bruderlin asks, extending his hand across the table.

I look at his outstretched palm, considering one last time what I'm getting myself into.

"I guess I'm in," I say, extending my hand. "Agent McGregor, reporting for duty."

Bruderlin slides a small card across the table. "This has the details of the event. We'll be in touch with more specific instructions."

I pick up the card, feeling the weight of it and what it represents in my fingers.

"So I guess I'm officially a spy now, huh?" I can't resist saying it out loud.

"You are a concerned civilian assisting with an investigation," Bruderlin corrects me firmly. "Not a spy."

"Right, got it. Concerned civilian. Not a spy." I give them a wink that I immediately regret when their expressions remain deadly serious.

"We'll be in contact soon," Showalter says, gathering his documents. "Remember, absolute discretion is essential."

I give them two thumbs-up as they file out of the room. They're probably already regretting coming to recruit me in the first place.

Welp. Too late now. Move over Sean Connery.

The first rule of flirting: look like you're enjoying yourself, even if you're terrified.

CHAPTER THIRTEEN

Anika

I f the universe wanted me to go somewhere fancy, it would give me better dresses that don't make me look like I've time-traveled from 1990.

"This is what desperation feels like," I mutter, holding up my mother's gauzy floor-length number she probably wore to a Stevie Nicks concert.

"What was that?" Ivy says through the phone while I balance it precariously between my shoulder and ear.

"Nothing," I sigh, rummaging deeper into my mother's closet.

"Well, as I was saying," Ivy continues, her voice tinged with that special brand of pregnant-woman determination, "Thomas is finally settled in Bern, and we need to set a date before this baby evicts me from my own body."

My fingers brush against something silky and white. My mother's wedding dress, complete with ginormous puffy shoulders. On the bright side, they could double as flotation devices in case of emergency.

I push it aside and come upon a silver sequined monstrosity that probably hasn't seen daylight since ABBA was topping the charts. "Mmm-hmm."

"Anika, are you even listening?" James chimes in, his British accent making everything sound both polite and accusatory at once. "Ivy's about to pop any day now. If you don't meet Thomas before the baby comes..."

"Yes! Dinner. Thomas. Date. I'm listening." I toss the sequined dress onto the growing pile of rejects.

Griffin invited me to some swanky black-tie investor thing, and I have approximately nothing to wear. Where does one even find a black-tie worthy dress in Grächen? It's not exactly Milan.

"You're backing out, aren't you?" Ivy's voice turns suspicious. "I can hear it in your voice."

I feel around and find something furry in the corner of the closet. "I'm not backing out," I lie, pulling the garment forward and frowning at an orange coat that might have been made out of a shag carpet. "I'm just...reassessing my availability."

"Well, un-reassess it." Her voice turns stern in that way only pregnant women can master. "Either you come to Bern to meet Thomas, or I will personally waddle down to Grächen and drag you to this dinner if I have to."

I sigh, dropping the shag carpet coat. "Wouldn't that be inconvenient with your enormous belly?"

I dig deeper into the abyss of bohemian fashion disasters that my mother calls a wardrobe, deluding myself that it might suddenly sprout a designer gown if I glare at it hard enough. Spoiler alert: it doesn't.

"So next Wednesday at seven," Ivy declares. "James is texting Thomas now."

"Mmm," I mumble noncommittally, pulling out a floor-length purple thing with embroidered moons and stars. It screams hippie chic. How am I supposed to attend a black-tie investor party while dressed like I read tea leaves for a living? Gold coins fringe the sleeves that clank when it slips on the hanger.

"Anika? What's that jingling sound?" Ivy asks.

"Just cleaning my closet," I lie, shoving the purple nightmare back where it came from.

I don't feel like explaining *why* I'm going through the closet. Telling Ivy about Griffin feels dangerous somehow, like naming a wish out loud might prevent it from coming true. If I don't tell anyone about these practice dates, then I won't have to explain when they end.

And they will end. That's the whole point.

No. I'm definitely *not* telling Ivy about Griffin. Or the party. Or the strange flutter in my chest whenever he smiles at me.

I hold a brown dress against me in front of the mirror that might actually work if I make a few minor (okay, major) alterations.

"Thomas is really excited to meet you. And James can make his famous lasagna."

"Actually..."

"No, No. I don't want to hear it," Ivy continues. "Once this baby arrives, James and I won't be available for another decade, minimum. So unless you want your first date with Thomas to be just the two of you with no buffer..."

"Next Wednesday might not work for me. The bar has been busy lately."

"Why are you suddenly hesitant?" Ivy presses. "Last time we spoke you seemed almost excited."

Because last time we spoke I wasn't spending every other day with a six-foot-something Canadian goalie who makes me forget everything else in my life.

"I know, I know. It's just...complicated right now."

What's complicated is that every time Griffin smiles at me, my stomach does this weird flippy thing that I'm pretty sure isn't indigestion. What's complicated is that I'm supposed to be learning how to date one man while I'm falling for another.

"Nothing is complicated about dinner," Ivy insists. "You show up, you eat food, you talk to Thomas. If you hate him, you never have to see him again."

My thoughts drift to Griffin, to his dimpled smile and ridiculous inspirational quotes. To the way his hand felt around mine at the restaurant. To the fact that none of these practice dates are preparing me for Thomas. They're making me wish Thomas didn't exist.

I toss the dress aside and slump onto the bed beside the mountain of fashion crimes. Who am I kidding? This thing with Griffin will soon be a memory. A very pleasant memory, yes. But what makes me think anything will ever happen with a man who's only teaching me how to date other men?

I stare at the ceiling wondering what I've gotten myself into.

"Anika? Are you still there?"

"*Ja*," I grumble.

"Oof, need to pee again," Ivy groans through the phone. "This baby is using my bladder as a trampoline."

"TMI, Ivy," I say.

"Don't think this conversation is over," she warns. "I will keep calling until we set a date for Thomas. Pregnancy has given me superhuman persistence and zero shame."

"Fine, fine," I mutter, knowing full well I have no intention of agreeing to anything.

"Gotta go before I wet myself! Love you, bye!"

The line goes dead before I can protest further. I toss my phone onto the rejected dress pile.

"Who was that, *Schätzli*?"

I bolt upright to find my mother leaning against the doorframe, a knowing smile playing on her lips. Her silver-blonde hair is twisted into a messy bun with what appears to be a paintbrush stuck through it. There's a smudge of yellow paint on her cheek that matches her flowing tunic.

"Just Ivy," I mutter, hastily shoving dresses back into the closet. "Pregnancy has made her extra bossy."

"And why are you destroying my closet?" She gestures to the fabric explosion with amusement. "Planning a fashion show?"

"I need a dress for...an event."

"With that handsome hockey player?" Her eyes light up like Christmas came early. "The one who brought flowers?"

"It's not what you think."

"Of course it is!" She claps her hands together. "Finally! My daughter is going on a date!"

I don't correct her. Explaining that Griffin is just my dating coach would require admitting I've never been on a real date at twenty-five, which feels more pathetic than letting her believe this lie.

"It's a black-tie thing," I mumble. "Nothing in your closet works unless I'm attending as the entertainment."

"So don't go." She shrugs, picking up a paisley kimono and

holding it lovingly. "Stay home. Work at the pub. Die alone surrounded by beer taps and drunk locals."

"*Mutter!*"

"What? I'm just saying what will happen if you keep finding excuses." She tosses the dress aside. "I'll cover the pub. You've hardly taken a night off in three years."

Except for the Visp game, she's right.

I chew my lip. "I don't know…"

"If you don't go out with that delicious hockey player," she says, narrowing her eyes, "I will rearrange your vinyl collection by color instead of alphabetically."

I gasp. "You wouldn't."

"Try me." She crosses her arms, smiling sweetly. "And I'll switch all your Smiths records with my Yanni collection."

Now that's just evil.

She dances around the room humming a Yanni song.

"I don't have anything to wear anyway," I say with resignation. "So there's no use talking about it."

She twirls mid-dance to face me. "Maybe we can ask around the village? See if anyone has something you could borrow?"

I nearly choke. "Absolutely not. I'd rather wear this…thing."

"What about Frau Heller?" she suggests, tapping her chin thoughtfully. "She has that fancy dress she wore to her grandson's wedding."

"*Mutter!*" My face burns. "I am not going door-to-door begging for dresses!"

The mental image alone makes me want to crawl under my bed and hibernate until spring. The village gossip mill would churn out engagement rumors before I even made it home with a borrowed gown.

My mother waves dismissively. "Pride won't keep you warm at night, *Schätzli.*"

I'm contemplating whether I could fashion something

presentable from the pub's curtains—they're burgundy velvet, very Maria von Trapp—when the doorbell's cheerful ring interrupts my fashion crisis. My mother practically skips to answer it, leaving me alone with the pile of colorful thrift store rejects. I hold the brown dress against me one more time, wondering if I could somehow transform it into something that doesn't scream "I make my own granola."

"Maybe if I cut off the sleeves and hem it above the knee..." I mutter, turning sideways. "And add a belt? And completely change the fabric, color, and design?"

"Anika!" My mother's voice sings from the hallway. "There's something for you!"

She reappears in the doorway, cradling an enormous white box tied with a black satin ribbon. "The delivery man just left this. It's addressed to you."

"For me?" I take the surprisingly heavy box and place it on the bed. "There must be some mistake."

"It has your name on it." She points to the elegant card tucked under the ribbon.

I carefully untie the bow and lift the lid. Nestled in layers of tissue paper is the most exquisite dress I've ever seen. It's a deep midnight blue, with a subtle shimmer that catches the light as I lift it from the box. It unfolds into a floor-length gown with a tasteful slit up one side and delicate beading across the bodice.

"Oh my..." My mother's hands fly to her cheeks. "It's stunning!"

I'm speechless, running my fingers over the silky fabric. The cut is classic, elegant.

"There's more!" My mother reaches into the box and pulls out a smaller package. Inside are strappy, black heels that look suspiciously like my size.

"How did he…" I whisper, slipping off my sock to compare my foot to the shoe. Perfect fit.

"Wait, there's another box!" Mother squeals as she pulls out a small velvet case.

This one contains a delicate silver necklace with matching teardrop earrings. Simple, nothing flashy or ostentatious. Just…lovely.

"Well, well," my mother says, a knowing smile spreading across her face. "I wonder who could have sent such a thoughtful gift? Perhaps a certain hockey player?"

I feel heat creeping up my neck. "The card doesn't say it's from Griffin."

"It doesn't have to, *Schätzli*." She taps the side of her nose. "A mother knows these things."

Every love story is just two people trying to dance to the same song.

CHAPTER FOURTEEN

GRIFFIN

M y entire world narrows to the vision stepping out of
the sleek black limousine I sent to pick her up.

Anika emerges onto the helipad like something from a
dream, and my brain short-circuits. Everything—the mission,
Malcolm Chase, the FIS agents lurking somewhere nearby—
evaporates like ice on a spring day.

Her hair tumbles in soft waves past her shoulders, catching
the last rays of sunlight. She's wearing a furry pink winter coat

that reaches her knees, but the blue dress I sent her peeks out beneath it.

Words catch in my throat as she steps onto the helipad.

Words. I need words. Any words.

"You're..." I swallow hard. "Wow."

Smooth. Real smooth.

Her face falls. "I knew I shouldn't have worn my mother's furry coat. But all I have are puffy ski jackets."

"No, no...it's just..."

"I'm sorry. I'm going to embarrass you in front of your colleagues."

"I can assure you, woman. The way you look...I don't think I want to take you anywhere."

She frowns, and I can see a slight panic in her eyes. I cup her chin in my hand. "But that's only because every other man at the party tonight will want you."

Her voice quivers. "We can't have that, can we?"

I shake my head slowly, dropping my gaze to her lips. "No, we cannot. I need every other man to know you're mine tonight."

"Is...is this part of the lesson?"

"Oh, honey, I'm just getting started."

The helicopter pilot clears his throat behind me, reminding us we have somewhere to be. Somewhere that involves me playing spy against my boss while pretending I'm just taking the most beautiful woman in Switzerland to a fancy party. No pressure.

"Your chariot awaits," I say, offering my arm. When she takes it, I nearly forget about Malcolm Chase, the FIS, and whatever financial crimes might be happening at this gala.

"You never said we'd be taking a helicopter," she says as she looks at the sleek machine. "I've never been in one before."

"I probably should've mentioned this is a helicopter ride," I say, helping Anika up the steps.

She clutches my arm with surprising strength, her eyes sparkling and excited. "Is this standard dating coach protocol?"

I laugh, settling in beside her. "The party's at a private ski chalet tucked away in the mountains just on the other side of the valley. Since there are no cars allowed in Zermatt, it's helicopter or skis."

"Ah yes, because skiing in this gown would be completely practical." She smooths the midnight blue fabric with a smirk. "Though I would've paid good money to see you try in that tuxedo."

Her smile is pure mischief.

The pilot turns around, giving us a thumbs-up. Anika's grip on my arm tightens.

"Don't worry, they'll wait until you're settled before starting the rotors. Wouldn't want to ruin that hair." I wink, then immediately wonder if that was too flirty.

"My hero," she deadpans, but her smile says she appreciates the gesture.

When the rotors start spinning and we lift off, Anika's entire face transforms. She presses her face against the window. The setting sun catches her profile, turning her skin golden and her hair into living flame.

"Griffin! Look at how small everything is!" She points excitedly. "There's S'Holzfass! And the trail where I caught you chopping wood half-naked!"

"I wasn't half-naked," I protest, but can't help grinning at her enthusiasm.

"Tell that to my retinas. They're still recovering."

The helicopter banks, and the Matterhorn comes into spectacular view. Anika gasps, reaching for my hand without thinking. Her fingers intertwine with mine, warm and soft.

"It's like a different world up here," she shouts over the noise. "Is this how you always travel? Private helicopters and limousines?"

"Only on Fridays," I deadpan. "Tuesdays are strictly hot air balloons."

She laughs, and I instinctively squeeze her hand.

"And on Thursdays you walk down the mountain trail to S'Holzfass to get beaten."

"I will try to keep far away from your fist."

"I meant beaten at cards."

The helicopter rises higher, and the Alps spread out beneath us in a breathtaking panorama of snowcapped peaks and valleys. Anika drinks in the view.

I can't help thinking about what the FIS agents told me about Anika after they ran their background check. Clean as a whistle, they said. No criminal record, no suspicious connections. Just a hardworking bartender who inherited her father's pub and makes a mean Old Fashioned.

I glance at her profile as she gazes out the window, and something twists in my chest. I want to tell her the truth about tonight—that I'm basically playing spy against Malcolm Chase, that there might be actual danger involved. I should tell her about the Ponzi scheme, about the FIS agents who will be watching us tonight, about how this isn't just a fancy date but potentially dangerous.

But the agents warned me in no uncertain terms to keep Anika blissfully unaware. And to be honest, seeing her like this, radiant with excitement, I don't think I could bring myself to shatter that. Instead, I just squeeze her hand and enjoy this moment of pure joy on her face, storing it away in my memory like the precious thing it is.

"It's incredible," she shouts, pointing to where the last rays of sun are hitting the Matterhorn.

"Yeah," I say, not looking at the mountain at all. I'm watching the way her eyes light up, how her lips part slightly in wonder, the delicate curve of her neck where the necklace I sent rests against her skin. "Absolutely magical."

The helicopter touches down on a private landing pad, and we're immediately greeted by staff in crisp black uniforms who escort us toward a massive stone structure nestled against the mountainside.

"You said we were going to a chalet," Anika says, craning her neck to take in the soaring stone facade with floor-to-ceiling windows reflecting the snowcapped peaks.

"Yes. A Swiss Chalet," I say with a big grin.

"Griffin, this isn't a chalet," she says with a laugh. "This is a château. You live in a chalet."

"What's the difference?" I ask, enjoying the way she rolls her eyes at me.

"About fifty million francs and fourteen bathrooms."

"Well I don't know about that, but in Canada, we have a chicken restaurant called Swiss Chalet," I admit. "They make this amazing Rotisserie Chicken Poutine. The best you've ever tasted."

Anika's face scrunches up like I've just suggested putting ketchup on fondue. "That is not Swiss food. That is a crime against Switzerland."

"It's delicious is what it is," I counter, guiding her to where an attendant is checking coats. "French fries covered in gravy and cheese curds, topped with rotisserie chick…en."

Words stick in the back of my throat as Anika slips off her coat to reveal the midnight blue gown. It cascades around her like liquid starlight, hugging curves I didn't even know existed beneath her usual jeans and flannel. The fabric makes her eyes impossibly blue. Not the pale blue of a spring sky but the deep, mysterious blue of a mountain lake. More beautiful than Banff.

"Holy…"

"Is this okay?" she asks, gesturing at herself with a nervous laugh that punches me right in the chest.

She does a little twirl, and the dress flares slightly, revealing a slit that makes her legs look endless.

"More than okay," I manage to say.

"Thanks," she says sheepishly, smoothing her hands over the silky material. "How did you know my size?"

I tap the side of my head. "Goalie instincts. We have to size up shots in milliseconds."

"You sized me up, did you?" Her eyebrow arches with that snarky challenge I've come to crave.

"Every chance I get," I admit, more honestly than I intended.

The coat check clerk smirks as she scans a claim code onto my phone, but I barely register her at all. I can't take my eyes off Anika.

We're then guided through massive wooden doors and enter a grand foyer with a chandelier that looks like it's made of actual ice crystals, casting rainbow prisms across the polished stone floor. The ceiling soars three stories up, with balconies overlooking the space from each level.

Everywhere I look, elegant people mingle. The sparkle of diamonds and black tuxedos, the tinkling of crystal glasses meeting in toasts. The space buzzes with conversation and laughter, punctuated by the gentle notes of a string quartet playing in the corner. Through the floor-to-ceiling windows, I can see snow beginning to fall, each flake illuminated by the outdoor lighting like tiny stars drifting down from the heavens.

"Wow," Anika whispers, her fingers tightening on my arm.

A waiter glides past with a silver tray of tiny, artfully arranged bites.

"What is this?" I ask, picking up something that resembles a miniature work of art more than food.

"Seared foie gras with black truffle and gold leaf, sir," the waiter replies.

Anika snorts softly beside me. I snag two, thanking the waiter before he moves on.

Anika examines hers critically. "This is also not Swiss food," she declares taking a tentative bite, then her eyebrows shoot up in surprise. "It's...actually good."

I escort Anika deeper into the gala, trying to look like I belong among these ultra-wealthy investors. The thing is, I do belong here. At least on paper. I invested in Titans stock just like everyone else in this room. The difference is, I'm supposed to be spying on the guy who signs my paychecks.

No pressure.

Anika's practically vibrating with excitement, her eyes darting everywhere, like she's trying to memorize every detail.

"So many beautiful people," she murmurs. "I feel like I'm in a movie."

"You'd be the star," I say before I can stop myself.

She blushes, the pink in her cheeks making her eyes even bluer.

"This dating coach thing is working too well. I might actually believe you."

"Good. That's the point."

My hand finds the small of her back as I guide her through the crowd. The silky fabric of her dress is cool beneath my palm, but I can feel the warmth of her skin underneath. My brain short-circuits for a second.

Focus, McGregor. You're here on a mission.

I scan the room, looking for any sign of Malcolm Chase or

the FIS agents who are supposedly here. The problem is, I have no idea what they look like. They could be anyone. The bartender, the woman in the gold dress laughing too loudly, the elderly gentleman examining a painting in the corner.

Or maybe the guy staring directly at us from across the room?

He's mid-forties, clean-cut in a way that screams "government official," and he's watching us with an intensity that makes the hair on the back of my neck stand up. I catch his eye and give him a subtle nod.

The man's face flushes bright red, and he quickly turns away, nearly spilling his champagne in the process.

Hmm. Either that's the worst secret agent in history, or...

"What are you looking at?" Anika asks, following my gaze.

"Nothing. Just that guy who was staring at you."

"At me?" She laughs. "I doubt it. Everyone here looks like they walked off a runway."

"Trust me, he was definitely checking you out."

A strange possessiveness surges through me, and I slide my arm around her waist, drawing her closer. She fits against my side perfectly, like she was designed to be there.

"What was that for?" she asks, eyes sparkling.

"Just making sure everyone knows you're with me tonight."

The gesture feels right, even though I have no claim to her. She's here for dating practice, I remind myself. For some other guy named Thomas. The thought makes something twist uncomfortably in my chest, and I pull her slightly closer. We're supposed to look like a couple, after all. But there's something undeniably real about the way my heart races when she leans into me.

A waiter glides by with a tray of champagne flutes, and I snag two, handing one to Anika. Her fingers brush mine, sending a jolt of electricity up my arm.

"To practice dates," I say, clinking my glass against hers.

"To practice," she echoes, but something flickers in her eyes that makes my heart do a double backflip.

We wander through the party, passing clusters of wealthy investors discussing portfolios and profit margins. I should be listening for information about Malcolm Chase, but I can't focus on anything except the woman beside me.

"So, this is how the other half lives," Anika whispers, as she takes in the crystal chandeliers and ice sculptures.

"More like the other one percent," I reply. "My mom would lose her mind in this place. She'd be wrapping appetizers in napkins to take home."

Anika laughs, the sound light and musical. "My mother would be interrogating the staff about their astrological signs."

"So," Anika says, leaning closer so I can hear her over the ambient noise. Her clean scent fills my senses. "Tell me something I don't know about Griffin McGregor."

"I can play the harmonica," I offer. "But only the first eight notes of 'Piano Man.'"

She laughs, the sound warming me more than the champagne. "Impressive. What else?"

"No, no. Now it's your turn," I say, leaning slightly closer. "Tell me something about you."

"There's nothing interesting to tell."

"Oh I think there is. What's with the 80s music obsession? Every time I come into S'Holzfass, it's like stepping into a time machine."

"What's wrong with 80s music?" She narrows her eyes defensively.

"Nothing! I just find it interesting. Most people our age are into…I don't know, whatever's trending now."

"Well, most people have terrible taste," she says with a shrug. "The 80s had the best music. New Order, Falco, Yaz…"

"Were you secretly born in 1971 and just aging really well?"

She laughs, the sound bright against the murmur of the party. "Maybe I'm taking after my mother. She acts like it's still the nineteen sixties. All peace signs and tie-dye. I think she was born in the wrong era." Anika takes another sip of champagne. "Maybe I was too."

"That explains a lot, actually," I say. "Why you're so different from everyone else I've met."

Her eyes soften for a moment before that familiar wall comes back up. "Different or weird?"

"In your case," I say, gently tucking a strand of hair behind her ear, "more like extraordinary."

Her eyes glimmer with something unreadable when I call her extraordinary, but then a ripple of movement flows through the crowd as the string quartet stops playing their tasteful chamber music. For a moment, only murmurs and clinks of champagne glasses float through the air. I cast my gaze around the room again, searching for Malcolm Chase among the elite crowd.

Then electronic music pumps through hidden speakers. The opening synthesizer notes of "The Safety Dance" by Men Without Hats.

Anika freezes, her face lighting up. "Oh I love this song!"

"Fun fact, did you know Men Without Hats is a Canadian band?" I ask, raising my voice over the music.

"You don't say." Her eyes sparkle with amusement. "No wonder I love it so much."

I notice her feet tapping against the polished floor, her fingers drumming on her champagne glass to the beat. She's trying to maintain her sophisticated composure, but her body clearly wants to move.

"You can dance if you want to," I quip, nodding toward the

center of the room where a few brave souls have started to sway.

Anika shakes her head, suddenly shy. "In front of all these people?"

"Who cares what they think?" I take her champagne glass and set it on a passing waiter's tray alongside mine. "Come on. Your practice date is requesting a dance."

She hesitates, glancing around at the sea of black-tie elegance. "I don't know..."

"What happened to the woman who broke into my cabin singing Blondie at the top of her lungs?"

Her cheeks flush pink. "She wasn't wearing a designer gown in a room full of millionaires."

The music builds, and I see her resolve crumbling. Her shoulders start moving almost imperceptibly to the beat.

"Your feet are already dancing," I point out. "The rest of you might as well join them."

Less than a minute into the song, something magical happens. Anika finds herself on the dance floor, her inhibitions seeming to vanish with each step.

"We can leave your friends behind," she sings, suddenly transforming into a 1980s dancing queen right before my eyes.

She bounces on her toes, her arms swing with enthusiastic abandon, and she does these little kicks, which shouldn't work with her floor-length gown but somehow do.

The formerly stuffy atmosphere of the gala suddenly turns into a disco as she spins, the DJ's lights becoming a halo of fire around her laughing face.

I stand frozen, watching her become this radiant creature of pure joy. My heart hammers against my ribs with such force I worry I might need medical attention.

"Griffin!" she shouts, grabbing my hands. "Come dance!"

I try my best to mirror her movements, but coordination on

ice doesn't translate to the dance floor. My limbs move stiffly, a beat behind the music.

"You're terrible!" she shouts over the music, laughing.

"I'm better on skates!" I shout back.

"Stop thinking about it! Just have fun!"

She demonstrates a move involving her arms waving above her head while her hips swing in a figure eight. When I try it, she laughs so hard she snorts, which only makes her laugh harder.

Her joy sparks something inside me. A wild, untamed happiness I haven't experienced since childhood. I find myself dancing without caring how I look, moving for the pure pleasure of movement. A few other couples join us on the floor, others move aside, giving Anika room for her increasingly enthusiastic moves. She kicks off her high heels, sending them sliding across the polished floor, and continues barefoot, now adding little jumps.

"S-A-F-E-T-Y!" she spells out with her arms.

I decide if you can't beat 'em, join 'em and launch into my best robot dance, moving my arms in mechanical jerks, moonwalking backward (or trying to).

Anika doubles over laughing, clutching her stomach. "What is THAT?"

"It's 'The Safety Dance!'" I defend myself, continuing my robotic movements.

Her laughter rings out, pure and uninhibited. She wipes tears from her eyes, careful not to smudge her makeup.

She moves closer, our bodies almost touching as we dance. Her cheeks flush pink from exertion, her eyes sparkle with happiness, and I realize I'm witnessing something rare and precious. Anika Gisler completely, genuinely happy.

I can't stop staring at her. The way her hair falls across her face when she dips her head. The delicate line of her throat when she throws her head back laughing. The way her hands move through the air like she 'just don't care'.

"Come on, goalie man!" she teases. "Keep up!"

I grab her hand and spin her around. When she returns to me, she's closer than before, her body brushing against mine. For a heartbeat, our eyes lock. Something electric passes between us. A current of understanding, of connection. Her smile softens, becoming something more intimate.

Our faces are so close I can see the flecks of gold in her blue eyes. We're both breathing hard, her chest rising and falling against mine. For one suspended moment, we're frozen there. Bodies pressed together, faces inches apart, the world reduced to just us two.

The music builds, and I pull Anika flush against me, dipping her low.

"Have I told you how exquisite you look tonight?" I breathe the words against the skin of her neck. I can feel her pulse quicken even as she's lost for words.

Then, with rapid synthesized claps, the music ends and the spell breaks. But I keep her close, unwilling to let go. Anika stares up at me, lips parted, eyes alight with wonder.

She finds her shoes and we make our way off the dance floor. Her cheeks are flushed, her eyes bright with something I don't dare name. I can't tear my gaze away from her face, memorizing every freckle, every eyelash, every curve of her lips.

"Where did you learn to dance like that?" I ask.

"From watching Molly Ringwald in *The Breakfast Club*. I've seen it maybe fifty times."

"Molly Ringwald wishes she had your moves."

Anika laughs, tucking a strand of hair behind her ear. "I doubt that."

"You're supposed to be learning from me," I say, voice dropping lower.

"Oh?" Her eyebrow arches. "What am I learning right now?"

"How to own a room." My hand finds her waist, pulling her close. "Everyone here can't take their eyes off you."

"Everyone?" she asks, and I hear the real question beneath.

"Especially me," I admit, my voice barely audible above the music.

"Griffin," she starts, but whatever she was about to say is interrupted when a familiar voice cuts through our moment.

"Griffin McGregor! What a delightful surprise!"

Malcolm Chase materializes before us, his expensive suit somehow shinier than everyone else's, his smile just as artificial as I remember.

"Mr. Chase," I manage, straightening my spine. "Good to see you."

"Please, call me Malcolm." His overly white veneers on full display as he shakes my hand. Then his gaze slides to Anika in a way that makes my arm hair stand on end. "And who is this vision?"

"My date, Anika," I say, pulling her slightly closer. "Anika, this is Malcolm Chase, owner of the Toronto Titans."

"Enchanted," Malcolm purrs, taking her hand and bending to kiss it. His lips linger a beat too long, and I feel my temperature rising.

Anika extracts her hand with practiced grace. "Charmed."

My jaw clenches so hard I'm surprised my teeth don't crack.

"I must say, you two were quite the spectacle on the dance floor." Malcolm's eyes rake over Anika again. "Where did you find such a talented partner, Griffin?"

"Just lucky, I guess," I say, fighting the urge to step between them.

Malcolm turns his attention back to me, his expression sharpening. "I didn't realize you were among our top investors. I don't recall seeing your name on the exclusive invitation list."

I force a casual shrug. "The Titans stock has been particularly interesting to follow."

"Has it now?" Something calculating flashes in his eyes.

"I try to get in on every opportunity I can. Hockey careers don't last forever, you know."

Malcolm raises an eyebrow, looking almost impressed. "Indeed. Smart man. Perhaps smarter than I gave you credit for."

"Don't let this goofy face fool you," I joke, immediately regretting it.

His lip twitches slightly, and after a beat of uncomfortable silence, he glances at his watch. "I should be moving along."

He begins to turn from us, but I can't let him go. The FIS agents prompted me to get in his inner circle at any cost. In a panic, I blurt, "My financial advisor has been particularly impressed with the offshore investments."

This stops him in his tracks. As a casual investor, I'm not supposed to know about the offshore shell companies.

He gives me a sideways glance. "Perhaps we should discuss your...investment portfolio over a drink sometime."

"Why not now?" I say, seizing the opening. "I'd love to hear more about future opportunities. Maybe join you at your table?"

Malcolm's smile tightens at the corners. "Another time, perhaps. I have many guests to greet tonight." He turns back to Anika with that predatory smile. "But do enjoy the party. The caviar is imported directly from the Caspian Sea. Nearly extinct, just like good manners."

With a final lingering look at Anika, he melts back into the crowd.

"Well, he's a delight," Anika mutters once he's out of earshot.

I laugh, tension draining from my shoulders. "That's Malcolm for you."

"Is he always so..."

"Slimy? Pretentious? Like he's mentally undressing every woman in the room?"

"I was going to say like a movie villain who bathes in the tears of his enemies, but yours works too." She wrinkles her nose. "How do you work for someone like that?"

"Technically, I work for the team," I say, guiding her toward a quieter corner. "Malcolm just signs the checks."

"Does he have 'Professional Slimeball' printed on his business card?"

I choke back a laugh. "Right below 'World's Most Punchable Face.'"

"Seriously," she says, twisting her lip. "I need to wash my hand. I can still feel his lips on it."

"Here," I say, taking her hand in mine. "Let me help with that." I brush my thumb over the spot where Malcolm kissed, as if erasing his touch.

Anika's eyes meet mine, and for a moment, everything else disappears again.

I can feel her pulse racing beneath my fingers as I trace circles on her wrist. Her skin is impossibly soft, and the way she's looking at me right now, eyes glittering, lips inviting, a delicate flush spreading across her cheeks, makes my heart do a triple axel in my chest.

I'm suddenly hyperaware of how close we're standing, how the soft lighting catches the gold flecks in her eyes, how her pulse flutters visibly at the base of her throat.

"Anika, I..."

"I need to use the restroom," she blurts out and pulls her hand away, tucking a strand of hair behind her ear. "Right now. Immediately."

"Oh. Sure." I step back, giving her space. "Just try not to serenade anyone with Blondie this time. These fancy people might not appreciate it as much as I did."

She gives me a little laugh that hits me square in the chest. "I'll try to contain myself."

Then she's walking away, and I'm helpless to do anything but watch.

The midnight blue dress cascades down her body, the slit revealing a tantalizing glimpse of leg.

The back dips low, and I suddenly have the overwhelming urge to trace the constellation of freckles across her back with my fingertips.

My heart does a somersault when she glances back over her shoulder, catching me staring. Instead of the snarky comment I expect, she gives me a small, almost shy smile that knocks the air right out of my lungs.

I watch her weave through the crowd, turning heads as she goes. But it's the confidence in her walk that really gets me. For someone who claims to be out of her element, she moves like she owns the place. Chin up, shoulders back, hips swaying just enough to make my mouth go slack. A few heads turn as she passes, and a possessive heat flares in my chest.

That's my date, I want to shout. Mine.

When she finally disappears around a corner, I realize I've been holding my breath.

Holy hockey sticks. I'm in deep trouble here.

This was supposed to be simple. Help Anika learn to date. Spy on Malcolm Chase. Get information for the FIS. But nothing about this feels simple anymore. Not when my heart races every time she looks at me. Not when I can still feel the warmth of her body pressed against mine after that dance. Not when the thought of her practicing these date moves with some random guy named Thomas makes me want to punch a wall.

I grab a glass of water from a passing server and down it in one gulp. The cold liquid does nothing to cool the heat spreading through me.

I can't do this anymore. I can't pretend I'm just her dating coach when every fiber of my being wants to be the guy she's learning for. I can't keep teaching her how to flirt and dance and hold hands with someone else when I want it to be me.

When she comes back, I'm telling her. No more games, no more practice dates. I'm laying it all out there. How I feel when she walks into a room, how her laugh makes my whole day better, how I've been falling for her since the moment she threatened me with a fish.

I grab another glass of water, mentally rehearsing what I'll say. Something smooth and charming that doesn't make me sound like a complete idiot. Something that won't scare her away.

But who am I kidding? This is me we're talking about. I'll probably blurt out something ridiculous like "I think about you approximately 23.5 hours a day" or "Your face is my favorite face."

Still, I have to try. Tonight. Before we leave this party. Before she goes on that date with Thomas. Before I lose my nerve.

I've faced down 100-mile-per-hour slap shots without flinching. I can handle telling a beautiful woman I'm crazy about her.

I hope.

The string quartet starts playing a tango, and I straighten my bow tie, eyes fixed on the corner where Anika disappeared. Any minute now, she'll walk back into view, and I'll tell her exactly how I feel.

No more coaching. No more pretending.

The kiss you rehearse is never the kiss you remember.

CHAPTER FIFTEEN

Anika

I'm having a full-blown panic attack in the world's fanciest toilet.

The bathroom door clicks shut behind me, and I slump against it, my heart doing the Macarena inside my chest. What just happened out there? One minute we're dancing to one of my favorite 80s songs, and the next minute I'm practically melting into him.

I push away from the door with a grunt. "This is not a real

date."

The bathroom is ridiculous. I mean truly, properly ridiculous. A crystal chandelier dangles from the ceiling. The walls are covered in what appears to be actual gold leaf. The sink looks carved from a single piece of marble, with gold taps shaped like swans. Even the toilet looks too fancy to actually use. Is this how rich people pee? The mirror stretches across an entire wall, framed in what looks like even more gold, making me wonder if I've accidentally stumbled into some modern-day Versailles.

I stare at my reflection. My cheeks are flushed pink, my eyes too bright. I look...happy. Dangerously happy.

"It's just dancing," I tell my reflection. "Just dancing with a man who smells like pine trees and looks at you like you're the Stanley Cup."

This bathroom has a chaise lounge. A chaise lounge! As if people regularly need to lie down while visiting the toilet. Next to the chaise sits a small table with fresh flowers and—I'm not joking—a bowl of individually wrapped Swiss truffles. I unwrap one and pop it in my mouth, because if I'm having a crisis, I might as well have chocolate while doing it.

The rich caramel melts on my tongue as I pace the marble floor in my borrowed shoes. This dress that Griffin sent...it's the most beautiful thing I've ever worn. And the way he looked at me when I stepped out of that limo...

No. No, no, no. I cannot think about that look. That look is dangerous. That look makes me forget about Thomas and dating lessons and everything else.

"He's your dating coach," I remind myself sternly. "He's teaching you how to impress another man."

But then I remember how his voice went all deep and rumbly when he told me I looked beautiful. How his hand kept finding the small of my back, like it belonged there...the way he twirled me across the dance floor like we'd been dancing together our whole lives.

"Ooohh!" I chirp, grabbing another chocolate. This one has a hazelnut center.

I've never felt this way before. Not ever. Not with anyone. My stomach flips every time Griffin smiles at me. My skin tingles where he touches me.

Is this what attraction feels like? Because if it is, how do people function? How do they go about their daily lives feeling like this and not spontaneously combust?

I fan my face with my hands. Is it hot in here, or is it just the memory of Griffin's breath on my neck?

I'm counting down the seconds until I have to go back out there and pretend I'm not falling for Griffin McGregor.

Because I'm not. I'm absolutely, positively not falling for him. That would be ridiculous. Catastrophic. The worst idea in the history of ideas.

I splash cold water on my wrists, but it does nothing to extinguish the warmth spreading through my body. Griffin's hands are still burning imprints on my waist, my back, my fingertips.

"Listen to me," I tell my reflection firmly. "This is practice. PRACTICE."

Griffin is being nice because that's his job as my dating coach. He probably acts this way with everyone.

My reflection looks unconvinced.

Besides, even if (and this is a massive if) he *did* feel something, he's leaving. Going back to Canada when the lockout ends. And I'm staying here. With the pub. With my quiet life.

The thought makes my chest ache.

A soft knock at the door startles me.

"Just a moment," I call, gathering my composure.

I straighten my shoulders and take one final look in the

mirror. The woman staring back at me looks like a princess. A slightly panicked princess who's eaten too many emergency chocolates, but a princess nonetheless.

"Time to go back out there and remember this isn't real," I tell her firmly.

But as I reach for the door handle, I can't help wondering. What if it could be?

I open the door, half-expecting to see Griffin, but he's not there. I'm so distracted, I nearly collide with a woman standing directly in my path.

"Sorry, my fault," I mumble, sidestepping to avoid her.

The woman doesn't move. She's elegant in a silver sheath dress that hugs her slim frame, her blonde hair pulled into a sleek chignon. Her cool, assessing eyes lock onto mine as her wine glass tilts, almost in slow motion.

Dark red splashes across the front of my beautiful dress.

I gasp, looking down at the spreading stain.

"Oh dear," she says, her British accent crisp. "What a terrible accident."

"It's okay, I can—"

Before I can even continue, a man in an impeccably tailored suit appears beside me, his hand gripping my elbow with casual authority.

"Excuse me, sir!"

The man's grip tightens just enough to signal this isn't a request. "Let's step back inside, shall we?" he says with a smooth British accent, steering me back inside the restroom.

The bathroom door clicks shut behind us, the man's broad shoulders blocking the exit, and with a casual flick of his wrist, he locks the door.

My pulse hammers in my throat. "What are you—"

"We have ninety seconds before the target suspects our presence," he says to the woman, completely ignoring me.

The woman stands between me and the sinks, while the man leans against the door. I'm trapped between them like a rabbit about to get eaten by wolves.

"What do you want?" I demand, my voice embarrassingly squeaky. "If you're planning to rob me, I should warn you I left my wallet at home."

The woman pulls a compact from her clutch and checks her reflection. "Your hockey player," she says, snapping it shut. "How well do you know him?"

I blink rapidly, trying to process. "I...We're just..."

"He's not who you think he is," the man says cryptically.

The air suddenly feels too warm, too still. "Griffin? What are you talking about?"

The woman leans closer. "Your *date* is in over his head, and he's playing a very dangerous game with people who don't lose gracefully."

"Who are you people?" I demand, thinking I could probably take these two on if it came down to it. I'd hate to fight in this dress though.

They exchange a look that communicates volumes in silence.

"Friends. Of a sort," the man says, which is absolutely not an answer. "And you should be grateful we found you first."

"First, before what?" My voice rises. "What is happening?"

The woman steps around me, encroaching upon my space until I back up against the vanity. "The less you know, the better. For both of you."

"Sixty seconds," the man says, checking his watch.

"Is this some kind of joke?" I ask, though nothing about their expressions suggests humor.

"Do we look like we're joking?" The man's voice drops lower. "You need to get your boyfriend out of here. Now."

"Griffin isn't my boyfriend," I correct automatically, then shake my head. "And why...?"

"Because," the woman cuts in. "he's either in danger or he is the danger. And you don't want to wait around to find out which."

The man steps closer to me. "There are forces at work here beyond your understanding, Miss Gisler."

My stomach drops. "How do you know my name?"

The woman's lips curve into something too sharp to be a smile. "We know a lot of things. Including that your...not-boyfriend...has entangled himself in something that could get him killed."

"Killed? Does Malcolm Chase have anything to do with this?"

My mind is racing. Griffin said something about an investment opportunity. And that Malcolm guy gave me the creeps.

"Malcolm Chase isn't who Griffin should be worried about," the man says, his voice low. "Just get the hockey player to take you home."

"And if I don't?" I challenge, though my voice trembles.

The man's smile is cold as winter. "Then we can't guarantee what happens next."

"To him...*or* to you," the woman adds.

The man unlocks the door. "Thirty seconds."

"Get him to leave," the woman warns. "Tell him you're ill. Tell him anything. Family emergency. Sexual proposition. Whatever works."

Ha! I've never been kissed. I certainly am not going to do...that.

"And don't mention anything about this conversation," the man adds. "The less he knows, the safer you both are."

"Why should I trust you? I don't even know who you are!"

"Because if you don't," the woman says ominously. "he might not make it back to Canada in one piece."

My stomach drops. "Are you threatening him?"

"Warning you," the man corrects. "There are people here tonight who would consider Mr. McGregor...expendable.

The woman reaches past me to wet a towel, hovering near my ear. "Remember," she whispers. "Say nothing about us."

Then, pressing the towel into my hands, she says, louder now, "For your dress. Club soda and salt when you get home."

"Time's up," the man says to the woman, straightening his already perfect tie. "Easterly exit in three minutes."

She nods, then turns to me. "Choose wisely, Miss Gisler."

"What do you mean choose wisely?" I ask, but the woman is already moving toward the door.

The man gives me one last look. "Get him out. Immediately. And Miss Gisler?" The man's eyes twinkle. "Trust no one else here. Including your date."

He opens the door, checking both ways before they both slip out, leaving me alone with the terrifying realization that Griffin has been keeping secrets.

What just happened? Who were those people? And what does Griffin have to do with any of this?

My dress is stained with red wine. I dab at it halfheartedly with the damp towel, but it's hopeless. At least the color isn't showing up too badly against the deep blue.

I need to find Griffin. Whatever those people were warning me about, I need to get us both out of here.

Taking a deep breath, I step back into the glittering party. Crystal glasses clink, laughter bubbles, and the orchestra plays something classical that sounds vaguely familiar. The music swells around me, couples spinning across the dance floor in a blur of designer gowns and tuxedos. Waiters glide between guests with trays of champagne. Everything looks exactly the same as when I left, but now it all feels...sinister. Like a beautiful mask hiding something ugly.

What have I gotten myself into? And more importantly, what has Griffin gotten himself into?

Trust no one else here. Including your date.

I scan the crowded ballroom for Griffin's tall frame, my eyes darting from face to face. Where is he? Did something happen to him already?

But the sea of black tuxedos and evening gowns blurs together.

A server passes with a tray of champagne. I grab a glass and drain it in one gulp, ignoring his startled look. Liquid courage. I need to find Griffin, tell him we need to leave, without revealing why. How am I supposed to do that? Not making an untoward proposition, I can tell you that much.

I push through clusters of laughing guests, murmuring apologies as I search. The orchestra's melancholy song perfectly matching my growing sense of dread.

Then I spot him across the room, his broad shoulders unmistakable even from behind. He's standing near one of the massive windows that overlook the snow-covered mountains, his back to me.

Relief floods through me. He's safe. He's right there.

Now, I just need to get him out of here before whatever danger those strange people warned me about materializes. I start toward him, rehearsing excuses in my head. Food poisoning? Migraine? Sudden urge to make out in the helicopter?

Then I see something that stops me cold.

Oh.

My feet freeze to the floor. The air rushes from my lungs as though someone's punched me in the stomach.

I blink hard, hoping I'm imagining things. That what I'm seeing is just a trick of the light, or too much champagne, or the stress of being threatened in a fancy bathroom.

But it's still there when I open my eyes.

The orchestra continues playing, but the music seems to fade away. The laughter around me becomes distant, like I'm underwater. All I can focus on is what's happening across the room.

My throat tightens. A strange, hollow feeling spreads through my chest.

He's not who you think he is.

I thought—

No. It doesn't matter what I thought. I was wrong. So very wrong.

I was so stupid. So, so stupid to think that tonight was magical.

But now I have a choice to make. Do I trust those strangers' warning and drag Griffin out of here? Or was their warning part of something else entirely?

Griffin turns slightly, and for a brief moment, our eyes meet across the crowded room. Something flickers across his face. Surprise? Guilt?

I back away slowly, nearly colliding with a dancing couple. I apologize and pivot, the room tilting sideways.

I need to get out of here. Away from this party. Away from Griffin.

Away from the truth that's staring me in the face.

I turn to look for the exit, but before I can do anything, a hand closes around my arm, and a voice whispers in my ear.

"I told you to leave, Miss Gisler. Now it's too late."

The man presses two fingers over his ear. "Meridian, we've got company."

The man's fingers dig into my arm like talons. "Let go of me," I hiss, trying to wrench away.

Instead of releasing me, he spins me around so forcefully I nearly lose my footing, pulling me against his chest in what must look like an intimate embrace to anyone watching. My hands instinctively press against his lapels to create distance, but he's as solid as a brick wall.

"Act naturally," he murmurs, his mouth close to my ear. "Smile. Dance. Don't draw attention."

He begins swaying us to the music, one hand splayed possessively across my lower back. My feet stumble as he continues to move us in time with the music.

"I don't want to dance with you," I whisper fiercely.

"Play along until I deem it safe," he orders, his eyes scanning the room over my shoulder.

I glance across the ballroom and spot Griffin. He's noticed us. His normally cheerful face has hardened into something I've never seen before. Jaw tight, eyes narrowed, brows drawn together in a severe line. He's already cutting through the crowd, moving with purpose in our direction.

Even from here, I can see the intensity in his eyes. The look on his face makes my stomach flip. It's protective, fierce, nothing like the playful, quote-spouting goalie who chops wood without a shirt on.

This is someone else entirely.

"My friend is coming," I warn the man. "And he doesn't look happy."

The man follows my gaze, his posture stiffening. "That complicates things."

"Good," I snap. "Now let me go."

The man stops dancing abruptly, his eyes scanning the room. "Listen carefully. There are four OMBRA operatives in this room."

"I don't even know what OMBRA is!"

"Keep your voice down," he hisses. Then, with surprising gentleness, he adds, "Come. I can get you out safely."

He's guiding me away from the dance floor, his hand firmly around my upper arm as we move toward a side hallway. I glance back and see Griffin pushing past a cluster of laughing guests, his eyes locked on us.

"Stop manhandling me," I snap, trying to wrench my arm free. "I can walk on my own."

His grip loosens slightly, but he doesn't let go as we move down a dimly lit corridor. "I'm trying to save your life, Miss Gisler."

"I just want to go home," I say, my voice smaller than I intend. "Alone. Without any man. Without any of...whatever this is."

He stops at an intersection of hallways, checking both directions before turning to me. For the first time, I notice the tiny scar bisecting his left eyebrow, the only imperfection in his otherwise immaculate appearance.

"There's a service elevator at the end of this corridor," he says, pointing to our right. "Take it down to the ground floor, then follow the exit signs to the staff parking area. There will be a black car waiting. The driver knows where to take you."

"I'm not getting in a stranger's car."

He sighs. "Fair enough." He tugs me down a different hallway. "This way."

I stumble after him, my heels clicking on marble as we move deeper into the mansion. The music fades completely, replaced by an eerie silence broken only by our footsteps and my slightly panicked breathing.

"Who are you?" I demand as he pulls me around another corner.

"Wilde," he says without looking back. That doesn't answer my question at all.

We reach an ornate wooden door at the end of a hallway lined with oil paintings of stern-looking men in hunting attire. Wilde pulls a small device from his pocket, runs it along the door frame, then nods to himself before turning the handle.

"After you," he says, gesturing me inside.

"No way. You first."

He smirks, then steps into what appears to be an opulent study. Floor-to-ceiling bookshelves line the walls, interrupted only by a massive stone fireplace. A heavy mahogany desk dominates the center of the room, surrounded by leather chairs.

"Nice place to hide a body," I mutter, following him reluctantly.

Wilde moves directly to a bookshelf, running his fingers along the spines. "Malcolm Chase likes his secrets," he says, pulling on a specific volume. Something about financial markets. "And his escape routes."

The bookshelf swings outward with a soft click, revealing a dark passageway beyond.

I take an instinctive step backward. "Oh, no. No way."

"It's the safest way out," Wilde insists. "This passage leads directly to the second helipad."

"How do you know about secret tunnels in Malcolm Chase's private mansion?"

"That's classified."

"Of course it is," I mutter.

Wilde reaches into his jacket pocket and pulls out what looks like a sleek metal pen. With a click, the end illuminates with a bright beam of light. He hands it to me. "Follow this tunnel straight through. After about fifty meters, you'll reach a junction. Take the right path, then the second left. That will lead you to a stairwell that comes out behind the main kitchen, near the service entrance to the helipad."

I take the light, turning it over in my hand. "Is this going to self-destruct in five minutes?"

"It's just a flashlight, Miss Gisler," he says, though I catch the ghost of a smile. "However, I wouldn't recommend disassembling it."

"Great. So it might explode."

"Your pilot will be waiting. Tell him 'eucalyptus,' and he'll take you directly home."

"Eucalyptus? Seriously?"

"It's a verification code. For your safety."

I glance down the dark passage, then back at Wilde. "You realize this is exactly how people get murdered in horror movies, right? Strange man leads woman to secret tunnel, gives her cryptic instructions, then locks her inside?"

"If I wanted to harm you, Miss Gisler, I would have done so in the bathroom."

"That's...not as reassuring as you think it is."

Wilde checks his watch. "We don't have time for this. Get to the helipad and wait for your pilot. He'll take you home."

"What about Griffin?" I ask, surprising myself with how much I care about the answer. There's also the little matter of leaving behind my mother's furry coat.

"We'll handle Mr. McGregor."

"Handle? That sounds ominous."

"Go," he says, his voice softening slightly. "Please."

"Right path, second left, kitchen, helipad," I repeat. "Eucalyptus."

Wilde nods. "Good luck, Miss Gisler."

Before I can say anything else, he's gently pushing me into the passageway. The panel slides closed behind me with a soft click, plunging me into darkness except for the beam of the flashlight.

"Well, this is just perfect," I mutter, aiming the light down the narrow stone corridor that looks like it belongs in a medieval castle and not a luxury ski resort. "Just follow the creepy British man's directions through the secret tunnel. What could possibly go wrong?"

Sometimes the most romantic thing
you can do is listen.

CHAPTER SIXTEEN

Anika's been gone for five minutes, which shouldn't worry me, but does. When she left so abruptly, I felt like I'd said something wrong, though I couldn't figure out what.

Maybe my dancing skills weren't as impressive as I thought? I should have gone with her, made sure she was okay. What kind of fake date am I? A pretty terrible one, apparently.

I decide to head to the bar. After all, if I'm playing spy for the night, I might as well lean into it fully. Nothing says I'm a super spy quite like ordering a martini at a fancy gala.

"Martini, please," I tell the bartender, a stoic man with a waxed mustache. I lean in slightly. "Shaken, not stirred." I've always wanted to say those words.

The bartender raises an eyebrow but nods without comment.

I resist the urge to adjust my bow tie or check for a hidden gun holster. Maybe I'm taking this spy thing a bit too seriously, but hey...When in Rome. Or rather, when in a billionaire's secret mountain lair.

I drum my fingers against the polished bar top, my eyes constantly sweeping the room for Anika. Once she gets back, I need to tell her the truth. This whole investor party story isn't going to hold water much longer, especially if Malcolm Chase starts acting suspicious. Anika's smart. Too smart to keep in the dark.

She deserves to know she's at a party crawling with spies and possible criminals. Plus, I'm betting those bartending skills of hers could come in handy. People spill all kinds of secrets to their bartenders. Something about the combination of alcohol and a sympathetic ear loosens even the tightest lips. Maybe she could work her magic on some of Malcolm's associates while I try to get closer to the man himself.

"Your martini, sir," the bartender says, sliding the pristine glass toward me.

I take a sip, enjoying the crisp bite of gin and vermouth. I like my beer just like any self-respecting Canadian, but I'd like to think I have a refined palate when the occasion calls for it. And tonight, playing spy in a designer tux, definitely calls for it. There's something satisfying about sipping a fancy drink in a fancy place wearing a fancy suit. Makes me feel sophisticated, like I belong among these high rollers instead of just being the guy who makes them all rich by winning hockey games.

"You look like a man with secrets."

The voice is like warm honey, accent vaguely European but impossible to place. I turn to find myself face-to-face with a knockout in a red velvet dress so form-fitting it defies physics and a neckline that plunges somewhere south of decency. Her dark hair cascades over one shoulder, and her eyes, almost black in this lighting, study me with amused interest.

"Nope," I reply, raising my martini slightly. "I'm an open book."

She laughs, a musical sound that seems to dance above the ambient noise of the party. "Let me guess. Shaken, not stirred?"

"Is it that obvious?"

"Just a hunch." She slides onto the barstool next to mine, crossing legs that seem to go on for days.

The bartender appears without being summoned. "Negroni," she orders, not taking her eyes off me. "With an extra dash of Campari." Then she leans in slightly and says with a dainty laugh, "Actually, I overheard you place your order."

My face turns hot. I *am* that obvious.

I take another sip of my martini. It tastes like what I imagine James Bond's cologne smells like. Smooth, sophisticated, and slightly dangerous.

"The trick is to pretend you like it until you actually do."

"I'm sorry, what?"

She nods at my glass. "Gin. Although I imagine that philosophy can be applied to many things."

"Oh? Like what?"

"Only unpleasant things." Her gaze rakes over me. "The pleasant ones require no pretending."

Her eyes hold mine a beat too long, and I clear my throat. I've seen this look before in VIP sections, at after-parties, in hotel lobbies. I've been around beautiful women my entire career. The hockey world is full of gorgeous women who hang around players, hoping for...well, whatever it is they're hoping for. A good time, Instagram photos, free drinks, or sometimes just the thrill of bagging an athlete. I've learned to spot the ones with agendas.

This woman definitely has an agenda.

The bartender delivers her drink, and she raises it in a toast. "To new friends."

I clink my glass against hers, studying her over the rim as I take a sip. She's gorgeous, sure, but there's something calculated about her charm.

"I'm Elodie," she says, extending a hand adorned with a single ruby ring.

"Griffin," I reply, shaking her hand briefly and then shift slightly, creating a bit more space between us. "I should mention I'm here with someone."

"Of course you are," she says, not moving away at all. "The lovely blonde in the stunning blue dress? I noticed you dancing. Not bad."

"Thanks." I glance toward the hallway where Anika disappeared. "She should be back any minute."

"I'm sure she will." She leans in, her perfume enveloping me...something exotic and spicy. "But she doesn't know why you're really here."

My spine stiffens. "I'm not sure what you mean."

"We don't have much time," she murmurs, lowering her voice.

"Excuse me?"

She glances around casually, then meets my eyes with sudden intensity. "Malcolm's inner circle is gathering in the east wing library in twenty minutes. If you want in, you need to be there."

My heart rate kicks up a notch. She must be one of the operatives Showalter mentioned. The agents did say they'd have people here, but they never mentioned who. I study her more carefully now, trying to determine if she's legitimate.

"You're with FIS?"

"Don't worry," she whispers. "We're on the same team. Just keep acting natural."

"I was told there would be agents here," I say carefully.

"And here I am." She takes a delicate sip of her negroni. "The question is, are you ready to do what needs to be done?"

I hesitate, looking around for Anika again. "I should wait for my date."

Elodie's perfectly manicured hand lands on my forearm. "Time is not a luxury we have, Mr. McGregor. Connections are being made as we speak. If you delay, you'll miss your opportunity."

But something feels off. Maybe it's the way she's looking at me, or maybe it's just that Anika's disappearance has me on edge.

"Malcolm doesn't strike me as the type to just let a hockey player into his secret meetings," I say.

"He's not. But lucky for you, I can be quite persuasive." She gestures to herself with a wry smile. "I can get you in. The rest is up to you."

"I need to at least find my date first," I say, standing up.

Elodie rises with me, her movements fluid and graceful. "Oh, I believe I saw her stepping outside for some air."

That doesn't sound like Anika. She was going to the bathroom, not the terrace.

"Don't worry," says Elodie, probably seeing the concern on my face. "See that man by the arching windows? The one with the gold-sequined suit jacket."

"Unfortunately, yes." What an eyesore.

"That's Cain Fawkes. He's Malcolm's loyal attack dog. If we want to get into that private meeting, you need to make a good first impression."

"I've never seen that man before in all my years with the Titans."

Elodie arches a brow. "Trust me. His job has nothing to do with hockey."

That thought is slightly unsettling, which means this Cain guy deals with Malcolm's illegal business.

"And how do you suggest we butter him up? Or am I going to regret asking?"

Her grin turns a little witchy. "Oh, I'm way ahead of you. Come on. I'll introduce you."

"But...Anika"

"We need to move now. Unless you're not as committed to this mission as your superiors suggested."

That stings my pride a bit. "I'm committed. But I need to let my date know where I'm going."

"No time," she insists, her hand now resting on my forearm. "And no phones. Malcolm has signal jammers throughout the building. Old-school paranoia."

I drain the last of my martini, still scanning the room for any sign of Anika. My gut is telling me to find her first, but my head is reminding me why we're here. Get close to Malcolm. Find out what he's up to.

"Five minutes," I tell Elodie firmly. "I'll give you five minutes, and then I'm finding my date."

She smiles, victorious. "That's all I need. Follow me."

I follow Elodie across the ballroom, weaving through clusters of Switzerland's elite while trying not to look like I'm being led to my execution.

Cain Fawkes stands by a massive window framed by velvet drapes, surveying the party like he's mentally calculating who to throw off the mountain first. Something about this whole situation feels off, like when you know a slap shot is coming but can't quite track where it's headed.

Every few steps, I glance over my shoulder, hoping to spot Anika. Nothing. Where did she go?

"Eyes forward, hockey boy," Elodie murmurs, her fingers digging into my arm like she's afraid I might bolt. Which, to be fair, I'm considering. "And smile. You look like you're marching to the penalty box."

"That's my concentration face," I protest but paste on what I hope is a charming grin.

She rolls her eyes, but there's a hint of a smile. "Just follow my lead and try not to say anything...hockey-ish."

"Hockey-ish? What does that even mean?"

"Cain!" Elodie's voice transforms into a light cadence as we approach Gold Sequin Jacket Guy. "I've been looking everywhere for you."

Cain Fawkes turns, and I immediately understand why Malcolm keeps him around. Despite the ridiculous jacket, everything about him screams that he breaks kneecaps for fun. His face has that particular hardness you only get from years of making people regret looking at him the wrong way. He's shorter than me by a good three inches, but the way he carries himself suggests he doesn't consider this a disadvantage.

His cold, calculating eyes flick from Elodie to me, narrowing slightly. "Elodie. Wasn't expecting to see you tonight."

His voice is surprisingly refined for someone who looks like he bench-presses small cars.

"Cain, darling!" Elodie purrs, releasing my arm to slide up to him. "That jacket is absolutely criminal. I'm blinded by your fabulousness."

"It's a Tom Ford," he says, straightening his back. "Limited edition."

"It's...very sparkly," I offer, which seems to be the wrong thing to say because Elodie jumps in smoothly.

"This is Griffin McGregor," she says, like she's presenting a prized show dog. "He's one of Malcolm's investors. And a hockey player."

The way she says "hockey player" makes it sound like an adorable hobby, like I collect stamps or build ships in bottles.

Cain's gaze narrows, his expression suggesting he's just found something unpleasant stuck to his shoe. "I know who he is."

"Then you know he's trusted." Elodie smiles sweetly. "Griffin is interested in exploring some of Malcolm's more... exclusive opportunities."

Cain looks me up and down. "Is that so?"

"That's right." Smooth, confident. "Always looking for smart opportunities."

Cain's eyebrow twitches. "Funny, I don't recall seeing your name on tonight's list."

Elodie slides her fingers under Cain's lapel. "I thought he might enjoy joining the discussion later."

Cain's eyebrows shoot up. "That discussion isn't for tourists, Elodie."

"I'm not a tourist," I interject, trying to sound casual. "I've got a decent chunk of change invested already."

"Hockey players," Cain scoffs. "You get a few million and suddenly think you're Warren Buffett."

"Who says I'm not?" I grin. "Have you ever seen us in the same room together?"

"Don't be rude, Cain," Elodie chides, leaning in to whisper something in his ear that I can't hear. His expression shifts slightly.

"Just eager to get in on the ground floor of whatever's next," I say.

Cain studies me for a long, uncomfortable moment, his expression unreadable. I maintain eye contact despite the growing certainty that this man has definitely made people disappear.

Finally, he nods. "Fine. If you want in, you follow my rules. No questions, no comments unless directly addressed. But if you say or do anything stupid, you're out."

"Scout's honor," I say, holding up three fingers.

"And lose the blonde," he adds, nodding toward where Anika disappeared. "This isn't bring your girlfriend to work day."

My stomach drops. "About that—"

"He understands," Elodie cuts in smoothly.

"Twenty minutes. East wing library," Cain says curtly. He walks away without another word, his gold jacket glittering.

"See? Easy," Elodie says, looking pleased with herself.

"Yeah, super easy," I mutter. "Now I really need to find Anika."

"We don't have time," Elodie insists. "We need to prepare."

"I'm not going anywhere until I know she's okay."

Elodie sighs dramatically. "Fine. You have ten minutes. Meet me by the grand staircase after that." She leans in, her lips almost brushing my ear. "Don't be late, Griffin. This is your only chance to get what you came for."

Just as I'm about to turn away, Elodie's fingers tighten around my lapels, yanking me closer with surprising strength.

"Wait," she says, her voice suddenly all business. "You can't go in there looking like this."

"Looking like what?" I glance down at my tux.

"Like you've been wrestling a bear." She clicks her tongue disapprovingly. "Honestly, men have no idea how to maintain themselves at formal events."

Before I can protest, she's tugging at my jacket, smoothing

invisible wrinkles. Her fingers snake around my neck, adjusting my collar.

"I'm pretty sure I look fine," I mutter, trying to step back, but she's got me locked in place like I'm caught in a face-off.

"Trust me," she says, her voice all honey-sweet. "You'll want to look like you belong in that meeting."

Her hands move to my hair, nails scraping lightly against my scalp as she rearranges what I spent twenty minutes getting just right in front of the mirror.

"There," she says finally, looking satisfied with her handiwork. "Now you look presentable."

And then, quick as a snake strike, she leans in and presses her lips to my cheek.

"For luck," she whispers.

"I think you've made your point," I say through gritted teeth, finally managing to put my hands on her shoulders and create some distance.

The words die in my throat as I catch a flash of strawberry blonde hair across the grand ballroom. Anika.

She blinks rapidly, lips slightly parted, and even from here I can see the color rising in her cheeks. Our eyes lock for one excruciating second, and I see the exact moment her expression shifts from shock to hurt to something worse. Cold resignation. Like she always expected this to happen.

"Anika!" I call out, but the room is too big, and my voice is swallowed by the orchestra.

She turns away sharply, disappearing into the crowd. I push forward, not caring who I bump into, but the sea of people seems to close around her like she's being swallowed whole.

Then, I spot her again, and my blood turns to ice.

Apparently, the universe has decided I haven't been punished enough tonight because some slick-looking guy in a tailored suit has appeared at her side. He says something that makes her pause and then slides an arm around her waist and pulls her into a dance. His hand splays possessively across her lower back as he guides her across the floor, all smooth and calculating.

My vision goes red around the edges. Who the hell does this guy think he is?

Couples blur past me as I weave between them, keeping my eyes locked on Anika and Mr. Smooth Criminal. He's leaning in close, whispering something in her ear. Her face is tense, unreadable. Is she enjoying this? Is she trying to make me jealous? Or is she genuinely into this guy?

"Griffin!" Elodie calls after me. "Don't blow this!"

I ignore her, pushing forward with single-minded determination. The only thing I'm blowing is my chance with Anika if I don't explain what just happened.

The guy dips her low, his lips inches from her neck, and something primal roars in my chest. I don't care who he is. His face is about to become intimately acquainted with the floor.

I shoulder past a waiter, my blood pounding in my ears.

All I can think about is getting to Anika before that suit-wearing jackass whisks her away completely. I feel a tightness in my chest that's spreading throughout my body like a vice. Nothing, not even the playoffs, has ever given me this much stress.

"Excuse me," I mutter, accidentally bumping into an elderly woman, who gives me a scandalized look. "Sorry, ma'am. Hockey emergency."

The rational part of my brain knows I have no right to be jealous. This isn't a real date. I'm her dating coach, not her boyfriend. But the caveman part of my brain is already plotting ways to separate this suave stranger from his perfectly styled hair.

I swear if he dips her one more time, I'm going to...

221

"Griffin!" Elodie's manicured fingers wrap around my elbow. "There you are."

"Not now," I growl, trying to shake her off without causing a scene. The last thing I need is to be that hockey player who made a spectacle at a fancy Swiss gala.

"You don't understand," she hisses, her voice dropping to a whisper. "Something urgent has come up."

I finally tear my eyes away from Anika to look at Elodie. Her expression is intense, almost desperate. "Look, I appreciate the spy games and all, but I need to talk to my date first."

"This isn't a game," she says. "You're causing a scene."

"I'll be at the meeting as planned if I can," I say firmly, extracting my arm from her grip.

I turn back toward Anika, scanning the dance floor frantically. The sea of tuxedos and evening gowns has shifted, and for a heart-stopping moment, I can't find her.

Then I see Mr. Perfect Hair though the crowd.

I quicken my pace, mentally rehearsing exactly how I'm going to introduce this guy's face to my fist, when a gold-sequined arm shoots out, catching me square in the chest.

"Going somewhere, Puck Boy?" Cain's voice drips with disdain.

"My date," I say, trying to sidestep him. My eyes remain locked on Anika, who's now being led off the dance floor.

Cain sneers, adjusting his ridiculous gold cuffs. "I told you to ditch her. Typical hockey jock."

"I was just about to tell her to take a hike," I lie, trying to peer around his ridiculously broad shoulders to keep Anika in view, but she's disappearing into the crowd. "It's just...too much champagne," I blurt out, making an exaggerated grimace. "Gotta take a wiz."

Cain's face remains impressively impassive. "Charming. You have fifteen minutes until the meeting."

"That should be plenty," I say, patting my stomach with a pained expression. "Unless there's a line, in which case…"

"If you're not there, don't bother showing your face around here again." He walks away with a sinister laugh. "Which would be fine by me."

I turn back toward where I last saw Anika, just in time to catch a flash of her dress disappearing down a hallway. With that guy.

Sometimes love sneaks in through the side door.

CHAPTER SEVENTEEN

Griffin

I've lost sight of Anika completely now, which means Mr. Tall Dark and Handsy has successfully spirited her away down that hallway. My imagination conjures increasingly dramatic scenarios. Is he kidnapping her? Seducing her?

That's it. I'm going to rip his arms off and beat him with them.

Too dark?

I push forward with renewed urgency, weaving through the last knot of guests, following where Anika disappeared. The hallway stretches before me, dimly lit and empty except for a few couples seeking privacy in shadowy corners. No sign of Anika.

"Anika?" I call out, not caring who hears me now. My voice echoes off the ornate walls.

I jog down the corridor, checking each branching hallway.

Nothing.

It's like she vanished into thin air. Or worse. Like she deliberately disappeared with *that guy*.

My stomach twists at the thought. Was she that upset about seeing Elodie with me? Upset enough to run off with the first smooth talker who offered an escape?

And it's not just jealousy, though there's plenty of that burning through my veins. It's worry. Something about that guy set off all my alarm bells. The way he appeared out of nowhere, how quickly he whisked her away...

I reach a junction where the hallway splits three ways. Left, right, or straight ahead? I have no idea which way they went.

"Eeny, meeny, miny...Oh, forget it," I groan, running a hand through my hair. I pick the right corridor, moving at a half-jog.

This hallway is even darker, lined with closed doors. I try the first handle. Locked. Same with the second and third. "Anika?"

Nothing.

The hallway is eerily quiet compared to the ballroom's vibrant chaos. My footsteps echo as I jog down the corridor, heart pounding in my ears.

"Anika!" I try again, louder this time.

A door creaks open to my right, and an older woman peers out, her face a map of irritation.

"Young man, this is not a hockey rink. Kindly lower your voice."

"Sorry, ma'am," I say, trying to peek past her. "Did you see a woman in a blue dress come this way? With a guy in a dark suit?"

She purses her lips. "I most certainly did not. Now, if you'll excuse me."

The door shuts firmly in my face.

I'm struck by the absurdity of potentially bursting in on some billionaire in the bathroom because I'm jealous of my fake date talking to another man.

But then I hear it. Anika's voice, faint but unmistakable, coming from around the corner.

I race down the hallway, rounding one corner, then another, just in time to see her dress vanishing through a doorway at the far end. The door closes with an ominous click.

"Hold on, Anika," I shout, breaking into a full sprint.

I reach the door and grab the handle, giving it a twist. Locked. I press my ear against the wood, straining to hear anything on the other side. Nothing but silence.

My mind races through possibilities, each worse than the last. Did she go willingly? Is she in danger? Or is this just a jealous overreaction because some guy swept in while I was busy with Elodie?

I step back, eyeing the door to see how hard it would be to break it down before Doctor Evil's younger, better-looking cousin whisks her away to his secret volcano lair.

I stare at the locked door, my brain frantically cycling through every spy movie I've ever seen. What would 007 do in this situation? Probably whip out some laser watch that doubles as a lock-picking device while delivering a witty one-liner about "getting the door."

"Okay, Griffin. Think. You've seen every spy movie ever made."

I pat my pockets, hoping for divine intervention in the form of lock-picking tools I don't own.

My search yields exactly zero spy gadgets. Just my wallet, phone, and a mint I pocketed at the bar. So much for my secret agent career.

"Maybe I could..." I trail off, remembering a scene from some movie where they slid a credit card between the door and frame. Worth a shot.

I slide my platinum card into the crack between door and frame, wiggling it up and down like I've seen in films. The card bends alarmingly but the door remains stubbornly locked.

"Come on, you've got a 100,000 limit. The least you could do is open a door," I grumble at the card.

After thirty seconds of embarrassing scraping sounds, I accept defeat and pocket my now-warped credit card.

My next brilliant idea involves throwing my shoulder against the door, which I immediately reconsider. If I dislocate something, Coach will have my head on a platter. And explaining a shoulder injury from playing amateur spy? Not a conversation I want to have.

"Maybe I could kick it down?" I wonder aloud, eyeing the solid wood skeptically. "That always looks so easy in movies."

I step back, eyeing the door with newfound determination.

It looks solid. Probably solid enough to break my foot if I try to kick it down. But Anika might be in trouble, and I can't just stand here.

"This is going to hurt," I tell myself, mentally preparing to channel my inner action hero. I take two steps back, lift my leg, and...

The door clicks softly and swings open on its own.

I lower my foot and peer into the darkness beyond. The room appears to be some kind of study. Leather-bound books line mahogany shelves, a massive desk dominates one corner, and the faint scent of cigars and expensive booze hangs in the air.

"Hello?" I call, stepping cautiously inside. "Anika?"

Silence greets me as I scan the dark study. My eyes dart to every corner, even checking the ceiling in case someone's pulling a Spider-Man and waiting to pounce. Nothing but ornate crown molding. A grandfather clock ticks ominously in the corner.

"This is getting weird," I mutter, moving deeper into the room.

Something's off. The air feels...disturbed, like someone just left.

I circle the room, checking behind furniture, under the massive desk, feeling increasingly foolish. What am I even doing? Anika's a grown woman who can talk to whoever she wants. Maybe they just moved to another room for privacy.

The thought makes my stomach clench uncomfortably.

Then, I notice it. The bookshelf against the far side of the office isn't quite flush with the wall. A sliver of darkness peeks through where it's slightly ajar.

"You've got to be kidding me," I breathe, approaching the shelf. "A secret passage? Really?"

I peer into the gap between the bookcase and wall. Cool air wafts from the opening, and beyond lies a dark corridor disappearing into shadows.

"This is either the coolest or the creepiest thing I've ever seen," I think, pulling the bookshelf wider. Anika went this way. I'm sure of it.

Here goes nothing. I tap the flashlight icon on my phone

and step inside. The passage stretches ahead, disappearing around a bend.

"Focus on the journey, not the destination," I chant to myself. Unsurprisingly, my grandmother's inspirational quotes aren't quite cutting it right now.

A dim light flickers somewhere deep in the passage. Anika?

I press on through the corridor, quickening my steps.

"Anika?" I call out, voice bouncing off stone walls. "If you can hear me, just know that I'm either rescuing you or making a complete fool of myself. Fifty-fifty at this point."

The passage slopes upward now, and a cool draft brushes against my face, carrying the faint scent of pine and snow. My pace quickens despite the voice in my head asking what exactly my plan is when I find her. Hey, Anika, sorry about that woman draping herself all over me like a cashmere throw. Totally not what it looked like. Also, why did you run off with a Bond villain?

The tunnel gradually widens, and up ahead, I spot a rectangle of silvery light. An exit?

I quicken my pace, nearly tripping over my own feet in my haste. As I approach, the light resolves into what appears to be a doorway leading outside.

I push through and find myself stepping onto a stunning terrace, framed by elegant arched columns and overlooking a sweeping view of the Alps. The night sky stretches above, scattered with stars. And there, silhouetted against the moonlight, stands Anika.

My breath catches in my throat.

She's facing away from me at the edge of a stone balustrade, her hair dancing in the wind, her gown rippling around her slender frame. She hugs herself against the cold, shoulders slightly hunched, looking impossibly small and vulnerable against the vast mountain backdrop.

"Anika?" I call softly, afraid she might disappear if I speak too loudly.

She turns, and something inside me shifts, like a goalie mask being lifted after a long, brutal game. The mountain air rushes into my lungs, sharp and sweet.

"Griffin?" Her voice carries on the wind, uncertain.

She looks like something out of a dream. The kind you wake from with your heart still pounding and your soul aching for something you can't quite name.

My pulse thunders in my ears. My hands actually tremble.

Thank goodness she's alone. No sign of that...guy. Just Anika.

I take a step toward her, the urge to wrap her in my arms nearly overwhelming. I want to bury my face in her hair, breathe her in, tell her that seeing her with another man made me crazy with jealousy. That I don't want to be her dating coach anymore. I want to be the guy she's learning for.

But her expression stops me cold. Those usually warm eyes are winter-lake frozen.

"What are you doing out here?" I ask, closing the distance between us. "And without a coat? You must be freezing."

I shrug out of my jacket and drape it over her shoulders.

The way it engulfs her smaller frame does something primal to my insides. My throat tightens as she pulls it closer around herself, her fingers disappearing in the sleeves.

"Why'd you run off like that?" I ask, trying to keep my tone light despite the worry that's been gnawing at me. "One minute we're having the time of our lives, the next you're gone. Did I do something wrong?"

Anika's laugh is hollow, nothing like her usual warm chuckle. "No, Griffin. I just thought the practice date was over."

"Over? We barely started."

She tugs my jacket tighter around herself, her voice calm but distant. "You seemed...occupied."

"Occupied? What are you—" Then it hits me. "Wait, you mean with that woman at the bar? That wasn't..."

Anika's eyes flick to my cheek, and she points one accusing finger. "You have lipstick. Right there."

My hand flies to my face, finding the exact spot where Elodie planted her kiss. Heat blazes up my neck. I frantically pull out my handkerchief and scrub at my skin.

"It's not what it looks like," I blurt, which, let's be honest, is exactly what guilty people say in movies right before they get dumped.

"That woman...She just grabbed me at the bar and..."

"And what? Fell face-first onto your cheek?"

"Ambushed me!"

Anika raises one perfect eyebrow. "Ambushed you? With her lips?"

"I was trying to find you when she pounced." I'm still scrubbing my face, probably turning it into a red, raw disaster zone. "Is it gone?"

Anika sighs. "Almost. You missed a spot." She points to the corner of my mouth.

"Did I get it now?" I ask, rubbing harder.

"Now you just look like you have a rash."

"I can explain," I start, but Anika holds up a hand.

"It's fine, Griffin." Her smile is polite, distant. The kind she probably gives to annoying customers at the pub. "I understand this wasn't a real date. We both know that."

"She's nobody," I say finally, my voice rough. "And for the record, I wasn't exactly thrilled to see you dancing with Pierce Brosnan's evil twin back there either."

"Who?"

"That guy you were with. The one who dragged you away. You gonna tell me who that was?"

Anika's expression shifts, becoming guarded. "I'm not sure I'm supposed to tell you anything about that."

"Not supposed to...What does that mean?"

Instead of answering, Anika pulls my jacket tighter around her shoulders. The odd way she's acting stirs something ancient and primal in me.

I almost don't recognize myself when I growl, "Did he threaten you?"

It takes her longer to think about that than I care for. "No. I mean, I don't think so."

"Anika, look at me. Did he hurt you? Because I swear, I will hunt him down."

"He didn't hurt me," she says quickly. "It's complicated."

"Complicated how?" I take another step closer, close enough to see the faint freckles across her nose. "Anika, I've been going out of my mind thinking you were in danger."

Her eyebrows shoot up. "In danger? From what?"

"I don't know! Secret passages? Mysterious men? You name it."

Anika's eyes flicker with something I can't read. "Griffin, maybe you should go back to Canada."

"Canada?" My voice rises despite my efforts to keep it level. "Anika, what's going on?"

She looks away, studying the mountains like they hold answers. "Nothing. Everything's fine."

"Then come back inside. I need to tell you something important," I say, stepping closer. "About tonight. What we're really doing here."

Her smile is gracious but guarded. "I'd rather not know too much about what you're doing. Or who you're doing it with."

The way she says it, like she knows something, makes my skin prickle.

Words fail me as I look at Anika. Really look at her. Moonlight catches in her eyes, reflecting flints of silver. Her lips, slightly parted, are tinged blue from the cold. She's never looked more beautiful or more real than she does right now, wrapped in my oversized jacket with her hair a wild tangle around her face.

I've never wanted to kiss anyone more in my entire life.

"Look, just wait inside until I finish some business I need to take care of, then I'll explain everything. Please?"

"Business?" A flash of something darkens her eyes before she schools her expression. "You mean with that woman in the red dress? Is that the 'business' you need to take care of?"

Wait a minute. Is she actually jealous? The thought sends a ridiculous thrill through me despite the gravity of the situation.

The corner of my mouth twitches up. "Are you jealous?"

"I am not." She lifts her chin, defiant.

"You are." I step closer, my heart racing. "Admit it. You like me."

She shrugs with exaggerated casualness. "Sure. You're a nice guy."

"No." I shake my head. "You like me, like me. More than a friend, more than practice dates."

I move forward until her back meets the stone balustrade. My hand finds its way to her jaw, cupping it softly. Her pulse jumps beneath my fingers. "Admit to me what you really think of me."

"I am Swiss," she says primly. "I have a neutral opinion of you."

I can't help but chuckle at her stubborn wit, even as my heart hammers against my ribs. "Well, I'm Canadian." I lean closer, drawn by the warmth of her skin and the challenge in her eyes. "So I feel the need to apologize for what I'm about to do."

Her eyes shimmer. "And what's that?"

"Give you the best kiss of your life."

"I've never been kissed," she says triumphantly, as if she's just won an argument. "So the bar is pretty low."

That stops me. I pull back slightly, searching her face. "Never?"

She shakes her head, a flush creeping up her neck.

I'm reeling. Her first kiss. The responsibility of that nearly knocks me sideways. "Then I better make it count."

I lean in slowly, giving her time to pull away or punch me if she wants to. She doesn't. Instead, her eyes flutter closed, long lashes casting shadows on her cheeks.

My lips brush against hers, gentle as a whisper. She's so still I wonder if she's breathing. I press a little firmer, and then...oh! She responds, her mouth softening beneath mine.

The first taste of her is like stepping into sunlight after months of darkness. Sweet, warm, life-giving. Her lips are soft, tentative at first, then increasingly bold as she follows my lead.

I cup her face with both hands now, thumbs brushing her cheekbones.

When she sighs against my mouth, it's like someone's knocked the wind out of me. A sucker punch straight to the solar plexus that leaves me dizzy and desperate for more. Her hands find my chest, fingers curling into my shirt like she needs something to anchor her in this new sensation, bunching the fabric between her knuckles until I can feel the warmth of her palms burning through the material. A small sound escapes her throat, half surprise, half pleasure, that vibrates against my lips and sends liquid heat coursing through my veins like wildfire. Igniting places I'd forgotten existed.

For someone who's never done this before, she's a remarkably fast learner. The initial hesitation in her movements has given way to something more curious, more confident. The way she tilts her head just so, the experimental pressure of her mouth against mine. It's intoxicating, watching her discover this part of herself against my lips, feeling the moment when instinct takes over and her body remembers what her mind never knew.

The world narrows to just this. Her lips against mine, the mountain air sharp in my lungs, her heartbeat racing beneath my palm as it slides to her neck. Nothing else matters.

Just Anika, melting against me like she was made for me.

I pull back just enough to catch my breath, resting my forehead against hers. Her eyes remain closed, lips slightly parted, cheeks flushed.

"You didn't punch me this time," I whisper, tracing the curve of her cheek with my thumb.

Her eyes flutter open, dazed and dark. "I'm still considering it."

I laugh, the sound carried away by the wind. "Worth it."

She smiles then, and something in my chest expands, warm and aching.

This wasn't part of the plan. None of this was part of the plan. I came to Switzerland to play hockey. Not to play spy. And not to fall for a woman who feels like forever in my arms.

"Griffin," she whispers. I love the sound of my name on her lips. "What are we doing?"

"I have no idea," I admit, tucking a strand of hair behind her ear. "But I don't want to stop."

A helicopter's distant whirring breaks the moment. Anika pulls away, wrapping my jacket tighter around herself.

"That's my ride," she says. "I have to go."

But I'm reluctant to leave this moment, this terrace, this

bubble, where nothing exists but us. I take her hand, threading my fingers through hers. "Not yet."

"Griffin, please."

"You can't just leave after...after that."

The helicopter's whirring grows louder, its searchlight sweeping across the terrace.

"I really have to go." She tries to pull her hand away, but I hold fast.

"Why? Because of that guy? Because of what you saw at the bar?" I step closer, ducking my head to meet her eyes. "Or because of what just happened between us?"

She looks away, her freckles like stardust in the moonlight. "All of it."

The mental clock in my head ticks louder. I'm supposed to be meeting Elodie soon for whatever secret spy business we're doing. If I'm late, the whole operation could fall apart. But letting Anika leave like this feels wrong on every level.

"Stay." I tug her gently toward me. "Please. We can leave together if you want. Forget the party, forget everything else."

Her laugh is soft and a little sad. "You can't forget everything else, Griffin. Can you?"

The helicopter hovers closer now, snow swirling around us in its artificial wind. My watch vibrates, announcing the top of the hour.

"Look, I can explain everything," I say, raising my voice over the noise. "Just not right now. Not here."

"I think that's my point." She finally pulls her hand free.

The accusation stings because it's true.

"Okay, yes, I have a meeting I need to get to." I run a hand through my hair, frustrated. "But it's not what you think. I'm not...I wouldn't..."

How do I explain that I'm playing spy without sounding completely insane? Or worse, like I'm making up excuses?

"I'm not above begging," I say finally, dropping to one knee dramatically. "Please, please, please stay. I'll buy you a pony. Two ponies. A whole stable of tiny horses."

A reluctant smile tugs at her lips. "Get up, you lunatic."

"Not until you agree to stay." I grab her hand and press it to my heart. "Feel that? That's what you do to me."

Despite everything, she laughs. A real laugh that crinkles the corners of her eyes.

"I'll learn to yodel. I'll memorize the entire Swiss national anthem. I'll..."

"Stop." She presses her fingers to my lips, and the simple touch sends electricity down my spine. "You're impossible."

"Give me one good reason why you can't stay."

She rolls her eyes. "I'm tired."

"Liar."

The helicopter touches down at the far end of the terrace, its blades slowing just enough for safe boarding. A man in a flight suit jumps out and waves us over.

Anika steps back, creating a gulf between us. "Griffin, you need to leave this party. Now. It's not...safe."

"Not safe?" I echo, frowning. "What did that guy tell you?"

She shakes her head. "I can't...Just trust me, okay?"

"I can't leave yet," I admit, hating the words even as I say them. "I have something I need to finish here."

She studies me for a long moment, then nods like she's made a decision. "Then I can't help you."

The helicopter pilot signals impatiently. Anika slips out of my jacket, pressing it into my hands.

"Anika."

"Goodbye, Griffin." She steps back, the wind whipping her hair around her face. "Thank you for the practice...well, you know."

The way she says it, like our kiss meant nothing, cuts deeper than any hockey stick to the ribs. I watch helplessly as she walks toward the waiting helicopter. She doesn't look back. Not even once.

"Not goodbye," I call after her. "See you later. Tomorrow. At the pub."

She doesn't answer, just climbs into the helicopter with surprising grace for someone in a floor-length gown.

The helicopter lifts off, taking Anika with it, and something in my chest constricts painfully. I stand there long after it disappears into the night sky, clutching my jacket in my hands.

Then, hating myself for it, I run back inside the mansion.

*Every goodbye sounds like a song
you've heard before.*

CHAPTER EIGHTEEN

K issing Griffin McGregor has ruined my life in exactly six different ways, and I'm still counting.

I peek through the tiny gap between the wine rack and the wall, barely breathing as Griffin's silhouette appears outside the frosted window on his way to knock on the pub door. Again. For the third time today.

My heart lodges in my throat.

"He's persistent, I'll give him that," Lars mutters, shuffling his Jass cards like he's done a thousand times before. Lars, Colin, and Evan sit at their usual table, acting as my human shield.

"Shh!" I hiss from my hiding spot. "He'll hear you."

Griffin knocks again, more insistently this time. The sound echoes through the pub, setting off those unwelcome butterflies in my stomach. "Anika? I know you're in there!"

"I don't understand why we're doing this," Evan says, laying down a card. "You two seemed cozy with each other before. What happened at that fancy party?"

What happened? Oh, nothing much. Just mysterious warnings from possible criminals, a femme fatal leaving her lipstick mark on Griffin's face, and a kiss that melted my brain.

"Nothing happened," I lie. "I just need space."

The truth is, I've been hiding from Griffin for three days now. Three days of ducking behind cheese displays at the market and taking alternate hiking routes. Three days of texting "go back to Canada" in various ways. Three days of replaying that kiss over and over until I want to scream into a pillow.

Three days of falling asleep with my fingers pressed to my lips...which is pathetic on levels I don't even want to examine.

Griffin's face appears at the window now, hands cupped around his eyes to see through the glass. I shrink further into my hiding spot, almost knocking over a bottle of schnapps in the process.

"For the love of..." Colin sighs, pushing back his chair. "I'll get rid of him."

Colin shuffles to the door and cracks it open just enough to block entry. I can't see Griffin's face anymore, but his voice carries clearly.

"Hey, I just need to talk to Anika for five minutes," Griffin says, pleading and determined.

"Bar's closed," Colin replies flatly.

"But you guys are in there playing cards," Griffin argues. "The lights are on."

"Private game night."

Lars and Evan exchange amused glances over their cards. They're the only customers I've allowed in today, partly because they're like uncles to me.

"Look, I know she's in there. Her mother said she was working tonight."

I'm going to kill my mother. Slowly. With her own patchouli incense sticks.

"Anika isn't available," Colin says, starting to close the door.

"Wait!" Griffin's foot appears, stopping the door. "Just tell her there's something important she needs to know about—"

"Goodbye, hockey man," Colin interrupts, finally shutting the door with a definitive click.

The lock turns, and he returns to the game like nothing happened, but I can feel all three men's curiosity radiating across the room.

"He looked terrible," Lars comments, not looking up from his cards. "Like a sad puppy."

"He's still out there," Evan reports, peering through the curtains. "Just...standing in the snow. Looking pathetic."

"Good," I mutter, though my stomach twists uncomfortably.

Colin looks up from his cards. "This is getting ridiculous, Anika. Why are you avoiding the boy?"

"I'm not avoiding him," I lie. "I'm just...busy."

Lars snorts. "You're acting like a teenager with her first crush."

"I am not crushing on Griffin McGregor!" I protest too loudly, making all three men explode into laughter.

"Of course not," Colin says, exchanging a look with the others. "That's why you're hiding behind the wine instead of

247

just telling him to go away like you do with every other man who bothers you."

I grab a cloth and aggressively wipe down the already clean bar. "It's complicated."

"Love always is," Evan says sagely.

"It's not love!" I protest too quickly. "It's...concern for his safety."

Lars snorts, which makes me want to throw a rag at him.

I sigh because there's no keeping secrets from these guys. But also because I need to process this whole crazy mess out loud, and I can't talk to my mom about it.

"Okay, I'll tell you, but you are sworn to secrecy, got it?"

The three men exchange knowing looks and cross their hearts, each swearing.

"I mean it," I warn. "This information can't go past these doors."

Lars zips his lips with his fingers and twists them at the corner like he's turning a lock.

"Okay, so there were these people at the gala," I continue, lowering my voice. "They cornered me in the bathroom and warned me that Griffin is mixed up in something dangerous. That he needs to leave Switzerland while he can."

"I do not like this," Evan says tentatively. "What do you mean dangerous?"

"They cornered you in the bathroom?" Lars exclaims. "Did you use your kung fu moves on them?"

"No! Will you let me finish?"

Colin waves his hand. "Carry on."

I clear my throat, buying some time to think of how much to tell them. "All I know is that there were probably bad people at that party. I think the owner of the Canadian hockey team is in some kind of weird cult, because Griffin said he had to go to a secret meeting."

"Freemasons?" Colin wonders aloud, then snaps like he's got the answer. "Illuminati."

"Could be," I say, "Or maybe there were drugs involved."

"Drugs?" Evan's eyebrows shoot up. "What kind of drugs?"

"I don't know," I say. "Pot?"

Lars throws his hands in the air. "Anika! You think your hockey man is a secret pot-smoking cult and THAT's why he's in danger and needs to leave?"

"Like I said. I don't know, really."

"So you hide behind the bar?" Colin raises an eyebrow.

"What else am I supposed to do?" I throw the rag on the counter dramatically. "March up to his cabin and say, 'Hey, some creepy strangers in a bathroom told me you're in danger, so please pack your bags and flee the country'?"

"Yes," all three men say in unison.

I open my mouth to argue, but the sound of something hitting the window makes us all turn. Griffin is standing outside, breath fogging the glass, writing something backward so we can read it from inside.

P-L-E-A-S-E

Then, below that, he repeats it in German.

B-I-T-T-E

"He is learning Swiss German well, really," observes Lars. "It would be a shame if he went back to Canada now."

I've never known a grown man could look like an abandoned puppy until now, but Griffin somehow manages it with devastating effectiveness.

His shoulders slump as he stands outside the window, his fingertips slowly sliding down the glass where he wrote "*BITTE*." The falling snow catches in his hair, making him look like some sort of tragic hero in a foreign film. For a moment, our eyes connect through the frosted pane, and I feel a physical tug in my chest.

He stares through the frosted glass for one more long moment before turning away. Then he's gone, trudging away through the snow with his hands shoved in his pockets.

"That was painful to watch," Evan says, breaking the silence.

"Happy now?" Lars asks, gathering his cards. "You've successfully broken the Canadian."

"I haven't broken anyone," I protest, but the words sound hollow even to me. "He'll be fine. Hockey players are tough."

"Not when it comes to matters of the heart," Evan says with the confidence of someone who's read too many romance novels. "I've never seen a man look so miserable."

"Good thing you're not interested in him," Colin adds with a smirk.

I throw a peanut at his head. "Don't you three have homes to go to?"

"And miss this entertainment?" Lars chuckles. "Besides, we still have half a game to finish."

"*Stöck*!" Colin announces, sliding a card across the table.

"That's not how you announce *Stöck*," Evan snaps. "You have to play both cards first."

"I know the rules," Colin grumbles. "I'm just trying to distract Anika from her broken heart."

"My heart is perfectly intact, thank you very much," I say. "Can we please talk about something else?"

"Like what?" Lars asks, taking a sip of his beer. "The weather? The latest internet gossip? The fact that you're letting the best thing that's happened to you in years walk away because some strangers in a bathroom told you to?"

"Yes!" I exclaim, pointing at him. "Exactly like that last one. Let's not talk about that."

Evan shakes his head. "Anika, when was the last time you were this interested in a man?"

"I'm not."

"Never," Lars interrupts. "The answer is never."

"That's it!" I snap, grabbing their half-empty beer glasses. "You're all cut off."

The three men exchange looks of mock horror.

"You wouldn't," gasps Evan, clutching his chest.

"Try me," I challenge, narrowing my eyes. "One more word about Griffin and you can play your Jass games somewhere else tonight."

Colin raises his hands in surrender. "Fine, fine. But when you're eighty and alone with seventeen cats, remember this conversation."

"One more word of advice and you're all banned for a week."

The threat works. All three men snap their mouths shut and return to their game, murmuring quietly among themselves. I pretend to be absorbed in my work, but my mind keeps replaying Griffin's dejected expression as he walked away. The way his eyes had pleaded with me. The way his lips had felt against mine at the gala...

Kissing a man should not feel like diving into a volcano, but here I am, three days later, still feeling the lava in my veins.

I shake my head to clear it. This is for the best. Whatever Griffin is mixed up in, it's clearly dangerous. Those people at the gala weren't joking. The British man's grip had been too tight, his eyes too serious. And the woman's whispered warnings too specific.

A sharp knock at the door makes me jump.

"For the love of—" I mutter. "He just doesn't give up, does he?"

Läck! I am way too jumpy these days.

"I'll handle it," Lars says, pushing back from the table. "I'll tell him you've moved to Antarctica."

He shuffles to the door, pulling it open with an exaggerated sigh. "*Nein, wir sind geschlossen.*"

But instead of Griffin's voice, I hear a different one. Smooth, cultured, and vaguely familiar.

"You're closed, are you?" he says casually. And he understands German, apparently. "I'm looking for Anika Gisler."

Lars's posture stiffens immediately as the man wedges himself through the door and into the pub.

Even from across the room, I recognize the silhouette. Tall, impeccably dressed, with that same authoritative stance that had cornered me in the bathroom at the gala. The British man. Wilde.

Lars glances back at me, eyebrows raised in silent question.

My stomach drops to my feet. What is he doing here? How did he find me?

Colin and Evan are on their feet now, sensing trouble. Evan discreetly reaches for the cricket bat we keep under the bar for emergencies.

"Don't come any closer," I warn, grabbing a bottle of Kirsch. "I have excellent aim and zero patience left today."

Wilde raises his hands in a placating gesture, but his eyes remain coolly amused. "I merely wish to speak with you, Miss Gisler."

My three self-appointed bodyguards immediately form a human wall between us. Lars puffs out his chest like an angry rooster. Colin crosses his arms, looking more intimidating than a man his age has any right to. Even Evan, who cried during a beer commercial last month, has his fists clenched. These men never feel the need to come to my aid. They know I can handle drunk, handsy customers. But something about Wilde has them on high alert. Or maybe it's what I told them about the pot cult.

"Whatever you're selling, we're not buying," Lars growls.

"Gentlemen," Wilde says, adjusting his cufflinks with casual confidence. "I merely need a moment of Miss Gisler's time."

"And who are you, exactly?" Lars demands.

Wilde's smile is practiced and polite. "An acquaintance."

Lars steps forward, planting himself directly in front of Wilde. "You will leave now."

"I assure you, gentlemen, I'm not here to cause trouble," Wilde says, his voice smooth as aged whisky. "I simply need a word."

"And I need a yacht in Monaco," Colin retorts. "We don't always get what we want."

I should be terrified, but there's something oddly comforting about three middle-aged guys ready to throw down for my honor. Still, I know Wilde isn't leaving without saying whatever he came to say.

"It's fine," I assure them.

The three men exchange doubtful glances but don't budge.

"You know this man?" Evan asks, looking skeptical.

"Well, not exactly." I give them a reassuring nod. "You can stand down. But don't go too far."

Lars narrows his eyes at Wilde. "We'll be right here. Watching."

"How reassuring," Wilde murmurs, straightening his already perfect tie.

The Jass players reluctantly retreat to their table, making a show of rearranging their chairs to face the bar. Evan places the cricket bat across his lap.

"I'd prefer to speak privately," Wilde says, his gaze sliding meaningfully toward the trio.

"No," I reply, crossing my arms. "They stay. Consider them my emotional support senior citizens."

Colin makes an offended noise from his table. "I'm only fifty-eight!"

Wilde's expression remains carefully neutral. "Very well."

"Also, there's a two-drink minimum," I add, slapping a cocktail napkin on the bar.

Wilde's mouth twitches. "I don't drink alcohol."

"Lucky for you, I serve more than just alcohol." I grab a bottle of Elmer Citro, cracking it open and setting it in front of him with a deliberate *thunk*.

Wilde glances at the green bottle, then at the Jass players (who are making no pretense of not listening), before finally sliding onto a barstool with the careful precision of someone who calculates every move.

"They're harmless," I say, following his gaze. "Unless you try anything weird. Then they'll beat you with playing cards. It's surprisingly painful."

"I'm sure," Wilde murmurs, taking a cautious sip of the citrus soda. His eyebrows lift slightly. "This is...unexpectedly refreshing."

"I know," I say. "Now, what are you doing in my bar? You have five minutes."

Wilde leans forward and looks me directly in the eyes. "His Majesty's Secret Service requires your cooperation."

Luck favors the stubborn.

CHAPTER NINETEEN

The Mountaineer rail through the Canadian Rockies is nice but it can't compare to gliding through the Alps to St. Moritz on this luxurious express train. I've done some pretty wild things in my life, but this takes the cake. Let alone how I'm currently sitting across from a real-life Bond Girl, getting briefed on the logistics of an espionage mission at a high-stakes poker game that I absolutely cannot afford to lose. Just your average Thursday.

Through panoramic windows that stretch from floor to curved ceiling, the snowcapped mountains parade past, and I wish Anika was here to share this view with me.

"Beautiful, isn't it?" Elodie coos, swirling her champagne. Her red fingernails match her lipstick, which matches the ruby pendant nestled at her throat.

"Yeah," I manage, tearing my gaze away from the window. "Hard to believe I'm about to commit fraud with this backdrop."

"It's not fraud when you're stopping a criminal, Griffin."

Easy for her to say. She's not the one about to go up against a guy who apparently runs a criminal empire disguised as a hockey franchise.

"I'm just wondering if there's a refund policy on this whole spy adventure," I mutter, watching a pristine alpine lake flash by. "Like, can I exchange it for something with less potential for...dying? Maybe something in the light reconnaissance department?"

Elodie laughs, but I'm getting more anxious the closer to St Moritz we get.

Our personal concierge approaches with a tray of appetizers that look too artistic to eat.

"The amuse-bouche features local Alpine cheese with honey glaze and black truffle," the concierge explains, which is fancy-speak for tiny portion, enormous price tag.

I thank him, wondering if my bespoke suit hides the home-grown Canadian hockey kid in me.

Once he's gone, Elodie leans forward, her décolletage strategically visible. "You seem tense, Griffin," she says, setting down her glass. "Relax. Enjoy the journey."

"I'm fine," I hiss, lowering my voice to a harsh whisper. "It's not like TEN MILLION FREAKING EUROS were just wired to my bank account or anything."

"Trust me," she cuts me off with a dismissive wave. "By the weekend, you'll be a hero. The money isn't real to these people anyway. It's just chips in their game."

"And I just have to...win?" I take another gulp of champagne.

"Let's go over the plan again," Elodie says, delicately selecting a slice of cheese. "When we arrive in St. Moritz, we'll check into separate rooms at the Palace Hotel. At nine, we meet our contact in the casino lobby."

"And they'll give me the...ear thing?"

She smiles indulgently. "The communication device, yes. It's virtually undetectable. Our surveillance team will have eyes on all cards at the table via hidden cameras. They'll feed you information through the earpiece."

"So I'm cheating," I say flatly.

Elodie's perfect eyebrows arch. "You're evening the playing field. Chase has been cheating for years. He's stolen pensions, life savings, children's college funds. Your hockey teammates' investments. Think of all the families who lost their savings."

I nod reluctantly. She's not wrong. But that thought still doesn't settle the churning in my stomach. How do secret agents sleep at night? I can barely get to sleep after a rough hockey game.

Elodie dabs her mouth with a napkin. "The FIS has been tracking Chase's financial movements for months," she explains. "This tournament is his attempt to recoup losses from his offshore accounts that are beginning to collapse."

The train curves around a mountain, revealing a valley so perfect it looks photoshopped. I should be enjoying this view. It's literally world-famous. But all I can think about is Anika. The way she looked at me before getting on that helicopter. The way she's been avoiding me since.

"Tell me about the tournament structure," I say, forcing my mind back to the mission.

"Texas hold 'em. Ten players. Ten million buy-in." Elodie's voice is all business now. "The final hand wins the whole pot."

I blow out a whistle. "That's...a hundred million euros."

"Indeed." She smiles thinly. "Chase has invited only his top investors. People who have the most to lose if his scheme is exposed."

"And what happens after I win?" I ask. "Assuming I do."

"You'll transfer the winnings to an account we provide. The FIS will have what they need to bring down Chase's entire operation and force him to cooperate in exchange for leniency."

I nod, but something still feels off. Probably just nerves. I can't even win at Jass.

"When this is over," she continues, "The money recovered will be returned to the investors."

"And my role will remain confidential?"

"Completely. You'll return to your hockey career, your cabin in Grächen, and your...bartender."

The way she says "bartender" makes my jaw clench. I think about Anika again. Her strength, her wit, the way she punched me after our almost-kiss. The memory makes me smile despite everything.

"Something amusing?" Elodie asks.

"Just thinking about home," I reply.

The train begins to slow as we approach another scenic stop. Outside, a postcard-perfect Swiss village nestles against the mountainside.

"We arrive in St. Moritz in two hours," Elodie says, checking her phone. "Any questions before we get there?"

Oh, I have SO many questions, but most of them aren't productive.

"What if I get caught?"

"You won't."

"But if I do?"

Elodie sips her champagne, her eyes unreadable. "Then FIS will disavow all knowledge of you, and you'll be on your own in a Swiss prison."

I laugh, then realize she's not joking. "Great."

"One more thing," she says. "No matter what happens over the next two nights, stick to the plan. No improvising."

"No improvising. Got it."

"And trust no one but me."

The train lurches slightly as we round a bend. I check my reflection in the train window. The man staring back at me looks like someone who knows what he's doing. It's a good disguise. Even though I'm used to wearing suits for the game, this one feels tighter. More constricting. I slide a finger in the collar and tug to ease the discomfort.

"You're fidgeting again," Elodie observes, crossing her legs with deliberate slowness. The slit in her dress reveals a dangerous amount of thigh.

"I'm not fidgeting. I'm...adjusting."

"And what exactly are you adjusting?" Her voice drops to a husky whisper.

"My entire life choices that led me to this moment," I mutter, reaching for my water glass instead of the champagne. I need a clear head.

Elodie leans forward, elbows on the table, chin resting on her interlaced fingers. "Tell me about yourself, Griffin McGregor. The man behind the hockey mask."

"Not much to tell. I play pro hockey, and love my Tim Hortons coffee. I'm a simple guy."

"Come now." She traces the rim of her glass with one perfectly manicured finger. "A professional athlete with your... physique must have quite the interesting life."

I shift uncomfortably. "Nope. Just sports, movies, and video games."

"I don't believe that for a second." Her foot brushes against my leg under the table. Not an accident.

"What about you?" I deflect, moving my leg out of her reach. "What does a secret agent do on her days off? Defuse bombs for fun? Parachute into restricted airspace?"

Elodie laughs, a practiced sound. "A girl has to have some secrets."

"So that's a yes on the bombs, then?"

The waiter arrives with our main course, saving me from whatever was happening with her foot. I focus intensely on cutting my steak.

"Tell me, Griffin," she says, her voice dropping to a sultry hum. "What's your tell?"

"My what now?"

"Your tell." Her eyes narrow playfully. "Every poker player has one. That little unconscious habit that gives away when you're bluffing."

"I don't have a tell."

"Everyone has a tell." She takes a deliberate sip of champagne, her eyes never leaving mine. "For instance, when you lie, your left eyebrow twitches ever so slightly."

My hand flies to my eyebrow before I can stop it.

Elodie chuckles softly. "I was guessing. But now I know."

"That's not fair," I protest, feeling my face heat up.

"Poker isn't fair. Neither is espionage." She studies me for a moment. "You are just too wholesome."

"Is that supposed to be an insult? Because where I come from, that's basically a compliment."

"In my line of work...it's a liability."

"Well, good thing I have you to teach me the finer points of dishonesty," I mutter.

"Indeed." She grins playfully. "Let's practice. Tell me a lie."

"What?"

"Tell me something that isn't true. Make me believe it."

I stare at her, bewildered. "Right now?"

"Yes, right now. Convince me."

I take a deep breath. "Okay. I...actually hate hockey. I only play because my parents forced me into it as a child and now it's my only skill."

Elodie's perfectly sculpted eyebrows rise. "Your left eyebrow twitched again."

"It did not!"

"It absolutely did. Try again. And you don't have to recite a novel. Short and sweet is best."

I sigh, running a hand through my hair. "Fine. I'm allergic to strawberries."

"Better." She nods. "But still not convincing. You're too stiff."

"This is ridiculous," I grumble. "I'm a goalie, not a spy."

"Tonight, you're both." She leans forward again, her voice dropping to a whisper. "Do you know what makes a good liar, Griffin?"

"An absence of moral fiber?"

"Belief." Her eyes lock with mine. "The best liars believe their own stories, if only for a moment."

The train enters a tunnel, plunging our cabin into momentary darkness. When the lights flicker back on, Elodie has moved to sit beside me instead of across.

"What are you doing?" I ask, suddenly aware of how small our private compartment feels.

"Testing a theory." She's close enough that I can smell her perfume. It's something expensive and sophisticated. "You see, I need to know if you'll break under pressure."

"I'm a goaltender. Pressure is my comfort zone."

"Is it?" Her hand lands on my thigh. "Because right now, your pulse is racing."

I carefully remove her hand. "That's just my natural reaction to possible imprisonment and financial ruin."

Elodie laughs, genuine this time. "You really are something else, Griffin McGregor."

"So I've been told."

"You're not what I expected," Elodie says.

"Let me guess. You were expecting James Bond, got Mister Rogers instead?"

"On the contrary." Her eyes travel over me like she's memorizing every detail. "Most men in your position would be... taking advantage of the situation."

"My position being...potential prison inmate if this goes sideways?"

She smiles. "I meant a handsome man, alone on a luxury train with a woman who finds him attractive."

I nearly choke on air. "Subtle."

"I'm never subtle when I see something I want." She places her hand on mine. Her touch is cool, calculated.

I gently withdraw my hand. "I'm flattered, but...no. Just no." I stand up abruptly. "If you'll excuse me, I need to use the restroom," I announce, desperate to escape this awkward situation. "Too much champagne."

"Of course." She slides back to her seat, crossing her legs. "Don't be long. We have strategy to discuss."

I nod and make my hasty retreat down the swaying corridor of the luxury train car.

The bathroom at the end of the car is mercifully empty and ridiculously fancy. I splash cold water on my face and stare at myself in the mirror. "What have you gotten yourself into?" I mutter. "Just wanted to play hockey, ended up in a spy movie."

After a few deep breaths, I exit the bathroom feeling

marginally more composed…until a man materializes from nowhere, blocking my path back to the compartment.

He's tall and bulky with close-cropped black hair. Built like a defenseman, with broad shoulders and a neck thick as a tree trunk. His face is so comically fierce, if he were an actor, he'd definitely get typecast as henchman number three. Right down to the thin scar that runs from his left temple to his jaw. And of course he's wearing all black, probably so he can hide bloodstains.

Also, he's holding a knife, pointing directly at me.

Not a cute little pocketknife either. This is a serious, *killed people in seventeen countries* kind of blade.

"Um, I think you have the wrong guy," I stammer, backing up slowly.

His face remains expressionless.

"Hockey man," he says in a thick accent I can't place. "You come with me now."

"I'm actually good right here, thanks," I reply, looking desperately for an escape route.

He responds by lunging at me with the knife.

I yelp and stumble backward, the blade missing my chest by inches. Thank goodness for goalie reflexes!

"Whoa! Personal space, buddy!" I shout, backing up as he advances.

He slashes again, this time aiming for my throat. I duck, and the knife embeds itself in the wooden panel behind me. While he's yanking it free, I bolt down the corridor in the opposite direction from my compartment.

"Help! Crazy knife guy!" I yell, but no one seems to notice.

The train takes a curve, throwing me off balance. I stumble into an empty compartment, which turns out to be a stroke of bad luck as Scarface follows me in, closing the door behind him.

"Look, I think there's been a misunderstanding," I try, raising my hands in surrender. "I'm just a hockey player."

"You talk too much," he growls, reaching into his jacket again.

This time he pulls out what looks like brass knuckles, but with nasty little spikes on them. Great. Because the knife wasn't enough.

He swings at my face. I duck, and his fist smashes into the window, cracking the glass. While he's momentarily stuck, I dive between his legs like I'm sliding to catch a puck.

I scramble to my feet and burst through the compartment door, sprinting down the corridor. Behind me, I hear him roar with frustration.

The dining car is ahead. I dash through it, dodging waiters carrying trays of champagne and apologizing profusely as I go, because I'm still a nice Canadian, even when running for my life.

I glance back to see Scarface hot on my heels, now flinging what appear to be honest-to-goodness ninja stars. One embeds itself in a cheese cart, sending a wheel of Gruyère flying.

"Sorry about the cheese!" I call out, ducking as another star whizzes past my ear.

I reach the end of the dining car and burst through to the next carriage—a sleeper section with narrow corridors. Perfect for a guy my size trying to outrun an assassin.

I squeeze past a couple returning to their compartment. "Excuse me, pardon me, killer behind us, maybe lock your door!"

The assassin shoves them aside and pulls out yet another weapon. Some kind of collapsible baton that extends with a flick of his wrist. He swings it at my head. I duck, and it smashes into a light fixture, sending sparks raining down.

"Do you just have an entire weapons store under your shirt?" I yell.

Somehow, I make it through the door at the end of the car, finding myself on one of those little platforms between train cars. Cold air hits me like a slap, and the ground below is rushing by at terrifying speed. Is this where I'm supposed to climb to the roof? Because my shoes have absolutely no grip.

Scarface bursts through the door behind me. His expression hasn't changed at all. He looks almost bored. Like he's thinking about his tax returns while trying to murder me.

Do villains file their taxes? I feel like that was a conversation James Bond had in one of the films.

"Can we talk about this?" I gasp, pressing myself against the railing. "I'm sure whatever I did to offend you, we can work it out like adults!"

He responds by swinging at my face.

I duck, and his momentum carries him forward. For one horrifying second, I think he's going to topple over the railing, and I actually reach out to grab him because, apparently, my survival instincts are broken. But he catches himself and whirls around, now blocking my access to the next car.

"Look, I'm sure you're a nice guy under all that leather!" I shout over the roaring wind.

He swipes at me again, and I jump back, my heel catching on something. I stumble, arms windmilling, and fall backward, and something triggers the door to open for me.

I land hard on my back.

This is another dining car, but a little less fancy, filled with passengers enjoying their lunch. Every head turns to stare at me sprawled on the floor.

"Sorry!" I call out, scrambling to my feet. "Just...enthusiastic about the dessert course!"

The henchman steps through the doorway, somehow making the simple act of walking look menacing.

In a panic, I look around for anything I can to defend myself and grab a silver serving tray off a nearby table and fling it like a frisbee. It spins through the air and...actually hits him square in the face.

He staggers back, giving me just enough time to sprint down the aisle.

"Sorry! Coming through! Emergency!" I shout, dodging passengers and knocking over some glasses. The resulting crash buys me a few precious seconds as the assassin has to navigate the sea of broken glass.

I burst through another door, finding myself in a luggage compartment. Stacks of suitcases line the walls, and there's nowhere to go but forward.

Scarface appears in the doorway behind me, a thin line of blood trickling from his nose where my improvised projectile hit him. He looks annoyed now, which is somehow more terrifying than his previous blank expression.

"Okay," I pant, backing up against the far wall. "Let's be reasonable here. Whatever they're paying you, I'm sure we can—"

He throws a knife.

I drop to the floor on pure instinct, and the blade embeds itself in the wall where my head was a split-second ago.

"That was EXTREMELY unnecessary!" I yelp.

He reaches into his jacket and, because the universe hates me, pulls out another knife.

I grab the nearest suitcase and hold it up like a shield just as he lunges. The knife punctures the leather, stopping inches from my face.

I drop the suitcase and grab the closest weapon I can find, which turns out to be a pink Hello Kitty umbrella.

"Stay back!" I brandish the umbrella, totally not as calm and collected as Colin Firth in the *Kingsmen* movie. His umbrella was bulletproof. "I'm warning you;, this opens with ONE CLICK!"

Scarface tilts his head, unimpressed.

"You die now," he announces.

"Can I at least know why?" I plead, swinging the umbrella. "Is it because I beat the Davos team last week? Their fans are passionate, but this seems excessive!"

He lunges. I sidestep. Barely.

"Can we just..."

The assassin takes out another knife.

"Seriously? How many of those do you have?"

I frantically look around for an escape route, but the door behind me is locked. Scarface is blocking the only way out.

"I'm really not worth killing," I babble. "I'm Canadian. The most dangerous thing I've ever done is eat gas station sushi!"

He cracks his neck left, then right in that universal bad-guy gesture.

This is it. I'm going to die on a luxury train in Switzerland.

I close my eyes and prepare for impact. They say right before you die, your whole life flashes before your eyes. But all I can think of is Anika. At least I got to kiss her. Once.

Then suddenly...CRASH!

The compartment door flies open behind Scarface, and a blur of red fingernails spins into the room. It's Elodie.

She launches into a spinning kick that connects with Scarface's jaw, sending him staggering sideways. Her evening gown somehow transforms into an outfit perfectly suited for combat, the slit in her dress now practical rather than just seductive.

"Duck!" she shouts.

I drop to the floor as she flips over my head, her stiletto heel catching Scarface under the chin. Ouch, that'll be another scar.

He quickly recovers and swings at her, but she catches his wrist mid-strike, twists it at an angle, and follows with an elbow to his throat.

"Should I...help?" I call out, watching as she somersaults over his shoulders.

"Stay!" she grunts, deflecting a punch that leaves a dent in the metal wall panel.

"I'm not a dog," I protest, then immediately duck back down.

Scarface, now full of rage, grabs Elodie by the throat, lifting her off the ground. I scramble to my feet, ready to tackle him, but Elodie wraps her legs around his arm, twists her body, and somehow flips him to the floor. But he grabs her ankle as he falls, pulling her down with him. He's on top of her now, throwing punches. But Elodie is quick, evading his blows.

I throw the umbrella at him, which bounces off his shoulder lamely, but at least it affords Elodie enough of a distraction to break free. She grabs the Hello Kitty umbrella and cracks it over his head, snapping it in two. Now I'm feeling sorry for the poor kid who will be very sad without her umbrella.

Henchman staggers back, finally showing signs of slowing down. But then he lunges at Elodie, catching the fabric of her dress and tearing it.

Time stands still as Elodie looks down at her dress and slowly looks back up at the assassin. Then with rage she had clearly been holding back, she pounces.

"This. Was. Valentino." Each word is punctuated by a devastating strike. Throat, kidney, knee.

Scarface stumbles back, searching his pockets for more weapons. But it seems he's fresh out.

Elodie catches her breath and with a steady, deadly voice says, "I've had quite enough of this."

She kicks off her heels in one smooth motion, sending one of them flying directly into his forehead.

I spot a fire extinguisher mounted on the wall and make a dash for it. "Elodie! Catch!"

I yank it free and toss it toward her, but Scarface intercepts it midair and swings it at Elodie's head.

She ducks, and the extinguisher smashes into the window behind her, cracking the glass.

"Sorry!" I call out. "I was trying to help!"

"Your help is noted!" she shouts back, delivering a rapid sequence of punches to Scarface's ribs. He staggers back, momentarily dazed, and trips, arms windmilling, and crashes into the already-cracked window. The glass spiderwebs further but holds.

The assassin hangs suspended in the shattered frame, jaw slack with surprise. Then Elodie pokes him in the chest with one perfectly pointed fingernail and lets gravity do the rest.

With curses that fade quickly into the distance, he disappears from view.

Elodie stands at the broken window, hair whipping in the wind, looking like a model in a music video.

"Well," she says, turning to me with perfect composure. "That was inconvenient."

I stare at her, mouth hanging open. "You just...He's...Did you kill him?"

Elodie brushes a strand of hair back into place. "He'll survive. Probably."

"Probably?!"

She shrugs, retrieving her heels. "Men like him. They are...resilient."

I stare at the broken window, then back at her. "You pushed him off a moving train!"

"Would you prefer I'd let him stab you?"

"But...the...window..." I sputter.

"Yes, it is quite drafty," she says, straightening her dress. "Come along, Griffin. We have a poker game to prepare for."

The secret to poker is smiling
when you shouldn't.

CHAPTER TWENTY

After our train adventure, Elodie and I arrived in St. Moritz with just enough time for me to be fitted with my spy gear. A nearly invisible earpiece that makes me feel like I have a mosquito permanently lodged in my ear canal. Agents Bruderlin and Showalter are in a secret room guiding me through tonight's events along with a professional poker player named Victor Hahn.

"Ready?" Elodie asks, adjusting my bow tie. She's acting far too familiar for my taste, but I suppose that's the undercover ruse.

"As ready as a goalie facing a five-on-three power play," I mutter.

She smiles like she understands the reference, but I know she doesn't. "Remember, I'll be right beside you. Your lady luck."

Our tournament is in a private room in the Casino St. Moritz. Two men guard a set of mahogany doors. They check our invitations, then step aside to let us enter.

The space is intimate but imposing. Dark wood paneling, plush carpet that swallows sound, and at its center, a sunken area with a large oval table covered in green felt. A bar wraps along the far side.

A man in a tailored suit approaches us. "Mr. McGregor, we've been expecting you. I am Joseph, the floor manager. The game begins in fifteen minutes."

"Thank you," I say as Joseph directs us farther into the room.

My earpiece crackles to life. "Testing, testing. Griffin, this is Agent Showalter. Can you hear me?"

I give a subtle nod, hoping the camera they've told me about catches it.

"Good. Don't respond verbally unless you're alone. Just scratch your chin if you understand."

I reach up casually and scratch my chin.

"Perfect. We're all set. The cameras are operational."

Eight players are already seated, each with a small mountain of chips before them.

And there, at the far end, sits Malcolm Chase, looking like the cat that ate the canary, washed it down with cream, and is now eyeing the goldfish. His silver-flecked hair is slicked back, and his eyes narrow when they land on me. He adjusts his gold cufflinks and gives me a smile laced with vitriol.

"Ah, McGregor," he says, his voice carrying across the room. "I was beginning to think you'd changed your mind."

"Wouldn't miss it," I reply, channeling every ounce of confidence I've ever felt making a save in overtime.

The floor manager gestures to the one empty chair. "Mister McGregor, if you please."

Elodie gives my arm a squeeze. "For luck," she whispers, pressing a kiss to my cheek that feels like a branding iron.

To Malcolm's right sits a Middle Eastern man with a beard trimmed like a topiary. He nods at me with cool assessment.

Next to him is the only woman at the table. A statuesque blonde with ice-blue eyes. She wears a simple black dress with a diamond choker. She kind of reminds me of Uma Thurman.

"That's Katarina Volkov," whispers the voice in my ear. "Russian oil heiress. Don't let her looks deceive you."

On my left, a young Korean man is lounging back in his chair, thumbs flying over his phone's screen.

"The man on your left is Ye-jun Song. Social media influencer. All he does is travel around the world playing in poker tournaments. That's pretty much his full-time job."

A gaggle of young Korean women (probably his entourage), watch him from across the room. Also glued to their phones.

And then, I notice the man taking his seat across from me looking impeccably British in a tailored suit. He's the guy from the gala who danced with Anika. The one who took off with her and sent her through that secret passageway. He catches my eye and gives me a barely perceptible nod. I don't like him. Not one bit.

Joseph, the floor manager, begins his spiel.

"Ladies and gentlemen, the game is no-limit Texas hold

'em. Five communal cards, two in the hole. Buy-in has been confirmed at ten million euros per player."

Ten million euros. Right. Totally fine. With nothing but plaques and chips stacked up in front of me, I can just pretend it's not real.

Joseph presents himself on top of the landing. "The banker, Monsieur Gerhardt, represents Credit Suisse and will be holding the stakes in escrow."

A thin man with wire-rimmed glasses steps forward, holding a sleek metal briefcase. "Good evening. I will be overseeing the funds for tonight's game." He places the briefcase on a small table beside the floor manager. "Each player has deposited ten million euros. Additional buy-ins of five million will be available by electronic transfer only. The funds will remain in escrow until the winner enters their password into the secure terminal."

He opens the briefcase, revealing a computer screen and keyboard. "The winner's funds will be transferred to any account of their choosing upon verification of their personal password."

He turns to the table. "We will proceed alphabetically. Mr. Chase, please be the first to enter your password."

Malcolm stands and approaches the briefcase. Gerhardt turns it away from prying eyes as Malcolm types. I catch a slight smirk on his face as he finishes.

"Monsieur Durand," the banker calls next. The man who danced with Anika stands up. So that's his name. Unless he's operating under a secret cover. Not that it matters to me. Whoever he really is will have the pleasure of getting acquainted with my fist later tonight. I shoot laser eyes into the back of his head as he hunches over to type in his password.

Elodie takes her place behind my chair, her hand resting

lightly on my shoulder. Her perfume is too strong for my taste. I prefer a woman with a natural scent.

My mind flashes to Anika. How her eyes crinkle when she laughs, how she brandished that trout the first time we met. What would she think if she could see me now?

"Mr. McGregor," the banker announces, snapping me back to reality.

I approach the briefcase, staring at the keyboard. What would a super-spy use as a password? What would be impossible to guess?

"Remember, something you can recall under pressure," Showalter whispers in my ear.

My fingers hover over the keys. Then I smile, thinking of Anika and type: H-O-P-P-S-C-H-W-I-I-Z

"Password accepted," the banker confirms.

I return to my seat, my heart hammering against my ribs like a slap shot. The chips in front of me represent more money than I've ever seen in one place. And somehow, I'm supposed to win it all while pretending I know what I'm doing.

"Breathe, McGregor," Showalter says. "We've got your back."

Once all the players have entered their passwords, the dealer announces, "The game will commence momentarily."

"Remember," Elodie whispers in my ear, her breath warm against my skin. "Everyone has a tell. Find it."

"The man to your right is Cletus Beauregard," Showalter informs me through the earpiece. "A Texan business mogul known for aggressive betting when he has middle pairs."

I glance at the stern-faced man with a Stetson cowboy hat, who nods curtly.

Then the dealer begins to shuffle.

"Blinds, please," the dealer announces. "Small blind, five thousand. Big blind, ten thousand."

I glance down at my chips, stacked in neat columns.

"Don't worry," Showalter says. "We've got eyes on everyone's cards. Just follow our lead."

The dealer slides two cards face down in front of me.

"Good luck, gentlemen," Chase says, raising his glass of scotch. "May the best man...or woman...win."

Or the man with the best surveillance equipment, I think.

"Play conservatively," Victor, the poker expert instructs. "Fold early. We're establishing your pattern."

I peek at my cards: seven of clubs, two of diamonds. Garbage.

"Fold," Victor confirms.

I toss my cards face down before the betting even reaches me. Durand studies me briefly, then returns his attention to his own hand.

The next hand brings me a queen and a jack, both hearts.

"Call the big blind, nothing more," Victor says through the earpiece.

I push forward chips worth one hundred thousand euros. The flop comes: Ten of hearts, Ace of spades, Three of diamonds.

"Check and fold if there's a raise."

I check. Katarina bets two hundred thousand. I fold, even though I had a potential straight draw. The woman smiles thinly at me.

"Good," whispers Victor. "Let them think you're cautious."

The dealer shuffles the cards and deals again.

I lift the corner of my cards just enough to see an Ace of hearts and a King of diamonds.

"Big slick," whispers Victor in my ear. "Raise three times the big blind."

I push forward a stack of chips. "Thirty thousand."

Malcolm's eyes flicker to mine, assessing. The Russian

heiress folds immediately. The Middle Eastern man calls. Malcolm raises to fifty thousand.

"Call," the voice instructs. "Don't show too much strength yet."

I match Malcolm's bet, and we watch as the dealer lays down the flop: Queen of hearts, Jack of hearts, Seven of clubs.

"You've got a straight draw and a flush draw," Victor says. "Check and see what Chase does."

I tap the table. Malcolm bets seventy-five thousand.

"Call again. You've got too many outs to fold."

The turn card is the Ten of Hearts. I now have a royal flush draw. The best possible hand if another heart comes, or a King or Ace.

"Check again," instructs Victor. "Let him hang himself."

I check. Malcolm pushes forward a stack of red chips. "One hundred fifty thousand."

"Raise to three hundred thousand," says Victor. "Show some aggression."

I count out the chips and slide them forward. Malcolm's eyebrow twitches. Oh! That's the first tell I've seen from him.

The river card is the Nine of Hearts.

"Call," the voice says without hesitation.

I push my chips forward. "I call."

Malcolm studies me for a long moment, then folds his cards face down. The dealer pushes the pot toward me, and I rake in the chips, trying not to smile too broadly.

"You're doing great," Elodie whispers, her hand squeezing my shoulder. "Keep it up."

That's when the room seems to shift on its axis.

The casino doors open, and Anika walks in. She's wearing a sleek black dress that hugs every curve, her hair is swept up, exposing the elegant line of her neck.

My mouth goes dry. Time stands still.

I can't focus. Not when Anika is walking across the room with deliberate grace, every eye following her progress. She doesn't look at me directly, but I know she's aware of my presence. There's a confidence in her stride that I haven't seen before. A subtle power that makes my heart race.

She passes behind my chair without acknowledgment, and I swear I feel the air crackle.

Then she circles the table and stops behind Durand. She leans down, her lips almost touching his ear as she whispers something. He nods once, his expression unchanged, his eyes never leaving his cards.

I grip my cards so tightly they bend. What is she doing here? And with him? My stomach churns with jealousy. Is this why she's been avoiding me? Has she been with this guy all along?

Anika straightens, gives Durand's shoulder a familiar squeeze, then glides to the bar where she orders a drink with a graceful gesture.

"Griffin!" the voice hisses. "It's your bet."

I blink, realizing the table is waiting for me. I glance down at my cards, then at the flop. I've completely missed what's been played.

"Fold," the voice in my ear says urgently. "You're distracted. Fold and regroup."

I toss my cards face down. "Fold."

Malcolm smirks across the table, clearly noticing my sudden change in demeanor. "Losing your nerve, McGregor?"

I force a smile. "Just getting started, Chase."

But my eyes drift back to Anika at the bar.

I'm suddenly sick of this whole charade. I wave the barman over. "Double shot of tequila. Añejo. No lime...Please."

Elodie's clicks her tongue. "Tequila? What happened to your martini, shaken not stirred?" There's a trace of amusement in her tone.

"Left it on the train with that assassin," I mutter, keeping my eyes fixed on Anika.

Elodie jabs my shoulder as if to shut me up even though I'm sure no one heard the assassin comment except the FIS agents listening in.

"Deal," Malcolm announces, his voice cutting through my distraction.

The cards slide across the felt. I pick mine up. Pocket aces. The best starting hand in poker.

"Raise to fifty thousand," Victor whispers urgently in my ear.

I glance at my cards again, then at Anika, with an intensity that makes my stomach knot.

"I fold," I announce, tossing my cards face down.

"What?" the voice in my ear explodes. "You had pocket aces!"

I casually reach up and adjust my ear, dislodging the device just enough to muffle the tirade.

Malcolm Chase chuckles. "The pressure getting to you already, McGregor? We've barely begun."

"Just stretching my legs," I say, standing just as the barman arrives with my tequila. I down it in one gulp, welcoming the burn that travels down my throat and settles in my empty stomach. The warmth spreads through my limbs, giving me a false sense of courage.

I make a beeline for the bar, where Anika is perched on a stool, her back deliberately turned to the poker table. She's sipping something amber-colored and pretending I don't exist.

"What are you doing here?" I ask, trying to keep my voice low and controlled.

She turns slowly, her expression perfectly neutral. "Having a drink."

"You know what I mean." I move closer, hissing under my

breath. "You've been avoiding me for days, and now you show up here? With him?"

Her eyes flick briefly to Durand, then back to me. "I'm not with anyone."

"Really? Because it sure looked like you two were pretty cozy."

A flash of irritation crosses her face. "This isn't the place, Griffin."

"Then where is the place? Your pub, where you won't let me in? Your phone, where you won't answer my calls? I thought we had something, Anika."

A flicker of something...regret? Longing...? crosses her face before she masters it. "You don't understand what's happening."

"Then explain it to me. Because from where I'm standing, it looks like you're getting awfully friendly with that guy."

She sets down her glass with a soft clink. "Why does it matter to you?"

"Why does it matter?" I repeat, my voice dropping to a dangerous whisper. I step closer, close enough that I can smell her perfume. Something subtle and clean, not the cloying musky bomb Elodie bathes in. "It matters because every time I close my eyes, I see you. It matters because seeing you with him makes me want to flip that poker table and carry you out of here over my shoulder. Because ever since you broke into my cabin with that stabby attitude, I haven't been able to think straight."

Anika's lips part in surprise at my intensity. "I'm not stabby."

"Look, I'm in the middle of a gagillion-euro poker game, and all I can focus on is the way you're whispering in that guy's ear." I lean in so there's practically no space between us. "So yeah, it matters to me."

"You can't just say things like that," she hisses.

"I haven't been able to think of anything else...but kissing you again," I admit.

Anika's breath hitches, but she keeps her composure. "That was practice."

"For who? Thomas? Or that guy over there glaring a hole in the back of my head?"

"Griffin, you need to go back to your game." She glances over my shoulder.

"The game can wait." I brace my hand on the bar, effectively boxing her in. "You've been ignoring me for days, and now you show up looking like that?" I gesture at her dress, the way it hugs every curve. "I'm not walking away until I get answers."

"I don't owe you explanations." She tilts her chin up defiantly.

"No. You don't get to push me away anymore." I lean in. "I nearly died on a train this morning, and you know what flashed before my eyes? Not hockey. Not my career. You. Just you."

Her eyebrows shoot up. "You whaaat?!"

"Someone tried to kill me," I say, noting how her eyes flicker with concern. "And all I could think was that I never got to tell you how I feel."

"And...how do you feel?" she asks, her voice carefully neutral.

I brush a strand of hair from her face, my fingers lingering against her cheek. "Like I've been guarding a net my whole life, and you just scored right through me."

She rolls her eyes, but I catch the slight upward tug at the corner of her mouth. "That's the cheesiest hockey metaphor I've ever heard."

"I've got more where that came from." I move even closer. "You're mine, Anika."

Her breath catches. "I am not yours. I am not anyone's."

"Yet," I add. "But I'm a patient man. I'll wait."

"There's nothing between us. Just air."

"Oh really?" I lean impossibly close, my mouth inches from her ear. "Your body said otherwise when I kissed you. The way you melted against me, the little sound you made in the back of your throat...That wasn't nothing."

She flushes pink to the roots of her hair. "Griffin!"

"I'm not letting you walk away again without hearing me out."

Her gaze flickers to the poker table, then back to me. "This really isn't the place for this conversation."

"Then let's go somewhere else. Right now."

"I can't just leave."

"Why not? What's keeping you here? Him?" I gesture toward Durand again, letting my anger rise.

"You," she says cryptically.

"I'm done playing games, Anika." My voice is firm, possessive. "I need you alone."

She rolls her eyes and turns back to the bar.

"No, not like that. Well, yes like that, but more importantly so I can explain everything. The helicopter, the gala...None of it was what it seemed."

She looks up at me, her expression guarded. "Then what was it?"

"Not here." I glance around. "Let's go up to my room."

She snorts. "So you can spin me more stories? I'm not naive, Griffin."

"No, you're not. You're the smartest woman I've ever met. That's why I need you to trust me just a little longer."

Anika shifts her gaze back to the poker table. "You should go."

"Not until you tell me what's going on," I say, my voice low and fierce. "That guy doesn't deserve you. He doesn't even know you."

"Griffin..."

"Tell me I mean nothing to you." My voice comes out louder than I intend.

"Shhh."

"Tell me, and I'll leave you alone forever."

Her eyes meet mine, and for a second, I see something raw and real there. "It's not what you think."

"Then what is it? Because the way you walked in this room, it looks like it is what I think."

"It's not."

"Then why are you here with him?"

She hesitates. "I can't explain right now."

"Try." I tilt her chin up, not caring who sees how close her lips are to mine. "Because the thought of his hands on you makes me want to tear this place apart."

Her breath hitches. "Griffin..."

"One word from you, Anika. One word, and I'll walk away from this table, from this game, from all of it. We'll get out of here and never look back."

"There you are, darling," a sultry voice interrupts. "You're needed at the table."

Elodie materializes at my side. Her hand lands possessively on my forearm, her nails digging in just enough to communicate her displeasure.

"The game is resuming," she whispers. "Malcolm is asking for you personally."

I don't turn around. "Give me a minute."

Anika's eyes dart between us, and though she tries to maintain her neutral expression, I catch the slight tightening around her mouth...her fingers gripping her glass. Something primal flashes on her expression before she masks it with cool indifference. She's jealous. The realization sends a ridiculous thrill through me that I probably shouldn't enjoy as much as I do.

Elodie smiles at Anika, all teeth and no warmth. "I don't believe we've been properly introduced. I'm Elodie."

"Anika." She extends her hand with deliberate politeness.

The barman approaches. "Can I get you something, madam?"

"A Negroni," Elodie says without taking her eyes off Anika. "With an orange twist, not lemon."

I try to subtly extricate my arm from Elodie's grip, but she holds fast, playing the role of possessive girlfriend.

"You have a bit of fluff," Elodie says, reaching up to brush at my ear. Her fingers find my earpiece, adjusting it back into place. Immediately, Showalter's agitated voice fills my ear again.

"—completely unprofessional! Get back to the table now, McGregor!"

"She's using you," Elodie hisses in my ear. "This is a distraction technique. Get back to the table."

I keep my eyes locked on Anika's, but her entire demeanor shifts. Her spine straightens, and a saccharine smile spreads across her face.

"Your accent is...interesting. Where are you from?" she asks Elodie. You are not Swiss."

Elodie's expression flickers briefly before resettling into its mask of cool confidence. "Everywhere and nowhere. My father was a diplomat. We moved constantly."

"That must have been very difficult as a child," Anika says.

Elodie's grip on my arm tightens almost imperceptibly. "It taught me adaptability. A useful skill."

I watch this verbal tennis match with growing confusion. The two women are sizing each other up, exchanging pleasantries loaded with subtext I can't quite decipher.

"Fascinating," Anika says, though her tone suggests it's anything but. "And what brings you to Switzerland? The skiing? The banking? The...hockey players?"

I swear I see Elodie's eye twitch at that last word.

"Business," Elodie replies curtly.

The barman returns with the Negroni. As Elodie reaches for her drink, I notice something on her wrist. The edge of a tattoo peeking out from under her bracelet. A small, dark symbol that looks like a stylized spider or maybe a star.

"And what kind of business is that?" Anika asks sweetly. Something's different about her tonight. Her face is still as adorable as ever, freckles dancing across her nose and cheeks as those big, beautiful eyes seem so innocent. But there's nothing innocent about the way she's questioning Elodie. She's calculated. Crafty.

It's hot.

But as effective as Anika's bold confidence may be, Elodie's training with the secret service gives her an edge. Without missing a beat, she answers with a straight face.

"Finance." Then, lifting her glass, says, "It was a pleasure to meet you, Anika. But I'm afraid I need to steal Griffin back to the poker game. The table is waiting, darling."

A gentle warning.

"I'm sure the...table can wait a little longer," I say, voice clipped.

"Go on," Anika says, waving her hand dismissively. "Don't let me keep you from your...business." She feigns a smile at Elodie as she says the last word. "I'll be right here, chatting with my new friend."

"I would like nothing more," Elodie says, tilting her head as if she's trying to figure Anika out.

I look between them, suddenly feeling like I've wandered into a minefield without a map. The air crackles with unspoken tension, and I have the distinct impression that whatever game these two women are playing is a lot cattier than that poker game across the room.

"Griffin," Showalter barks in my ear. "The hand is starting. Get back to the table now."

I'm so tempted to rip the earpiece out and throw it in Elodie's Negroni, consequences be damned. Let Malcolm keep his millions. Let the FIS find another patsy. To tell Elodie to back off, to make it crystal clear to Anika that there's nothing between us. But something in Anika's expression stops me. A subtle warning, perhaps.

"Go play your game, Griffin," Anika says. "They're waiting for you."

"Fine," I mutter, extricating myself from Elodie's grip. "I'll be back," I tell Anika, trying to convey with my eyes all the things I can't say aloud.

I step back, feeling like I'm physically tearing myself away from her.

"Take your time," she replies, raising her glass in a mock toast. "Don't worry about us...girl talk, *ja*?"

As I walk back to the game, I just catch Anika saying, "Sooo, I'd love to hear more about your travels. You must have so many interesting stories."

I take my seat at the table, my mind racing. Out of the corner of my eye, I see Anika leaning casually against the bar, chatting like she's just met her new BFF. But I know something's up with those two beautiful, dangerous women. Each with their own agenda. I just need to figure out what Anika's is.

Home is wherever someone saves
you the last cookie.

CHAPTER TWENTY-ONE

Anika

I swirl the dregs of my champagne, replaying tonight's casino drama. Griffin started the poker tournament looking like a runway model in his tuxedo. I mean, he was smoking hot.

Don't judge. I have a weakness for men in finely tailored suits.

But by the end of it, he'd cycled through ten shades of green. Sigh. He still looked good though.

"You seem distracted," Wilde says, cutting into my thoughts.

We're tucked away in a corner of the hotel restaurant open for wealthy patrons even though it's the middle of the night. Money talks, so I've learned.

"I'm thinking about the game," I admit, stabbing at my untouched chocolate mousse. "Griffin kept touching his ear whenever he was bluffing. And when Malcolm went all-in with those kings, Griffin looked like he was going to throw up."

"Yet he's still in the game," Wilde observes, sipping his sparkling water with lime.

Barely.

For five excruciating hours, I watched from the bar as he nearly lost everything during the first few hands, then clawed his way back with a series of lucky draws. I thought he was finished when the Texan called his bluff. Griffin just sat there like a deer in headlights until the dealer started tapping the table.

Around 2 AM, when Griffin's chip stack had dwindled to a pathetic little mound compared to Malcolm Chase's towering fortress, the dealer finally announced the game would resume tomorrow at dusk.

"He's down to what, fifteen percent of his original chips?" I scrunch my nose. "I don't understand why his sponsor couldn't find someone who actually knows how to play poker."

Wilde's mouth twitches in what might almost be a smile. "Don't underestimate him just yet. They're feeding him moves."

"What do you mean...feeding him moves? He's terrible."

"Not necessarily. I've seen this strategy before. Malcolm Chase is feeling a little too overconfident right now. But when they resume the game tomorrow, I think you'll see a whole different side of Griffin McGregor."

"So you think someone is helping him cheat."

His expression darkens. "Which is precisely why we need information on the woman who calls herself Elodie. What did you learn when you spoke to her?"

I snort. "Other than she's beautiful, dangerous, and has her claws in Griffin? Nothing much. She shut down the conversation before I could get anything useful."

"You kept her attention long enough for us to clone her phone. That's all we needed."

I blink. "Wait, you did what? When?"

"That's classified."

Of course it is.

Wilde taps his fingers on the table. "We need to know who they're working for."

"I thought you said they were spotted with the Swiss Secret Service earlier tonight."

Wilde just scowls into his sparkling water.

"And what exactly does that woman want with Griffin anyway? I've seen the man trying to fight off two guys in my bar. Trust me, he's no Chuck Norris."

I take a sip of my water, hoping it might help me process the absurdity of this situation. I think about Griffin, his golden retriever enthusiasm, his ridiculous inspirational quotes. The man is basically a walking sunbeam. The idea of him involved in something sinister is ridiculous.

"I need you to get into her room," Wilde says. "Find her devices, communications, anything that might give us some intel."

I blink. "And how exactly am I supposed to do that?"

Wilde gives me a pointed look that makes my cheeks burn. "Through Mr. McGregor's adjoining suite, of course."

"No," I say flatly. "Absolutely not."

"You have his trust."

"I am not seducing Griffin to get into Elodie's room!" The

couple at the next table glances over, and I lower my voice to a hiss. "That's...that's completely unethical!"

"I never said anything about seducing him." Wilde hums as he studies my reaction. "Though your mind went there rather quickly, didn't it? Interesting."

"I...well...I only meant..." I stutter. "Just find someone else. Scratch that. Don't find someone else. There will be nobody going into Griffin's hotel room tonight or ever."

"Miss Gisler, people's lives depend on this. Including his."

A chill runs through me. "You're serious."

"Deadly." His eyes lock with mine. "I wouldn't ask if there were another way."

He reaches into his coat pocket and slides something across the table. "I've taken the liberty of booking you the suite across from his."

It's a key card. But there's something underneath. Two tiny silver objects no bigger than earrings. Barely visible against the white tablecloth.

"What are these?" I ask, though I already know.

"Tracking and listening devices. State of the art. Completely undetectable by standard sweeping equipment."

"Bugs? Are you serious right now?"

Wilde's voice is matter-of-fact, like he's asking me to pass the mustard. "Plant one on McGregor. The other needs to find its way into Elodie's possession. Preferably on something she'll take everywhere. Her purse, jewelry case, cosmetics bag... anything she won't leave behind."

I push the devices back toward him. "This is insane. Griffin's a nice guy. He might have questionable taste in music, but he's just...he's..."

"Dangerous," Wilde cuts in, his expression hardening.

"That's ludicrous. He's about as dangerous as a golden retriever puppy."

Wilde slides the bugs back to me. "Your feelings for him are clouding your judgement. But...right now, you're our best asset."

I laugh bitterly. "Asset?"

"Miss Gisler." His tone sharpens. "I understand your reluctance, but Mr. McGregor could be involved in something that threatens international security."

"Then why don't you let me tell him? Warn him?"

"I assure you, we have compelling reasons."

"Like what?"

"Classified." His expression doesn't change. "The less you know, the safer you'll be."

"Maybe Griffin knows something that could help."

Wilde's expression hardens. "Absolutely not. For all we know, McGregor could be willingly working with the target and compromise my cover as Durand."

I shake my head vehemently. "No. Not Griffin."

"You've known him, what? A few weeks?"

I scoff. "I've known you for all of five minutes."

Wilde must see the doubt in my eyes. "Help us, and we can protect him...if he deserves protection."

"And if he doesn't?"

"Then at least you'll know the truth."

I stare at the listening devices for a long moment. The right thing to do is clear. I should walk away right now. Go back to my simple life in Grächen.

But what if Wilde is right? What if Griffin is in danger?

"Fine," I say, finally pocketing the bugs. "How exactly am I supposed to get into Elodie's room through McGregor's suite. What if the adjoining door is locked?"

"Your keycard will open anything with a card reader. It's been...enhanced."

"Of course it has," I mutter.

Wilde's gaze shifts to something behind me.

"You have a visitor," he says quietly, standing up.

I turn to see Griffin across the restaurant, approaching our table, his face a storm cloud. He's still in his tuxedo, though his bow tie hangs loose around his neck, and those perfect curls are now sticking up in adorable disarray.

Not that I should be noticing how hot he looks when he's this angry.

Wilde places a few crisp bills on the table. "I'll be monitoring the situation remotely. If anything goes wrong, call room service and ask for banana peppers. That's your distress signal."

Wilde gives me a curt nod and walks away as Griffin barrels through the room like a freight train, neck muscles coiled with barely-contained rage. His eyes are locked on Wilde, tracking him like a predator.

As Griffin pivots to pass my table, I grab his arm, feeling the solid warmth beneath the fine fabric of his tuxedo. "Griffin, stop!"

He tries to shrug me off, but I tighten my grip, practically hanging off his bicep. People are starting to stare.

"Let me go, Anika," he growls, still watching the exit where Wilde vanished. "I just want to have a friendly chat with your dinner companion."

"You can't just attack people in a five-star hotel!"

His eyes dart between me and Wilde's disappearing form. "Watch me."

"No. You're making a scene." I press both hands against his chest, which feels like pushing against a brick wall. "Sit. Down."

For a terrifying moment, I think he might actually lift me out of the way. Instead, he exhales through his nose and drops into Wilde's vacated chair.

"Tell me who that man is," Griffin demands, his jaw clenched.

I push the untouched chocolate mousse toward him. "Have some dessert. Your blood sugar is clearly low."

"Anika." His voice is deadly serious in a way I've never heard before. He grips the edge of the table, knuckles white. "Who. Is. He?"

My heart hammers against my ribs. This is not the Griffin I know. This is someone else entirely, and it should terrify me. Instead, I feel a traitorous heat spreading through my body.

"Who is he?" Griffin repeats. "Is he working for Chase? Against him? What's your relationship with...what's his name again?"

"Just a poker player. Like you."

Griffin's eyes narrow. "He's not your type."

"How would you know?"

"Because I'm your type," he says, with such conviction I almost believe him. "I've been looking for you everywhere since you left the poker room. Why did you disappear like that?"

I swallow hard, searching for a believable lie. "I was craving chocolate."

"Don't play cute." He leans forward, elbows on the table. "What are you doing in St. Moritz...with him?"

I let out a frustrated breath. "Why do you even care? You've had Elodie practically glued to you all night."

"Elodie is..." He hesitates, and something flickers across his face. "I'm not saying I don't trust you. I'm saying I don't trust him."

"Well, I can handle myself. I've been doing it for years without your help, thank you very much."

Griffin's voice drops to a dangerous whisper. "Did he touch you?"

"What?" The question catches me off guard.

"Just answer carefully," he says, voice dropping to something primal. "Because if he did, I'll make sure he can't use that hand for a very, very long time."

Heat flushes through me. Half indignation, half something else I don't want to examine too closely.

"You're completely overreacting," I say, forcing a laugh that sounds hollow even to my ears.

"No. I'm reacting exactly enough to make sure he never comes near you again."

Griffin's jaw tightens, a muscle twitching along his temple. His eyes fix on mine, and the raw possessiveness I see there makes my breath catch. I've seen Griffin focused on the ice, but I've never seen him like this. Primitive and dangerous.

Wilde's warning echoes in my head.

Griffin could be dangerous.

"He didn't touch me," I say firmly. "And even if he did, that would be none of your business."

Griffin's eyes flash. "It absolutely would be."

"Griffin, what's gotten into you?"

"I saw the way he was looking at you." His eyes scan my face like he's searching for something. "If he so much as looks at you wrong...it won't end well for him."

A waiter passes by, giving us a wide berth, and I realize we're creating a scene. I grab Griffin's hand and pull him toward a far wall beyond the bar, away from the curious stares.

"You can't fight everyone who talks to me," I whisper-shout once we're semi-private.

His eyes darken. "Watch me."

"Griffin," I say through gritted teeth. "You need to calm down, right now."

"Tell me who he is," he insists. "And why are you meeting him in St. Moritz? Did he bring you here?"

"It's none of your business who I meet or why."

"Tell him you're taken," he says suddenly. "Then tell him by who."

I blink, caught off guard. "I'm not taken."

His eyes lock with mine, steely and unwavering. "Aren't you?"

The intensity of his stare makes my stomach flip. It would be so easy to give in to whatever this is between us. But...Okay, I can't exactly think of a reason why I shouldn't let him kiss me silly right here, right now. Clearly there's something wrong with me.

He rubs his face, his voice softening just a fraction. "Look, you left the gala and ignored my texts for days. Then you show up here, in St. Moritz of all places, and now you're having intimate, late-night dinners with a strange guy...with admittedly great hair?"

"Griffin!"

"You're not leaving with him tomorrow after the game," he says, cutting me off. "That's not a request."

There's something in his voice. A note of desperation beneath the command that makes me pause.

"What are you really doing here, Griffin?" I ask quietly. "Because whatever it is, it's clearly way over your head."

Something shifts in his expression. A flicker of vulnerability beneath the jealousy.

"I'll tell you everything," he says finally. "Just...Let's go somewhere private to talk."

I gulp, thinking of all the wrong things. "Your...room?"

"No. Not my room. The...walls are too thin. Your room."

My mind races as I realize I've backed myself into a corner. I need to get into Griffin's room to plant the bugs, not bring him to mine.

"Actually," I say, stalling. "I think your room would be better. I, uh...my room is a mess."

Griffin's jaw tightens, a darkness crossing his features. "Your room is a mess because he's in it, isn't he?"

"What? No."

"That British guy," he practically growls. "Durand. Is he in your room right now?"

"Of course not!" I sputter, genuinely offended. "Why would you even think that?"

"Because you're acting strange, Anika." He steps closer, invading my personal space in a way that makes my heart stutter. "Evasive."

"I'm not being evasive!"

"Then let's go there. Now." His voice leaves no room for argument.

I press my lips together,

"Look, Griffin, it's late. We're both tired."

"He doesn't deserve to be in the same room as you," Griffin interrupts, his voice dropping to something dark and possessive. "And if he forgets that, I'll remind him."

"There's no one in my room," I snap, frustration bubbling up. "And even if there was, it wouldn't be your business."

"It absolutely would be," Griffin says, his voice dropping dangerously low. "I don't share."

Heat floods my cheeks with something I refuse to acknowledge. "Share? Share what exactly? I'm not yours to share!"

"You didn't see it, but I did. The way he watched you tonight."

"This is ridiculous," I mutter, brushing past him toward the elevators. I jab the button with more force than necessary, fuming.

Griffin follows, his long strides easily catching up. "Anika, wait."

"I need to go to bed. Alone," I emphasize, glaring at him. "And you need to get some rest before tomorrow's game."

The elevator arrives with a cheerful ding that feels wildly inappropriate for the tension crackling between us. I take a step inside, hoping he'll take the hint and stay behind.

When Griffin moves to follow me, I place my hand against his chest, feeling his heart pounding beneath my palm.

Instead of backing away, Griffin places his hand over mine, trapping it against his chest.

Then he steps forward, backing me inside the elevator. He towers over me, his body radiating heat and his eyes burning with something that makes my knees weak.

"We're not done talking about this," he says, backing me against the mirrored wall. His hands plant on either side of my head, caging me in with his considerable height and breadth.

The proximity is overwhelming. I can count every eyelash, see the faint stubble on his jaw, smell the faint trace of whiskey on his breath. For one wild moment, I think he might kiss me again. A part of me—a reckless, stupid part—hopes he will.

Instead, I duck under his arm and step to the front of the elevator. "Yes, we are."

I should be alarmed. I should push him out of this elevator. Instead, my traitorous heart gallops in my chest begging for more, more, more.

And then his mouth is on mine, hot and demanding. This isn't the gentle, questioning kiss from the helipad. This is possession, pure and simple. His hands cradle my face as he deepens the kiss, and for one shameful moment, I melt into him.

His body presses against mine, solid and warm, and I find my hands sliding up his chest to his shoulders. My fingers brush against his collar, then dig into his shoulders as the elevator lurches upward, matching the swooping sensation in my stomach. Griffin's mouth moves hungrily against mine, like he's starving and I'm the only thing that can satisfy him.

His hands slide down to my waist, pulling me impossibly closer.

I arch into him, my fingers tangling in those perfect curls I've been dying to touch since the first day I saw him.

"Anika," he groans against my mouth, the sound vibrating through me like electricity.

His hands travel down, one settling at the small of my back while the other traces the curve of my hip. Each touch leaves a trail of fire in its wake. I'm melting, dissolving, becoming something molten and desperate in his arms.

The elevator continues its ascent, each floor chiming softly in the background. A countdown to when this madness must end. But I don't want it to end. I want to stay suspended in this moment forever, where there are no spies or schemes or bugs to plant. Just Griffin's mouth hot against mine, his hands mapping every curve.

My fingers slip beneath his shirt, feeling the warm skin there.

I should push him away. I should remember why I'm here. But Griffin's touch is intoxicating. It makes me feel reckless.

I find myself yanking him closer, nipping at his lower lip.

He makes a sound somewhere between a growl and a moan that just sends me...Where it sends me, well that's a question for future Anika.

"I've been wanting to do this since the moment you broke into my cabin," he murmurs against my jaw, trailing kisses down my neck.

"I didn't break in," I gasp as his teeth graze my pulse point. "I had the key."

"Semantics." His laugh is a warm puff of air against my skin. "You were still trespassing."

"Are you going to punish me?" The words slip out before I can stop them, husky and inviting.

He pauses just long enough to look at me. His eyes darken to midnight. "Is that what you want?"

My heart hammers wildly. Yes. No. I don't know. I can't think straight with him looking at me like that.

Griffin's fingers trace my collarbone, dipping lower to the edge of my dress.

Then his mouth is on mine again, hungrier this time. My back presses against the mirrored wall as his hands roam restlessly, like he can't get enough. One slides up to cradle my jaw while the other moves to my hip, his thumb tracing maddening circles there.

My fingers tangle in his hair, and he makes a sound deep in his throat that sends liquid heat coursing through me. The rational part of my brain grows fainter with each passing second.

Griffin breaks away only to trail kisses down my neck, his stubble creating a delicious friction against my skin. I gasp when he finds a particularly sensitive spot just below my ear.

"Found it," he whispers smugly, and I can feel his smile against my skin.

I tug his hair in retaliation, which only makes him groan and press closer. His body is solid and warm against mine, and I can feel his heart hammering in his chest, matching the frantic rhythm of my own.

The elevator slows, a subtle shift that signals we're approaching a floor. Griffin doesn't seem to notice, his arms curling around my waist, lifting me slightly so I'm on my tiptoes.

With a cheerful ding, the doors slide open.

"Oh my!" a female voice gasps.

We spring apart like guilty teenagers. An elderly couple stands in the hallway, the woman's mouth forming a perfect O of surprise, the man's bushy eyebrows shooting up toward his receding hairline.

"We'll just take the next one," the man says, adjusting his glasses as if he's not quite sure what he's seeing.

My cheeks burn as I smooth down my dress. Griffin looks deliciously disheveled, his hair mussed from my fingers, his lips slightly swollen.

"So will he," I say, shoving Griffin toward the door.

He stumbles backward, looking adorably confused as he finds himself standing beside the elderly couple.

The woman gives Griffin an appreciative once-over, then winks at me with a knowing smile.

"Smart girl," she whispers. "Always leave them wanting more."

"Anika, wait..."

"Goodnight, Griffin," I say firmly, jabbing the 'close door' button repeatedly. "For what it's worth, I hope you win tomorrow."

The doors slide closed on Griffin's stunned expression. I collapse against the wall, my heart pounding from that earth-shattering kiss, which was...unexpected. Overwhelming. Perfect.

As the elevator continues upward, I pull one of the bugs from my pocket, turning it over in my fingers.

"If you're listening, Wilde," I whisper to the tiny device. "Mission accomplished. I successfully planted the device on Griffin. One bug down, one to go."

Every bruise has a story, and most of them are funny later.

CHAPTER TWENTY-TWO

Griffin

The poker table blurs around me as my mind drifts back to last night's elevator encounter. Her lips on mine. Her taste, her touch, the way she pressed against me. The soft sounds she made when I kissed her neck. Then abruptly shoving me out into the hallway, leaving me aching and confused.

The climb up six more flights of stairs afterward hadn't been my idea of a romantic ending. Neither was getting jumped by one of Malcolm Chase's goons on the twenty-first floor landing.

I'm still puzzling over the whole situation when Chase clears his throat. "Your bet, McGregor. Unless you're folding?"

I snap back to reality, where four grim-faced players watch me like hawks circling prey. My chip stack sits pathetically small compared to the mountains in front of Chase and the Korean player, Mr. Song. There are only five of us left in the game, down from ten players. Me, Chase, Mr. Song, the Texan, and that smug-faced Brit, Durand. If that's even his real name.

"Counting your losses already?" Chase smirks, tapping the table near my dwindling chips.

"Counting the ways I'll spend your money," I reply, forcing a confident smile despite the dire odds.

Victor, the professional poker player in my ear keeps assuring me I can still win this, but I'm starting to wonder if he's been day-drinking.

"I raise," announces Mr. Song, his shiny manicured fingers pushing forward a small mountain of chips. His social media followers would eat this moment up.

"Rough night, McGregor?" Malcolm smirks across the table. "That's quite a cut you've got there. Stairs can be treacherous, no?"

I touch the fresh gash above my eyebrow, courtesy of his stairwell goon. "Walked into a door."

Malcolm's eyes glitter with cold amusement. He knows. Of course he knows. His henchman probably called him right after I left the guy half-unconscious sprawled across the emergency exit landing.

"Must've been quite a door," Malcolm murmurs, turning a chip over and over again at his fingertips.

I force a smile. The memory flashes vivid. Stumbling up the stairs, still dizzy from Anika's kiss. When a shadow detached from the wall. The glint of steel. My hockey reflexes kicking in as I ducked, the knife missing my eye by millimeters.

"A straight draw," whispers Victor in my ear. "Play it cool."

Easy for him to say. He's not sitting across from his boss, who sent an assassin to attack his star goalie.

Chase leans back, his expensive suit jacket unbuttoning to reveal a tacky green silk vest underneath. The man dresses like a cartoon villain, complete with a pocket square matching his tie. How have I not noticed that before?

He catches me looking and smiles like that shark in *Finding Nemo*. "Are we playing cards or having a staring contest, McGregor?"

Fish are friends. Not food.

I stare at my cards. Not spectacular, but not terrible either.

The flop reveals a Queen of Spades, Ten of Hearts, and King of Spades. My pulse quickens. I might actually have something here.

"What's it gonna be, boy?" The Texan taps his thick fingers on the felt. "We don't have all night."

My earpiece crackles. "Stay in. Song is bluffing. He's got nothing but air and overconfidence."

I glance at Mr. Song, who's busy taking selfies.

"I'll see your bet," I tell Song, pushing forward a matching stack of chips. "And raise you another fifty thousand."

I glance across at Elodie, who gives me an almost imperceptible nod.

"You want to dance, Canadian?" Song asks, peeking over his phone. "Let's dance." He actually dances in his chair, singing a K-pop song to himself, and shoves forward his remaining chips.

Durand studies his chips, his face unreadable. His eyes flick toward the bar where Anika stands. My stomach clenches. Why does he keep looking at her? Something's off about that guy. He's not who he says he is.

"Mr. Durand?" the dealer prompts.

Durand sighs dramatically. "I believe discretion serves me better tonight." He tosses his cards face-down on the table.

The Texan grunts something unintelligible and raises.

Chase leans back in his chair, observing me with the calculating stare of a predator.

"I'll call," he says smoothly, matching the bet.

Now it's my turn again. Victor whispers urgently, "Go all in. Trust me. The Texan's bluffing with garbage."

"All in," I announce, shoving my entire stack forward.

A ripple of excitement passes through the spectators lining the walls of the private gaming room. Among them, I spot Anika by the bar, stunning in a silver cocktail dress. Our eyes lock for half a second before she turns away, pretending I don't exist.

Women. One minute they're kissing you senseless in an elevator, the next they're conspiring with mysterious British Pierce Brosnan wannabes.

"Bold move, McGregor," Malcolm says with a sly grin. What a tool. He really thinks he's going to win this thing.

"Like my grandma always says," I reply with a wink. "Go big or go home."

If the man paid any attention to the Titans games, he'd know I play to win.

"Show your cards, gentlemen," the dealer announces.

We reveal our cards. My flush beats Chase's two pair, but Mr. Song turns over pocket aces, giving him a set of three.

But the Ace of Spades on the river completed my flush while improving his hand to three of a kind. Not enough.

"Flush beats three of a kind," the dealer announces. "Mr. McGregor wins this hand."

The Texan slams his fist on the table hard enough to make the chips jump.

"Sorry, boys," I say, "The ice isn't the only place I can win."

Mr. Song stands, adjusting his glasses and designer jacket.

"This has been most illuminating," he says, his thick Korean accent clipped. "My followers will find my misfortune quite amusing."

He pulls out his phone, positions it for a selfie with the poker table behind him, and begins recording...in perfect unaccented English."

"Omigosh, you guys! I can't believe what happened! Poker vibes were not on point today! Hashtag poker fail. Hashtag High Roller Problems. Hashtag Win Some You Lose Some. Hashtag Still Richer Than You."

He flashes a peace sign, captures his sad face for posterity, and continues his performance. "Make sure to swipe up for my Patreon! Love you all! Hashtag Poker Life."

"We will take a fifteen-minute break," the dealer announces.

The Texan pushes back from the table, his face red as a watermelon.

Chase maintains his composure, but his knuckles whiten as he grips the edge of the table.

He narrows his eyes at me. "Luck favors the bold. Or perhaps...the assisted?"

My stomach drops. Does he suspect the earpiece? He doesn't wait for my answer before he gets up to go for a smoke.

As the players disperse, Song continues his theatrical social media meltdown, now filming himself walking backward out of the private room. "Remember to like and subscribe! Even when you lose ten million euros! Hashtag Real Life. Hashtag Transparency Matters."

With a small bow to the remaining players in the room, he exits, followed by his entourage of women.

Rising from my chair, I feel the room spin slightly. Four

hours of intense concentration plus whatever happened in that stairwell has my head pounding.

I glance toward the bar. Anika is gone. So is Durand. A cold feeling settles in my gut. I'm about to run outside when Elodie materializes at my elbow.

"Quite the comeback," she says. "Your luck seems to have turned."

"Luck had nothing to do with it," I hiss. "And you know it."

Elodie's nails dig into my arm like a bird of prey.

"I need some air," I announce, peeling her fingers off my arm one by one. "And possibly a tetanus shot."

"Don't wander too far," she singsongs. "You have a game to win."

"Wouldn't miss it for the world," I say with a grin guaranteed to annoy. "Beating Malcolm Chase is rapidly becoming my favorite hobby."

I make my escape, weaving through the casino's labyrinth of slot machines and blackjack tables, scanning faces in the crowd. No sign of Anika or her mysterious British companion. My earpiece crackles with static, someone speaking too far from their microphone, maybe. I yank it out and stuff it in my pants pocket. The casino's oppressive luxury is beginning to suffocate me.

Outside on the terrace, the crisp air slaps my face. Stars pepper the night sky above St. Moritz, impossibly bright and breathtakingly beautiful. My breath clouds in front of me, reminding me I left my jacket inside.

A figure stands alone, silver dress shimmering in the moonlight. Anika. She's hugging herself against the cold, her bare shoulders pebbled with goosebumps.

My heart does a stupid little flip. So much for my legendary calm under pressure.

"Fancy meeting you here," I say, approaching slowly like she might bolt. "Come here often?"

She turns, moonlight catching the planes of her face. "Griffin."

The way she says my name sends warmth coursing through me despite the cold.

"Where's your British bodyguard?" I ask, scanning the terrace.

"He's not my bodyguard." She wraps her arms around herself, fighting off the chill.

Without thinking, I sweep a stray hair from her cheek. She doesn't pull away.

"You're bleeding again," she murmurs, studying the cut above my eyebrow. Her fingers hover near the wound without touching. "I heard you got attacked last night. In the stairwell."

My hand automatically rises to the cut above my eyebrow. "News travels fast."

"Are you okay?"

"Never better. My face broke his fist, poor guy."

She rolls her eyes but can't quite suppress her smile.

"How did you know about the stairwell?"

"Wil...er, I mean the British man told me." She turns toward the mountains, moonlight catching her profile.

"The British man? Durand? Did he orchestrate the attack?" The question slips out before I can stop it.

Anika stares at me, eyes narrowing. "Why would you think that?"

"Because this whole situation reeks worse than hockey gear after playoffs. Because Durand appears everywhere I go. Because you're suddenly buddy-buddy with him at the same poker game I'm at when you wouldn't give me the time of day for days."

Her mouth tightens. "It wasn't Durand."

"How can you be so sure?"

"Because he was trying to help you." She turns fully toward me now, eyes blazing. "He ran up twenty-one flights of stairs to make sure you weren't murdered."

"Twenty-one flights? Impressive cardio regimen."

"By the time he reached the landing, you'd already…" She makes a punching motion with her fist.

"So, he was there. And didn't even say hallo gov'na."

"He said you handled yourself well." Her lips twitch. "I'm quite impressed you managed without a woman stepping in to save you."

"Hey, now."

"Am I wrong?"

"No," I admit, laughing despite myself. I'm no fighter. On the ice, I avoid confrontation. Off the ice, I'm the guy who apologizes when someone else steps on my foot. "Between you kung fu fighting those bar goons and Elodie going full Lara Croft on an assassin, pushing him off a moving train…"

"Elodie did what?"

"I thought I told you about the train."

"You did but…" Anika blinks rapidly. "I guess I didn't let you tell me the details."

"Well, I ducked a lot while Elodie did all the ninja moves."

She bites her lip, suppressing a smile. "Not exactly James Bond material, are you?"

I hang my head. Sixteen-year-old Griffin would be so disappointed in me right now. "No, I suppose not."

A shooting star streaks across the sky, gone before I can point it out. Wishes wasted.

"Besides," I continue. "Fighting isn't exactly in my skill set. I'm more of a lover than a fighter."

Her cheeks flush beautifully.

"Griffin, I…"

"Excuse me, Mr. McGregor?" A uniformed concierge stands at the terrace entrance. "The game will resume in five minutes. Your presence is requested."

"Of course." I nod, not taking my eyes off Anika. "Be right there."

The concierge retreats, leaving us alone again.

"Anika, about last night."

She places her finger against my lips. "Go win your game, Griffin."

"And after?"

A smile plays at her lips. "After, we talk."

"Promise?"

Warmth blooms in my chest as she says, "And I will take the train back to Grächen with you."

The poker room hums with quiet tension when I enter. Three faces turn toward me with barely concealed contempt. Durand, Malcolm, and the Texan, all hoping I wouldn't return.

"McGregor." Malcolm nods. "We thought you might have decided to quit while you were ahead."

"And miss the chance to see your face when I win? Not a chance." I slide into my chair, attempting to channel my inner Sean Connery but feeling more like Austin Powers.

The dealer shuffles the cards. "Gentlemen, shall we continue?"

The line to my poker coach has gone silent. My hand instinctively reaches for my ear, finding nothing. The earpiece. It's gone.

Wait. I took it out of my ear when I went outside.

I pat my pocket. But it's not there either.

My stomach plummets through the floor. I frantically check my other pockets, pretending to get comfortable. Nothing.

"Problem?" Malcolm asks with a wolfish grin.

"Not at all." I force a relaxed expression while internally screaming. The earpiece must have fallen out somewhere between the terrace and here.

Elodie floats over.

"Everything all right, darling?" she whispers, her hand brushing my shoulder.

"Lost my...good luck charm," I mutter.

"A word in private please," she says to the table. "It's a personal matter."

"We ain't waitin' much longer," says the Texan.

"Excuse me, gentlemen." I rise, following her to a corner of the room.

When she's convinced we're out of earshot, she glances around, whispers, "When?"

"I don't know...it must have fallen out on the terrace during the break."

Her voice drops to a deadly whisper. "Do you understand what's at stake?"

"I'm perfectly aware of that, thank you," I hiss.

Elodie's face turns to granite. "We need to stall, retrace your steps. Look everywhere. I'll go visit those bozos upstairs to inquire about a replacement."

"Gentlemen, I'll be dealing the next hand if everyone is ready," the dealer announces. "If all players would please take their seats."

Malcolm swivels in his chair, eyebrow arched. "Either take your seat or forfeit, McGregor. We don't have all night."

His smug face makes me want to punch something. Preferably him.

"I'll wing it while you go get another earpiece," I whisper to Elodie.

Elodie's eyes widen to anime proportions. "Wing it? Are you insane? You'll lose everything!"

"What choice do we have?" I whisper urgently. "Unless you want to feed me answers through interpretive dance, I need that earpiece."

"This is the third one you've lost," she reminds me harshly. "They don't just sell those at the corner market."

"I'm sorry. No one told me not to wear it in the shower. And the second one wasn't entirely my fault."

I suppose I can't exactly hold it against housekeeping for wiping down my nightstand when I forgot to put the "do not disturb" sign on my door while I went out for lunch. They were just doing their job, after all. And those earpieces are so tiny. I blame Agent Showalter for not giving me something to store it in. Like a ring box or something.

Elodie's face hardens. "Without guidance, you'll lose everything in thirty minutes."

"Your pep talks need work." I glance at the table. "Look, the sooner you go upstairs, the sooner you'll be back."

Elodie glances toward the table where three pairs of eyes watch us with varying degrees of suspicion. "Fine. Play conservatively. Fold early. Understand?"

"Got it."

"Hurry up, Canadian!" The Texan pounds the table with his meaty fist.

Elodie slips out of the room, and I return to the table and settle into my chair. "Sorry about the delay, gentlemen. Ready to play some cards?"

I have a hundred inspirational quotes about confidence. Grandma has a hundred more. But I can't think of a single one right now.

"Technical difficulties?" Malcolm asks, eyebrow raised as he arranges his massive chip stack.

"Nothing serious." I arrange my pathetically small pile of chips into neat stacks. "My Lady Luck needed...to refresh her makeup."

"Luck," Durand says with a British sniff. "Is for amateurs."

The Texan grunts in agreement.

"Five hundred thousand to start," announces the dealer.

Cards whisper across the green felt. I lift the corner of mine. Jack of Clubs, Seven of Diamonds. Not great, not terrible. What would the voice in my ear say?

The Texan bets aggressively on the first hand, and I fold early. Malcolm wins with a straight, his smile stretching across his face as he rakes in the chips.

"First blood," he murmurs, stacking his winnings.

Three more hands pass this way. Me folding early, protecting my dwindling chip stack while praying for Elodie's return. My strategy consists entirely of don't-lose-everything-before-help-arrives.

Durand studies me with unsettling intensity. Can he tell I'm flying blind now?

"Everything all right, Mr. McGregor?" he asks in that infuriating British accent.

"Peachy," I say with a tight smile.

I scan the room for Elodie. No sign.

My eyes meet Anika's across the bar. She's gnawing her lower lip. Seeing her calms me somehow. Even with no earpiece and Malcolm breathing down my neck, her presence steadies me.

The next hand brings me a pair of nines. Better, but nothing spectacular.

Durand raises pre-flop. The Texan folds immediately.

Malcolm calls. My turn again.

"Call," I say, matching their bets.

The flop comes. Ace of Clubs, Seven of Spades, Two of Hearts. Nothing helps my nines.

Durand bets big. Malcolm considers, his fingers playing with a chip, before calling.

My nines suddenly seem pathetic. "Fold."

The door opens, and Elodie slips back in. Her face is pale. When our eyes meet, she gives an almost imperceptible shake of her head.

No earpiece. I'm done for.

The game continues, more intense now. Durand plays cautiously, winning small pots, folding frequently. Malcolm becomes more aggressive, trying to bully us with large bets.

An hour passes. My fortunes continue to slide. Across the room, Elodie grows increasingly agitated, crossing and uncrossing her legs, checking her watch.

I glance again at Anika, who straightens suddenly at the bar, her expression shifting from worry to determination.

She mouths something. I squint, trying to decipher her silent message.

Win.

With one word, my brain clicks into hockey mode. The same clarity washing over me before big games. The buzzing doubt vanishes, replaced by the same laser focus I have on the ice.

Who needs an earpiece when you have someone believing in you?

My grandma's words come flooding back to me. *Whether you think you can or think you can't, you are right.*

That's a Henry Ford quote for ya.

I take a deep breath. Close my eyes for a moment.

In goal, I read patterns. Body language. The slight shift in a forward's weight before he shoots left. The fraction-second hesitation before a wrist shot becomes a pass.

I open my eyes and really look at my opponents.

The Texan scratches his left eyebrow when he's bluffing. Malcolm's mouth tightens almost imperceptibly when he's confident in his hand. Durand...reveals nothing, which is information in itself.

Two more hands. I start playing strategically, folding when uncertain, betting small when confident. My chips stabilize.

"Raising the blinds," the dealer announces.

With the blinds raised, each hand costs me a small fortune just to see my cards. I count my remaining chips. Enough for maybe five, six hands at most. This is the time when even great players crumble under pressure. They start making desperate moves, trying to double up quickly, and instead crash out with nothing.

Not me. Not today.

"Five hundred thousand," Malcolm announces, tossing chips into the pot.

Sweat beads down the Texan's forehead as he contemplates his options. His left eyebrow twitches. Once, twice. I suppress a smile. He's bluffing.

"Call," he says eventually, adding his chips to the growing pile.

Durand matches the bet.

My turn. The flop gave me top pair with a straight draw.

"Call," I say, matching their bets.

The dealer burns a card and reveals the turn. A King of Hearts.

The Texan bets two hundred thousand. Malcolm raises to five hundred thousand. Durand calls with a casual tilt of his head.

I glance at Anika again. She's perched on the edge of her barstool, barely breathing.

"Call," I announce, adding my chips to the pot.

The dealer reveals the river card. A three of clubs.

The Texan bets aggressively. Three million. Malcolm counters with six million. Durand matches Malcolm's bet without batting an eye.

The spotlight of pressure burns on me. With no voice in my ear, no secret advantage, I'm naked against these pros. Yet something clicks. Just like when I finally got my groove as a goaltender. That moment of clarity. I feel like I'm underwater and everything is happening in slow motion. My eyes move between the Texan, Durand, and Malcolm. The Texan's face has gone still, except for the vein pulsing in his temple. Durand remains maddeningly unreadable. Malcolm looks downright gleeful. He totally thinks he's got the winning hand, so the least I can do is mess with him.

"Decisions, decisions," I murmur, arranging my chips.

"Well, McGregor?" Malcolm snaps. "Last chance to fold with some dignity."

"Do you ever watch the Titans games?" I press. "If you did, you'd know I never give up."

Anika stands at the bar, one hand pressed against her collarbone. She gives me the tiniest of nods.

"I'll see your six million," I announce, pushing a stack of plaques into the center.

The Texan lets out a low whistle but doesn't hesitate. "I raise one million more."

Durand lifts an eyebrow, the first real expression I've seen on his face all night. "Call," he says smoothly, matching the seven million.

Malcolm chuckles. "Gentlemen, we're finally getting serious." He makes a show of counting out his chips. "I'll see your seven million and raise you...two million more."

"Nine million," the dealer confirms.

The bet comes around to me again. The tension cranks up another notch. My collar feels suddenly tight against my neck. Sweat beads on my forehead.

"The bet is nine million to you, Mr. McGregor," the dealer says.

My mouth goes dry. The weight of every decision I've made in my life seems to funnel into this single moment. I need to trust my hockey instincts. The Titans never won a game just sitting there playing it safe.

"All in," I announce, pushing my entire stack forward.

A collective gasp ripples through the room.

"Thirty-eight million, five hundred thousand." I dig into my pocket and toss my lucky Canadian Loonie into the pot. "And one Canadian dollar," I add with a wink at Anika.

"The bet is thirty-eight million, five hundred thousand...and one Canadian dollar...to you, Mr. Chase," the dealer announces.

The Texan barks out a laugh. Durand's lip quirks upward.

"You must have quite a hand, McGregor," he says. "Or perhaps you're desperate."

I shrug. "Only one way to find out."

"One can only wonder," Malcolm says coolly. "Where does a hockey player like you get off betting his life savings on a poker game? Or do you have a silent benefactor in that pretty little bartender?"

It takes every ounce of control not to fly across this table to strangle that creepy grin out of him. But for Anika, and only for Anika, I'll settle for strangling all the stolen money from him and then hand him over to the Feds. So I play it cool. For now.

"Tell me, Malcolm," I say. "Can I expect another Christmas card this year with you and your perfect family on the front? Or will you send a Season's Greetings from you and your sidepiece?"

Malcolm's top lip twitches, a rush of blotchy red creeping up his neck to his eyeballs.

He glowers at me murderously as he shoves all his chips forward, knocking over his neat piles in the process. "All in."

"Mr. Chase is all in for forty-four million, two hundred thousand," the dealer confirms.

Malcolm holds up his hand to the dealer. "Wait." He reaches into his pocket, producing a sleek key fob.

"Sorry, I don't carry Canadian Loonies. But in the spirit of your dramatics..." He tosses the fob onto the pile. "My Bugatti La Voiture Noire."

The dealer looks uncertainly between us. "Sir, the house rules do not allow..."

"The house will accommodate me," Malcolm snaps. "Won't you?"

The floor manager hurries over, whispers something to the dealer, who nods reluctantly.

"The vehicle has been accepted as part of the wager," the dealer concedes.

The Texan guffaws and pushes his entire stack forward. "Blast it all. I reckon you Canadians are bluffing."

"All in for twelve million," the dealer confirms.

After a moment's hesitation, Durand announces, "For a Bugatti, I'm all in as well."

"All in for ten million, three hundred thousand," the dealer says.

I keep my expression neutral despite my racing pulse. If I'm wrong about this...

The room falls silent, everyone collectively holding their breath.

"Gentlemen," the dealer announces. "Please reveal your cards."

The Texan goes first, turning over a king and a seven. The dealer slides the cards around to accommodate his hand.

"Two pair, kings and sevens."

Durand reveals a jack and a nine. "Straight, five to nine."

Malcolm's smile grows impossibly wicked as he turns over his cards. A pair of kings.

"Full house, kings full of sevens," the dealer announces.

All eyes turn to me. Malcolm already has one hand stretching toward the pot.

My heart hammers in my chest as I flip my cards. Queen and Ten of Hearts.

The dealer's voice doesn't even quiver when he says, "Royal flush in hearts."

Malcolm's face drains of all color.

"The winning hand belongs to Mr. McGregor," the dealer confirms.

Malcolm's eyes burn with rage. "You cheated."

"Careful, Malcolm," I warn. "Those are serious accusations in a place like this."

His jaw works silently, fury radiating from him in palpable waves.

"The house recognizes Mr. McGregor as the winner of the main pot and all side pots he is eligible for, awarding him a total of one hundred and five million euros," the dealer announces formally. But then breaks his stoic facade as he adds, "Also, one Canadian dollar and a Bugatti La Voiture Noire."

I slide a one million euro plaque toward the dealer as I depart from the table. "For your trouble," I say.

The dealer accepts it with a graceful nod. "Most generous, sir."

The Texan ambles over, ruddy-faced and surprisingly cheerful for someone who lost millions. He extends a meaty hand.

"Son of a gun! I haven't seen poker played like that since my daddy won a ranch in '82." His handshake nearly dislocates my shoulder. "You played us like fiddles. No hard feelings here. When you're beat, you're beat."

"Thanks," I manage, flexing my fingers to ensure they still work. "You played a great game."

"Hell, I played like a drunk armadillo compared to whatever voodoo you pulled off." He laughs, slapping my shoulder hard enough to rattle my teeth. "Well, I'm fixin' to hit the bar and drown my sorrows in bourbon. Next time you're in Dallas, you look me up. Cletus Beauregard. My poker nights could use some fresh blood."

Across the room, Malcolm lunges for his Bugatti key fob on the table, but a security guard intercepts his arm.

"Sir, all items in the pot belong to the winner."

Malcolm's face contorts. "Do you have any idea who I am?"

The guard remains impressively stoic. "Yes, sir. You're the gentleman who no longer owns a Bugatti."

Malcolm yanks his arm free, straightens his jacket with an aggressive tug, and storms toward the exit. The doors bang open as he plows through them.

"Mr. McGregor." The floor manager appears at my side. "Congratulations on your win. The banker will see you whenever you're ready to transfer the funds."

"We'll go straight away," Elodie says beside me. "No time like the present."

Over her shoulder, I catch sight of Anika slipping toward the door. Our eyes lock across the room. She gives me a small, mysterious smile before vanishing into the corridor.

My heart does a cartwheel in my chest. What was that smile? A congratulations? A goodbye? A see-you-later-for-elevator-makeout-session-part-two?

Durand stands rigid near the bar, not watching Anika leave,

but studying Elodie and me with laser focus. His expression is calculating. Intense.

"Everyone's watching us," I whisper to Elodie as we exit.

"Let them watch," she replies coolly. "You're a hundred million euros richer. People always stare at winners."

"Right this way, please." The floor manager leads us up the steps to an elevated section of the room where the banker waits. His steel briefcase containing the computer setup with encryption software sits open on the table.

"Password, please," he requests, turning the keyboard toward me.

My mind conjures Anika's face at the hockey game, holding her homemade sign, screaming "*Hopp Schwiiz*!!" while jumping up and down.

I type H-O-P-P-S-C-H-W-I-I-Z, smiling at the memory.

The screen flashes confirmation with a soft beep.

"Thank you." The banker nods. "Now, where would you like the funds transferred?"

Elodie leans forward, inputting bank information she has memorized, apparently.

"Everything in order?" I ask casually.

"Perfect," Elodie responds. She smiles at the banker. "When will the transfer complete?"

"Immediately," he confirms. "The funds are now being processed."

I thank the man, and we make our way to the exit. Once we're out of earshot, Elodie turns to me, her expression softening slightly. "Thank you, Griffin. On behalf of the Swiss Federal Intelligence Service, I want to express our deepest gratitude for your cooperation."

"Happy to help catch a crook," I say cheerily. "So what will happen to all that money?"

"It will be held up as evidence for a time. But once we can

trace Mr. Chase's accounts, it will be distributed among all his fraud victims."

"That makes it all worth it."

She winks at me. "I like to think so."

The floor manager reappears, holding my lucky Loonie and the Bugatti key fob on a small tray.

"Your personal effects, sir." He presents them with a slight bow. "We will oversee the vehicle transfer paperwork on your behalf. We've also taken the liberty of upgrading you to our Alpenglühen suite for the remainder of your stay. Our finest accommodation."

"Alpenglühen," I repeat, mangling the pronunciation. "Sounds fancy."

"It's named for the red glow on the mountains at sunset. Seven thousand square feet of luxury, private hot spring bath on the balcony overlooking the lake, and a complimentary bottle of Dom Pérignon awaiting your arrival."

"Sweet." I grin. "Does it come with those little chocolates on the pillows?"

The joke is lost on him as he tips his head and walks briskly away.

Elodie checks her watch. "If you'll excuse me, I should retire for the evening. It's been...eventful." She offers her hand with cool professionalism. "Congratulations again on your win."

"Thanks for your...coaching." I wiggle my ears slightly, referencing the missing earpiece.

She gives an elegant shrug. "You managed perfectly well without us in the end."

As she glides away, Durand detaches from his spot by the bar, following her at a discreet distance.

All I want now is to find Anika, sweep her into my arms, and celebrate properly. Ideally with a repeat of that elevator makeout session, minus the abrupt ending and subsequent stairwell assault.

"Mr. McGregor!"

I whirl around to find Agents Bruderlin and Showalter approaching from a side corridor, looking surprisingly casual in evening wear. Bruderlin sports a midnight blue tuxedo while Showalter rocks a perfectly tailored charcoal suit.

"Holy smokes, you clean up nice," I blurt. "Much better than those off-the-rack suits from before."

Bruderlin chuckles. "Undercover work has its perks."

"We came to congratulate you," Showalter says, extending his hand. "Impressive performance. Especially after losing the earpiece."

I shake his hand. "Sorry about that."

"No need to explain," Showalter cuts me off with a wave. "Even though our operative upstairs nearly had a coronary."

"Poor guy was screaming into his microphone for twenty minutes," Bruderlin adds with a smirk. "Kept insisting you fold every hand."

I wince. "Would've been nice advice to hear."

"But unnecessary, as it turns out." Showalter claps my shoulder. "You proved quite capable on your own."

"You made a professional poker player out of a job," Bruderlin says.

"So what happens now?" I ask. "Chase gets arrested?"

The agents exchange glances.

"Chase vanished through a service entrance," Showalter says. "But we've frozen his accounts and flagged his passport. He won't get far."

Showalter straightens his already impeccable tie. "We wanted to say goodbye. Our involvement here is officially concluded."

"So this is it?" I ask. "No more spy stuff?"

"No more spy stuff," Bruderlin confirms with a rare smile. "You can go back to catching pucks instead of international criminals."

"Though you've proven surprisingly adept at both," Showalter adds.

"Does this mean I can keep the Bugatti?"

The agents exchange another look.

"Consider it hazard pay," Bruderlin says dryly.

My jaw drops. "Seriously?"

"The paperwork to seize it would be a nightmare," Showalter explains. "Besides, Malcolm Chase no longer legally owns it. You won it fair and square."

"Or as fair as one can win anything with government agents feeding you poker moves," Bruderlin mutters.

"Hey, I won without the earpiece in the end!"

"Indeed, you did," Showalter acknowledges. "Which brings us to our final point. Nobody can know about our operation. The FIS involvement remains classified."

"My lips are sealed," I promise, making a zipping motion across my mouth. "No one would believe me anyway."

"Mr. McGregor, it's been...interesting," Bruderlin extends his hand again.

"Likewise, Agent Bruderlin."

As they walk away, Showalter calls over his shoulder, "Enjoy your retirement from espionage."

I watch them disappear around a corner, then sprint toward the elevators.

Upstairs, I burst into my room, grabbing my duffel bag and stuffing clothes inside. My brain spins with possibilities for the evening ahead. Champagne on the balcony? Room service? Or skip straight to kissing Anika senseless?

A cool draft catches my attention. The adjoining door to

Elodie's room stands open, swinging slightly from the air current from the hallway.

I approach cautiously, knocking on the doorframe. "Elodie?"

Silence greets me. I push the door wider, revealing an immaculate room. Bed made, surfaces clear, closet empty.

She's gone. Not a trace remains, as if she never existed.

Every blind date is a spy mission in disguise.

CHAPTER TWENTY-THREE

Anika

My mind calculates the minimum polite interval required before I can fake a headache and flee this date.

"So anyway, about the drainage issues in modern landscape architecture..." Thomas drones on, his fork poised midair with a chunk of chocolate cake. He hasn't taken a bite in three minutes, too busy explaining water runoff coefficients.

I nod and smile mechanically while sneaking glances at Ivy,

who's perched on the sofa across from us. She winces slightly, rubbing her side where the baby must have kicked. Poor thing looks like she swallowed a beach ball. A very large beach ball. With another smaller beach ball inside it. James hovers nearby, checking his phone every thirty seconds as if expecting labor to begin via text message.

"So I told my supervisor the drainage system simply wouldn't work with that gradient," Thomas continues, finally forking a bite of chocolate cake into his mouth. "The water would pool at the eastern corner, creating a marshy area no one wants in their garden."

I nod and smile, mastering the art of appearing interested while my mind wanders to a certain Canadian goalie with dimples deep enough to drown in. Griffin would have told a joke by now.

"Fascinating," I murmur, taking a sip of water. "The drainage systems in Switzerland are quite efficient."

Thomas perks up like I've offered him the keys to landscape architect heaven. "Are they? I'd love to hear about Swiss irrigation techniques!"

What would Griffin say to this? Probably something absurd like "In hockey, we prefer our irrigation frozen to make the puck slide better!" Followed by one of his ridiculous inspirational quotes. My lips curl involuntarily at the thought.

"Anika?" Ivy's voice snaps me back. "Are you listening?"

"Sorry, what?" I blink rapidly.

"I asked if you'd like more wine," James repeats, bottle hovering above my nearly empty glass.

"No, thank you," I reply. I'm driving home...preferably soon.

Ivy shifts uncomfortably on the sofa, rubbing her massive belly. "So, Thomas, Anika runs the best pub in Grächen."

"Really?" Thomas perks up slightly. "I imagine the accounting must be challenging for a small business."

"It keeps me busy," I offer blandly.

The conversation flatlines again. I desperately search for something interesting to say, but my mind drifts back to three days ago. Griffin's victory smile after winning the poker game, the way his eyes lit up when he offered to show me his suite.

"Would you like to see my upgraded room?" he'd asked, leaning against my doorframe. "They've given me the Alp glow suite or whatever it's called. Supposedly there's a hot tub on the balcony and complimentary champagne."

I'd already changed into my unicorn pajamas by then, hair piled messily atop my head. But more importantly, I didn't trust myself alone with him in a luxury suite with champagne and a hot tub.

"Tempting," I'd replied. "But I've already committed to this glamorous evening ensemble."

His laugh had warmed me from head to toe.

"Anika?" Ivy prompts again, eyebrows raised.

"Sorry," I mumble. "Long week."

Thomas is still droning on about something, but I'm not sure what he's saying. It's like his lips are moving, but what comes out are just jumbled words. I feel bad for feeling this way. I really do. But the man is just so...boring.

Ivy catches my eye and winks. She thinks this is going well. She doesn't realize I'm mentally calculating how many kilometers separate me from Griffin's cabin right now.

"Ivy, do you need anything?" I ask, noticing her shift positions for the fifth time in as many minutes.

"I'm fine," she insists, wincing slightly. "The little footballer is practicing penalty kicks on my bladder, but otherwise perfect."

James places a protective hand on her belly. "Perhaps we should wrap up soon, love. Doctor said to rest."

Yes! Let's wrap it up.

"Nonsense! I want to hear more about Thomas and Anika hitting it off!" Ivy beams at us like we're characters in her favorite romance novel reaching the good part.

Thomas smiles politely. His teeth are nice. His hair is nice. Everything about him is...nice. And therein lies the problem.

I can't help but to compare him with Griffin. His boundless enthusiasm, his perpetual optimism, the way his eyes light up when he talks about hockey and chocolate and his favorite movies.

The drive back from St. Moritz plays in my mind. Griffin behind the wheel of his insanely posh new Bugatti, explaining as much as he could about his mission, although much of it was classified.

What he really wanted to discuss was what happened between us.

"About that kiss—" he'd started.

I'd cut him off immediately. "We got caught up in the moment. The danger, the excitement. It wasn't real."

His eyes never left the road, but his knuckles whitened around the steering wheel. "Felt pretty real to me."

"You're going back to Canada when the NHL lockout ends," I'd reminded him. "And I'll still be here, running my pub."

He'd reached over to hold my hand in that moment, not saying another word for a long while. His hand, so large and sturdy, felt right.

"Anika?" Ivy's voice cuts through my daydream. "Where did you go?"

I blink rapidly. "Sorry, what?"

"I asked if you'd like to show Thomas around Grächen sometime," Ivy repeats, her eyes narrowing suspiciously. "He mentioned wanting to try snowshoeing."

"Oh." I fumble, catching Thomas's hopeful expression. "I, um...Snowshoeing is nice," I respond lamely.

Ivy shoots me a death glare across the coffee table. I can practically hear her thoughts. *Try harder!*

"Thomas is designing a beautiful community garden in Bern," James offers desperately.

"With excellent drainage," Thomas adds proudly.

I nod appreciatively, wondering if Griffin made it back to Visp for his regular practice routine. He mentioned something about tomorrow's game against Davos.

Ivy suddenly gasps, her hand flying to her stomach.

"Contractions?" James asks, already on his feet.

"No, no," she waves him down. "False alarm. Baby just kicked my bladder. Shall we put on some music?"

James rises from the couch and turns on his Bluetooth speaker system. "I've got it, darling. Any preferences, Thomas?"

"Anything composed before 1900, really," Thomas answers with a dismissive wave of his hand. "The structure, the discipline of it. Modern music lacks the architectural elegance of classical compositions."

My eyes roll so hard I nearly see my own brain.

"The repetitive nature of contemporary music is its downfall," Thomas continues, warming to the subject. "Especially those dreadful synthesizers from the 1980s. Three chords played over and over, no complexity whatsoever."

Oh heck no. He did not just insult 80s music.

Ivy shoots me a panicked look, knowing full well my record collection is my pride and joy. This man just declared war on Falco, Yaz, and New Order in one breath.

"And Eurovision?" He throws his hands up. "Don't even get me started."

Ivy's eyes bulge out. Her jaw practically hitting her enormous belly. One does not disrespect Eurovision. He might as well be burning the Swiss flag.

What was that secret signal James told me to make? Tug my

earlobe? I give James a bulgy-eyed look and tug. He just looks back blankly. I tug my ear again. He looks to Ivy, then back to me with the most confused expression I've ever seen.

"You know," I say, placing my napkin beside my half-eaten cake, "I need to use the restroom."

Ivy shoots me a pleading look as I stand. "You know where it is. Down the hall, first door on the right."

I nod, uselessly yanking my earlobe at James, and escape the living room. Instead of turning right, I veer left toward the front door, slipping outside into the cool evening air.

Inhaling deeply, I close my eyes and let the crisp night fill my lungs. When I open them, a familiar silhouette across the street catches my attention.

A sleek Bugatti sits parked under a streetlight, its metallic surface gleaming like black ice.

No. He wouldn't.

But he absolutely would.

I stomp across the street in my nice dinner boots. Griffin glances up, spots me coming, and his face breaks into that stupid, beautiful smile with those stupid, beautiful dimples. He unfolds his tall, beautiful athlete body out of the car, closing the door to lean on it casually with a sheepish grin.

"Well, hello there," he says, dimples appearing like exclamation points. "We gotta stop meeting like this."

"What are you doing?" I hiss.

Griffin runs a hand through his hair. "I was...driving by?"

"You were driving by Ivy's house in Bern? Three hours from Grächen? At nine thirty on a Tuesday night?"

He winces. "Sounds implausible when you put it like that."

"Are you stalking me?" I demand, crossing my arms.

"Stalking is such an ugly word." His eyes flicker over my dress, appreciation evident. "You look beautiful."

"Don't change the subject." But warmth floods my cheeks anyway. "You need to go home."

"How's the date going?" he asks, completely ignoring my directive.

"None of your business."

"Is he funny? Charming?" Griffin leans closer, his voice dropping to a conspiratorial whisper. "Does he make your heart race in elevators?"

"That's not fair."

"He looks boring," Griffin says flatly. "Like, professionally boring. Like he studied at Boring University with a double major in Dullness and Watching Paint Dry."

A laugh escapes before I can stop it. "He hates 80s music."

"No! Come on," Griffin says. "Let's ditch this snooze-fest. We could go to my cabin. Put on some Depeche Mode."

For one dangerous second, I actually consider it. The cabin with its cozy fireplace...and Griffin making me laugh. Making me feel alive. But I'm on date with Drainage Thomas, unfortunately.

"I can't," I say firmly. "Ivy and James set this up. It would be rude."

"Does Thomas know you secretly love The Cure?"

"Stop it."

"Does Thomas know how brave you were in St. Moritz, helping to bring down a financial criminal?"

The memory of the poker game flashes through my mind. The tension, the danger, Griffin's triumphant smile when he won.

"Thomas is safe," I whisper. "He won't leave when the lockout ends."

Griffin's smile falters for a fraction of a second. "Some things are worth the risk, Anika. More than one hundred million poker chips and more than my lucky Loonie."

The front door of Ivy's house opens, spilling warm light onto the sidewalk. I hear James calling my name.

"I need to go," I say, stepping back from the car.

Griffin nods, understanding in his eyes. "For what it's worth, I hope you have a terrible time with Thomas."

A laugh escapes me. "That's horrible."

"I'm a horrible person." He grins. "But I'm your horrible person if you want me."

I roll my eyes but can't suppress my smile. "Goodbye, Griffin."

I cross the street but don't go back in the house until I see the Bugatti pull away slowly, its taillights disappearing around the corner with "Don't You Want Me" by The Human League blasting from the speakers.

I wait until Griffin's taillights disappear completely, straining my ears until the last notes of The Human League fade into the night. Part of me hopes Griffin is circling the block, waiting for me to change my mind. The other part hopes he's driving straight back to Grächen, because I can't trust myself around him.

I take a deep breath of the cold evening air, savoring these final moments of freedom before returning to Thomas and his riveting theories on proper soil permeability.

Wonderful, stable, excruciatingly dull Thomas, who won't kiss me senseless on helicopter pads or drag me into international espionage. Thomas, who won't make me feel alive and terrified all at once. Thomas, who won't break my heart when he flies back to Canada.

I sigh heavily, turning back toward Ivy's house with the enthusiasm of someone approaching a root canal. Maybe I can develop a sudden migraine. Food poisoning? Spontaneous combustion?

The sound of footsteps behind me registers a split second before a large hand clamps over my mouth.

*The heart is like soup—it warms
best when shared.*

CHAPTER TWENTY-FOUR

Muscle memory kicks in before my brain catches up. My father didn't spend years drilling kung fu forms into me for nothing. I pivot, redirecting his momentum while simultaneously driving my elbow backward into a solid ribcage. Air whooshes from his lungs as he doubles over. I follow with a knee to his face that sends him staggering backward.

His partner doesn't hesitate. He lunges, aiming a punch at my head that would have knocked me unconscious if it connected. I sidestep, catching his extended arm and send him stumbling into a row of hedges. A swift kick to the back of his knee drops him to the ground.

The first man recovers quickly, producing something from his jacket pocket. A syringe. My stomach drops. Whatever's in that needle, I definitely don't want it in my bloodstream.

"Why are you making this difficult?" he hisses, circling me cautiously now.

I shift my weight to the balls of my feet, keeping both men in my peripheral vision while executing a perfect spinning kick. My boot connects with his wrist, sending the syringe flying into the bushes. He curses and throws a wild punch that misses my head by centimeters. I counter with three rapid strikes. Nose. Throat. Sternum. He collapses to his knees, gasping for air.

The second man charges again. I use his momentum to flip him over my hip. His massive body slams against the sidewalk. Basic judo throw, but it works every time on overconfident men who underestimate five-foot-seven women.

I don't wait to see if he gets up because syringe guy is coming at me now. We exchange a flurry of blows. His attack more conventional street fighting, mine the disciplined forms of Wing Chun. I parry his jab, counter with a palm strike to his nose. Something crunches. He howls, blood streaming down his face.

"Sorry about that," I mutter, then drive my knee into his groin.

I hear Ivy's front door opening again. "Anika?" James calls out.

The distraction costs me. The second man, still on the ground, grabs my ankle with both hands. I lose my balance, hitting the sidewalk hard. Pain flares through my elbow and hip. I kick upward, catching him squarely in the jaw. His head snaps back with a satisfying crack.

Lights flick on in neighboring houses. A dog starts barking. The syringe man is recovering from the blow to his family jewels, and I've run out of time for this nonsense.

I sprint down the street, my dress hiked up to my thighs. Behind me, I hear cursing in three different languages. My lungs burn as I round the corner, scanning frantically for somewhere to hide. A noise behind me. They're giving chase. I dart between parked cars, zigzagging through the residential neighborhood to lure them away from Ivy's house.

A motorcycle engine roars to life behind me. I risk a glance over my shoulder and see both men mounting black bikes.

Then, headlights illuminate the street ahead. The unmistakable synthesizer of "Don't You Want Me" growing louder as the lights get closer. A sleek black Bugatti screeches to a halt beside me, passenger door flying open.

Griffin. The absolute idiot didn't leave after all. He leans across the seats, his expression dead serious for once.

"Need a ride?"

I dive into the car without hesitation. "Go!"

I barely have time to slam the door before Griffin floors the accelerator, sending me slamming back into the leather seat. The Bugatti leaps forward with a growl.

"You came back," I gasp.

"I was circling the block," Griffin admits, eyes locked on the road.

The Bugatti's engine screams, gaining speed, straight toward the motorcycles.

"Are you insane?" I shriek, clutching the dashboard. "They're right in front of us!"

"Trust me," Griffin says with disturbing calm.

At the last possible second, motorcyclists' wrench their handlebars in opposite directions, tires smoking as they skid sideways, barely missing us. Griffin whips the wheel, drifting around the corner as the centrifugal force presses me against the door.

"Seatbelt," Griffin reminds me cheerfully, as if we're headed to Sunday brunch instead of fleeing hired goons.

I fumble with the buckle, finally clicking it into place as we take another corner. "Who are those guys?"

"Probably Chase's men," Griffin says, checking the rearview mirror. "He wasn't happy about losing all that money."

"You think?" The sarcasm drips from my voice.

The motorcycles appear behind us, gaining ground. Griffin floors it, sending us hurtling down a narrow residential street.

Griffin grins, dimples making an appearance. "You're cute when you're scared."

"I am not scared," I snap. "I'm terrified."

The Human League fades out and Yaz's "Only You" fills the car with its melancholy synthesizer. My heart does a ridiculous little flip at the familiar opening notes.

"Is this..."

"Oh, just a playlist I made for you," Griffin admits, keeping his eyes on the road. "Songs to Make Anika Ditch Her Boring Date. I may have spent three hours crafting the perfect 80s mix to lure you away from Thomas."

Something warm, and dangerously close to affection, spreads through my chest. This ridiculous man made me a mixtape. Like we're teenagers in 1985.

"You planned to serenade me with Yaz?" I ask, trying not to sound as touched as I feel. "Do you have a boom box and a trench coat in the trunk?"

"Maybe. Wait until you hear track fourteen. It's 'Somebody' by Depeche Mode."

"I love that song!"

A motorcycle appears suddenly on our left, the rider's face

hidden behind a black helmet. Griffin swerves sharply, throwing me against the door.

"Sorry. I know you like Yaz, but it's a bit of a mood whiplash." He tosses his phone into my lap. "Playlist two. Quick!"

I swipe through while bracing myself against the door as Griffin takes another sharp turn.

"Playlist two?"

"Yeah, the one called Spy Business."

Of course he has a playlist called Spy Business. I tap it just as the motorcycles pull alongside us. One rider reaches for our door handle. Griffin jerks the wheel, forcing them to fall back.

Gritty electric guitar blasts around us. The display on his phone reads "James Bond Theme" by Oakenfold. It's all, aggressive big beat drums and surf guitar combined with the brassy horns of the 007 theme. The quintessential soundtrack for a high-speed car chase.

Griffin's face lights up with boyish delight. "That's more like it!"

The motorcycles split up, one pulling ahead while the other falls back. They're trying to box us in.

"Hold on," Griffin warns, then slams on the brakes. The motorcycle behind us nearly crashes into our bumper but swerves at the last second.

Griffin immediately accelerates again, turning sharply onto another street.

"Where did you learn to drive like this?" I demand as he executes a perfect drift around a fountain in a small plaza.

"Mario Kart," he answers without missing a beat.

Griffin jerks the wheel left, sending us down a narrow alley barely wide enough for the car. The stone walls scrape against the side mirrors, making me wince.

"Sorry, baby," Griffin whispers, and I'm momentarily confused until I realize he's talking to the car.

We emerge onto a wider street, but our reprieve is short-lived. Both motorcycles appear again, closing in from different directions.

"We can't outrun them," I say, scanning the streets for police, or help, or anything.

"We don't need to outrun them," Griffin replies cryptically. "We just need to outsmart them."

He makes a sudden turn onto a pedestrian-only shopping street, the car bouncing over the decorative cobblestones. Thankfully, it's empty at this hour.

"So," Griffin ventures a sidelong glance at me with a lopsided smile. "Thomas, huh? Still think he's a better date than me?"

"Eyes on the road!" I shout as he narrowly misses side-swiping a parked car.

"I couldn't decide if showing up at your date was romantic or creepy."

I can't help it. I burst out laughing, the tension of the chase dissolving into hysterical giggles.

"Definitely creepy," I manage between gasps of laughter. "But I'll allow it."

Griffin's eyes meet mine for a split second, and something electric passes between us before he returns his attention to the road. My traitorous heart does a dangerous little flip.

A crash from behind breaks the moment. One of the motor-cycles has rammed our bumper.

"Oh no, you did not just do that," Griffin shouts over the music, accelerating down the street.

The Bugatti responds like it was built for this very moment, hugging the road as we zoom past the historic buildings of Bern's Old Town.

"Take a right here!" I yell, spotting a narrow street I recognize. "It leads to the river!"

Griffin yanks the wheel hard.

"So? You never answered my question." Griffin takes a turn without slowing down.

"What question?"

"How does this compare with your date with Thomas?"

I stare at him in disbelief. "Are you seriously asking about my date right now?"

"Just making conversation." He shrugs, checking the rearview mirror. The motorcycles are gaining.

"He hates Eurovision," I blurt out.

"What? NO. Not Eurovision!" He takes another turn. "As a Canadian, I am personally offended for Celine Dion."

We emerge onto the road running alongside the Aare River and Griffin accelerates again. The motorcycles appear behind us, determined to close the gap.

"The bridge!" I point ahead to where the road crosses the river.

Griffin guns it toward the bridge. "How dare he disrespect our Celine?"

One of the motorcycles pulls up beside us again. Without thinking, I roll down my window and launch my boot directly at his face. He swerves wildly, nearly toppling before regaining control.

"Did you just take off your shoe and throw it at him?" Griffin asks, incredulous.

"They're killing my feet!" I shout, already removing my other boot.

The second motorcycle pulls alongside us on Griffin's side. I see the rider reaching for something in his jacket.

"Duck!" I scream.

Griffin hunches down just as I hurl my remaining boot

across him and out his window. It catches the rider in the shoulder.

"Your aim is terrifying," Griffin says, straightening up as the motorcycle falls back.

Griffin punches the accelerator, and the car leaps forward with a roar.

"Griffin!" I gasp. "There's a dead end ahead!"

Where the road meets a pedestrian bridge, concrete barriers block vehicle access. Griffin's face remains eerily calm.

"Do you trust me?" he asks, eyes never leaving the road.

"No!" I shout, bracing myself against the dashboard.

He laughs as we speed toward certain death. At the last possible second, he wrenches the wheel, sending us sliding sideways into what looks like a delivery entrance beside the barrier. The Bugatti's tires scream as we drift through the narrow opening with millimeters to spare.

The motorcycle isn't so lucky. The rider tries to follow our maneuver but clips the edge of the barrier. The bike goes down, sending him sliding across the pavement.

"One down!" Griffin announces triumphantly.

The remaining motorcycle is still behind us, but Griffin seems unconcerned, finally emerging onto the bridge spanning the Aare River.

"I mean, the audacity! Celine is a national treasure." Griffin is halfway across the bridge now.

Without warning, he slams on the brakes and spins the wheel, executing a 90-degree turn that leaves us facing the oncoming motorcycle. The rider hesitates, clearly not expecting this maneuver.

Griffin revs the engine threateningly, like a bull pawing the ground before a charge.

"What are you doing?" I ask nervously.

"Playing chicken," Griffin replies, then floors it.

We hurtle toward the motorcycle, which is barreling toward us in the middle of the bridge. At the last possible second, the rider panics and swerves, losing control on the narrow bridge. The motorcycle skids sideways, then topples over the edge into the icy river below with a splash.

Griffin regains control, slowing the car to a reasonable speed as we merge onto a main road. The James Bond theme reaches its crescendo as he calmly turns down a side street and kills the lights.

"And that," he says, turning to me with a satisfied grin, "is how you lose a tail."

My heart hammers against my ribs. I'm not sure if it's from the chase, the near-death experience, or the man beside me looking unfairly handsome while committing multiple traffic violations.

"You're insane," I tell him, but can't keep the admiration from my voice.

"Maybe," he agrees, reaching over to trace his thumb down my cheek. "But ya gotta admit. I'm more fun than Thomas, right?"

I bite my lip to keep from smiling. "The bar is very low."

Griffin's expression softens. "Sorry about crashing your date."

"No, you're not."

"You're right," he chuckles. "I'm really not."

Deeming it safe again, Griffin casually rolls onto the road that leads toward Grächen.

"You'll stay with me tonight," he says, serious now. "It's not safe for you to go home."

The Bugatti's headlights illuminate the snow-dusted path as we approach Griffin's cabin. My bare feet are propped on the dashboard, my body still vibrating with leftover adrenaline.

The dark silhouettes of pine trees seem like a secret hideaway after the madness of the evening. Secluded, and blessedly free of motorcycle-riding henchmen.

"You're sure more assassins didn't follow us?" I ask, scanning the shadows.

"Positive." Griffin kills the engine. "Though I'm pretty sure Thomas is still yammering on and on to an empty chair."

I snort. "Poor Ivy. She'll never forgive me."

Griffin jogs around to my side, opening the passenger door. "Let's get you inside before your toes freeze."

Without warning, he scoops me up in his arms. I yelp in surprise. "What are you doing?"

"Being chivalrous," he announces proudly. "You're barefoot, there's snow on the ground, and I'm a gentleman."

"You really don't have to carry me," I mumble into his shoulder, though I make no attempt to wiggle free. His arms feel secure around me, and after tonight's excitement, I find myself relaxing into his hold.

Griffin carries me to the front door, fumbling with his keys while still holding me. It takes three attempts before he manages to unlock it, and I bite back a smile at his determination not to put me down.

The cabin glows with welcoming warmth when Griffin pushes the door open. He sets me down gently on the braided rug just inside, his hands lingering at my waist a moment longer than necessary.

Griffin moves efficiently around the cabin, turning on lamps, adjusting the thermostat.

"You should probably call your mom," Griffin says. "Those guys might try your place next."

My stomach drops. I hadn't thought about that. "I left my phone at Ivy's."

"Use my phone. It's on the counter."

I dial my mother's number from memory, praying she answers. She answers on the first ring.

I keep my tone casual as I explain I'm staying with a friend tonight. I carefully avoid mentioning motorcycle chases or assassination attempts. She worries enough about me as it is.

As I speak, my eyes follow Griffin around the cabin. He moves with unexpected grace for such a large man, his shoulders rolling beneath his Henley as he crouches at the fireplace, stacking logs with those thick, competent hands.

"Yes, Mama. I'll be careful," I promise, watching Griffin rip up some newspaper and stuffing it under the logs.

Somehow this all feels oddly domestic. The way he lights a match. How his profile glows as the fire catches, small flames licking up around the kindling. Griffin stays there, coaxing it larger, adding another log when the first ones catch. There's something mesmerizing about watching him work.

"Stay with Helga tonight, okay? Just...as a precaution."

Griffin glances up, catching me staring. Instead of looking away, I hold his gaze. Something electric passes between us before he smiles softly and returns to his task.

"No, I'm fine," I assure my mother. "Just a feeling. Please, Mama? For me?"

She finally agrees, though not without questions I have to creatively deflect. I give her my love and hang up the phone.

"She's going to stay with her friend," I tell Griffin.

He turns from the fireplace, and his expression softens when he sees me. "Come sit by the fire while I get you something warm to wear."

He disappears down a hallway and returns with a pair of thick wool socks and a Toronto Titans sweatshirt.

"Here," he offers. "They'll be huge on you, but they're warm."

I take them gratefully. "Thank you."

In the small bathroom, I slip out of my dress and pull Griffin's sweatshirt over my head. It falls almost to my knees, the sleeves hanging well past my fingertips. I roll them up and pull on the socks. They're massive on my feet, pooling around my ankles like fuzzy leg warmers, but gloriously warm.

When I return to the living room, Griffin has changed into flannel pajama pants and a different Titans shirt. His eyes flicker briefly over my body before he nods to the sofa. "Make yourself comfortable while I put on some music. Do you want anything to eat?"

"I couldn't eat a thing. My stomach is all knotted up from the car chase."

"Mine is too. But for...other reasons."

I sink onto his sofa, letting that little comment slide into the ether while he taps around on his tablet screen. "Somebody" by Depeche Mode plays on a big Bluetooth speaker.

Griffin turns, looking absurdly pleased with himself. "Track fourteen, as promised."

My heart does something complicated in my chest.

Griffin approaches slowly, extending his hand. "Dance with me?"

I hesitate. "Griffin..."

"Just one dance," he says softly. "After the night we've had, don't we deserve that much?"

I place my hand in his, allowing him to pull me to my feet. His other hand settles at my waist, warm and solid. We sway together in front of the crackling fire as the vocals and simple piano accompaniment wrap around us. The music is so beautifully melancholy and heart-wrenching, I almost want to cry.

We dance for a moment, the firelight painting everything in amber and gold.

"I was so worried about you," Griffin whispers against my hair, his arms tightening around me as we sway to the music. "When I saw those men grab you..." His voice catches. "I'm so sorry, Anika. This is all my fault."

I pull back to look at him. The genuine anguish in his eyes.

"Your fault? How is any of this your fault?"

"I dragged you into this mess with Chase." His thumb traces circles on my lower back, seemingly unconscious. "I should have known he wouldn't just accept losing millions without retaliating."

"I'm a big girl, Griffin. I make my own choices."

"You wouldn't be in danger if it weren't for me."

"I chose to help, remember?" I tilt my head back to meet his eyes. "Nobody forced me."

"Still." His voice is rough with emotion. "Those men could have hurt you. If I hadn't circled back..."

"But you did." I place my palm against his chest, feeling his heart thump steadily beneath my fingers. "You were there when I needed you."

Griffin's hand covers mine, pressing it more firmly against his heart. "That's what scares me. What if next time I'm not? What if you get hurt because of me?"

The firelight casts his face in warm shadows, highlighting the worry lines around his eyes. He looks different without his usual carefree smile. More vulnerable, more real.

I rest my head against his chest again, exhausted from the night's excitement. Griffin smells like expensive cologne and mint toothpaste, with a hint of something uniquely him beneath it all. His heart thunders steadily against my ear. Or maybe that's my own pulse I'm hearing.

"Should we call those FIS agents? Let them know Chase is sending people after us?"

Griffin sighs. "I never had their contact information. They always reached out to me, never the other way around. I've tried looking up their department, but it's all classified. No public contact information."

"That's convenient."

My body feels more fatigued with each passing minute, the adrenaline finally draining away.

"We'll figure it out tomorrow," Griffin says. "Right now, you're safe here."

I nod against his chest, feeling oddly at peace despite everything. His heartbeat provides a steady rhythm beneath my ear. We continue swaying long after the song ends. I feel my eyelids growing heavy, and I can't suppress a massive yawn.

Griffin chuckles. "Am I boring you? Should I talk more about landscaping and classical music?"

I swat his arm. "Stop it. I'm just crashing from a long day. Blind dates, car chases, and kung fu fights take a lot out of a girl."

"You were amazing, by the way," he says, admiration clear in his voice. "The way you fought those guys off...I've never seen anything like it."

"My father believed every woman should know how to defend herself," I explain through another yawn. "He started teaching me when I was six."

Griffin's hands move to my shoulders, gently steadying me as I sway slightly. "Come on, sleepyhead. You need rest."

He leads me down a short hallway to the bedroom, a small, cozy space with wooden beams and a sloped ceiling. It's simple but clean, with a wooden dresser and a small bookshelf. Even though this is Walter's cabin, I can tell Griffin put his own mark on it. A large bed covered in a thick handmade quilt dominates most of the room. One bed. Of course. One very inviting bed that suddenly seems both enormous and tiny at the same time.

The realization hits us both.

"I'll take the sofa," Griffin offers immediately.

"Don't be ridiculous." I counter, too exhausted to feel awkward. "The sofa is too small for you. We're adults. We can share a bed without things getting complicated."

His eyebrows shoot up. "You sure?"

"Unless you snore. Then all bets are off."

Griffin laughs, the tension broken. "No snoring, I promise."

I collapse onto the bed, not bothering to pull back the covers. "Get in bed," I mumble, my eyes already closing. "I'm not kicking you out of your own bedroom."

After a moment's hesitation, Griffin stretches out beside me, careful to maintain a respectful distance. The bed dips under his weight, inevitably rolling me slightly toward him. Neither of us moves to correct it. The silence stretches, punctuated only by the occasional pop from the dying fire in the living room.

Eventually we slide under the covers, leaving a gap between us. But as the clock inches toward morning, that distance disappears. Almost unconsciously, I reach for Griffin in the dark, curling against his side. He hesitates for just a moment before wrapping his arm protectively around me, my head resting on his chest.

"This okay?" he whispers.

"More than okay," I sigh.

His fingers trace lazy patterns on my back through the sweatshirt.

"I have a game tomorrow," he murmurs into my hair. "Against Davos."

"Mmm," I acknowledge sleepily.

"Promise me you won't go to the bar."

"Griffin…"

"Please, Anika. Those guys are still out there. The bar is the first place they'll look for you. Come to the game instead. I'll leave tickets for you."

"The inventory delivery comes at ten tomorrow," I explain groggily. "I need to sign for it or lose my deposit."

Griffin sighs. "Then I'm coming with you."

"You have morning practice."

"After practice. Before the game."

"No, I need to go home for clothes and shoes. And a shower. I'll ask Lars or Colin to meet me there."

"You'll come to the game after?"

"Mmm." I yawn again, already half asleep. "We'll figure it out tomorrow."

Griffin's fingers find mine, intertwining them. "I just want you safe."

"I know," I whisper.

We fall silent, our breathing synchronizing. Griffin's arm tightens around me, and I nestle closer, feeling oddly at home. His steady heartbeat lulling me toward sleep.

"Anika?" His voice rumbles under my ear.

"Mmm?"

"Thomas doesn't deserve you."

I smile against his shirt. "Neither do you."

Just before sleep claims me completely, I feel Griffin press a gentle kiss to the top of my head. The last thing I register is his whispered words.

"I've got you, Anika. I promise."

Hope is louder than fear, even if it whispers.

CHAPTER TWENTY-FIVE

GRIFFIN

Nothing beats the sound of twenty thousand Swiss fans screaming your name. Well, that's not exactly true. I'd much prefer the sound of one Swiss fan in particular...

Nope. Gotta keep my mind clear.

The scoreboard glows 3-3 with forty seconds left in the third period. Sweat drips into my eyes as I crouch in goal position, my focus narrowing to the puck flying across the ice.

Davos's star forward dekes left, then charges right, his stick a blur as he winds up for what would be the game-winning shot.

My muscles burn from two periods of relentless play, but I've settled into that perfect zone where everything slows down, where I can track the puck like it's moving through Canadian maple syrup.

The puck launches toward me. I stretch, my glove hand extending impossibly far, and snag it mid-air. The crowd erupts.

"McGregor! McGregor!" they chant as I toss the puck to the referee.

I tap my stick twice on the ice. A signal to my defensemen. Christoph receives the pass from the ref and rockets it to Peter, who finds Tyler streaking up the boards. The fans rise to their feet as Tyler crosses the blue line with fifteen seconds left.

"Go, go, go!" I yell, though no one can hear me over the deafening roar.

Tyler passes to Peter, who fakes a shot before sliding the puck to Christoph. The seconds tick down. Ten...nine...

Christoph winds up from the point, but instead of shooting, he passes to Peter, who's snuck behind the defense. Peter redirects the puck into the net as the buzzer sounds.

The arena explodes. My teammates pile onto Peter while I skate the length of the ice to join the celebration. Peter headlocks me while Tyler sprays me with water.

"Did you see Campbell's face when you robbed him?" Tyler laughs. "Thought he had you beat glove-side!"

I grin through my mask. "Old Calgary boys never reveal their secrets."

The crowd continues to roar as we line up for handshakes. When I reach Dex in the line, he gives me an extra-hard slap on the pads.

"Highway robbery," he mutters good-naturedly. "Dinner's on you next time."

I wink. "Worth every franc."

After media scrums and cool-down stretches, I shower and change into street clothes. My phone buzzes with texts. Three from my agent about endorsement offers in Switzerland, one from Sawyer congratulating me on the shutout, and nothing from Anika. I hadn't expected her to use the ticket I'd left for her, but I'd still like to know she's safe back at my cabin. As soon as I turn the heat on in my car, I'll call her.

I push through the stadium exit doors, into the cool night air. The parking lot stands nearly empty now, save for a sleek black sedan idling near my car.

My steps falter.

Agents Bruderlin and Showalter stand beside my car (not the Bugatti, which I need to put in the shop) with grim expressions. My stomach drops. Something went wrong. Elodie? The money? Malcolm Chase? Anika? Or did they hear about the high-speed chase through Bern last night?

"Mr. McGregor," Bruderlin says with a nod. "Nice game."

"Thanks." I shift my bag to my other shoulder. "Is everything okay?"

"We need to talk," Showalter replies gravely.

So he *did* hear about the high-speed chase.

"Listen, I know I broke a few traffic laws, but..."

A third figure emerges from the shadows behind them. My blood runs cold.

"Durand?" I blurt. "What is he doing here?"

Bruderlin clears his throat. "This is Agent Wilde, Mr. McGregor. He's with—"

"MI6," Wilde finishes. "Sorry for the theatrics at the casino. Professional hazard."

My brain scrambles to process this. "MI6? As in, James Bond MI6?"

"We're considerably less flashy in real life," Wilde says dryly.

"So, your name isn't Durand?"

"No."

Bruderlin clears his throat. "There's been a complication."

My stomach drops as my thoughts fly to Anika. "What kind of complication?"

"Perhaps we should discuss this somewhere private," Durand...I mean...*Wilde* suggests.

I cross my arms. "Here is fine."

Showalter sighs. "The woman you knew as Elodie? She's gone. And so is the one hundred four million from the poker game."

The world tilts slightly. "What do you mean, gone?"

"We mean," Wilde says, "she never deposited the money into the FIS accounts. She transferred it elsewhere and disappeared."

"She's gone," Bruderlin interjects. "Vanished."

"But she's FIS," I protest. "She works for you!"

The three agents exchange loaded glances.

"She doesn't work for us," Bruderlin says slowly. "We believed she was FIS, but..."

"She played us all," Showalter interrupts.

Wilde steps closer. "'The woman you know as Elodie is actually Renata Nero. Known in certain circles as simply Nero. A high-level operative within the OMBRA crime syndicate."

My equipment bag slips from my shoulder and thuds to the ground. "OMBRA? Like some evil SPECTRE organization?"

"Precisely." Wilde nods. "We've been tracking Nero's movements across Europe for years but never had an identity on them or even knew if they were a man or a woman. Until now. I suspected her OMBRA involvement at Malcolm Chase's gala, but the tattoo on her wrist tipped me off on her true identity."

Showalter pulls out his phone, showing me a surveillance photo of Elodie leaving the casino, already sporting a blonde wig.

"Wait," I say, a horrible thought forming. "If she's not FIS, was she ever protecting me from assassins?"

Wilde's eyebrow rises. "Assassins?"

"On the train to St. Moritz. A man attacked me with knives and those metal punch things."

"Brass knuckles?" Showalter supplies.

"Right, those. Elodie...Nero...whatever her name is, she saved me. She fought him off."

The three agents exchange significant looks.

"What?" I demand.

"It seems likely," Wilde says carefully, "that was staged to gain your trust."

My mind reels. "She threw a man off a moving train to gain my trust?"

"Probably an OMBRA associate who jumped safely into water," Wilde explains. "It's a common tactic."

"She stole one hundred four million dollars," I whisper.

"Euros," Wilde corrects. "And yes."

I feel like I'm going to throw up. "So what happens now? Chase gets away with his Ponzi scheme?"

"MI6 has no interest in Chase or the one hundred four million," Wilde says simply. "That's FIS territory. My mandate is dismantling OMBRA. But since Nero has absconded with Swiss intelligence funds, we're joining forces."

"We'll need your continued cooperation," Showalter says.

I laugh bitterly. "You've got to be kidding me."

"She'll contact you again," Wilde says with certainty. "When she does, we need you to play along."

"What about Anika?" I ask suddenly. "Is she in danger?"

Something flickers across Wilde's face.

I narrow my eyes. "What aren't you telling me?"

Showalter shifts uncomfortably, not meeting my eyes. "About Miss Gisler..."

The world narrows to a pinpoint. Blood roars in my ears.

"What about Anika?" My voice sounds strange, distant.

"She's gone missing," Wilde says, his words hitting me like a cold knife to the chest. "She never opened the pub this afternoon, yet the doors were wide open and there were signs of a struggle. We believe OMBRA has taken her."

Not all spies carry guns; some carry hearts.

CHAPTER TWENTY-SIX

The afternoon air is frigid as I approach OMBRA's fortress. The decommissioned glacier observatory looks like something ripped straight out of a villain's Pinterest board. All sleek metal and glass perched impossibly on the jagged edge of the Monte Rosa Massif, right on the border of Switzerland and Italy.

"McGregor, status check." Wilde's voice comes through my earpiece.

"Freezing my butt off, thanks for asking."

I didn't sleep last night. Instead, I spent hours in a tactical briefing, learning entry points, exit strategies, and contingency plans. The instructions were clear. Use my connection with Nero to approach the fortress openly. Don't attempt entry. Wait for MI6 to engage, then ski down to the extraction point.

Early this morning, just as expected, Elodie...Nero...(still getting used to that) sent me an encrypted text message, almost as if she'd known I'd try to rescue Anika. I was told to come alone. The whole thing smells like a trap.

"Remember your instructions," Bruderlin cuts in. "No heroics."

"Got it. Get in, get out, no stopping for gift shop souvenirs."

A red light blinks on at the observatory's entrance.

"Movement at the main door," I whisper.

"Maintain position," Wilde orders.

"Copy," I mutter, checking my watch.

The gadgets they've given me seem woefully inadequate. But at least the watch is a fancy Swiss timepiece, courtesy of FIS. It supposedly contains a tracking device, electromagnetic pulse generator, and can shoot a tiny grappling hook. I practiced with it for approximately eight minutes before we deployed, so naturally, I'm an expert now.

A pair of OMBRA guards patrol the snowy perimeter below, assault rifles slung across their chests. They glance up occasionally, scanning the cliffs.

"Guards circling," I whisper. "Window closing."

"Stand firm. Wait for my signal."

Another minute ticks by. The guards move closer to my position. If they catch me lurking around instead of acting like an invited guest, they'll shoot now and ask questions later.

"Target approaching checkpoint alpha," a voice murmurs. "Stand by, McGregor."

"They're going to spot me," I hiss.

"Hold position!"

One guard stops, shielding his eyes to peer up at the ridge where I'm hiding. He nudges his partner, pointing in my direction.

"I'm compromised," I mutter.

"Do not move!" Wilde orders.

The guards raise their rifles.

"Sorry, can't hear you," I say, dislodging the earpiece. "Must be the altitude."

I make a split-second decision, launching myself toward the fortress entrance.

I slide through the entrance, expecting gunfire or alarms. Instead, I'm greeted by silence so complete it feels manufactured. No bullets in my back...yet.

The heavy metal door slides shut behind me with an ominous click, and the hallway stretches before me with dim blue lights running along the baseboards. I press forward, ducking into alcoves when I hear distant footsteps. I'm channeling every spy movie I've ever seen, which means I'm basically an expert at infiltration now.

I pause at an intersection, listening. Left or right? Both corridors look identical.

"When in doubt, go left," I mutter, not entirely sure where I got that from. Let's be honest. Probably a 007 movie.

Two more lefts and a right later, I realize I'm hopelessly lost. The observatory's interior is a labyrinth of identical hallways and unmarked doors. I duck into another alcove as footsteps approach, then fade away.

In my head, I'm absolutely crushing this spy thing.

I slip into what looks like a control room. Computer screens line the walls, displaying schematics and data streams I don't understand. Backing out of the room, I continue down the corridor, which widens into a large circular chamber.

I take three steps in when a soft whirring sound makes me freeze. The lights are powering up one by one around the perimeter of the room. I throw up a hand to shield my eyes, blinking rapidly against the glare.

"I hope you're enjoying your self-guided tour."

As my eyes adjust, I make out Nero standing on a raised platform across the room wearing an immaculate white pantsuit. Her dark hair cascades over one shoulder, and her smile is both welcoming and dangerous. Four armed guards flank her, weapons at the ready.

"Hello, Elodie," I say, trying to keep my voice steady. "Or should I call you Nero?"

"You can call me whatever you like. I've gone by many names." She says with a thin laugh, approaching with the casual confidence of someone who knows they hold all the cards. "Though I must say, I'm rather fond of how you say 'Elodie.'"

"Where's Anika?" I demand, cutting to the chase.

Nero circles me slowly, like a shark. "All in good time, Griffin. We have so much to catch up on first. I've been waiting for your arrival."

"Let me guess. You're about to offer me a drink while petting a white cat?"

Her laugh is genuine this time. "You've watched too many movies. Though I do appreciate a man who understands the classics."

She gestures expansively. "Please, walk with me. I so rarely get visitors who appreciate fine architecture."

I stand my ground. "I didn't come for a tour."

She counters with a smile. "Come. I insist."

Two guards step forward, making it clear this isn't actually a request. I follow her through another doorway, my mind racing to formulate an actual plan.

"This is our primary operations center," Nero explains as we enter a massive room filled with people working at computer stations. Giant screens cover the walls, displaying global maps with pulsing red dots scattered across them. "From here, we monitor every OMBRA operation worldwide."

"Impressive setup for a criminal organization," I say, scanning the room for possible exits.

"Criminal?" She laughs. "Such a limited perspective. OMBRA...it's more of a revolution."

"Right. Revolution. Got it." I nod, casually reaching up to adjust my earpiece, turning it back on.

"Don't bother," Nero says, noticing my movement. "The entire facility is encased in a Faraday cage and surrounded by six feet of reinforced concrete. No signals in or out without my authorization."

"Where is she?" I demand, my patience wearing thin.

"Still so focused on the bartender," Nero sighs. "I thought hockey players had better attention spans."

"I'm not playing games, Nero."

"But you are, Griffin. You've been playing since the moment you set foot in Switzerland." She moves behind her desk and activates a holographic display. "Let me show you something interesting."

She presses a button on the wall, and a hidden door slides open.

My heart pounds as I expect to see Anika, maybe bound or injured. Instead, it's just another corridor.

She leads me into another room with a long glass table displaying 3D holograms of financial markets. People in minimalist black clothing analyze data streams flowing around them.

"For centuries, the elite have hoarded wealth through manipulation and exploitation," Nero explains, waving her hand through the hologram, which ripples at her touch. "OMBRA is simply rebalancing the scales."

"By stealing billions?" I ask.

"By reclaiming what was stolen first," she corrects. "The funds from your little poker game are already working against corporate greed."

I raise an eyebrow. "So you're Robin Hood now?"

"More ambitious than that." She smiles. "Robin Hood maintained the system while offering temporary relief. We're dismantling it entirely."

"So you're the good guys? That's why you kidnapped Anika?"

She smiles enigmatically. "A necessary step to bring you here. You should be flattered. Few outsiders ever see this facility."

The tour continues. She shows me everything with the pride of a CEO giving a board presentation. It's becoming clear she's either recruiting me or planning to ensure I never leave to tell anyone about this place.

"You've been busy," I say as we enter what appears to be her massive private office. Floor-to-ceiling windows reveal a breathtaking view of the Alps. "But you still haven't told me where Anika is."

Nero sits behind her desk, gesturing for me to take the chair opposite her. The guards remain at the door.

"Anika is safe," she says.

"I want to see her," I demand.

"And you will." Nero leans forward. "But first, let's discuss why you're really here, Griffin."

"I came for Anika."

"Did you?" She tilts her head. "Or did you come because you

recognized something in me? Something familiar?" She smiles. "We're not so different, you and I."

I almost laugh. "Pretty sure we're completely different. I play hockey. You build secret lairs in mountains."

"We both saw a broken system and chose to operate outside it," she counters. "You left the NHL because the owners were corrupt. I operate outside of conventional finance for the same reason."

"I didn't leave the NHL," I point out.

"Is that so?" She stands, walking to a cabinet where she pours two glasses of amber liquid. "You were willing to break rules, cheat at cards, all for what you believed was justice."

She offers me a glass. I don't take it.

"You'll forgive me if I don't drink anything you offer."

"As you wish." She takes a sip from one glass. "Though poisoning you would be terribly unimaginative, don't you think?"

"I wouldn't put it past you with that cliché villain act."

"OMBRA isn't just an organization, Griffin," she explains, reclining back. Now I really do expect her to swivel in her chair petting a cat.

"It's the future. While governments squabble over borders and resources, we're building something that transcends those outdated concepts. The FIS manipulated you, just as the NHL manipulated its players," she continues. "But OMBRA offers something different. True autonomy."

"What is this? A job interview?"

"Perhaps." Her eyes glitter with amusement.

"Thanks, but I'm not interested in joining your supervillain club."

Nero laughs. "Supervillain? You truly are adorable. Yes, the word Ombra means 'shadow,' but we're not lurking in dark corners. OMBRA is what the light can't touch."

"Very poetic," I mutter. "Now where's Anika?"

"So single minded, Griffin. It's not very becoming."

"I want to see Anika," I repeat. "Now."

Nero studies me for a long moment, then taps her bracelet. "Bring Miss Gisler to my office," she says. Turning back to me, she smiles, and I see a flicker in her eyes before I feel a large presence behind me followed by a sharp pain in my skull. Then everything goes dark.

Every great escape starts with laughter.

CHAPTER TWENTY-SEVEN

Two goons march me into what appears to be a luxury hotel lobby, even though it's probably just where my kidnappers like to play video games. It's all gleaming marble floors, floor-to-ceiling windows with panoramic views, and modern art pieces that dot the walls. Some kind of avant-garde water feature trickles softly in the background.

And there, slumped in a chair unconscious, is Griffin. His

wrists are zip-tied to the arm rests. His head lolls to one side, a trickle of blood running from his temple down his jawline.

"Griffin!" I lunge forward, but the two men clamp down on my shoulders. "Let me go!"

Griffin's eyelids flutter at the sound of my voice. He looks disoriented for a moment before his gaze locks onto mine. Recognition floods his face, followed by panic. He immediately strains against whatever binds him to the chair.

"Anika? Are you okay?"

"Am *I* okay? You're bleeding!"

He blinks, seeming to register the situation fully. "Only a little. Hockey players bleed all the time."

Even concussed, he manages to make me roll my eyes.

"What a touching reunion."

I turn to see Nero, or Elodie, or whatever her name actually is sitting behind an enormous glass desk. She wears an immaculate white suit and severe stilettos.

"What did you do to him?" I demand.

"Nothing permanent." She waves dismissively. "Please, sit."

The goons push me into a chair across from Griffin.

Griffin wiggles against his zip ties. "Why are we here? What do you want?"

"Nothing from you, actually." Nero smiles. "You two were simply...in the way."

"Let Anika go," Griffin demands, his voice gaining strength. "She has nothing to do with this."

Nero ignores him and presses a button on her desk. The room's lighting dims as a holographic display activates in the center of the room, displaying the Davos World Economic Forum logo.

"Next month," she announces like she's giving a TED talk, "the most powerful people in the world will gather in Davos. Presidents, prime ministers, CEOs. All in one place."

Griffin and I exchange glances. Here comes the villain monologue.

"Let me guess," I interrupt. "You're going to hold them hostage for one million dollars?"

"One *billion* dollars," Griffin adds, channeling his Doctor Evil impression.

Nero's eye twitches. "This isn't *Austin Powers*. My plan is far more sophisticated."

She swipes her hand across the air, and the hologram changes to display microscopic robots crawling across what appears to be brain tissue. I suppress a gag.

"Nanobots," she explains, her voice rising with excitement. "Delivered through the air filtration systems, activated by specific neuro-frequencies. Once deployed, every leader at the forum becomes my puppet."

Griffin stifles a laugh. "Sorry, did you say mind control nanobots?"

"Mock if you must," Nero continues, unbothered. "But while you've been skating around on the ice, I've been developing technology beyond your comprehension. The nanobots are merely phase one."

She expands the hologram again, showing people across the globe with glowing eyes.

"All World Economic Forum Young Global Leaders have unwittingly received a dormant code during routine check-ups. On my signal, synchronized coups will occur worldwide."

Griffin and I exchange glances. His expression says what I'm thinking. This woman is off her rocker.

"So, basically Skynet," Griffin mutters. "And you came from the future to kill Anika and me before we have a son that will destroy your operation."

My whole face brightens. "You want to have kids with me?"

"I want everything with you," he says with the most

dazzling smile I've ever seen. It would be romantic if we weren't being held hostage.

Nero steps between us, blocking my view of Griffin. She really hates that he cares for me.

"Have you heard of Project Blue Beam, Mr. McGregor?"

"Can't say I have," he replies. "Sounds like a toothpaste commercial."

The hologram shifts again to show what appears to be images of spaceships in the sky.

"Is that...an alien invasion?" Griffin asks incredulously.

Nero starts pacing the room.

"Project Blue Beam is a classified technology capable of creating any illusion anywhere on Earth. Imagine the possibilities! Alien invasions, natural disasters, political assassinations. I could create mass hysteria with the flip of a switch."

Griffin snorts, which earns him a withering glare from Nero.

"So you're going to...fake an alien invasion? Why?" I ask, trying to keep up.

"The masses will believe anything they see." She spins around, arms spread wide. "Fear is the greatest weapon, and it will be mine to wield. Governments destabilized by events which never physically occurred. The possibilities are endless. And the best part? Because of the mind-control nanobots, nobody will know I'm the one who holds the strings."

Griffin clears his throat. "This all sounds very...creative. But what exactly do Anika and I have to do with your, uh, world domination plan?"

Nero stops, blinking as if remembering we exist. "Nothing, actually. You were just collateral damage."

I furrow my brows. "You kidnapped us for nothing?"

"Well." She shrugs. "Griffin is quite the pretty little bauble. I might keep him and do away with you."

She walks back to her desk and presses a button. "Now, if you'll excuse me..."

Two more guards enter the room.

"Take them to holding until I decide what to do with them," Nero orders.

"I'm sorry," I whisper to Griffin as the guards cut his zip ties, haul us to our feet, and take us away.

"About what? Getting kidnapped? Not your fault."

"No, about Thomas. I shouldn't have gone on that date."

Griffin blinks. "We're discussing this now?"

"Well, we might die, so..." I shrug.

"We're not going to die. Not today. Any chance you've got some kung fu moves up your sleeve?" he whispers.

"I'm good, but not that good."

I counted at least ten guards on this level alone.

We're marched down a sterile white corridor, and Griffin's eyes never stop scanning our surroundings. The two burly guards keep their weapons trained on us, maintaining a professional distance.

"How badly are you hurt?" I whisper, eyeing the dried blood on Griffin's temple.

"Only a bump on the head. Nothing compared to taking a slap shot to the face."

The guard shoves Griffin forward. "No talking."

Griffin stumbles but recovers with surprising grace. As he rights himself, I notice him fiddling with his watch. An expensive-looking gadget with too many dials for telling simple time.

The guards stop us in front of a reinforced door. One punches a code into the keypad while the other keeps his gun trained on us. The door slides open to reveal a small, windowless room with two metal chairs bolted to the floor.

"In," the taller guard orders.

Griffin steps forward first, suddenly tripping over his own

feet and collapsing against the guard. "Sorry! Hockey injury. Knee gives out sometimes."

The guard shoves him off with a grunt.

But Griffin presses something on the side of his watch, and a tiny whooshing sound fills the air. A nearly invisible wire shoots out, wrapping around the guard's ankles. Griffin yanks, and the man crashes to the floor with a surprised yelp.

I drive my knee into the second guard's groin (I've discovered I really like that move). He doubles over, and I bring my elbow down on the back of his neck. He crumples beside his friend.

Griffin stares at me, mouth agape. "Remind me never to upset you."

"You can thank me by getting us out of here."

Griffin presses another button on his watch, and both guards convulse briefly before going still.

"Did you kill them?"

"Electromagnetic pulse. They'll wake up with headaches." Griffin peers outside. "Coast clear. Let's move."

We sprint down corridors, ducking into alcoves whenever we hear voices. Alarms begin blaring, red lights flashing overhead.

"They know we've escaped," I pant.

We skid around a corner, nearly colliding with a startled technician, who drops her tablet with a clatter.

"Sorry!" Griffin apologizes before shoving her into a supply closet and jamming the handle with a broom.

"Canadians," I mutter. "Even breaking out of an evil lair, so polite."

We navigate through a maze of utilitarian hallways until we reach an emergency exit. Griffin checks his watch again.

"Wilde and the cavalry should be here any minute. When we get outside, we need to move fast."

The moment we push through the exit door, more alarms blare behind us. Cold air slaps my face as we sprint across the snow to a ridge overlooking the steep descent.

Griffin pulls me toward a snowbank, where two pairs of skis wait, partially buried. "I stashed these earlier, just in case."

"You brought me skis?"

"And a matching jacket." He tosses me a hooded parka identical to his, with a red maple leaf emblazoned on the back.

I slip it on as Griffin helps me into the ski bindings. "Why the matching outfits? Starting a Canadian cult?"

"We're going to have company coming down that mountain. They'll all be wearing these."

No sooner do we click into our skis than an alarm blares from inside the fortress. Guards pour out onto the snow, pointing and shouting.

"Go!" Griffin shouts.

We launch over the platform edge, plummeting several feet before our skis hit powder. My knees absorb the impact as we carve down the mountain face, zigzagging between rock outcroppings. The mountain drops away beneath our skis, snow spraying in our wake as we navigate sharp turns down the near-vertical slope.

Behind us, engines roar. I glance back to see men on snowmobiles in pursuit, because of course evil henchmen have motorized ski bikes. Others strap on skis, sliding down after us.

"Don't look back!" Griffin shouts. "Just follow me!"

We slalom between jagged rocks and towering pines, the distance between us and our pursuers shrinking with each turn.

"Stay close!" Griffin shouts over the wind.

I follow his lead, weaving between trees as armed men on skis pursue us. The *whump-whump-whump* of helicopter blades grows louder overhead.

"We're surrounded!" I yell.

Griffin points ahead. "Not for long!"

The helicopter appears over a ridge, and for a terrifying moment, I think it's OMBRA, until figures in matching maple leaf jackets leap from the open door, landing on skis. They immediately spread out in formation.

"Friends of yours?"

"Our decoys," Griffin says, pulling me sharply right as our pursuers hesitate, confused by the sudden multiplication of targets.

The decoys converge with us, creating a diversion. We split, merge, cross paths. The guards falter, unable to track which maple leaf jacket contains their targets.

An explosion rocks the mountain behind us. I glance back to see smoke billowing from the OMBRA fortress. MI6 making their move on Nero.

The slope steepens. We pick up speed, crisscrossing with the skiers in maple leaf jackets, who mirror our movements. Behind us, the OMBRA skiers split up, trying to track each jacket.

A man on a ski bike roars toward us. One of our allies pulls something from his pocket—a small metal ball—and tosses it under the approaching vehicle. It sparks, and the bike veers wildly before crashing into a snowbank.

"Where do they get these toys?" I shout.

"Spies-R-Us!"

The pursuit grows. More OMBRA guards join the chase on skis, getting close.

"We've got company!" I shout.

"Split up at the next ridge!" Griffin calls over the wind rushing past our ears. "Crisscross patterns!"

A man skis alongside us. It's Wilde.

"Hand her off," he calls to Griffin.

Griffin squeezes my hand. "Go with him. I'll lead them away."

"But—"

"Trust me."

Wilde pulls me away before I can respond. We veer sharply into a narrow chasm.

"In here," Wilde commands, ushering us into a crevice barely visible among the rocks. "They'll pass right by."

Sure enough, the pursuers roar past our hiding place, chasing the decoy agents still zigzagging down the slope. I watch the chase continue. Despite the identical outfits, I spot Griffin instantly by his distinctive hockey player's stance. His weight centered low, powerful turns, with the same confident edge he shows on the ice.

The pursuing guards close in. One by one, the agents peel off in different directions, each followed by a cluster of confused pursuers. Eventually, only Griffin remains, trailed by three guards on snow bikes.

Griffin speeds toward the edge of a massive drop, gaining momentum rather than slowing. The three pursuers close in, weapons raised.

"No, no, no," I whisper.

He picks up speed, heading straight for the cliff's edge.

"What is he doing?" My voice rises in panic.

I race to the edge of a parallel ridge, watching in horror as Griffin speeds toward the precipice without slowing down.

"Griffin!" I scream uselessly as he launches off the cliff edge, soaring into open air. For three heart-stopping seconds, he's in free fall.

Then, with a snap, a parachute deploys above him. Brilliant red and white, a giant maple leaf unfurling above him. That lovely, ridiculous man has the Canadian flag printed on his parachute. The guards skid to a halt at the edge, unable to follow.

Relief floods through me so intensely my knees nearly buckle.

"Rather dramatic, isn't he?" Wilde comments, appearing beside me.

The helicopter swoops down, hovering near our position. Wilde signals with a laser pointer, and the craft descends toward a small clearing.

"Time to go," he shouts over the noise. "Your boyfriend is meeting us at the rendezvous point."

We ski to the clearing, where the helicopter awaits with rotors whirring. Wilde helps me aboard first, then follows me inside. The craft immediately lifts off, banking sharply away from the mountain.

We descend toward a snowy, open space where I can see Griffin's parachute already collapsed on the ground. He's unbuckling his harness when we touch down.

I don't wait for the rotors to stop. I leap out, stumbling through the snow toward him, my skis long abandoned.

"You idiot!" I yell, throwing myself into his arms. "You magnificent, ridiculous idiot!"

Griffin catches me, his arms strong and secure around my waist. His face is flushed from cold and exertion, snowflakes clinging to his eyelashes.

"I love you," I blurt out, surprising myself as much as him. "I love you and your stupid hockey quotes and your crazy stunts and—"

He cuts me off with a kiss that warms me from the inside out. His lips are surprisingly soft against mine, a sharp contrast to the rough stubble grazing my chin. My heart stutters, then races, and I melt into him completely. Griffin's arms tighten around me, pulling me closer until I can feel the rapid rise and fall of his chest against mine.

I've spent twenty-five years avoiding this very thing, building walls around myself, and here comes this goofy Canadian crashing through them like they're made of tissue paper. My fingers find their way to the curls at his collar, still damp from snow and sweat, and I hold on as if he might float away if I let go.

When he finally pulls back just enough to rest his forehead against mine, his hands frame my face, thumbs brushing away the tears I hadn't realized were falling. His brown eyes are dancing with joy and surprise and delight. It makes my stomach flip in the most wonderful way.

"If this is my reward," he says, pressing another kiss on the tip of my nose. "I might have to jump off more cliffs."

"Welcome to Italy," Wilde announces dryly as he walks past us. "Follow me."

Wilde leads us through knee-deep snow, toward an amphibious all-terrain vehicle with massive tires.

"Sit tight," Wilde says, handing us thermal blankets. "This transport will take you to a secure location in the valley."

He checks his watch. "I'm heading back up to coordinate the raid. With any luck, we'll have Nero in custody within the hour."

"I don't suppose there's a cappuccino waiting at this secure location?" Griffin asks, completely serious. "We are in Italy after all."

I stare at him in disbelief. "We just escaped an evil lair by skiing down a mountain with armed guards chasing us, and you're thinking about coffee?"

Griffin shrugs, flashing that dimpled smile that makes my stomach do somersaults. "I miss my Timmies."

"What is...Timmies?" I ask.

"Tim Hortons, of course. Best coffee on the other side of the Atlantic."

"I beg to differ," Wilde says, right before shutting the door. He slaps his hand on the driver's window, signaling to head out, then ambles back through the snow.

The helicopter rotors whir to life as Wilde climbs aboard. Through the thick windows, I watch it lift off and disappear over the mountain ridge, heading back toward the OMBRA fortress.

The big beast of a vehicle we're in lurches forward, and Griffin immediately drapes an arm around my shoulders, like it's the most natural thing in the world. My body relaxes into his side.

"So," he says, his dimples appearing as he grins down at me. "Dating lesson recap. Skiing away from international criminals. Good date activity or bad date activity?"

I laugh despite myself. "I think I'm going to have to fire you as my dating coach. You're terrible at it."

"What? Why?" His mock outrage is almost convincing. "I thought the whole rescue from evil lair thing would earn me bonus points."

"Getting kidnapped wasn't exactly part of the dating curriculum I signed up for." I nudge his ribs playfully. "Plus, I'm pretty sure most blind dates don't go parachuting off a cliff."

"Poor Thomas doesn't stand a chance." Griffin doesn't look remotely sorry.

"I'm now utterly ruined for boring landscape architects."

"I maintain I was an excellent coach. My student just fell for the teacher instead of the other guy."

Through the window, I watch the majestic mountains retreat as we descend into the valley.

"What happens now?" I ask, suddenly serious. "When this is all over?"

Griffin considers this, tucking a strand of hair behind my ear. "Well, I was thinking we could start with that cappuccino."

"And after that?"

"After that?" He smiles, and I see our future reflected in his eyes. "I think we still need to take down Malcolm Chase. Are you ready for one last adventure?"

"Hmmm. Maybe I'll sit this one out, if you don't mind."

He leans down and kisses my nose. "I don't mind."

If you fall, make it look like you were meant to.

CHAPTER TWENTY-EIGHT

I t turns out Swiss precision also applies to revenge—executed exactly at 5:30 AM with a side of hot chocolate and *schadenfreude*.

Once again, I'm freezing my butt off in the snow, preparing a raid on a criminal mastermind. I better not make a habit out of this.

This time, it's Malcolm Chase's obscenely ridiculous alpine

chateau, and I'm with my ragtag group of friends. Hockey players, wives, and one Irish mobster.

The mountain sun hasn't fully risen, casting everything in a bluish predawn glow. Chase's outdoor Christmas lights are still on, but it's not Santa entering the house this morning. I feel like that guy in *Die Hard* even though Christmas Eve isn't until tomorrow.

"You sure about this, kid?" Showalter asks, checking his watch for the fifth time in two minutes. He's decked out in tactical gear while I'm wearing jeans and a heavy Titans jacket. "You can still wait in the van."

"Absolutely sure. Malcolm Chase stole from my teammates, manipulated the league, and indirectly got my girlfriend kidnapped by international criminals. This is personal."

I nod toward my friends. "Besides, I've got my support system."

When I called for backup, I expected maybe two or three friends to show up. Instead, I got the entire hockey mafia. Behind me stands the most unlikely strike force ever assembled. Half the Titans roster, three hockey wives, one hockey girlfriend (soon to be fiancée), one parrot, and an Irish mobster in a flat cap.

Otto the parrot chooses this moment to squawk from Maggie's shoulder, causing several FIS agents to jump.

"Squawk off, Malcolm!"

"Otto! Shh!" Maggie covers his beak gently. "Sorry, he gets excited during raids."

"During raids?" Showalter raises an eyebrow. "How many raids has this bird been on?"

Otto begins to sing "Bad boys, bad boys..."

"Ummm, none at all," Maggie lies. "He's neeeeever been on a raid."

Sawyer's uncle Whitey adjusts his Peaky Blinders cap and

cracks his knuckles. "Reminds me of the Belfast job in '99," he muses with his thick Irish brogue. "Except we had less sports equipment and more explosives."

Sawyer's sister Siobhan elbows her uncle. "We're here in an advisory capacity only, remember?"

"Right, right." Uncle Whitey mimes zipping his lips. "Advisory only."

Owen adjusts the GoPro strapped to his chest while Emily fiddles with the settings on her phone. "This is so going on my blog," she whispers. "Anonymous source reveals Ponzi scheme takedown."

I squint at her. "You still have that blog?"

Her eyes dart to the side. "Uh, no."

"Remember sleuthing around the Blizzard Dome in the middle of the night?" Owen grins at his wife.

"Just like old times," Emily squeaks, popping on tiptoe to kiss Owen.

Showalter looks incredulously at the whole group. "Who are you people?"

Colette raises her hand. "I'm a high school English teacher."

"And I'm with her." Hendrix paces nervously, constantly patting his jacket pocket.

Hendrix has been acting strange since he arrived yesterday. I know he's got an engagement ring burning a hole in his pocket. He plans to propose tomorrow on Christmas Eve at the Gornergrat.

Colette watches him with amusement. "Are you sure you're nervous about the raid and not something else?"

Hendrix nearly jumps out of his skin. "What? No! I mean, yes! The raid. Totally the raid."

"Real smooth, bro," Liam snickers, elbowing his brother. "The Nebraska Knights send their regards to this scumbag, by the way."

The scumbag, of course, is Malcolm Chase. Liam is here standing in solidarity with his brother and all us Titans. He's even sporting a Titans jersey, which is big of him considering the Knights are our sometimes rivals.

I take a deep breath, the cold air sharp in my lungs. Somewhere in Toronto, another team is preparing to raid the Blizzard Dome offices. A third group is positioned outside Chase's Toronto residence. Three simultaneous strikes to ensure he can't escape or destroy evidence.

"You good?" Owen asks, noticing my expression.

"Are you kidding? After taking down OMBRA, this is a walk in the park."

Mikael Laakso stands rigid as a statue, eyes fixed on Chase's mansion. The retired captain's jaw clenches with every breath. "Six years," he growls. "Six years watching him underpay staff and squeeze every penny while preaching fiscal responsibility."

His wife Hannah loops her arm through his. "And now you get to see him in handcuffs."

Coach Knight smacks a hockey stick against his palm rhythmically. "Should've known something was fishy when he started pushing player investment opportunities. Not exactly standard owner behavior."

Kevin Tate checks his phone. "Leigh says to kick his booty extra hard for making her miss this. Baby's not due for three weeks, but she's not taking chances."

Maggie laughs. "She said booty? That's so Leigh."

"We're parents of toddlers," Kevin deadpans. Our whole vocabulary consists of potty, ouchie, and uppy uppy."

"Awww that's so adorable," Emily coos. Owen suspects she has baby fever.

Siobhan types on her tablet. "I've got eyes on his security system. Ready to disable on your signal." She looks up. "Also, nobody tell the FIS I'm doing this. Super illegal."

Showalter pretends not to hear her. "Plausible deniability," he mutters.

Uncle Whitey adjusts his flat cap. "In me day, we'd just go in swingin'," he says with his thick Irish brogue. "None of this digital nonsense."

"In your day," Sawyer counters, "phones were still attached to walls, Uncle Whitey."

"And we liked it that way, boyo!"

"Everyone remember the plan?" I ask, surveying my friends.

Kevin Tate nods. "Distraction at the front gate while FIS enters through the back."

"And no punching," Liam adds, glancing pointedly at his brother Hendrix. "No matter how much Chase deserves it."

"Speak for yourself," Hendrix mutters.

Showalter's headset blinks a red light. He listens, then gives me a curt nod. "Toronto teams are in position. We move in thirty seconds."

I raise my stick slightly, and fifteen hockey sticks rise in unison behind me. We must look absolutely ridiculous. I love it.

Coach Knight grips his stick tightly, knuckles white. "Twenty-five years coaching, and I've never wanted to check someone into the boards more than Malcolm Chase."

Uncle Whitey cracks his knuckles. "Remember, lads and lasses, go for the kneecaps first."

"We're not actually assaulting anyone," Showalter clarifies with alarm. "This is a legal operation."

"Right." Uncle Whitey winks. "Legal kneecapping."

"Remind me why we brought the actual mobster?" I whisper to Sawyer.

"Irish charm," Sawyer winks. "Plus, he knows a guy who knows a guy who can make Chase's offshore accounts very uncomfortable."

"Fifteen seconds."

Hannah pulls out her phone, snapping a quick photo of our assembled group. "This is going to break social media when it drops."

"Delete that," Mikael growls.

"Just kidding, Stern Daddy." Hannah winks, tucking her phone away. "This is just for the Christmas card."

Mikael shoots her a hard look, and she throws up her hands. "Kidding!"

"Ten seconds," Showalter whispers and nods to Siobhan.

Siobhan glances up from her tablet. "Security disabled. Cameras looping empty footage. And I've frozen the backup generators. He's digitally blind."

I glance at my friends...my family really...all wearing Titans colors like we're about to hit the ice together. A wave of gratitude washes over me.

"Five...four..."

Uncle Whitey spits and adjusts his cap.

"Three...two..."

Sawyer and Owen exchange a fist bump.

"One...Go time."

Showalter signals his agents, who move efficiency toward the mansion's various entrances. We follow behind like a bizarre parade.

As we approach the front door, Showalter holds up a hand. "We go in first, secure the scene, then you follow. Clear?"

Uncle Whitey chuckles. "Sure, lad. Whatever you say."

The FIS team breaches the door with a battering ram.

"FEDERAL INTELLIGENCE SERVICE! NOBODY MOVE!"

The FIS agents sweep through Malcolm's mansion, room by room. Their tactical lights create eerie shadows as they call "Clear!" through their comms.

"Clear to proceed." Showalter signals the all-clear for us to enter as they move to the back and side exits.

We enter the mansion like a bizarre sports-themed SWAT team. The place is a monument to excess. Vaulted ceilings, marble floors, custom woodwork everywhere. It's the kind of wealth that only comes from stealing other people's money.

"Split up," I direct. "We need to find Chase before he destroys anything important."

Our group fans out through the mansion's first floor. I hear doors banging open, closets being checked. Otto provides a running commentary of "Where's daddy? Where's daddy?" as Sawyer and Maggie search the kitchen.

Uncle Whitey whistles low, running his finger along a gold-trimmed sideboard.

"Place like this, the silverware alone would fetch six figures," he muses, eyes twinkling.

Sawyer coughs loudly. "We're here to witness justice, Uncle Whitey. Not steal the spoons."

"Speakin' academically, boyo. Just keepin' me skills sharp."

Mikael stalks through the living room, examining framed photos of Chase with various celebrities and dignitaries. "Look at this," he growls, picking up a photo of Chase with the commissioner. "Smiling while he robbed us blind."

Hannah rubs his arm. "At least now everyone will know the truth."

Hendrix paces anxiously, still patting his pocket. "Can we hurry this up? I've got things to do."

"Like propose?" I whisper.

He shushes me. "Dude! Not so loud!"

"Your secret's safe," I assure him. "But everyone knows. You're about as subtle as a freight train."

Colette appears beside us. "What are we whispering about?"

"Nothing!" Hendrix squeaks.

Owen and Emily return from the east wing. "Eight

bedrooms, six bathrooms, and a home theater that seats twenty," Emily reports. "No sign of Chase."

"He must've known we were coming," Kevin says, looking disappointed.

I shake my head. "No. He's here. I can feel it."

There's only one place he could be.

"The study," I announce. "I know where he is."

Everyone stops and turns toward me.

"Follow me."

I lead the group through the mansion's twisting corridors, past priceless art and gaudy displays of wealth. The farther we go, the more I recognize from that night. The night Wilde sent Anika down that tunnel. How things have changed since then.

"There." I point to an ornate door at the end of a hallway. "He's in there."

We approach quietly, and I press my ear against the door. Paper shredding. Furious typing. Muttered curses.

I look back at my friends, all wearing identical expressions of determination, and nod. Then I throw open the door.

Malcolm Chase stands over a paper shredder, feeding documents into it like he's Oliver Freaking North. A computer screen flickers with deletion progress bars. He freezes mid-shred, face pale as fourteen people and one bird file into his study, forming a semicircle around his desk.

"Going somewhere, Malcolm?" I ask pleasantly.

His eyes dart between us and the bookcase against the far wall.

"What is the meaning of this?" he sputters, dropping the papers and adjusting his silk robe like we've interrupted his morning tea rather than his crime spree. "This is a private residence!"

Only then does he recognize everyone wearing Titans jerseys. "Jablonski? O'Malley? Ellis?" Then his eyes narrow on me. "And you, McGregor. What the hell are you doing in my home?"

"What am I doing? Well, let's see." I tap my stick against my palm. "First, I won back the money you stole from investors. And now, I'm here to watch you get arrested."

Malcolm inches toward the bookcase as he speaks. "This vendetta against me is absurd. I've only ever acted in the best interests of the Toronto Titans."

"Is that why you created a Ponzi scheme disguised as team stock?" Owen asks.

"Or why you've been siphoning money into offshore accounts for years?" Hendrix adds.

"This is absurd." Chase tries to regain his composure. "I'm a respected businessman."

"Not for much longer," Mikael says, expression cold.

"You underpaid the female staff for years," Hannah says.

"Just ask Nancy Lambert," Emily adds.

Malcolm scoffs. "Nancy Lambert is in jail, where she belongs. My lawyers will have this sorted by lunch."

"I'd like to see them try." Siobhan steps forward, tablet in hand. "I've accessed your encrypted servers. All eighteen of them, including the ones in the Caymans you thought were untraceable."

Malcolm pales. "I don't know what you're talking about."

"I sent copies to the FIS, FBI, CSA, and NHL Commissioner's office," she continues. "Oh, and I tweeted your offshore account numbers. They're trending."

Sawyer grins at his sister. "She's wicked smart."

Uncle Whitey laughs, adjusting his flat cap. "Listen here, ya posh eejit. I've been runnin' circles around the Garda since before ye were in short pants, and even I know better than to keep incriminatin' evidence in me own feckin' house!"

Otto squawks from Maggie's shoulder: "Busted, nerd!"

Malcolm jumps. "What the hell is that?"

"This is Otto. He's an African Grey parrot," Maggie says proudly. "And he catches bad guys for kicks and giggles."

Malcolm's composure cracks. "You have no idea who you're dealing with."

"Actually, we do," Kevin says, clicking his tongue. "A greedy man, who thought he could steal from hockey fans."

"Bad idea," Coach Knight adds, tapping his stick against the floor. "Very bad idea."

"You won't get away with this," Malcolm snarls. "I have connections."

"Are you sure about that?" Emily chirps. "I just checked my phone. The NHL Board of Governors has called an emergency meeting. You're about to be the former owner of the Toronto Titans."

"You can't prove anything."

Uncle Whitey shakes his head. "Oh, shut yer gob, ya manky wee scrote. Ye wouldn't last one day in Southie."

"We have the transaction records," I say. "Every dollar you siphoned from investors, including your players."

"And the emails," Siobhan adds. "The ones where you called the players 'overpaid muscle with the collective IQ of a hockey puck.'"

Owen gestures to everyone present, still recording on his GoPro. "That's funny, because this overpaid muscle just helped take down your empire."

Mikael crosses his arms across his chest. "I spent six years as captain watching you squeeze every dollar from this team while paying female staff half what they deserve."

"I have no control over the going wage in Canada," Malcolm spits.

"How about we let the public decide?" Hannah chimes in.

"Your social media nightmare starts in approximately three minutes."

"You people have no clue about running a multi-million-dollar sports franchise," Malcolm sputters.

Coach Knight laughs. "Son, I've spent decades managing team budgets on a shoestring. I understand enough to know when someone's skimming off the top."

"The lockout was just a distraction," Liam realizes aloud. "You needed time to move assets offshore before anyone noticed."

"You orchestrated everything," Emily observes. "The CBA negotiations, the NHLPA. You poked the bear."

Chase inches toward the bookcase, trying to be subtle. "This is preposterous. I demand you all leave immediately."

"Looking for your escape tunnel?" I ask quietly. "The one behind the bookcase?"

Malcolm makes a break for it, lunging toward the bookcase and yanking on a disguised lever. The shelves swing open with a mechanical hum, revealing a dimly lit corridor.

He darts inside, only to crash directly into Showalter and two FIS agents coming the other way. They pull Malcolm back into the study.

"Malcolm Chase," Showalter says, handcuffs already out. "You're under arrest for securities fraud, embezzlement, money laundering, conspiracy to defraud, and operating a criminal enterprise across international borders."

"Nobody makes a fool of me," he spits, glaring at me.

I can't help but smile. "You've done a good job of that yourself."

Uncle Whitey chuckles while helping himself to Malcolm's cigars. "In the old country, we at least had the decency to be proper criminals."

"Thank you, Uncle Whitey," Sawyer says. "That's quite enough from you."

Chase glowers at Whitey and Sawyer as the agent secures his wrists behind his back.

"Your assets have been frozen," Showalter informs him. "Your accounts are being audited as we speak."

"I want my lawyer," Chase mutters.

"That can be arranged," Showalter says, nodding to his agents. "But you should know we've already raided your Toronto offices and residence simultaneously. We have everything."

"We'll need statements from all of you," Showalter says to our group.

As Chase is led away, he stops beside me. "This isn't over, McGregor."

"Actually, it is," I reply with a grin. "Merry Christmas, ya filthy animal."

I've always wanted to say that.

As the agents march him toward the door, Malcolm looks back at us with pure hatred.

Uncle Whitey offers a cheerful little wave goodbye. "Don't drop the soap, ya donkey!" he calls after them.

We all watch Malcolm get escorted out, and suddenly the victory high fades into something else. We all exchange awkward glances, the same question hanging in the air.

"So...what happens to the Titans now?" Owen finally asks, voicing what we're all thinking.

Reality starts sinking in.

"The league will probably appoint some interim management group," Coach Knight says, running a hand through his silver hair. "Seen it before when owners get into trouble."

"What if they relocate the team?" Emily asks, glancing worriedly at Owen. "It's happened before."

Hendrix looks like he's about to hyperventilate. "Are we about to be sold to some random billionaire who'll move us to somewhere in the desert?"

Colette places a hand on his arm to settle him. "That's not going to happen."

"They can't move the Titans," I protest. "Toronto's hockey town."

Sawyer nods. "The fan base is too strong. But there's still going to be chaos."

"What about our contracts?" Kevin asks quietly. "If there's no owner..."

"League honors them," Coach Knight assures him. "But it'll be a mess for a while."

A somber silence falls over the group. We'd taken down a criminal but possibly put our team's future in jeopardy.

"Actually," Mikael clears his throat, "I've been thinking, and I came up with...an idea you might think is nuts." He holds his hands up like he's about to propose something crazy. "But, hear me out first."

Some hearts beat faster when the music is slightly sad.

CHAPTER TWENTY-NINE

Anika

I slam my forehead back onto the sticky table with a melodramatic thud. The cool wood feels nice against my skin, which is probably why I've been face-planting here for the past hour. The wood grain has probably tattooed itself onto my forehead, but I don't care. Let it mark me.

I become one with the table as "Heaven Knows I'm Miserable Now" by The Smiths starts playing for what must be the fortieth time today.

"*Gott im Himmel!*" Lars throws his Jass cards down. "Anika, please. We cannot take any more of this sad English man singing about his problems."

I lift my head just enough to glare at him. "Music helps me process my emotions."

"Process?" Colin cries. "You've been processing the same four minutes of music for three hours."

"It speaks to me," I mumble, dropping my forehead back onto the table with a dull thunk.

Evan rises from his chair, marching toward the stereo's remote control. "This ends now."

I scramble upright. "Touch the control and I will ban you from S'Holzfass for eternity."

"We're your only customers right now," Lars points out. "And we've endured sixty-seven plays of this misery anthem."

"Would you prefer I put The Hurting album on again instead?" I ask, arching an eyebrow.

"NO!" all three men shout in unison.

Colin clasps his hands together in prayer. "We beg of you, no more Tears for Fears."

"I feel like it is raining inside S'Holzfass," Lars adds.

I slump in my chair. "Good. The outside should match my inside."

"Why don't you try something more upbeat?" Evan suggests gently. "Like ABBA?"

"ABBA?" I sputter, sitting upright now. "Do I look like I'm in an ABBA mood?"

The three men study me from across the room, taking in the dark circles under my eyes.

"Are you going emo?" Lars asks, squinting at my black sweater, which matches my black jeans and black boots.

"Perhaps." I run my fingers along one of my braids. "I'm considering coloring my hair black. To match my soul."

"Oh good Lord," Colin mutters.

"I could channel my inner Wednesday Addams," I continue.

"Wednesday who?" Evan asks.

"She's my role model," I say without a trace of irony. "Emotionally unavailable and dead inside."

Their faces transform into masks of horror.

The Smiths song finally ends, but I've set it on repeat, so Morrissey starts crooning about misery again. Lars throws a coaster at the speaker, missing by a mile.

I plop my forehead back onto the table with unnecessary force.

"Ow," I mutter.

"Anika," Colin says, walking over to my table. "This has gone on long enough."

I flop my head to the side and press my cheek against the wood. The grain pattern makes these little swirly designs if you stare long enough. It's mesmerizing in a sad, pathetic way.

"I told him I love him," I whisper, my voice cracking. "Like an idiot. And he didn't say it back. He said NOTHING."

Colin sits down across from me, folding his hands like he's about to deliver a sermon. "Men are stupid."

"The stupidest," Lars says with authority. "We don't process emotions in real time."

"Griffin's probably kicking himself for not saying it back," Evan adds.

"It doesn't matter. He's back in Toronto now. The lockout is over. He's returned to his glamorous hockey life with his glamorous hockey friends."

"Anika," Lars says firmly. "Griffin is coming back, ja?"

I lift my head, wiping my nose with the back of my hand. "It's been almost a month. He said he'd be gone for a week, maybe two."

I stare into the distance. "It's a very, very mad world." Then I plop my head back down with a theatrical thump.

"Oh for the love!" Lars starts.

"Does Griffin at least call you?" Evan asks.

I mumble something into the table.

"What was that?"

I sigh. "Three times a day," I admit begrudgingly. "Sometimes four."

"And he texts you constantly," Colin adds.

"It's only a matter of time before he forgets me."

"So, the man calls you multiple times daily from another continent," Colin summarizes slowly, like he's talking to a child. "And you think he's forgotten about you?"

My chin wobbles traitorously. "Memories fade, but the scars still linger."

"Oh no, she's quoting lyrics again," Colin mutters.

"Are you quoting Tears for Fears right now?" Lars asks incredulously.

I ignore him. "Will I ever love again?"

Evan stands up abruptly, almost toppling over his chair. "This has gone far enough. We're staging an intervention."

"I don't need an intervention." My lips slide over something sticky on the table surface as I speak but I'm too dramatic to care.

"Lars," Evan continues. "You know what to do."

Lars shoves his chair back and vaults over the bar. He adjusts his collar, rolls up his sleeves, and cracks his knuckles.

"What do you think you're doing?" I demand, lifting my head fully off the sticky table.

Lars just winks, tossing a bottle over his head in an arc and catching it with his other hand. He's not even looking! He starts pouring various liquids into a cocktail shaker.

My jaw drops. "Since when can you..."

He rolls the shaker behind his neck, over his shoulder, catches it with his elbow, bounces it to his other hand, and shakes it like a maraca.

"Are you secretly Tom Cruise?" I mutter, watching him flip two more bottles in the air at once.

Colin and Evan clap enthusiastically as Lars continues his bartending spectacle, juggling tumblers, spinning in place, catching bottles behind his back, and tossing ice cubes into glasses from three meters away.

"I am so confused right now," I say, wiping what I think might be beer residue from my cheek.

Lars finishes with a flourish, pouring the colorful drink into a hurricane glass and decorating it with a pineapple wedge, a cherry, and one of those tiny umbrellas I didn't even know we had.

He slides it across the bar, then carries it over to my table when I don't make a move to get it.

"For you, *Fräulein*," Lars says, placing it in front of me with a bow.

I eye the drink suspiciously. "What's in it?"

"Happiness," Lars replies. He does this interpretive dance thing with his hands, waving around the drink as he scoots backward.

"What's going on?" I ask, suddenly alert. "Why are you all being weird? Weirder than usual, I mean."

Lars goes back to the bar to clean the tumblers. "Who else will keep the bar running while you're not here?"

I blink at him. "My mother."

The three of them burst into uproarious laughter.

"Your mother?" Colin wheezes, wiping tears from his eyes. "She smokes out all the customers with her incense. Then falls asleep."

"I have no customers. Just you three."

Evan snorts. "Not when Lars is behind the bar. He draws in the tourist crowd."

"Americans love it," Colin nods enthusiastically. "They leave enormous tips."

"Wait until Saturday night. Standing room only." Lars grins, spreading his arms wide. "Welcome to S'Holzfass After Dark."

"The...what?" I sputter.

"While you've been going to hockey games, working with spies, and catching criminals, we've been running the place," Colin explains.

"You've WHAT?" I screech.

"Lars does his bottle tricks; the tourists love it," Evan continues. "They take videos, post them online. The place has gone viral."

"Viral?" I stare at Lars. "You run my bar when I'm not here?"

"Someone has to," Colin says. "Last Saturday, we had people lined up outside. Lars did that fire trick thing."

"Fire trick?" I echo weakly.

"*Ja*, with the cinnamon and the whoosh." Evan gestures wildly with his hands.

"We've had to hire two more servers just to keep up with the crowd," Colin adds. "They're all coming in later. We open at seven now."

"You HIRED people? For MY bar?" I'm practically shrieking now.

"Your mother approved it. To be fair, you weren't exactly in a hiring state of mind," Lars points out. "You've been too busy listening to your sad songs."

"I'm being replaced," I murmur, staring into the middle distance.

"No," Lars protests. "We just wanted to help you out, really."

I slump in my chair, feeling even more dejected than before.

Not only am I lovesick and abandoned, but my bar is apparently thriving without me. Lars has been secretly extreme bartending while I've been playing the part of a Bond Girl.

"You're a better bartender than me, Lars."

Lars softens. "Anika, nobody makes a Schorle like you."

"A monkey could make a Schorle," I say flatly.

A profound despair mixed with a measure of rebellion hits me, and I might be losing it, but I stop the music mid-song and just as quickly switch to "It's the End of the World as We Know It" by R.E.M. and crank up the volume full blast.

I feel like I could scream, but all I do is laugh maniacally.

This might scare the guys more than anything, but at this point, I have no cares. Just abandon.

I take a sip of Lars's cocktail (which turns out to be delicious), and shout over the music.

"Hey," I yell, pointing at each of them in turn. "If you ever see aliens in the sky, don't believe it!"

They stare at me blankly.

"It's MIND CONTROL!"

I half expect them to take me to the loony bin when the door opens from outside. Cold air rushes inside and in walks my mother, wrapped in multiple colorful scarves. Her presence instantly fills the room with the scent of patchouli.

She surveys the scene of me sprawled at the table, the blaring music, my puffy eyes, and narrows her gaze.

"*Liebchen*," she says, studying me with her head tilted. "When was the last time you showered?"

I ignore her question, taking another sip of Lars's excellent cocktail. "The government is using holograms to stage fake alien invasions, Mama. I've seen the technology."

My mother purses her lips. "This is worse than I thought." She rummages through her massive woven bag and produces a small amber bottle.

I watch in horror as she uncorks the bottle. "Mama, no!"

"Mama, yes."

Before I can escape, she's dousing essential oil liberally onto the crown of my head, then sprinkles it all over me like she's basting a turkey. The pungent, earthy smell engulfs me, mingling with what I now realize is probably my own funk. I'm simultaneously mortified and oddly comforted. It smells like my childhood.

I sputter, wiping my face. "Thanks, Mama," I say dryly. "Now I smell like a 1960's record store."

"Perfect," my mother says, looking satisfied. "You love record stores."

The Jass players snicker, which earns them a withering glare from my mother.

"You three," she says, pointing at them. "Out."

"But—" Lars starts.

"Now. All of you!"

Evan puffs up his chest. "But we're in the middle of an intervention."

"Fine job you are doing." She makes shooing motions with her hands. "Out!"

Lars glances back at me with a wink before my mother physically pushes him through the doorway.

"Mama," I say once they're gone. "Why didn't you tell me about Lars taking over the bar?"

"Why would I?" She shrugs, reaching over to pause the music, pocketing the remote. The silence is deafening. "You were busy adventuring with the Canadian."

I drop my face into my hands. "This is ridiculous. I've been replaced by Lars and his bottle tricks."

"*Liebchen*," she says softly. "Enough of this wallowing."

"I'm not wallowing," I protest. "I'm embracing a life of solitude. I will be an old spinster."

"You're just scared." My mother's eyes soften. "You've spent so long taking care of everyone else, you've forgotten how to let someone take care of you."

"I didn't even know we had tiny umbrellas," I mumble.

"Listen to me, Anika," she says, patting my cheek. "Life is too short for this sadness. The universe has plans for you."

I sigh heavily. "I told him I loved him."

"I know."

"He said nothing."

"Your father did not say 'I love you' back to me for six months. Then one day, he built me a bookshelf and said, 'For your poetry books.' That was his way."

I slump in my chair. "He hasn't called today."

"No," she agrees, a small smile playing at her lips. "He hasn't."

There's something in her tone that makes me look up sharply. "Mama, what did you do?"

She rises from her chair with a mysterious smile, walking to the door. "Give him a chance to explain before you jump to conclusions."

The door opens, and there he is.

Griffin.

My heart flips in my chest as he stands there, snowflakes dusting his shoulders, his cheeks flushed from the cold. He's wearing a blue knit hat pulled down over his ears, and his dimples wink as he smiles at me.

"Hi," he says simply.

My mother slips out behind him, closing the door with a soft click.

I stare at him, afraid to blink in case he vanishes. "You're here."

"I'm here."

He remains rooted by the door, almost as if he's tentative to come in.

"For how long?"

"That depends." He takes a step toward me. "On you."

"Me?"

"Well, first of all, I want to tell you why I've been gone so long."

"Oh? If you're here to say goodbye properly, you didn't have to fly across an ocean. A text would have sufficed."

He chuckles, shaking his head. "I'm not here to say goodbye."

"You're not? Then why…"

"I bought the team," he interrupts. "Well, not just me. Owen, Sawyer, Hendrix, and a few others. We pooled our resources and bought the Titans."

I blink at him. "You…what?"

"We own the Titans now," he says, grinning.

I stare at him, stunned. "You…own a hockey team?"

"That's why I couldn't come back right away," he explains. "There was a mountain of paperwork, negotiations, league approvals. I wanted to tell you in person, and I made sure the news didn't leak until I could get back here."

This is good news. It really is. And I'm happy for him. But something inside of me just broke, and I feel a knot forming in my throat.

"Very cool," I say, forcing tears down. "I'm so happy for you."

He studies my face. "But?"

"But nothing. This is incredible news."

"You look like you're bracing for something."

I sigh, wrapping my arms around myself. "I'm just being realistic. You'll be heading back to Toronto soon, I guess? Now that everything's finalized?"

"Well," he says, taking another step closer. "That's the thing. I don't have to."

I blink at him. "What?"

"I live here now," he says with a bright smile. "Well, not here in your place specifically. Though I'm open to that arrangement too."

"You what?"

"I don't have to be in Toronto to own a sports team."

He's close enough now that I can smell his clean scent, which is warring with my hippie commune bouquet.

"My life is wherever you are," he whispers.

My heart thuds painfully against my ribs. "You can't stay in Switzerland. Your career..."

"Is wherever I want it to be," he interrupts gently. "I can play for Visp permanently if I want. Or retire.

I stare at him, baffled. "You'd...stay here? For me?"

"In a heartbeat."

"Griffin," I say sternly. "You can't give up your NHL career. That's insane."

"I'm not giving up anything if I get you."

My throat tightens. "Don't say things like that."

"Why not? It's true."

"Because!" I throw my hands up. "You can't just abandon your life for me. I won't let you."

"So you're insisting I go back to Canada?"

"Yes! Absolutely," I declare, even as my heart rebels against the words.

"Fine," he says with a slow nod. "Then I guess I'll just have to take you with me."

I stare at him. "What?"

"If you insist I go back to Toronto," he says, leaning forward over the table, "then I'll have to take you with me. Because I'm not going anywhere without you."

"Griffin!"

"When you told me you loved me on that mountain," he continues, his voice low and intense. "I was too stunned to say anything. I wasn't even sure I heard you right, especially after almost getting killed. And I thought maybe it was just...I don't know, a trauma response."

"It wasn't," I whisper.

"I know that now." Griffin comes closer, pulling me up from my chair. His hands are warm against mine. "I love you, Anika."

My heart thuds against my ribs. "You do?"

"Hopelessly. I never want to be apart from you again. I'm not going back to Toronto without you."

I feel tears welling up in my eyes. "But...I can't just leave. I have the bar, and—"

"We'll run the bar!"

The door suddenly bursts open, and the Jass players tumble in, red-faced and shivering.

"Sorry," Lars gasps. "It's freezing out there."

"We were listening at the door," Colin admits shamelessly.

"You better go with him," Evan exclaims. "Or we'll throw you over his shoulder ourselves."

I stare at them. "I can't expect you to run my bar."

"We already do," Lars points out.

"I can do the bookkeeping," Colin says.

"I can be manager and bouncer," Evan adds.

"And I," Lars says with a grand gesture, "will continue to dazzle the tourists with my fire tricks."

"See?" Griffin grins. "Problem solved."

"But...my mother," I protest weakly. "I can't leave her alone."

Griffin clears his throat. "Actually, I was hoping she might want to come too. I've already looked into visa options."

"No thank you," comes my mother's voice as she breezes

back in. "I'm quite happy here in Grächen. I could use some peace and quiet for once."

I turn to stare at her. "Mama? You were listening too?"

"Of course." She waves a dismissive hand. "The whole village is listening."

I glance toward the windows and, sure enough, several curious faces are peering in. They duck out of sight when I spot them.

"As long as Griffin promises to take your record collection with you," my mother continues. "I'm looking forward to listening to Yanni in peace."

I look around at all of them, feeling overwhelmed. "What would I even do in Toronto? I'd want to earn my keep."

Griffin's eyes light up. "You could open your own kung fu studio. Or teach women self-defense." He squeezes my hands. "And we'll spend summers here when hockey season is off. Switzerland is my second home now."

A tear slides down my cheek, and he catches it with his thumb.

"And who knows what the future may bring?" His eyes twinkle. "The world might need saving again someday."

I laugh despite myself. "So what, we'll be international crime-fighters in our spare time?"

"Why not? We make a pretty good team. I'm hoping MI6 will trick out my Bugatti with spy gadgets."

I look down at our intertwined hands, then back up at his hopeful face. Everything inside me is screaming to say yes, to take this chance, to leap into the unknown with this man who loves me.

"Okay," I whisper finally.

Griffin's face breaks into the biggest smile I've ever seen. "Okay?"

"Yes," I say, stronger this time. "I'll go with you."

He pulls me into his arms, lifting me off the ground and spinning me around.

I pull back from Griffin's embrace, suddenly very aware of my unwashed state. The potent mix of patchouli oil, sticky beer residue from the table, and what might be three days of no showering hits me with full force.

"Wait," I say, taking a step back. "You might want some distance. I smell like a health food store that's been set on fire."

Griffin's eyes crinkle at the corners as he tugs me back into his arms. "I don't care."

"Griffin, I haven't showered in…well, I can't remember."

He tugs me closer. "I spent fifteen years in hockey locker rooms. Trust me, you smell like a spring meadow in comparison."

"I'm serious," I protest, even as he pulls me into his arms. "I'm a biohazard."

"Anika," he says, his voice dropping low. "I flew across an ocean just to hold you. I'm not waiting another minute."

And just like that, my heart liquefies completely.

Then, his lips are on mine, and everything else melts away. My embarrassment, the watching eyes, the fact that I'm probably leaving a grease print on his pristine jacket. None of it matters when I'm in his arms.

"*Mach Platz!*" Lars suddenly shouts, clapping his hands. "Make room!"

Colin and Evan spring into action, pushing tables and chairs to the edges of the room to create a makeshift dance floor in the center of S'Holzfass.

A gritty fuzzed-out guitar riff fills the bar, and I immediately flash back to that embarrassing first meeting at Walter's cabin. I spin around to see my mother at the bar, holding the stereo remote with a mischievous grin as "One Way or Another" blasts through the ancient speakers.

Griffin wags his brows. "They're playing our song."

I narrow my eyes at him. "You!"

"I might have put in a song request." He shrugs, looking adorably sheepish. "I texted your mom from the train."

"The bathroom song?" I can feel heat rising to my cheeks. "From when we first met?"

"May I have this dance?" he asks, reaching for my hand.

"I should warn you," I say as Griffin pulls me into the center of the room. "I take my '80s dancing very seriously."

"Oh, I know," he says as I launch into my Molly Ringwald dance.

His dimples deepen as he drags his gaze down my body, then back up to my eyes. Then, fueled by whatever crazy energy he brought with him, he joins me, stepping side to side, swinging his arms, and bouncing on his toes.

I raise my brows. "Not bad."

"I like to call this The Carlton," he says with a big grin.

"You're ridiculous," I giggle, but I can't stop.

The song hits its chorus, and the entire bar seems to vibrate with energy. Evan and Colin each grab one of my mother's hands, tugging her onto our makeshift dance floor as she laughs and laughs. I haven't seen her this happy in years.

"S'Holzfass hasn't been this lively since the '90s!" my mother shouts over the music, twirling past me with her arms outstretched.

Oh how I wish Father could see us now.

Some curious villagers who were peeping through the windows have wandered in now, drawn by the music and the impromptu dance party.

"S'Holzfass After Dark is officially open!" Lars announces, leaping behind the bar. He immediately starts his routine, flipping bottles over his head, juggling cocktail shakers, and setting something on fire that definitely shouldn't be on fire.

Griffin spins me around, and I crash against his chest, breathless and giddy. His hands find my waist, steadying me.

"Are you sure about this?" I ask, looking up at him. "Taking me with you to Toronto? Splitting your time between two continents?"

Instead of answering with words, Griffin cups my face in his hands and kisses me. It's soft and sweet at first, then deeper, more urgent. The room and everyone in it fades away until there's nothing but Griffin, his lips on mine, his hands in my hair.

"One way or another," Griffin murmurs against my lips, "I was always going to find you. Even if it took a high-stakes poker game, crashing your blind date, and skiing off a cliff to make it happen."

I throw my head back laughing. "The spy who loves me."

"The *man* who loves you," he says, pulling me impossibly close. Then, with a rumble in his chest, he adds, "But this man is for your eyes only."

"I guess your mission is accomplished...as my dating coach," I tease, tapping my finger against Griffin's chest. "You taught me how to get a guy."

Griffin pulls back just enough to look at me, those dimples deepening as he grins. "Oh, I don't know about that. There might be a few more...advanced lessons we haven't covered yet."

I loop my arms around his neck, pressing closer. "Well, I've always been an excellent student. Very dedicated to my studies."

"Is that so?" His eyes darken as his hands slide lower on my waist.

"Absolutely. Top marks in everything I attempt."

Griffin's smile turns wolfish. "In that case, Miss Gisler, class is officially in session."

Life is short, eat ice cream.

EPILOGUE

Griffin

I swear time moves differently around Anika. One minute we're planning our summer escape to Switzerland, and the next I'm watching her twirl in a sunbeam on Queens Quay. My heart does this weird flippy thing it never did before I met her.

The past five months have been the best of my life. Anika has adapted to Toronto living like a native and has already made a lot of friends. Hard to believe we'll be in Switzerland next week, hiking those same trails where we first met. She's said she would love to stay here full time, but I promised her summers in Switzerland, and I can hardly wait.

We took a break from all the extra errands we must do before we leave and came out to the waterfront. The breeze feels like heaven on this hot, humid day, and nothing but a cold sweet treat could make this sticky afternoon more bearable.

"There it is!" I point down the quay to Scoops & Dreams, my favorite ice cream shop in Toronto. "Home of the best ice cream in Canada."

Anika squints at the colorful storefront, skepticism written all over her face. "You say this about every food place you take me to."

"And have I been wrong yet?"

"Swiss Chalet," she replies without missing a beat.

"Hey, their quarter chicken dinner is a Canadian institution."

"Griffin," Anika says, her accent thickening with indignation. "It is not Swiss! The name is false advertising."

"You mentioned that." I grin, kissing her forehead. " About seventeen times to our server."

"The chicken was good," she concedes graciously. "But why call it Swiss?"

"You ate it, though."

"Out of politeness. And hunger." She bumps her hip against mine. "The things I do for love."

The word 'love' from her lips still sends electric currents straight to my heart. Five months in Toronto, and I catch myself wondering if she'll wake up one morning missing her mountains and regretting following me here.

"What's happening in your head right now?" Anika squeezes my hand. "You went somewhere else."

"Sorry." I kiss her knuckles. "I'm just excited for you to try this place. It'll change your life."

"Like you did?" She stands on tiptoes to peck my cheek.

Inside Scoops & Dreams it smells like fresh waffle cones and sugar, with a hint of caramel wafting from the kitchen. The shop buzzes with summer energy. Kids with sticky faces, teenagers being loud teenagers, parents bribing toddlers with sprinkles. Outside, Toronto bakes under the June sun, making ice cream not a luxury but a necessity. Anika scans the chalkboard menu, biting her lip as she reads the forty-plus flavors.

"Hmm, very impressive variety."

"Better than your Italian gelato?" I ask, knowing full well I'm poking the bear.

She straightens up, eyes narrowing. "Let's not say things we cannot take back."

The teenage girl behind the counter smiles at our banter. "First time here?"

"For her," I say. "I'm a regular."

"He brings all his women here," Anika stage-whispers to the girl.

"Only the special ones who I save from supervillains," I counter.

The girl's eyes volley back and forth between us almost comically.

"I need to use the restroom before we order," Anika announces suddenly. "Where is it?"

The girl points toward the back. "Through that hallway on the left."

Before Anika turns to go, I can't help myself. "Hey, the acoustics are great in there if you want to belt out some Blondie!"

She pats my cheek. "You tell this joke every time I use a public restroom."

"Because it's hilarious."

"It's really not." She kisses me quickly. "But you're cute when you think you're funny."

As she walks away, I call after her. "What flavor would you like? Or are you neutral since you're Swiss?"

Anika spins around, walking backward. "Griffin! I am Swiss. Nothing but chocolate will do."

The counter girl stares at me. "Is she really going to sing in our bathroom?"

"Probably not," I laugh. "It's an inside joke."

As Anika disappears around the corner, I can't wipe the stupid grin off my face, still marveling at how lucky I am.

I order two waffle cones and wait for Anika to return, anticipating her reaction. Scoops & Dreams is famous for their enormous portions. Even the smallest scoop they offer is bigger than my face and I'm here for it.

When Anika emerges and sees the giant waffle cone, she drops her jaw and laughs.

"This is ridiculous," Anika says, accepting her chocolate monstrosity with both hands. "Nobody needs this much ice cream. We should have split one."

"Speak for yourself." I pull my waffle cone protectively closer to my chest. "Remember what I told you in St. Moritz? I don't share."

We step outside into the warm afternoon. The summer sun beats down on Toronto's waterfront, perfect ice cream weather. Children squeal on nearby swings, tourists snap photos of the harbor, and a street performer plays saxophone that floats on the breeze.

"You should see your face right now," I chuckle, watching Anika concentrate on keeping her chocolate tower from toppling. "You're looking at that cone like it's as big as the Matterhorn.

"Very close," she says, laughing, and my heart swells at the sound of it.

A drip of ice cream slides down the side of Anika's cone, and she catches it with her tongue. My brain short-circuits momentarily at the sight.

"Verdict?" I ask, watching her expression carefully.

She considers the ice cream with the seriousness of a wine sommelier. "Mmm. Good. Creamy."

"But?"

"But gelato in Florence still wins." She shrugs apologetically.

"Impossible standards," I groan.

We stroll along Queen Quay, navigating the afternoon crowd. Anika loops her arm through mine, careful not to bump our ice creams together. After months in Toronto, she still marvels at the city's vastness compared to Grächen.

I hold out my waffle cone with its towering scoop of maple walnut. "Want a taste?"

She eyes it suspiciously. "You want me to try yours?"

"Why not? Sharing is caring."

"But you don't share. I remember St. Moritz too, Griffin."

I shrug, feigning nonchalance while my pulse jackhammers, my thoughts racing to that night in the elevator. "I'm feeling generous today."

Anika takes a small lick. "Mmm. Very good." She offers her cone in return. "Your turn."

"No thanks." I twist away from her chocolate mountain. "I've had that flavor before."

Anika narrows her eyes. "Since when do you turn down chocolate?"

"I'm pacing myself."

"You're acting weird." She studies my face closely. "Are you up to something?"

"Me? Never."

"HA! Now I know something's up." She points her cone at me accusingly. "You're plotting something."

My heart hammers against my ribs. I try to keep my voice steady. "Can't a guy just enjoy some ice cream without an interrogation?"

"This better not be another spy adventure," she warns.

I laugh nervously. "No spy stuff, I promise."

Anika steps in front of me, walking backward so she can see my face. The move is so confident, so Anika. No fear of bumping into anything because she simply expects the world to move out of her way. Usually it does.

"You're not a very good liar," she says. "What aren't you telling me?"

I dodge the question by pointing toward the water. "Hey, check out that sailboat!"

Anika rolls her eyes but turns to look anyway. A white sailboat cuts through the harbor, its sail billowing in the summer breeze. The distraction works momentarily as we continue our stroll, ice cream dripping faster than we can lick it away. A ferry packed with tourists heads toward Toronto Islands. Everything appears perfect except my anxiety level, which escalates with each lick Anika takes of her ice cream. Then I notice she's slowing down but the chocolate mountain barely diminished.

"This is too much." She holds up her still-massive cone despite her valiant efforts to conquer it. "I cannot finish."

"Amateur," I tease, working steadily through my maple walnut scoop. "You can't give up now."

"Nobody can finish this amount."

"I can. See?" I take a huge bite off the top of my cone to demonstrate. The brain freeze hits me immediately.

Anika skips ahead. "I'm going to throw it away."

"No!" I say too slowly, the brain freeze thwarting my efforts.

But before I can stop her, Anika pivots toward what she thinks is a trash can—but isn't. I stare in horror as she cheerfully stuffs her half-eaten ice cream cone through the swinging flap of a bright red Canada Post collection box, and it disappears with a soft *plop*.

My heart stops.

"WHAT HAVE YOU DONE?" I screech, dropping my own cone and lunging toward the mailbox. Several passersby turn to stare.

She licks a chocolate smudge from her thumb, completely unfazed. "I threw it in the trash. Why are you yelling?"

"That's not—" I grab my head with both hands. "That's not a trash can!"

"It looks like a trash can." She glances back at the red box, comprehension dawning slowly on her face. "Oh."

"Oh? OH?" My voice rises an octave. "That's a postal collection box! You just mailed ice cream!"

"Oh. Well, I am sure postal workers have delivered worse things."

"Anika! The Canadian postal service doesn't deliver ice cream!"

Anika's cheeks turn bright red. "Will we be fined? Arrested?" She glances around furtively. "Should we run? Pretend we know nothing?"

I press my face against the mail slot, peering into darkness. "We need to get that cone back."

"Why? It's already ruined." Anika's eyes dart around, then back at me. "I still think we should run."

"No, you don't understand." I press my forehead against the cool metal of the mailbox. "There was something in your cone."

"Besides ice cream?" Her voice turns wary.

"I hid something in there."

"Something in my ice cream?"

"It wasn't IN your ice cream," I explain, my cheeks burning hot. "It was wrapped in plastic and pushed into the bottom of the waffle cone."

"Griffin." Her voice drops dangerously low. "What was in my cone?"

I take a deep breath. This is not how I planned this. Not even close. "A ring."

"A what?"

"A ring," I say louder, my face burning hot. "An engagement ring."

Anika's jaw drops. She stares at the postal box, then back at me, then at the postal box again. "You... hid an engagement ring... in an ice cream cone?"

I nod miserably.

Anika stares at me, her mouth opening and closing without sound.

"Say something," I plead.

"You put jewelry... in food?"

"It seemed romantic in my head!" I throw my hands up. "I had this whole plan. The ice cream, then a walk to the island ferry, sunset proposal overlooking the city skyline. Now it's melting inside a federal mailbox, probably ruining someone's birthday card."

"You hid jewelry. In food I was eating. What if I had swallowed it?"

"It was in a little waterproof container!" I defend myself. "And I was watching carefully."

Anika presses her palms against her eyes. "This is insane."

"I know. I'm sorry. My grandmother always says—"

"If you quote your grandmother right now, I'll push you into that fountain."

My shoulders slump. "I'll call the post office on Monday and explain."

"No. It could be long gone by then."

She glances around, spots a meter maid writing parking tickets, and marches straight toward her. I trail behind, convinced we're about to be arrested for mail tampering.

"Excuse me," Anika says to the uniformed woman. "My boyfriend has done something very stupid. You see, I thought that mailbox over there was a trash and—"

The meter maid looks up, unimpressed. "Ma'am, I can only help with parking violations."

She walks away shaking her head.

I turn back to the postal box, examining it from every angle. The mail slot stares back, mocking me. "There's got to be a way to get it out."

I attempt to slide my arm through the narrow opening, but it's hopeless. My bicep won't fit past my elbow. "Too small. I'm stuck with my hockey player build."

A woman pushing a stroller slows down to stare at us. I can't blame her. I'm practically hugging the postal box while Anika paces in small circles.

"Let me try." Anika pushes me aside, flexing her fingers. Her slender arm disappears into the slot up to her shoulder, her face pressed against the metal. "I can't reach the bottom."

She withdraws her arm, now covered in postal grime. "We need something long and grabby."

"Long and grabby?" I repeat. "Like what?"

"I don't know! One of those claw machines from the arcade?" She snaps her fingers. "Where's your spy watch?"

"I returned it. The FIS was very insistent about getting their toys back."

Anika purses her lips. "So what do we do? Call a locksmith? The fire department? Break into it with a crowbar?"

"Let's not add felony charges to our day."

We stare at each other for a moment before Anika bursts into laughter, doubling over with her arms wrapped around her stomach.

"It's not funny," I protest, but her laughter is contagious and soon I'm smiling despite myself.

"It's very funny," she gasps between laughs. "It's the most Griffin thing ever."

Her laughter echoes down the street, bright and clear. I watch her with ice cream smudged at the corner of her mouth and marvel once again at how a bathroom break changed everything.

"Love you," I say simply.

Anika's eyes soften. "I love you too."

We grin at each other like idiots. Six months together, and my heart still hammers whenever she smiles at me.

"We need to get it back," she says, suddenly serious. She marches up to the mailbox and peers through the slot. "I can't see anything."

"The collection times are listed on the box. Maybe we can intercept the mail carrier?"

She circles the mailbox, testing its weight and stability. "Can we tip it over?"

"It's bolted to the ground," I say, tugging futilely at one corner. "And tampering with mail is a federal offense."

I pace in front of the mailbox, weighing my options.

"You know," Anika says casually. "If you still want to propose today, you don't need a ring."

I stop pacing. "What?"

"The ring is a symbol. Nice, but not necessary." She shrugs. "I would have said yes anyway."

My heart thunders in my chest. "Would have?"

"Will." She smiles. "When you ask properly."

I stare at the mailbox for a beat, then at Anika, and everything clicks into place. My original plan might be drowning in melted chocolate, but inspiration strikes like a perfectly aimed slap shot.

"Stay right here," I command, pointing to the spot where she stands. "Don't move."

I sprint down the sidewalk toward a street vendor selling souvenir keychains. The woman barely has time to say hello before I grab a tiny metal CN Tower from her display and slap down a twenty.

"Keep the change!" I shout, already racing back to where Anika waits, arms crossed, eyebrows raised.

Pedestrians dodge out of my path as I skid to a stop and drop to one knee directly in front of the mailbox. I position myself between Anika and the red metal box, extending the miniature CN Tower in my outstretched palm.

"Anika Gisler," I announce, loud enough for curious onlookers to hear. "I present to you this mailbox and this extremely overpriced souvenir as symbols of my eternal devotion."

Her mouth twitches with suppressed laughter. "The mailbox?"

"Yes." I gesture grandly toward the postal container. "Like this sturdy Canadian structure, my love for you remains fixed and immovable. It accepts whatever you give it, even if sometimes it's chocolate ice cream when it shouldn't be."

A small crowd gathers. Someone whistles.

"Griffin, what are you doing?" Anika hisses, cheeks flushing pink.

"Improvising," I whisper back before continuing my speech. "This mailbox holds our future inside it. Literally. But also metaphorically."

She rolls her eyes but smiles. "You're ridiculous."

"I might not know how to keep track of important jewelry, but I promise to learn how to be the husband you deserve. No more hiding rings in desserts. No more international spy adventures. Instead of me teaching you how to date, I'm hoping you'll teach *me* how to be the partner you need."

My knee digs into the concrete sidewalk. A toddler points at me. His mother shushes him.

"So, will you marry me and give me new lessons on how to be your husband? The real ring is currently covered in chocolate and stuck to someone's electric bill, but I promise to retrieve it or replace it or whatever you want."

Anika extends her hand, wiggling her fingers impatiently. "Give me your silly tower."

I slide the keychain ring onto her finger where it dangles loosely.

"Yes," she says simply. "I will marry you."

I leap to my feet and sweep her into my arms, spinning us both in a circle. Setting her down, I kiss her chocolate-flavored lips.

"But we're still getting my real ring out, right?"

"Yes, I'll get your ring out even if I have to camp here until an official shows up."

"Or we could call the post office," she reasons.

"SHE SAID YES!" I bellow suddenly, causing Anika to jump. My voice echoes across the waterfront as I pump my fist into the air. "SHE SAID YES TO MARRYING ME!"

A smattering of applause breaks out from the curious onlookers who witnessed my makeshift proposal. An elderly couple gives us thumbs up. Two women filming on their phones cheer loudly.

"Griffin," Anika hisses, her cheeks blooming pink. "People are staring."

"Let them stare!" I sweep her into another hug, lifting her

feet off the ground. "I want the world to know that the most beautiful woman in the world agreed to marry me!"

A bearded man wearing cargo shorts nudges his companion. "Isn't that the goalie from the Titans? McGregor?"

"The guy who bought the team during the lockout?" his friend whispers back, not quietly enough. "I think it is."

Anika covers her face with her hands, peeking through her fingers. "This is so embarrassing."

"Embarrassing? This is the greatest moment of my life! Apart from when you broke into my cabin to pee, of course."

"Please stop telling strangers that story."

I notice a postal worker approaching, dressed in the familiar uniform, wheeling a cart behind him. He frowns at the small crowd gathered around his collection box.

"Excuse me," he says, jingling a large key ring. "I need to get through to collect the mail."

Anika and I exchange panicked glances.

"Sir," I say, stepping forward and dropping my voice. "Before you open that box, I should warn you there's... a situation inside."

The postal worker sighs deeply. "What kind of situation?"

I grimace, twisting my lips. "You might want to wear gloves for this."

The End

Want more Griffin and Anika? Subscribe to my newsletter and I'll send you a bonus scene straight to your inbox.

https://www.subscribepage.com/dgbonus

THANK YOU

Thanks for reading this book. I hope you enjoyed it as much as I've have and the great pleasure it was creating and getting to know Griffin and Anika. They are so dear to my heart now.

Your honest review will help readers choose Dating Goals as their next obsession.

Turn the page to find more books by Gigi Blume...

THE GIGIVERSE

TORONTO TITANS HOCKEY SERIES

Grump and Ten (Novella)

Head Over Skates

Offside Bride

Cross Check Christmas

Dating Goals

BACKSTAGE ROMANCE SERIES

Confessions of a Hollywood Matchmaker

Love and Loathing

Secrets of a Hollywood Matchmaker

Driving Miss Darcy

The Friend Act

PRECIO BROTHERS SERIES

Messy Love

The Hate Zone

Nacho Boyfriend

Just Amigos

STANDALONE

Bewitching the Ghost

ACKNOWLEDGMENTS

I want to express my gratitude to everyone who helped bring this book into fruition—particularly my core group of author friends for their unwavering support and encouragement:

My local OC (and visiting) Galentine's Gal Pals, who are loads of fun and always down for Thai food and donut runs. IYKYK

My long distance girlies, especially Carina Taylor who keeps me motivated and is the best sounding board (sorry about my rants sometimes), and Kelly Fletcher, who I could spend days with, talking shop and drinking margaritas.

Special thanks to my PA and editor Kristyn Fortner. You have the patience of a saint.

For all the readers who share my books on social media. You are so important!

And last but not least, for the readers who believed in this project enough to support it through preorders.

Your contributions helped keep me motivated to make this book the best it could be.

In no particular order (because you're all number one in my eyes):

Desirée, Manda, Abby, Annelies, Robyn, Krista , JP, Tamara, Devon, Becca, Allegra, Lynette, Mollie, Charlie, Lissa, Kaci, Hayley, Erica, Lesley, Caitlyn, September, Kristyn, Amanda, Megan C, Mimi, & Mary Beth K.

GET TO KNOW GIGI

Gigi is a USA TODAY bestselling author and hopeless musical theatre nerd who has perfected the art of lollygagging.

Former professional wedding singer, Gigi lives in Southern California with her personal chef (AKA husband) and two weird and awesome kids who have grown into wonderful, artistically talented young adults.

Quoting movies, Shakespeare, and pop culture with her kids is one of her favorite pastimes. A Hufflepuff and die-hard Whovian, she's convinced magic is really a thing, still believes in Santa Claus, and finds miracles everywhere.

When Gigi's not writing about swoony book boyfriends and the women that bring them to their knees, she likes to re-read Pride and Prejudice, embarrass her offspring, and get distracted by her dogs.

You can find more info and titles at gigiblume.com